Praise for the works of Stephanie Laurens

"Stephanie Laurens' heroines are marvelous tributes to Georgette Heyer: feisty and strong." *Cathy Kelly*

"Stephanie Laurens never fails to entertain and charm her readers with vibrant plots, snappy dialogue, and unforgettable characters." *Historical Romance Reviews*

"Stephanie Laurens plays into readers' fantasies like a master and claims their hearts time and again." *Romantic Times Magazine*

Praise for The Beguilement of Lady Eustacia Cavanaugh

"This fast-moving historical romance features more than a few delicious twists that represent Laurens at her best, serving up her fine blend of romance and intrigue in such a way that her readers have learned to expect the unexpected." *Angela M., Copy Editor, Red Adept Editing*

"In her lyrical new romance, New York Times Bestselling Author Stephanie Laurens masterfully weaves a taut tale of fiery passion, soaring love, and spellbinding intrigue set against the impeccable manners and mores of nineteenth-century England." *Rene R., Proofreader, Red Adept Editing*

ABOUT THE BEGUILEMENT OF LADY EUSTACIA CAVANAUGH

#1 New York Times *bestselling author Stephanie Laurens continues the bold tales of the Cavanaugh siblings as the sole Cavanaugh sister discovers that love truly does conquer all.*

A lady with a passion for music and the maestro she challenges in pursuit of a worthy cause find themselves battling villains both past and present as they fight to secure life's greatest rewards—love, marriage, and family.

Stacie—Lady Eustacia Cavanaugh—is adamant marriage is not for her. Haunted by her parents' unhappy union, Stacie believes that, for her, marriage is an unacceptable risk. Wealthy and well-born, she needs for nothing, and with marriage off the table, to give her life purpose, she embarks on a plan to further the careers of emerging local musicians by introducing them to the ton via a series of musical evenings.

Yet despite her noble status, Stacie requires a musical lure to tempt the haut ton to her events, and in the elevated circles she inhabits, only one musician commands sufficient cachet—the reclusive and notoriously reluctant Marquess of Albury.

Frederick, Marquess of Albury, has fashioned a life for himself as a musical scholar, one he pursues largely out of sight of the ton. He might be renowned as a virtuoso on the pianoforte, yet he sees no reason to endure the smothering over-attentiveness of society. Then his mother inveigles him into meeting Stacie, and the challenge she lays before him is…tempting. On a number of fronts. Enough for him not to immediately refuse her.

A dance of subtle persuasion ensues, and step by step, Frederick finds himself convinced that Stacie's plan has real merit and that it behooves him to support her. At least for one event.

Stacie's first musical evening, featuring Frederick as the principal performer, is a massive success—until Fate takes a hand and lands them in a situation that forces them both to reassess.

Does Frederick want more than the sterile, academic life he'd thought was for him?

Can Stacie overcome her deepest fears and own to and reach for her girlhood dreams?

Impulsive, arrogant, and used to getting his own way, Frederick finds his answer easily enough, but his new direction puts him on a collision course with Stacie's fears. Luckily, he thrives on challenges—which is just as well, because in addition to convincing Stacie that love can, indeed, conquer all, he and she must unravel the mystery of who is behind a spate of murderous attacks before the villain succeeds in eliminating all hope of a happy ending.

A classical historical romance set in London and Surrey, in the heart of the ton. Third novel in The Cavanaughs—a full-length historical romance of 122,000 words.

OTHER TITLES BY STEPHANIE LAURENS

The Untamed Bride

The Elusive Bride

The Brazen Bride

The Reckless Bride

The Adventurers Quartet

The Lady's Command

A Buccaneer at Heart

The Daredevil Snared

Lord of the Privateers

The Cavanaughs

The Designs of Lord Randolph Cavanaugh

The Pursuits of Lord Kit Cavanaugh

The Beguilement of Lady Eustacia Cavanaugh

Other Novels

The Lady Risks All

The Legend of Nimway Hall – 1750: Jacqueline

Medieval (As M.S.Laurens)

Desire's Prize

Novellas

Melting Ice – from the anthologies *Rough Around the Edges* and *Scandalous Brides*

Rose in Bloom – from the anthology *Scottish Brides*

Scandalous Lord Dere – from the anthology *Secrets of a Perfect Night*

Lost and Found – from the anthology *Hero, Come Back*

The Fall of Rogue Gerrard – from the anthology *It Happened One Night*

The Seduction of Sebastian Trantor – from the anthology *It Happened One Season*

Short Stories

The Wedding Planner – from the anthology *Royal Weddings*

A Return Engagement – from the anthology *Royal Bridesmaids*

UK-Style Regency Romances

Tangled Reins

Four in Hand

Impetuous Innocent

Fair Juno

The Reasons for Marriage

A Lady of Expectations An Unwilling Conquest

A Comfortable Wife

THE BEGUILEMENT OF LADY EUSTACIA CAVANAUGH

THE BEGUILEMENT OF LADY EUSTACIA CAVANAUGH

Copyright © 2019 by Savdek Management Proprietary Limited

ISBN: 978-1-925559-18-7

Cover design by Savdek Management Pty. Ltd.

Cover couple photography and photographic composition by Period Images © 2019

First print publication: July, 2019

Savdek Management Proprietary Limited, Melbourne, Australia.

www.stephanielaurens.com

Email: admin@stephanielaurens.com

The names Stephanie Laurens and the SL Logo is a registered trademarks of Savdek Management Proprietary Ltd.

❀ Created with Vellum

CHAPTER 1

MARCH 5, 1844. ALBURY HOUSE, UPPER GROSVENOR STREET, LONDON

*L*ord Frederick Kingsley Montgomery Brampton, seventh Marquess of Albury, walked into his mother's sitting room in his London house to discover his parent sitting in an armchair, sipping tea and showing no sign whatever of being close to imminent demise.

Not that Frederick had actually expected his mother to be at death's door, yet every time he responded to one of her vague summonses, which invariably hinted at the onset of a grave decline, only to find her as robust as when he'd last seen her, relief ghosted through him; one day, he knew, the summons would be real.

Today, however, as his mother's gaze fell on him, she brightened and smiled. "Ah, Frederick—you've come. Yes, I know—I'm a sad trial, but I assure you, I was feeling utterly wretched and faint yesterday, quite unable to lift my head. Yet this morning, I awoke, and the faintness had passed."

"For which I must be thankful, Mama." His mother was still a handsome woman with her silvery hair confined beneath a lace cap and her tall figure elegantly and fashionably gowned. Frederick bent and kissed her lined cheek, then nodded in greeting to the other occupant of the room, his mother's longtime companion, Mrs. Emily Weston, who was seated on the chaise beside his mother's favorite wing chair. "Good morning, Emily. I trust you're enjoying your customary rosy health."

That appeared to be the case; Emily's eyes were bright, her peaches-

and-cream complexion all but glowing. Ten years younger than his mother's fifty-six years, Emily had been the marchioness's trusted friend and confidante for the past decade and more.

Failing to hide an understanding smile, Emily inclined her head. "Indeed, Frederick, I'm very well." Emily's gaze returned to his mother, as if waiting for a shoe to fall.

On following Emily's gaze, Frederick caught a glint of calculation in his mother's eyes. That she'd called him up for some purpose from his preferred abode of the marquessate's principal seat, Brampton Hall in Surrey, wasn't a surprise. What that purpose was...

He sank into the wing chair on the other side of the hearth, fixed his mother with a weary look, and in a resigned tone, inquired, "What is it this time, Mama?"

His mother blinked her eyes wide. "Whatever do you mean, dear boy?" With barely a pause, she went on, "Tell me, how are things faring at Brampton?"

So, it's to be like that, is it? Stifling a sigh, he replied with what patience he could muster; his mother would reveal her hand when she was ready and not before. As it happened, he would have returned to town in a week's time to attend an event; responding to her summons hadn't truly put him out.

His mother ran through her usual questions regarding the estate, the staff, and the tenants, then angled a look at Emily.

Emily duly caught his gaze. "Are you pursuing any particular musical text at the moment?"

Suppressing a frown, he answered; the question was guaranteed to distract him and pass the time—there were few weeks in the year when he wasn't either studying or on the trail of some ancient musical text. The history of music—of ancient music in particular—had been his abiding interest since he'd left Eton. Yet Emily being prompted by his mother to ask such a question now, rather than, for instance, in the drawing room before dinner, suggested she was intent on keeping him in the sitting room—presumably because the reason for her summons was about to manifest.

Two minutes later, Fortingale, the butler, appeared and announced, "Lady Eustacia Cavanaugh has called, my lady." With a bow to Frederick, Fortingale added, "My lord."

A single glance at his mother's face was enough to inform Frederick that Lady Eustacia was, indeed, the reason his mother had inveigled him into returning to the capital.

Her eyes lighting as if Lady Eustacia's arrival was a delightful surprise, his mother declared, "How lovely! Do show her ladyship in, Fortingale."

Fortingale bowed and withdrew.

Rising in anticipation of the lady's entrance, Frederick shot his mother a narrow-eyed look. He'd thought she'd given up all attempts at match-making years ago. Apparently not, yet if she thought time had eroded his defenses, she was destined to suffer comprehensive disappointment.

Piqued over having been jockeyed into a meeting for which he had absolutely no desire, with his temper stirring, he turned toward the door as Fortingale opened it and ushered in...a vision.

Lady Eustacia Cavanaugh was, without a doubt, the most vibrantly attractive lady Frederick had ever laid eyes on.

With only the most cursory of curious glances his way, she glided forward and curtsied gracefully to his mother. "Lady Philippa. Thank you for receiving me."

Beaming, his mother held out a hand. "It's a pleasure to welcome you, my dear."

Lady Eustacia straightened and clasped his mother's hand.

With her free hand, his mother waved at him. "You must allow me to present my son, Albury."

Eyes of a soft periwinkle blue lifted to Frederick's face. Lady Eustacia's gaze was open, direct, and surprisingly, devoid of guile.

She carried herself well, with her head held high on a long, slender neck. Her face was heart-shaped, her nose straight, her lips lush and full. Her features were finely drawn, the lines worthy of a master painter, and her pale, porcelain-fine skin with its milk-and-roses complexion was utterly without flaw. She was, at best, of medium height, and her figure was voluptuously curvaceous, yet it was neither her features nor her curves that rendered her so eye-catching. That effect—that jolting impact—was primarily due to her coloring, to the dramatic contrast between her pale complexion and her glossy locks the color of the richest mahogany, those large, soft blue eyes, heavily fringed by sweeping black lashes and set beneath delicately arched dark brows, and the crushed-strawberry delight of her seductively beckoning lips.

Frederick sensed his resistance wavering and promptly strengthened it; the lady might be stunning, but given his mother's hand in arranging this meeting, Eustacia Cavanaugh had to bode ill for him. More, as his mind refocused on self-preservation, he realized who she was; he invested in syndicates run by Lord Randolph Cavanaugh, and unless Frederick missed his guess, Lady Eustacia had to be Rand's younger sister.

That meant she was the daughter of a marquess and the half sister of Ryder Cavanaugh, the current Marquess of Raventhorne, and thus belonged to the same rank of the nobility as Frederick himself.

She inclined her head to him and curtsied, sinking to precisely the correct degree. "Lord Albury."

"Lady Eustacia." Ingrained good manners had him clasping and bowing over the hand she offered—long, delicate fingers sheathed in soft skin—only to feel a distinct spark of connection, a definite jerk on his sensual chain.

Really?

Everything male in him immediately fixated on her. As she straightened, he saw consciousness flash behind her eyes and a hint of color tinge her cheeks, but then her lashes lowered, and she drew back her hand, and he was forced to let her fingers slide from his.

Intriguing.

Swiftly, he ran his gaze over her; she was fashionably attired in a walking dress of bright cherry red, which made the most of her dramatic coloring yet was distinctly severe in cut and style, almost repressively so. Although he paid scant attention to female fashions, he was fairly sure the current trend for walking dresses wasn't quite so buttoned up.

"And yes, Frederick"—his mother's voice drew his attention from whence it had wandered—"I confess that the suspicions you're harboring are entirely correct."

He was fairly certain that was the case; Lady Eustacia wore no ring, so was presumably unmarried, and therefore, given her station, let alone her connections, she numbered among the ladies he could not seduce.

His mother rolled on, "Lady Eustacia approached me regarding a matter involving you and music. I requested your return to town so she might put her notion to you directly."

He stiffened as the words registered, and his resistance roared back to life. He could guess what was coming; had Eustacia been of lesser rank, he would simply have said "No" and walked from the room. But she was Rand's sister—Ryder's sister; he had to be polite.

Schooling his expression to one of cool implacability, he refocused on

Eustacia Cavanaugh's arresting face and arched an arrogant, distinctly chilly, intentionally intimidating interrogatory eyebrow.

To his surprise, she regarded him with a directness that would generally be considered overbold, and a frown lurked in the depths of her blue eyes.

Stacie had thought she'd prepared herself for this meeting—that she'd come with her arguments well-rehearsed and perfectly structured to overwhelm the defenses of a reclusive, resistant, recalcitrant, and thoroughly difficult-to-sway nobleman—only to have her concentration fractured by the utterly mundane touch of his fingers closing around hers.

Despite her years of experience within the ton, the resulting flare of sensation—the shock of it rippling over her senses—had been unprecedented and intensely unsettling.

She'd been warned he was handsome, but no one had mentioned how disturbingly attractive he was in the flesh. Sable-brown hair fell in fashionably cropped locks about his well-shaped head, framing a wide forehead, while his clean-shaven face bore the hallmarks of his ancestry—well-set, heavy-lidded eyes beneath strong eyebrows and fringed by thick, dark lashes, combined with chiseled cheekbones, a strong aquiline nose, and a square chin—although the firm yet sensual line of his lips didn't quite match the rigid austerity of the planes of cheek and brow.

He was on the tallish side, with broad shoulders, narrow hips, and long, lean legs, and was impeccably attired in a black coat of the finest superfine worn over pristine ivory linen, a pale-gray-silk waistcoat, and well-fitted buckskin breeches. He had, apparently, just driven up from the country, yet not a speck of dust marred the glossy surface of his black boots.

All the above created a visual distraction, but it was the intensity in his gaze and the sense of a powerful personality behind his light-brown eyes that transfixed her senses; his very presence captured her attention in a way she'd never before encountered.

But she'd worked and schemed to get this meeting. She couldn't afford to waste the opportunity, especially as, judging by the icy reserve that now cloaked him, she wouldn't get a second chance.

"Lord Albury," she began.

"Lady Eustacia," he immediately responded, in an aloof and utterly bored tone that all but screamed she was wasting her time.

But she wasn't a lady easily cowed; she seized the opening. "Please—

call me Stacie." She held his gaze and relaxed her lips into a charmingly inviting smile. "Everyone does."

He didn't blink. "I've rarely thought of myself as 'everyone.'"

So he's determined to be difficult. Her smile deepened; two could play that game. "Indeed, you are quite unique, my lord"—from the corner of her eye, she saw his mother battle to stifle a snort—"which is the primary reason I've sought this meeting, so that I may lay before you a proposition that I believe will appeal to your musical interests."

He cast about for some sharp riposte, but what could he say? In the end, he arched a languid brow, inviting her to proceed.

"As you're doubtless aware, for many years—decades, in fact—ton hostesses have made a point of hiring foreign musicians to perform at all their musical events throughout the Season." That wasn't what he'd expected her to speak of; she detected faint confusion surfacing behind his eyes. Holding his gaze, she continued, "Those musicians come from France, Italy, Spain—even Germany and Russia. Indeed, many of the current crop of musicians lauded on the Continent were, as they say, 'discovered' here. They arrived in England as mere hopefuls and, through becoming the protégés of powerful hostesses, built a following here and, eventually, returned to their own country with money, experience, and a reputation they wouldn't otherwise have gained."

He was frowning faintly. "I'm aware of how the world of music operates, Lady Eustacia."

"Stacie," she reminded him. "And I expect you are. But have you ever considered the consequent plight of our local English musicians?"

He blinked, and she went on, "Consider, if you will—our musicians do not travel to the Continent. Even if they made the journey, while there are similar musical events—salons, musicales—held in all European capitals, the performers for those are drawn from the ranks of local musicians who have returned after making their name in England. London—and Edinburgh, admittedly, but given the sheer number of events, London most especially—is the crucible in which musicians' fortunes are forged."

He nodded somewhat curtly, but he was listening now. When she'd appealed to his mother, her companion, and his sisters regarding her scheme, all had agreed the idea was brilliant, but that it was impossible to get Albury to do anything he did not wish to; apparently, he was one of those men who was highly resistant to being managed and, conversely, always insisted on getting his own way.

However, his cooperation was vital for the achievement of Stacie's goal and her pursuit of the purpose in life she'd crafted as her own—an undertaking that suited her perfectly, given her longstanding appreciation of and devotion to classical music performances.

In light of that, she'd elected to view recruiting Albury as a challenge to her manipulative wiles, a legitimate use of the innate talent she'd inherited from her mother. At least in this, she could put that native skill to good use.

"As I'm sure you'll agree," she went on, "we English are not devoid of musical talent—your own ability gives that the lie." She didn't dare shift her gaze from his eyes; she was still feeling her way with him, trying to gauge his reactions via his irritatingly impassive countenance. "However, exceptional musical talent is not in any way linked to wealth or social rank. Consequently, while through a handful of long-ago performances in your mother's and sisters' drawing rooms, you attained fame"—his face abruptly hardened, and she held up a placating hand—"a fame I accept you did not seek and have little use for, but that, nonetheless, you easily gained, worthy English musicians from less-exalted social ranks find the hostesses' doors are closed to them, and therefore, the ton's eyes are shut to them. They have no opening—no stage on which they might prove themselves and so achieve the standing of soloist. No matter how wonderfully talented they are, the best our local musicians can hope for is a position in one of the theater orchestras or as one of a group of chamber musicians, playing hidden away in alcoves at the lesser balls."

From the corner of her eye, she could see his mother and Mrs. Weston avidly following the exchange, but there was no point appealing to them for assistance. Her plan—her purpose—would live or die on her ability to convince Albury to throw in his lot with her.

After several seconds of holding her gaze—with absolutely no sign of softening in his face—his lashes flickered, and he tipped his head. "I'm aware the situation is as you describe."

But what do you propose to do about it? hung in the air between them —precisely the invitation she'd angled for.

She tipped up her chin and met his unvoiced challenge. "It's my ambition to advance the prospects of local English musicians by using my social standing to create opportunities to display their talents before the haut ton."

Real interest—an arrested sort of interest—flared in his eyes; she'd broken through his walls—or at least found a chink in his armor.

"In short," she went on, "I propose to host musical evenings, featuring as performers the best local musicians one of the premier music schools in London has to offer."

When she paused, his eyes slowly narrowed, signaling that, in envisioning such an event, he perceived the obvious weakness in her plan.

Meeting his increasingly suspicious gaze, she gently smiled. "Of course, not even my name and the backing of my supporters would be enough to fill my rooms for a program featuring only unknown local performers."

The penny dropped; he straightened, resistance and rejection flashing across his face.

Before he could say no, she ruthlessly pressed on, "And that, Lord Albury, is why I wished to lay my plan before you and, in the name of our best local musicians, appeal to you to support my endeavor by agreeing to perform as the essential drawcard for such events."

Frederick wanted to say no. To simply refuse and...move on to discussing something else with the surprisingly engaging—attractively confounding—Lady Eustacia. Stacie.

Instead, he stared at her as the realization sank in that he honestly didn't know how he wished to respond to her invitation.

He'd been annoyed by her conspiring with his mother to gain this meeting, but the irritation was fading. If she'd tried to contact him directly, he wouldn't have agreed to see her; perhaps he should be thankful she hadn't thought to approach him through Rand or Ryder. And she'd confounded him with her request—an appeal to his better self that was shockingly well-aimed.

Her argument regarding local musicians was logical, well-based, and struck a chord with him, yet he was equally drawn by her physical attributes and by her determination to place her argument before him and attempt to lure him into breaking his self-imposed rule of playing only for himself or for scholarly purposes.

Yet his suspicions remained; that she was unmarried, attractive, of his own social class, and had approached him through his mother signaled that this was a matchmaking attempt, albeit one of significantly greater subtlety than any previous tilt at him.

He was perfectly aware that he ranked very highly as an eligible parti —yet surely, so must she.

She wasn't that young; from her assured behavior, he judged she was at least twenty-five years old. So why wasn't she married?

If they'd been alone, he would have asked her—to confound her as much as to hear what she would say. Yet if she was avoiding marriage, then presumably she harbored no matrimonial intentions toward him; indeed, she'd given no sign of trying to lure him in that way, which suggested that her quest to help local musicians was her true purpose in confronting him.

He had no intention of agreeing to her request, yet he didn't want to refuse her outright—not before learning more about her scheme. The prospect might prove to be as intriguing as she was, and Lord knew, he was bored.

Jaded and bored.

Even though he hadn't been looking for diversion, Lady Eustacia— Stacie—had given him something novel to think about.

He held her gaze and coolly stated, "I acknowledge the validity of the points you've made. I'll consider your proposal and inform you of my decision in due course."

Would she argue and try to press him?

She didn't shift her eyes from his; behind the blue of hers, he saw calculation—an assessing consideration she didn't try to hide.

Then, to his considerable surprise, her lashes veiled her eyes, and she inclined her head. "Thank you, my lord."

Stacie returned her gaze to his face. "The musicians of London and I will await your decision in the hope that you will see your way to lending your support in an arena and in a way only a nobleman of your particular talents can."

With that parting shot, she forced herself to turn to his mother and, gracefully, take her leave. While uttering the customary phrases, she swiftly reviewed the short meeting. Unless she'd misread him, Albury's response had been a test of sorts; exactly what he'd been angling to determine, she didn't know, but she'd got the clear impression that he'd expected her to argue further—so she'd done the opposite.

With him, she was reduced to operating on instinct; she hadn't been able to get any clear indication of his thoughts so had been forced to forsake logic and fall back on her innate abilities.

He might not have agreed to her proposal, but he hadn't refused yet; at the very least, she would get another chance to persuade him to her cause.

A cause that, sadly, would go nowhere without his active involvement. His and only his; his agreement to perform was crucial to her success, to her achieving the goal she'd set herself. Consequently, in pursuit of his agreement, she was willing to play a long game. What she'd seen and learned of him in this meeting had confirmed that persuading him to perform at her musical evenings would require unwavering persistence and commitment to her goal. Luckily, she'd been born with the former, and the latter had grown to an unshakeable resolve.

At the last, she turned to him and offered her hand. "Lord Albury."

He clasped her fingers, and his golden gaze trapped hers. For a second, he hesitated, then said, "If I'm to call you Stacie, then perhaps you should call me Frederick."

Those were close to the last words she'd expected him to utter; they distracted her from suppressing her awareness of him—from steeling her senses against his physical impact—and her fingers quivered beneath his before she ruthlessly hauled her mind back to its task. Stilling her fingers, too wary to take her eyes from his, she inclined her head. "Frederick, then. Until next we meet."

A slight lift to one eyebrow signaled that he'd heard her unstated challenge, then he inclined his head and released her hand.

With her heart unexpectedly thudding, she flashed the marchioness and her companion a grateful smile, then turned and walked to the door. A footman opened it, and sufficiently satisfied with her first tilt at Albury—Frederick—with her head high, she sailed through and found the butler waiting to see her out.

Frederick watched the door close behind Stacie Cavanaugh and owned himself puzzled—by her behavior and by his.

Until next we meet. Obviously, he would be seeing her again—and most likely, without his mother in attendance.

Speaking of whom…

He turned his head and directed a pointed look at his parent. When all she did was blink at him, he arched his brows in patent longsuffering, then with a nod to her and Emily, made for the door.

To his no doubt abiding distraction, he was actually looking forward to crossing paths with Lady Eustacia—Stacie—again.

When the door closed behind Frederick, the marchioness turned and exchanged an intrigued look with Emily. "Well!" the marchioness declared. "That went a great deal better than I'd expected."

Emily nodded. "He didn't just say no."

"Indeed." The marchioness's expression turned pensive. After several moments sunk in thought, she mused, "I did wonder, when Stacie appeared on the doorstep, as it were, if that might be a sign. If any lady has proved as resistant to the notion of marriage as Frederick, then surely it would be she."

"One has to admit that they seem to share a great many interests, including avoiding the altar."

The marchioness nodded. "I do believe, Emily dear, that Fate might have finally taken a hand and steered Stacie into Frederick's path."

"Or him into hers, as the case may be."

"Regardless"—the marchioness sat up, determination infusing both her spine and her expression—"Stacie Cavanaugh is unquestionably the best prospect for a daughter-in-law yet to come our way. We must stand ready to do whatever we can to assist in securing such a desirable result."

Two mornings later, at an hour when the majority of the ton could be relied on to still be in their beds, Frederick rode his favorite black gelding into the park. He enjoyed the early-morning silence, and once deep in the park, where the sounds of the awakening city were even more muted, he could almost imagine he was at Brampton Hall, engulfed in the soothing peace of the countryside.

The few other riders about at that hour weren't interested in socializing any more than he was. With a nod or a salute, they passed each other on the sward or waited for their turn to thunder down the tan of Rotten Row.

He'd galloped down once and was returning to the head of the track, close by Apsley House, when his gaze fell on the distinctive cherry-red riding habit of a female rider perched atop a good-looking, frisky bay mare.

Stacie.

His lips started to curve before he'd realized. He began to straighten them, then surrendered and let his faintly cynical smile show.

She halted a little way from the track and scanned the riders; her gaze reached him, and after a second of studying him, she sent the mare his way.

She circled and fell in alongside as he held his black to a long-legged walk.

He was conscious of her gaze running over him.

When he turned his head and looked at her, she inclined her head. "Good morning, Frederick."

"Stacie." Viewed in retrospect, it was odd they'd advanced so quickly to a first-name basis. He cocked a brow at her. "Tell me, was using first names a deliberate ploy to make me look upon your proposal more favorably?"

She widened her eyes at him. "Of course. First names get one past the awkwardness of lord this and lady that, and I would prefer that you didn't view my proposal in the light of social interaction."

"Indeed?" He paused, then felt compelled to ask, "How would you prefer I viewed it?"

She'd looked ahead and now raised her chin. "As an invitation to contribute to the greater good in a field in which you harbor real interest."

He pondered that, then tipped his head her way. "Good answer."

"Thank you."

They joined the small queue of riders waiting to gallop down the tan track.

There was sufficient space between them and the riders ahead and those behind for their conversation to remain private; he waited for her to ask for his decision regarding her request, but again, she surprised him.

Her gaze on the riders before them, she watched with apparent interest as each group or rider took their turn and—for the most part— shot off down the track.

Then it was their turn. He glanced her way and arched a resigned brow. "I presume you don't gallop?"

Most young ladies toed the line laid down by the influential hostesses who ruled the ton and deemed a public gallop a sign of unfettered wildness.

Her gaze trained down the track, she smiled. "How many grandes dames do you imagine are watching?"

Then she tapped her heel to the mare's flank, and the bay shot forward.

After a split second of shocked surprise, he loosened the black's reins and set off in pursuit. Whoops from the gentlemen who'd been behind them in the queue echoed in his ears as he flew down the tan in her wake.

His black was the stronger horse, but the bay was fleet of foot and carried a lighter rider who, he had to admit, knew how to ride. He caught up to her only on the last stretch. She threw him a laughing—challenging

—glance, then leaned forward, and they raced neck and neck to the end of the tan.

They shot off the track and wheeled to the right, onto the grass, and slowed.

Frederick stared at her, conscious of the wild thunder of his heartbeat, of the sheer exhilaration that coursed through his veins.

She tipped back her head and laughed, rather breathlessly, then shot him a smiling glance. "Thank you. That was fun."

He shook his head at her and set the black to walk beside her bay. "Do your brothers know you ride like that?"

"Who do you think taught me?" She looked ahead, still breathing deeply enough to have him battling the urge to stare at her chest rather than her face. "When I was younger, Rand, and sometimes Kit, too, used to let me sneak out and ride with them at this hour." She nodded ahead, and he saw a mounted groom waiting under a tree. "I still occasionally ride at this time—much better than later, when there are too many of the ready-to-be-censorious about."

Frederick waited, but when she set course for her groom, transparently intending to leave the park, he heard himself say, "I wondered when you would reappear. I have to own to being impressed you thought to seek me out here."

She shrugged. "I asked your mother if you rode in the mornings. It seemed a reasonable venue in which to meet, in case you've come to a decision regarding my proposal."

He noted she'd slid around asking outright if he'd decided. "I'm still considering it."

She acknowledged his reply with a tip of her head, then as they neared her groom, she drew rein and met his gaze. "In that case, I'll leave you to the rest of your morning."

Gracefully, she half bowed.

Instinctively, he returned the gesture with elegant flair. And said nothing at all.

With a subtle smile, she turned away and set her mare trotting.

Frederick watched as she rode toward the Stanhope Gate, with her groom falling in behind her.

Until next we meet had been the words that had sprung to the tip of his tongue, but he hadn't uttered them.

He remained inclined to refuse her request, yet some impulse argued increasingly stridently against that tack. Whether that impulse was fueled by his suspicion that her proposal almost certainly had merit and he should, therefore, seriously consider it or merely by a wish to see what her next tactic might be, he couldn't have said, yet he doubted this morning would be the last he saw of her.

Theoretically, she might change her mind and pursue some other less-reticent principal performer. Against that, she patently knew what a draw-card he would be—an arrogant assessment, perhaps, yet entirely justified. Given he'd sequestered himself from the ton for more than a decade, refusing to play at even his mother's or sisters' events, his earlier performances had attained a near-legendary status.

If he deigned to sit before a piano at a ton event, the hordes would gather.

Despite his entrenched resistance to her scheme to use him and his talent to draw attention to that of other musicians, he couldn't fault her reasoning. Or her consequent plotting.

He stirred, shook his reins, and set the black walking homeward.

And inwardly admitted that, in viewing the upcoming days, the most intriguing prospect exercising his mind was what Stacie would do next.

∼

The following afternoon, Frederick opened the door to his favorite book-shop and strolled inside.

A bell jangled loudly. After closing the door, Frederick paused to breathe in the aroma of parchments and glue and the musty scent that spoke of aged, even ancient, tomes.

The poky little shop off Leicester Square was the domain of Mr. Griggs, musical bibliophile extraordinaire. Shelves covered both side walls, reaching up into the shadows, and four freestanding rows of shelves ran parallel to the walls down the length of the shop, creating alleys so narrow that Frederick had to turn slightly sideways to negotiate passage to the counter at the rear of the room.

Daylight barely penetrated that far; when he reached the counter, Frederick saw that, as usual, Griggs had a shielded lamp burning.

Frederick hadn't muted his steps, yet only when he leaned on the counter did Griggs, a curmudgeonly sort, place a thick finger on the page he was reading and look up.

Recognition flowed over Griggs's heavy features, and he grunted. "It's you."

Unperturbed by the reception, Frederick smiled. "Good afternoon, Griggs. How's business?" That was Frederick's customary invitation for Griggs to bend his ear about whatever books on musical history had recently fallen into the old man's hands.

Frederick had been haunting Griggs's shop ever since he'd discovered it in his teens. Many of the volumes that now graced his library had passed through Griggs's hands.

"Well enough." Griggs pushed off the stool on which he'd been perched and bent to reach beneath the counter. "I 'spect you'll want to take a look at these books I got in from a contact in Switzerland." Griggs rose, bearing a foot-high stack of unusual-sized volumes covered in old leather. "In German, they are, but you can read that, can't you?"

"I can, indeed," Frederick said as Griggs placed the stack on the counter and handed over the first volume. Frederick took it, opened the cover, then arched his brows and shot Griggs a look. "A thesis?"

Griggs nodded and hiked himself back onto his stool. "Seems some university library was wanting to thin their shelves. My contact couldn't believe his luck."

"Hmm." Frederick turned the pages with care. The discards of learned institutions had supplied a goodly number of the most valuable volumes in his collection. The thesis in his hands concerned Hellenic composers of the fifth century and focused on musical forms created for stringed instruments. Closing the book, he nodded. "I'll take this one." He reached for the next book on the pile.

He worked steadily through the stack, selecting three volumes to add to his hoard, then settled to haggle with Griggs. After they'd reached an accommodation satisfactory to both, Griggs rehid the books Frederick had rejected and, taking his selected three, retreated through a curtained doorway into the private area of the shop to wrap and tie the books.

Frederick picked up a recently released tome on Romanian music. He was flipping through it when the shop door opened, setting the bell raucously jangling. A second later, the door closed, then light footsteps sounded and skirts swished as someone—some lady—made her way to the counter.

About to set aside the book, Frederick froze. It couldn't be—could it?

"Griggs? Are you there?"

He recognized the voice and turned to face Stacie as she stepped out of the central row of shelves.

She met his gaze, and although her brows rose, he saw no hint of real surprise. She dipped into a graceful curtsy. "My lord."

He bowed. "Lady Eustacia." Back to formal address; they were in public, after all.

Instead of remaining focused on him, her attention deflected toward the curtain as Griggs came lumbering out, the wrapped package of Frederick's books in his hands.

At the sight of Stacie, Griggs's face lit up to such an extent that Frederick blinked and stared.

"Ah—it's you, my lady." Griggs beamed. "Come to check on that order, have you?"

"I have, indeed." Stacie returned the old man's smile. She'd been following Frederick, biding her time, wanting the perfect location in which to approach him yet again; she'd been delighted to see him going into Griggs's, allowing her to use her entirely genuine connection with Griggs to conceal her determined pursuit. Or at least confuse the issue. "I don't suppose there's any chance the book's arrived?"

"Sadly, it hasn't, my lady." Griggs set down a package of books on the counter in front of Frederick. "But my man in Paris says he knows just where to get it. A week or so, and it should be here."

She sighed. "I'll just have to possess my soul in patience." She looked at the package of books on the counter, then raised her gaze and met Frederick's eyes. "What did you buy?"

He hesitated for an instant, but then replied, "A thesis on Hellenic stringed instrumentals of the fifth century, a guide to old Romany folk tunes, and a treatise on the Renaissance composers who performed at the Medici court." Before she could comment, he asked, "What book do you have on order?" With a faint lift of his brows, he added, "Who knows? I might have a copy, either here in town or in Surrey."

She let her smile deepen. "It's *Courvoisier's Arrangements for Harp* —a collection of works, French, from the Languedoc region."

"I see. Sadly, I don't number that volume among my collection. Do you play the harp?"

She laughed and shook her head. "Not nearly well enough. But these particular arrangements form the accompaniments to a collection of troubadour songs, and I do occasionally sing."

Honest interest flared in his eyes.

"It's my belief," Griggs put in, leaning on the counter, "that we don't hear enough of those old songs. Of course, most of them are long."

Frederick nodded. "Troubadour songs generally tell a story—that was the reason they were sung—and that makes them significantly too long for modern audiences."

"There's the language as well," Stacie said. "Most need to be translated, and that's rarely done well."

A three-way discussion ensued, one Stacie couldn't have planned better had she tried.

But eventually, after they'd pulled apart the topic of the modern performance of troubadour songs until there was nothing left to be said, Frederick straightened and picked up his wrapped books. He caught her eye. "Is your carriage nearby?" When she nodded, he said, "I'll escort you to it."

Perfect. All she needed was a moment in which to gauge his direction vis-à-vis her proposition.

Gaily, she farewelled Griggs and led the way up the central aisle. She shifted aside and allowed Frederick to open the door for her, then stepped onto the pavement and paused.

After closing the door, he halted beside her. He studied her for an instant, then asked, "Do you always wear red?"

Not the comment she'd expected and doubtless designed to throw her off her stride. She lightly shrugged. "I'm told the color suits me." She arched a brow his way and waited to see if he would respond.

After a second, he glanced around. "Your carriage?"

She smiled and waved at the sleek black carriage her coachman had drawn up to the curb twenty yards away. As they started in that direction, she airily said, "I assume you've yet to make up your mind over anchoring the performances at my musical evenings."

They reached the pavement beside the carriage, and he paused and looked down at her, his golden eyes meeting hers. Several seconds ticked by, then he replied, "Just so. I've yet to make up my mind."

She bit her tongue to hold back a tart quip that she'd always heard that hers was the indecisive sex.

Without shifting his gaze from hers, he reached out, opened the carriage door, and with a flourishing bow, gestured her inside.

With a graceful dip by way of farewell, she moved past him and climbed the steps.

When she turned and sat, he closed the door, then stepped back. At the last, as her coachman gave the horses the office and the carriage started to roll, Frederick raised a hand in salute—almost as if he hadn't been able to stop himself.

She leaned back against the squabs, replayed the exchange, then grinned.

He might not have agreed—indeed, for reasons known only to him, he might be deliberately leading her on and have no intention of agreeing to her request—but as long as he hadn't refused and denied her, hope remained.

That was good enough—encouragement enough—for her; she'd been warned wearing him down would take time.

The next day, Frederick lunched at his club, the Athenaeum, with his two closest friends, George Fitzsimmons, Lord Farleigh, and Percy Hawley, Viscount Piper. They'd been friends since Eton and met frequently whenever all three were in town.

Yet even while, relaxed and indulgent, Frederick listened to his friends' news and smiled at their jests, he was aware of a gnawing wish to be elsewhere, crossing verbal swords in a more stimulating—in multiple ways—encounter with a certain lady.

He couldn't recall ever being prey to such a distraction before and determinedly ignored the feeling.

Eventually, however, with a meeting with his man-of-business looming, he left the others in the smoking room and quit the hallowed precincts of the club.

After farewelling the doorman, he descended the steps to the pavement and turned toward Pall Mall—only to be brought to an immediate halt by a curvaceous lady in a stylish emerald-green carriage dress, who stood directly in his path.

Frederick arched a brow at her. "No red today?"

Her luscious lips curved. "No lady wishes to be predictable."

"I see." He found himself smiling back, captured by the light in her eyes. "And what brings you here?" He glanced around. "This is not an area generally frequented by ladies of the ton."

"Business," she replied, but didn't elaborate, leaving him to conclude that her business was with him. "I gathered that, when in town, you eschew the ton's balls and parties. Consequently, when I saw you exiting the club, I thought to seize the chance to inquire whether you had yet seen your way to agreeing to my request."

"I..." Frederick paused, surprised to discover that he didn't know how he wanted to answer—to agree or to refuse her. "In all honesty," he said, "I'm still considering your proposal—I haven't yet made up my mind."

And he hadn't.

Prior to meeting her, his response to such a request would have been an immediate and immutable negative. Now... Was he truly flirting with agreeing to her scheme?

He refocused on her face—on her dramatically vivid features—and saw them lighten, as if some inner glow had bloomed. Hope. She was hoping he would agree, and she truly wanted him to perform for her.

His reaction to the sight, to being the cause of that softening in her face, unsettled him.

He suddenly realized he was standing on the pavement within yards of the club's doors, and several who knew him, including George and Percy, might exit and come upon him and her at any moment.

Her periwinkle-blue eyes, bright and alert, were searching his face.

Rather than meet her gaze, he glanced toward Pall Mall and Waterloo Place beyond. "I take it your carriage is nearby?"

She waved to the west. "Just along Pall Mall."

He gestured in that direction. "I'll walk you to it."

With a graceful inclination of her head, she turned, and side by side, they walked to the corner and crossed the street. They'd almost reached the pavement on the other side when a youth wearing a courier's vest and carting a heavy leather satchel darted past, dodging between pedestrians as he raced to make his deliveries.

The lad bumped Stacie, knocking her off balance. Into Frederick.

He caught her elbow and steadied her.

Despite the flow of others all around, he was acutely aware of the tension that shot through them both—the sudden hitch in her breathing, the shockingly abrupt focusing of all his senses on her—and the impulses having his fingers clamped about her elbow sent surging through him. He wanted to draw her closer—a lot closer.

They gained the pavement safely, and he forced his fingers to ease and let her go.

She paused to look down and twitch her skirt straight. "Thank you." Her tone was even, but distinctly breathless.

He waved ahead, and they walked on, toward a black carriage that bore the Raventhorne coat of arms and stood waiting by the curb.

Determined to appear unaffected, Stacie raised her chin and ventured, "Please know you have only to ask if you require more details of my proposal in order to make your decision."

They reached the carriage and halted beside it. She raised her gaze to Frederick's face and told herself that when he'd steadied her, his touch hadn't held anything more than the usual protectiveness men like him—like her brothers—displayed toward ladies of their class; there was no reason to read anything more into the action.

His golden-brown eyes held hers. After several seconds, he replied, "If I need more information, I'll let you know—when next we meet."

Subtle challenge glowed in his eyes.

That seemed a propitious moment to part. Her footman had already opened the carriage door. With an easy smile and a dip of her head, she steeled herself and gave Frederick her hand and allowed him to help her up.

She settled on the seat, and the footman closed the door. Once again, as the carriage started rolling, Frederick raised his hand in a salute—this time, the gesture appeared more natural. More intentional.

When next we meet.

She wondered when that would be—specifically, how long she should wait before engineering another meeting.

Impatience urged her to track him down the next morning, but caution of a different stripe raised its head.

She examined the lingering constriction about her lungs and the strange breathlessness it caused, considered the tightness still afflicting her nerves, and wondered if, in seeking to lure Albury from his self-imposed social seclusion, she might have bitten off more than she'd expected.

Regardless, he was the only performer who could guarantee her scheme's success; she was committed to her purpose and was determined to triumph.

CHAPTER 2

*T*wo days later, Frederick strolled down Oxford Street on his way to Arthur's Music Emporium. After dwelling on the music sheets he hoped to find, it was a short step to considering what pieces he might play should he agree to be a part of Stacie's scheme.

He hadn't initially imagined he would agree, yet increasingly, he couldn't see himself disappointing her. He had a long acquaintance with importuning females; most, he found irritating in the extreme. Stacie, however, hadn't fallen into the trap of being too pushy and overstepping his line. She'd laid her request before him and, thereafter, had done nothing more than give him opportunities to accept, rather than badger him, seeking to make up his mind for him.

Indeed, he felt perfectly certain she'd crafted her approach deliberately to avoid provoking him into digging in his heels and categorically denying her. His mother and sisters must have warned her that was a real danger, so she'd taken steps to find her way around it. Her actions displayed a greater degree of intelligence and subtlety than ladies usually deployed in dealing with gentlemen, certainly those of his class, and that, in turn, left him more inclined to give her request genuine consideration.

The prospect of agreeing had slid across his mind more than once in the past days. However, no matter the likely positive outcomes—namely him spending more time basking in the warmth of Stacie's smiles and helping worthy fellow musicians—the drawbacks were significant. Him agreeing to perform at her function would open the floodgates to requests from his mother, his sisters, and every connection he possessed; they would all demand and expect him to perform for them as well, and he would have to expend considerable effort—and bear with significant aggravation along the way—to hold against them. He could and would do it, but just thinking of the battle made him weary.

In addition to that, performing in the ton again would inevitably reignite society's avid interest in him. Every grande dame and hostess, let alone every gossipmonger, would want to know how Stacie had lured him out of his self-imposed exile.

When gauged against those negatives, the positives didn't seem weighty enough to tip the scales.

Admittedly, he wouldn't be playing any composition of his own; he hadn't composed a single piece since the long-ago debacle that had prompted his retreat from the drawing rooms.

The thought drew his mind back to his hypothetical question of what he would play were he to agree to Stacie's request. Raising his gaze, he saw the board hanging above Arthur's door just ahead; he would cast his eyes over the new pieces Arthur had got in and see if any appealed.

Frederick opened the glass-paned door beneath the ornately lettered sign and walked inside. Light streamed through the south-facing windows; he closed the door and surveyed the rows of tables hosting countless thin-walled wooden boxes filled with sheet music. Arthur's had been a favorite haunt of his since before he'd been sent away to school, and every time he'd returned to London, he'd agitated until either his father or mother had brought him there to find and purchase fresh pieces to attempt.

The proprietor, Arthur Arthur, had been a canny judge of customers even then; he'd always given Frederick his personal attention, and on his part, Frederick hadn't been reticent over learning all he could from someone who truly knew music.

Smiling in anticipation of a pleasant interlude exchanging knowledge and opinions with Arthur, Frederick ambled down the central aisle toward the distant counter, set to one side at the rear of the shop; as he went, he glanced at the music sheets displayed on either side.

The shop was long; he was halfway down the aisle before he looked ahead and saw a lady standing before the counter in earnest conversation with old Arthur.

A lady with glossy dark-auburn hair and familiar curves, today clothed in a walking dress the color of burnished gold.

Frederick slowly continued down the aisle, quietly marveling. How had she known he would turn up there?

She couldn't have—which suggested she had her own reason for calling at Arthur's.

Curiosity burgeoning, Frederick went forward to join her.

As he approached the counter, Arthur's eyes shifted his way, then the old man's face creased in a genial smile.

Following Arthur's gaze, Stacie turned, and her eyes widened in genuine surprise. "Good afternoon, my lord." She glanced back at Arthur, then returned her gaze to Frederick. "I take it you're a patron of this august establishment, too."

"Indeed." Frederick halted at the counter, nodded a greeting to Arthur, then met Stacie's eyes. "I've been coming here since schooldays." He arched a brow at her. "You?"

She smiled. "Since I was in the schoolroom."

"Aye—I've known you both since you each were only just tall enough to see over this counter." Old Arthur patted the worn countertop and smiled at them. Then he said to Frederick, "I was just telling her ladyship here that I've heard we should have the next installment in Mendelssohn's 'Songs without Words'—Book Five, that'll be—later this year."

Frederick looked at Stacie. "Have you been collecting them?"

She nodded. "And you?"

"Of course—it's Mendelssohn and friends. So what did you think of Book Four?"

"I particularly like the adagio and the allegro vivace from that collection."

He nodded approvingly. "They do stand out."

She opened her blue eyes at him. "What composers do you favor?"

Unsurprisingly given the company, that question led to a lengthy discussion of the comparative merits of the compositions of composers ranging from Beethoven to Schubert, Liszt, Schumann, and Chopin, to the aforementioned Mendelssohn.

Frederick finally admitted a partiality for Schumann's "Fantasie in C Major." "That reminds me—I've been meaning to pick up a copy of Chopin's 'Ballade Number Four.'" He looked at Arthur. "I don't suppose you have one?"

Arthur grimaced. "I'd love to oblige, my lord, but that one's hard to come by. I don't have a copy in stock."

Frederick tapped the counter. "Put one on order for me, please."

"Of course, my lord." Arthur reached beneath the counter and brought out his order book.

Frederick felt Stacie's gaze and looked her way, brows arching in question.

She smiled. "If you're keen to try your hand at it, I have a copy, I'd be happy to lend it to you."

He waited, but she didn't put any condition on the offer. Didn't utter the words *if you'll agree to play at my recital.*

Slowly, his eyes locked with hers, he inclined his head. "Thank you. I might just take you up on that."

"Right, then." Arthur shut his order book. "As usual, I'll send notes around to you both when your pieces come in."

The door of the shop opened, admitting a harassed-looking lady and two schoolboys. The boys were arguing over who had priority in choosing what music they should take to their tutor's next lesson.

Arthur's attention shifted to the newcomers.

Frederick lightly touched Stacie's arm. "If you're ready, I'll see you to your carriage."

"Thank you." She exchanged a brief farewell with Arthur, Frederick did the same, and together, they stepped away from the counter. Skirting the trio heading purposefully toward Arthur, they made their way up the aisle.

Frederick lowered his head and his voice and asked, "What did you order?" He genuinely wanted to know.

"Mendelssohn's 'Carnavale.' I realized I don't have a copy."

He reached for the door handle and looked at her. "So you play the piano?"

She met his eyes briefly, a laughing light in hers. "Yes, but nowhere near as well as you."

He held the door for her, then followed her through and drew the door shut behind him. Releasing the knob, he murmured, "That doesn't actually convey a great deal—not many people do."

She laughed—and the sound danced over his senses. To his ears, the timbre was all bells, a lilting peal that lured and seduced.

She threw him a glance over her shoulder, her eyes alight with a similar allure. "And that, my lord, is why I'm intent on securing your services in support of those local musicians deserving of the patronage of the haut ton."

He halted on the pavement beside her and openly studied her.

She tipped her head and let him; she didn't look away.

Despite keeping his distance from society, he knew the haut ton—the gilded circle into which he and she had been born—well enough to know that she didn't quite fit. She wasn't the average young lady, intent only on securing a good marriage, be it a love-match or not. Her ambition was something quite different—she had a purpose that revolved about helping others and, more, served the greater good of music in general. That purpose was her driving force, and he had to admire her for that—had to admire her strength and devotion to a cause he could only applaud.

After several seconds, the glow in her face faded, and she asked, "Have you decided yet?"

He quashed the temptation to admit he had. "You're not going to give up, are you?" He wanted an excuse to surrender and give in—to appease that part of his mind that still insisted agreeing was a very bad idea.

She widened her eyes at him. "No." Then she added, "You are the performer I need to make my scheme a success. You and only you will do —so no, I will never give up trying to persuade you."

He held her gaze, then ventured, "I'm still not convinced. Not completely."

Stacie stared into his golden eyes. Although she could read little in them, she felt certain she'd understood him correctly. "You're saying that you're teetering on the cusp of agreeing, but that I need to provide some-thing more—some more compelling argument—to push you over the edge."

He considered her for a moment, then replied, "A somewhat lyrical assessment, but essentially correct."

A challenge, then—one she needed to meet to get what she wanted. She wracked her brains...then smiled and refocused on his eyes. "Very well. I suggest you accompany me on a visit to the institution currently vying with the Royal Academy for the title of premier music school in London and meet the local musicians I'm seeking to advance with my scheme."

Through her tone and the tilting of her chin, she made it clear that was her counterchallenge.

He searched her eyes, her face, then with his own expression studiously impassive, nodded. "All right." He arched his brows at her. "When should we go?"

～

The following afternoon, Stacie loitered on the pavement outside St Martin-in-the-Fields. The music school attached to the church had a lengthy history of fostering local London musicians.

She felt oddly tense, as if she had her fingers tightly crossed. She sensed she was close—so very close—to getting Frederick's agreement to play his part in her scheme, yet she wasn't certain that steering him through the school, having him meet the master and survey the work the school did, would prove sufficient to get Frederick over what he'd all but admitted was his last remaining hurdle.

Scanning the throng filling Trafalgar Square, she waited. Then she spotted him weaving elegantly through the crowd, heading directly for her.

By the time he stepped free of the milling horde, she'd plastered a bright smile on her face. "Good afternoon."

He half bowed. "As promised, here I am." He glanced behind her. "Do we enter through the church?"

"No." Turning, she gestured to the narrow street that ran down the side of the church. "The diocese runs several schools. Most, including the music school, are presently housed in this building." She indicated the large building on the other side of the street. "The music school is the third door along."

He nodded and walked beside her down the cobbled lane. When they reached the relevant entry, identified by a small plaque on the wall alongside, he reached past her and opened the door, then followed her inside.

Stacie led the way to a counter at the back of the small foyer. Beyond the barrier, two secretaries were busily working at a pair of desks; both looked up and, recognizing Stacie, smiled.

The older woman rose and came to the counter. "Lady Eustacia—how lovely to see you again."

"Good afternoon, Mrs. Withers." She waved at the presence by her side. "This is Lord Albury. I believe Mr. Protheroe is expecting us."

Frederick shot her a sidelong glance, but she made no move to meet it. After leaving him yesterday, she'd called on Protheroe to warn him of the importance of putting his and his students' best feet forward by way of convincing Frederick to participate in her scheme.

"Indeed, my lady." Mrs. Withers dragged her gaze from Frederick. "The master mentioned it—I'll just check that he's ready to receive you."

Mrs. Withers came out from behind the counter, bustled down the corridor to Stacie's right, tapped on the first door, then stuck her head inside. Stacie and Frederick were too far away to make out any of the whispered exchange, but Stacie could imagine Protheroe hurriedly tidying away the countless pages of music and correspondence that habitually covered his desk.

After several moments, Mrs. Withers drew back and beamed at Stacie and Frederick. "My lady, my lord. The master will see you now."

Stacie smiled and glided forward. On reaching the door, she walked into the room and halted before the desk behind which Protheroe—to her eyes, plainly nervous—stood waiting to greet them; she caught his eye and smiled encouragingly. The master was a slightly built man of about thirty-five years—a younger son of the gentry—with a steady gaze, a sure way with his juniors, and a profound understanding of all branches of music. His position as master wasn't a sinecure but had been granted on the basis of his achievements; he was considered by many to be a gifted teacher and a sound and well-liked administrator.

Frederick followed her into the room and halted beside her. A click sounded as Mrs. Withers closed the door.

"Lady Eustacia." Protheroe bowed to her, then to Frederick. "Lord Albury." Straightening, Protheroe fixed his gaze on Frederick's face. "Might I say, my lord, how very honored the school and, indeed, I myself are to have you visit?"

From the corner of her eye, Stacie saw Frederick blink—and held her breath. His mother and sisters had warned her that he could be diabolically cutting to those he saw as attempting to toady up to him. Would she have to step in and shield Protheroe?

But after a second's hiatus, Frederick only inclined his head in acknowledgment of the veiled tribute. "Lady Eustacia has piqued my interest with her description of the musicians here, Mr. Protheroe, and through my visit, I hope to see enough of their abilities to judge her devotion justified."

To Stacie's relief, Protheroe rose to the occasion. "My lord, I have no hesitation in recommending any of our seniors to your notice. All are of a standard that—given the chance—they could shine. Perhaps I might take you through our regimen of instruction in the senior year so you have an understanding of the various disciplines our students study, and then I can answer any questions you might have." Protheroe waved to the two chairs angled before the desk. "Please, sit."

Frederick held her chair for her, then elegantly sat in its mate.

Protheroe subsided into his chair, clasped his hands on the blotter, and launched into a patently rehearsed yet informative description of the teaching practices employed within the school. Frederick heard him out, then posed several questions, to which Protheroe had ready answers; the exchange was too technical for Stacie to follow, but from watching Frederick's face, she judged that Protheroe hadn't merely satisfied Frederick but had managed the difficult task of impressing him.

Her heart started to rise in hope.

Eventually, Frederick said, "Your curriculum is plainly sound and, as you say, closely mirrors that taught at the Royal Academy. Ultimately, however, the proof lies in the results."

"Quite so, my lord. I would be happy to take you on a short tour to meet some of our advanced students—those who have, essentially, completed their studies and are polishing their skills in the hope of finding a position with one of the country's orchestras or, failing that, in some other ensemble."

Frederick indicated his agreement with that plan and rose. As Stacie got to her feet, he met her eyes. "Are you coming?"

"I've already met all the senior students. I'll trail behind."

He tipped his head in acceptance and joined Protheroe, who waved Frederick to precede him out of the door.

Frederick waited in the corridor for Protheroe to join him. He'd noticed the framed certificate on the wall that declared Protheroe a graduate of the Royal Academy. On top of that, he'd been impressed by the breadth of the man's musical understanding; it remained to be seen if Protheroe's pupils measured up to the same standard.

The master led him to a small room in which three pupils were practicing a violin concerto. All three lifted their bows at Protheroe and Frederick's entrance, then lowered their instruments and bowed. To Frederick's approval, Protheroe introduced him merely as a potential benefactor and indicated that the boys should proceed. Along with Protheroe, Frederick stood by the wall just inside the door and listened.

After a moment, Stacie slipped into the room and joined them, but by then, Frederick had been captured by the music.

He was a longtime member of the Royal Philharmonic Society and had studied, albeit privately, with tutors from the Royal Academy of Music. His connections in the musical sphere ensured he always knew of any major musician who appeared in London or, indeed, anywhere in England. He came up to town whenever any major artist was performing and, through the years, had attended innumerable concerts and recitals.

He'd heard many concert-grade violinists; indeed, during his version of a Grand Tour, one dictated by musical performances, he'd even heard the great Niccolò Paganini play. While none of the three violinists before him were likely to attain Paganini's virtuosity, to Frederick's highly educated ears, all three were definitely up to concert-level performance. As all looked to be in their early twenties and equally transparently were not the sons of gentlemen, that was no mean feat.

Although Frederick had attended several excellent concerts in St Martin-in-the-Fields, he'd never thought to wonder where the performers hailed from; even if he had, he would have assumed they were graduates of the Royal Academy. Similarly, whenever he attended the opera or the theater, the orchestra in the pit was simply there—a fixture.

But such orchestras were composed of individual musicians, all striving to make a living through their art. And realistically, given the relatively low number of Academy graduates per year, less well-heeled schools such as this one had to be the source of many of the professional musicians who entertained the populace throughout the country.

The three violinists performing before him were, in his judgment, worthy of greater recognition than a position in some pit in a provincial theater.

The three reached the end of a movement, and Protheroe spoke up. "Thank you, boys. That was excellent. We'll leave you now."

The boys lowered their instruments and bowed again. Frederick inclined his head, then followed Stacie and Protheroe from the room.

Protheroe took him to listen to a group of cellists, then a pair of flautists, before they sat in on a rehearsal for an upcoming recital at Apsley House. "The Duke of Wellington has long been a supporter," Protheroe murmured, "but as he is a bachelor, playing at his events rarely leads to subsequent engagements in wider society."

Frederick felt Stacie's pointed look, but didn't need to meet it to understand Protheroe's point. Until musicians caught the eyes and ears of major ton hostesses, engagements for the salons and musicales through which solo artists made their name were unlikely to come their way. They might manage ensemble engagements to play at balls or soirées, but the pinnacle of society performance would remain beyond their reach.

That was what Stacie was aiming to change with her musical events.

It was a cause he could all too easily see himself supporting.

But...he needed to think carefully before he leapt. He hadn't forgotten the intensity of the mania that had engulfed him all those years ago; he definitely didn't want to have to weather such an experience again.

When Protheroe sent Frederick a questioning look, he nodded, and the three of them quietly left the rehearsal room. After shutting the door behind them, Protheroe looked at Frederick and lightly grimaced. "I know your personal interest lies in the pianoforte, but sadly, none of our graduate pianists are scheduled for practice sessions today."

Frederick inclined his head. "A pity. However, I believe I've seen enough to judge that"—he glanced at Stacie—"as Lady Eustacia maintains, this school is producing soloists worthy of the ton's attention."

Stacie's eyes lit; he could almost see delight flaring in her eyes.

Before she could ask if that meant he'd decided to agree to play at her events, he temporized, "I must now think hard about how best I might support your endeavors." He transferred his gaze to Protheroe. "I congratulate you on all you're achieving here. I expect Lady Eustacia will inform you of my ultimate decision."

At the edge of his vision, he saw the light in Stacie's eyes fade, and she looked at him in a puzzled, curious way.

Protheroe, however, was accustomed to such equivocal responses; with no sign of disappointment, he bowed and said, "If there's any further information I can provide, my lord, you have only to ask."

Four young cellists, barely taller than their instruments, were gathered in the hallway a little way along and were regarding Protheroe expectantly.

He glanced at the boys and smiled, then turned back to Frederick and Stacie. "My next class." Protheroe looked at Stacie. "If you know your way back…"

She smiled and assured him she did.

With another bow, Protheroe left them. Frederick watched him gather his pupils and noted with approval the boys' transparent eagerness to start their lesson—the sign of an excellent teacher.

Then he turned to Stacie and found her regarding him through narrowed eyes. He arched his brows at her.

"You're being difficult."

He humphed and waved her toward the front foyer. "I have my reasons. And if it's any consolation, on the strength of what I've seen today, I'm inclined to agree to your request—I just have to convince myself that doing so will not feature as the most stupid decision of my life."

She would have been in the schoolroom when the debacle occurred, and even if his mother and sisters had told her of it—and he wasn't sure they would have—they had never comprehended the depth of his revulsion; he seriously doubted Stacie had any inkling of what she was asking him to do.

But when, frowning, her gaze on his face, she opened her mouth to inquire, he tersely shook his head. "No—I'm not going to explain."

He looked ahead and heard her softly humph, but she glided beside him along the corridor and around the corner into the hallway that led to the front foyer.

The familiar chords from the opening of the adagio molto from Beethoven's "Piano Sonata Number 21" reached them, and Frederick halted. Head tilting, he listened; whoever was playing was accomplished. Not in Frederick's league—but only a few rungs below.

Without conscious direction, his feet followed the music to a door along the corridor. Silently, he turned the knob, then slipped through the doorway, into a small practice room housing a grand pianoforte. He paused against the wall, holding still so as not to disturb the young man who was playing with admirable passion and laudable technique.

The piano faced down the room; if the pianist lifted his eyes, he would see them. But his focus was all for the ivory keys beneath his fingers, his concentration absolute.

Frederick sensed Stacie beside him, but didn't take his eyes from the young man—he was in his early twenties at most. His shaggy brown hair fell across his brow, not quite reaching his eyes; from where he stood, Frederick could see the young man's cuffs were worn, and his coat was little better than threadbare.

But he could play.

Frederick ghosted along the wall until he reached a spot where he could see the pianist's hands. Long, strong fingers tickled the keys, their span impressive and their placement assured. Chord after chord rang clearly, well-executed, yet...

The young man reached the end of the adagio and, after the usual pause, commenced the rondo—and Frederick couldn't help himself. "No." He stalked forward as the young man started in surprise and lifted his hands and the music cut off. "Your balance isn't correct," Frederick continued. "Your left hand is overpowering your right."

The young man frowned. "I'm left-handed."

"So?" Frederick curtly gestured for him to move along the piano stool. "Ultimately, you play by ear—it shouldn't matter which is your dominant hand. Listen." He set his fingers to the keys. "This is how it should sound."

He didn't need the music sheets; he opened himself to the music and let it pour through him, guiding his fingers on the keys.

He played the rondo from start to finish, then lifted his hands and turned to see the boy staring at the keys with his mouth partly open. "Do you see—or rather, did you hear?" Frederick asked.

Slowly, the boy nodded. "Yes," he murmured. Then with greater confidence, he repeated, "Yes." Impulsively, he shifted along as if to bump Frederick aside and reclaim the keyboard, then froze and colored and glanced at Frederick. "May I?"

Frederick slid to the end of the stool and gestured to the keys. "Try it again. Just the rondo. You had the adagio perfectly gauged."

The lad set his hands to the keys, paused, then started playing.

Silent and still, Stacie remained by the wall and watched and listened —and gave thanks. She could *see* the musician in Frederick rise to the fore and take charge. He watched the young man's hands with an eagle eye, and when the piece ended and the young man raised his hands from the keys and looked, Frederick nodded approvingly. "Much better." He hesitated for only a second, then asked, "Do you know Schubert's 'Fantasy in F Minor?'"

His eyes lighting, the young man nodded. "I've played it, practiced it, but I'm not as good as you."

"No, you're not, but playing with pianists like me will improve your touch, which is what you need to work on. So." Frederick nudged the young man along. "I'll let you have the easier part." He set his fingers to the keys. "Ready?"

Somewhat nervously, the young man nodded—and Frederick launched into the piece and swept the younger pianist into it by sheer force of personality.

Stacie listened and marveled. It felt like a blessing to be able to hear such music at close quarters, to be able to watch and see the performers, Frederick with his fingers dancing unerringly over the keys, and the lad matching him—drawn in his wake by the power inherent in the composition.

Finally, the music ended, and she softly sighed.

The young man swung to face Frederick, stars in his eyes. "Are you a new teacher?"

"No. I'm Albury." Frederick rose and looked down at the younger man. "But you and I will play together again. What's your name?"

"Brandon, sir. Brandon Miller."

"Well, Brandon Miller, I strongly advise you to continue practicing. Your technique is excellent and your playing is, too, but your touch doesn't so much need work as you need to learn to trust in your feelings about how the music should sound and let that guide you."

"Thank you, sir. I'll do as you say."

With a nod of farewell for his newfound acolyte, Frederick walked to where Stacie waited and tipped his head toward the door. The strains of the Beethoven rondo, played with noticeably better balance, followed them into the corridor.

Stacie glanced at Frederick's face; his expression was once more austere and impassive—utterly impossible to read. While he'd played, his features had been mobile, reflecting the emotion he invested in his play-ing; it was almost shocking to realize how definite and absolute the wall he usually maintained between him and the world actually was.

In the foyer, when she would have paused at the counter, he grasped her elbow and steered her directly toward the door.

"Goodbye, Mrs. Withers!" Stacie called over her shoulder.

She saw Frederick's lips tighten, but he didn't slow—not until they were through the door.

Then he halted on the cobbles, released her elbow, and looked down at her. "Did you arrange that?"

She blinked up at him. "The young pianist?"

When he curtly nodded, she shook her head. "No." Then she confessed, "But if I'd known that was what it would take to tip you into agreeing to play, I would have."

He sighed, closed his eyes, and pinched the bridge of his nose.

She studied him, then finally felt it was safe to ask, "You are going to play at my musical event, aren't you?"

He lowered his hand, opened his eyes, and looked at her—for all the world as if he was irritated, but, she sensed, not with her. "God help me, yes. I'll play at your damned event. Those young men in there are good —in time and with the right experience, some might even achieve great-ness. Brandon Miller isn't up to my standard yet, but he's ten years younger. With the right encouragement, he could have the world at his feet."

Frederick watched her face transform—with joy, delight, and not a little relief. To his eyes, she all but glowed with happiness; the sight stole his breath and left him giddy.

"That's wonderful! I'm so glad you agreed to come and see the school and the pupils. Protheroe will be in alt."

"I daresay." Frederick steeled his senses and took her arm again. "But I would prefer you refrained from informing Protheroe for the moment. Give me a few hours to come to grips with my decision."

She cast him a look, but her smile didn't dim.

As they reached her carriage, she told him, "You hearing Brandon Miller playing just as we were leaving was obviously serendipity at work."

He didn't answer, just helped her into the carriage; he was going on to his club. He needed a drink. Several drinks. "We can meet tomorrow and decide on the details." He closed the door and saluted. "I'll see you then."

Smiling, she leaned out of the open window. "Until then."

He stepped back and watched the carriage roll away.

She'd ascribed him hearing Brandon Miller playing at the very moment his guard was at its lowest to serendipity.

He deemed it fate.

CHAPTER 3

*a*fter a restless night during which every possible scenario in which Frederick might change his mind and decide against supporting her scheme had played in a continuous loop through her head, Stacie called at Albury House as the clocks chimed ten-thirty—the earliest hour at which she could possibly call on a gentleman.

It was also an hour at which Frederick was highly unlikely to have left the house.

Indeed, on being admitted by the butler, who recognized her from her previous visits, she stepped into the front hall to see Frederick leisurely descending the main stairs. He saw her and paused, then resumed his unhurried descent.

Stacie surrendered her half cape, then turned to face Frederick as he neared. "If I could beg a few minutes of your time, my lord, I believe we have several matters to discuss."

One brow faintly arching, he halted before her and reached for her hand. "Good morning, Lady Eustacia."

Damn! "Indeed, my lord. Good morning." She allowed him to take her hand and bow over it, while she sank into an appropriate curtsy.

As they straightened, he met her eyes; the line of his lips was not quite straight. Releasing her, he waved toward the drawing room. "I do have a few minutes I can spare. Perhaps we might sit and address your 'matters.'"

Frederick ushered her into the drawing room. As he passed Fortingale, caution reared its head, and he murmured, "No need to shut the door."

He was perfectly certain Stacie had no notion of using propriety to trap him into offering marriage—in fact, now he thought of it, her lack of matrimonial interest in him was one of the things he found most refreshing about her—but others in his household might not be so inclined to overlook an opportunity such as discovering them together, in private and under his roof. Other gentlemen had found themselves leg-shackled for less.

True to his reading of her, she glided into the room and, with a swish of her skirt—today's in a rich shade of plum—claimed a seat on the chaise. He crossed to one of the armchairs opposite, sat, and looked at her, transparently waiting for her to speak.

A slight frown creasing her brow, she offered, "The first thing I believe we should decide on is how many events to include in the first year of our campaign."

He blinked. "Campaign?" He straightened as a feeling awfully like panic gripped him. "I thought we were speaking of one event—a single evening of music."

Her frown growing more definite, she aimed it at him. "As must be obvious even to you, a single event—an isolated evening—would achieve very little." She gestured dismissively. "A single evening would hardly be worth our time. We need to present our selected musicians to the ton at large, and while I admit I might have used the term 'event,' singular, I always envisaged a campaign." She met his eyes. "In terms of achieving our goal of introducing worthy young musicians to the notice of the ton, the only approach that will work is an organized sequence of events—in other words, a campaign."

"No." Adamantly, he shook his head. How had he got roped into this? Just the thought of performing at multiple events made him shudder. "No campaign." He held up a finger. "One event, nothing more."

"Frederick—that's nonsensical." Openly exasperated, she stared at him. "If you can perform at one event, given your ability, how much more effort would it take to perform at several more, spaced out over an entire year?"

She was right, of course; in terms of effort, the difference was negligible. But that wasn't the problem, and he wasn't about to explain.

His jaw set, he met her eyes. "The simple fact is, I don't want to appear before the ton at all. However, after seeing the need, I agreed to one—singular—event. That's all I'm prepared to play at."

Stacie narrowed her eyes on his face, with its hard edges and implacable expression. She'd thought she'd won his agreement to provide the drawcard she needed for her campaign and wasn't about to meekly surrender that position.

Head tilting, she studied him. *I don't want to...* Those were the crucial words in his refusal. So what would motivate a man like him to change his mind?

Inspiration struck, and she smiled.

His eyes narrowed in response, and she battled not to grin. "I happen to know that the Raventhorne Abbey library holds a collection of medieval musical texts—all originals—as well as five folios of very old sheet music."

The interest that lit his golden eyes was impossible to mistake.

More confidently, she went on, "If you agree to perform at least one piano sonata at six events spread out over the coming year, I'll arrange for you to borrow those texts and folios."

He stared at her for several moments, then asked, "Have any other scholars studied those volumes?"

"As far as I'm aware, they've been moldering in the abbey library for decades, certainly since before I was born. My great-grandmother was the one who bought them—she had an interest in music, too. No one in the family between her and me has been of a musical bent, so I suspect the books and folios have simply sat on the shelf."

"But you've looked at them?"

She nodded. "And I can report that they're in excellent condition."

Frederick felt his resistance wavering, weakened by the desire to see those old texts and folios. "Three events spread over the year, and I play whatever piece I choose."

Her eyes narrowed again. "Four events over a year, with a performance at least as long as a sonata, but you get to select the piece or pieces." She paused, then added, "That's my final offer."

He would have laughed except he truly wanted to get his hands on those texts, let alone the folios. Often, significant discoveries were unearthed in just such out-of-the-way and forgotten private collections. His gaze locked on her face, he considered the stubborn set of her chin, the adamantine glint in her eyes. "I suppose," he mused, more to himself than her, "that once I weather the first event, we'll know how to handle it."

She frowned in puzzlement. "Handle what?"

He paused, then replied, "The over-avid interest of the ton's ladies. Trust me, I know of what I speak."

She wasn't about to be distracted. "So are we agreed? Four events on the terms I stated?"

He inwardly sighed. He wanted access to those tomes; who knew what they might contain? "Very well. Four events over the year, a sonata-length performance at each, with pieces chosen by me."

The clock on the mantelpiece chimed eleven times; he glanced at it, then looked at her and rose. "If that's all, I have an appointment I must keep."

"All? But...we've only just started." Dismayed, she looked up at him. "We need to discuss how the events will run, what form will best suit to introduce the younger musicians, the timing and length of performances, whether we should restrict the repertoire or at least impose some guidance as to what style of pieces should be played." She flung up her hands. "There are countless details we need to decide, and not least of those is the date for our first event."

He frowned; she was right, and he didn't want her making those decisions alone. He met her eyes. "I'm due at the museum at half past eleven—a private viewing of an exhibition of ancient musical instruments and artifacts. The curator is an old friend, and he's invited all the scholars of ancient music to peruse the exhibition ahead of the public opening tomorrow." He paused, wondering at the impulse prompting him, yet went on, "You could accompany me—we can discuss the details of these events of yours in the carriage on the way, and you might find the exhibition of some interest."

Her eyes opened wide, then her features eased, and she nodded with becoming eagerness and rose. "Thank you. I accept your invitation. I had heard of the exhibition and hoped to find time to attend. We can take my carriage—it's waiting outside."

He inclined his head and waved her to the door, and she turned and walked beside him.

"I've never been to a private viewing before," she said as they passed into the front hall. "I daresay it will be much less crowded."

"Very much less crowded." Frederick took the short cape Fortingale offered and draped it over Stacie's shoulders. "That's one of the reasons every single musical scholar worth his salt will be there." He turned with her toward the door. "It's our chance to pore over things in relative peace."

She slanted him a glance as they passed through the door Fortingale held open. "Scholars and crowds don't seem to mix."

"Indeed."

They descended the steps, and he handed her into her carriage and followed.

The instant he sat beside her, the reality of them being in such close confines impinged, but there was nothing for it but to rein in his senses and pretend not to notice the way her breathing had changed.

The two of them traveling together in a carriage in broad daylight would raise no eyebrows, especially given their ages and their destination; that wasn't the problem. Frederick determinedly ignored the brush of her skirts against his thigh and calf and the entrancing perfume that rose from her skin and hair to wreathe through his brain and tried his damnedest to keep his mind from the too-fast rise and fall of her breasts, from dwelling on the faint breathiness that had afflicted her as, speaking a touch too quickly, she launched into a discussion of the style of event she considered most suitable for their purpose.

He focused and listened and, when appealed to, duly gave his opinion. As the carriage rattled through Mayfair and on toward Great Russell Street, they traded ideas and suggestions on all the topics she'd mentioned and several others besides. Somewhat to his surprise, he discovered her opinions generally had merit and often mirrored his own. More, when he opposed some point, she proved to be flexible and willing to accommodate his sometimes-eccentric wishes.

All in all, dealing with her was less of a trial than he'd anticipated, to the point where he admitted, "On reflection, your proposed campaign of four events spread through the year will be ideal not only for introducing our selected musicians but also for establishing the concept of events based on local talent rather than the imported variety in the ton's collective mind."

"Precisely." The carriage turned in to Great Russell Street, and she swayed, her shoulder briefly pressing against his arm. A second later, she cleared her throat, raised her chin several degrees, and stated, "I truly believe that, incorporating all the details we've discussed, our campaign will make best use of our inherent strengths—combining your reputation as a reluctant maestro with my social standing and connections within the haut ton."

He nodded and sat forward as the carriage slowed. "All in support of our local musical prodigies."

The carriage halted, and he opened the door and stepped down, then turned and gave her his hand and helped her down the carriage steps.

The august façade of the British Museum rose before them, a flight of stone steps leading up to the porticoed porch. He steeled himself—there really was no acceptable alternative—and offered his arm, and she placed her hand on his sleeve.

Stacie tried not to focus on the steely strength of the arm beneath the fine fabrics of his sleeves; at least, now they were out of the carriage, she could breathe. As they climbed the steps, she observed, "Now we've established that we are, more or less, of the same mind regarding our events, we can devote ourselves to the delights of the special exhibition without distraction."

Other than the distraction he himself posed, but she'd simply have to make the best—or perhaps the least—of that.

He tipped his head. "Indeed." And ushered her through the heavy doors and into the ornate foyer.

The exhibition—*Musical Instruments and Artifacts of Bygone Ages*—was housed in the East Wing. The curator—Frederick's friend—stood waiting to greet them at the top of the stairs, outside the main chamber.

The curator—Wiggs—was delighted to see Frederick and welcomed them both effusively. When Frederick introduced her, Stacie exchanged polite nods with Wiggs, but his attention immediately reverted to Frederick; she struggled to hide a smile at Wiggs's near-hero-worship of the rather stiff and distinctly reluctant man at her side.

Until that moment, she hadn't really thought about Frederick's standing among his scholarly peers; her focus had been on his musical talents. But judging by Wiggs's borderline-obsequious behavior, Frederick occupied a position among musical scholars that attracted a similar degree of awe as his reputation as a pianist.

And although he hid it behind an urbane veneer, his uncomfortableness with Wiggs's near-gushing reached her clearly.

Lord Frederick Brampton was...shy?

That seemed highly unlikely, yet...

Then others came up the stairs, and Frederick seized the moment to excuse them and move into the exhibition hall, and Stacie tucked away her unexpected insight for later examination and gave herself over to the wonders arrayed before them.

She'd seen old musical instruments before, but these were ancient, and most were in exquisite condition. She was fascinated by the delicate ornamentation on lutes and variations of the same, and on the few keyboard-like instruments present. Noting her interest, Frederick called her attention to some of the precise detailing she initially missed; she quickly realized his knowledge was broad as well as deep and bombarded him with questions, to all of which he proved to have the answer.

They circled the cases arranged in the main hall, then passed into the first of the five surrounding rooms also devoted to the exhibition's displays. The crowd was sparse, with few ladies present; most of those invited to the special showing appeared to be scholars ranging from earnest youths to crusty ancients almost as old as some of the instruments.

Many recognized Frederick, directing polite bows and nods his way; only a few approached to exchange greetings and a comment or two before moving on.

Stacie had long since drawn her hand from Frederick's arm and become a lone agent in her quest to see everything of note, and over the minutes, her senses had settled, her awareness diverting to all on which her eyes were feasting.

She had her palms flattened on the wooden frame of a case holding an exquisite Persian lute and was leaning over, peering through the case's glass top, when Frederick appeared beside her—close beside her—and her senses leapt and all but somersaulted.

Before she could straighten, he leaned close, his arms and chest all but caging her, and she lost her breath and all ability to protest.

Apparently oblivious, his face nearly level with hers, he pretended to examine the lute and murmured, "We have company."

His breath wafted across her cheek, and she set her teeth against a telltale shiver.

"My apologies," he continued, sotto voce, "but I'll have to introduce you."

Their gazes supposedly trained on the lute, they both slowly straightened. Mystified, she turned toward him and searched his face. His features were set, his expression at its most haughtily aloof. His gaze was fixed past her shoulder, and she turned to see who had elicited such a cool reception.

A couple were approaching—a tallish gentleman not quite as tall as

Frederick, with a more barrel-like chest and, while quietly well-dressed, lacking Frederick's ineffable elegance, was escorting a shortish lady, neatly and conservatively gowned in dark-blue twill. Like Stacie, the lady wore no bonnet, and her dark hair was gathered in a matronly knot at her nape.

Arm in arm, the pair came forward and halted a yard away.

The gentleman nodded to Frederick. "Albury. Well met. I believe you'll remember my wife."

"Brougham." Gracefully, Frederick inclined his head, then half bowed to the lady. "Lady Brougham. Delighted." Straightening, Frederick gestured to Stacie. "You must allow me to present Lady Eustacia Cavanaugh."

Stacie smiled and gave Brougham her hand, then exchanged greetings with his wife.

"Tell me, Lady Eustacia," Lady Brougham said, "do you have an interest in musical instruments?"

"I do, as it happens," Stacie replied, "although my interest is generally focused on modern-day specimens."

Lady Brougham smiled understandingly. "Indeed, but the instruments displayed are very pretty, are they not?"

"So I've discovered." Stacie shifted to face her ladyship, leaving Frederick to interact with Brougham. "Do you have any special interest in the exhibits?"

"No." Lady Brougham glanced at her spouse, who was now engaged in a somewhat stilted exchange with Frederick. "I come more in support than with any genuine interest, although in this case, I must admit the artistry of the ornamentation on some of the pieces is eye-catching."

Stacie and Lady Brougham turned to view Frederick and his lordship as Brougham said, "Have you read the treatise Jolyneaux published last week?"

"I have, indeed." To Stacie's surprise, there was ice in Frederick's voice. "I can't say I'm impressed—his conclusions seem entirely at odds with the latest discoveries."

Brougham looked taken aback. Before he could gather his thoughts and respond, Frederick reached for Stacie's arm, directed a nod at Lady Brougham, and a rather more curt one at Brougham. "If you'll excuse us, we need to get on."

Stacie smiled charmingly at the Broughams and allowed Frederick to lead her away. He remained stiff, even after he released her elbow. When he volunteered nothing, she glanced at him and arched a pointed eyebrow.

His lips tightened, then he reluctantly offered, "Brougham and I have known each other since Eton. He's a rival of sorts."

"Ah." Stacie wasn't sure how that translated into the rigid awkwardness both men had displayed, but it wasn't her place to prod. Instead, she scanned the nearer exhibits, then waved at one and directed her steps that way. "What an odd-looking..." She halted beside the glass case, looking down at what appeared to be a strange cross between a cello and a lute, but with many more strings and a curious sounding box. She frowned at the thing. "Is it a form of lute?"

Frederick halted beside her. "Not exactly. It's a sarangi from India. It's said to be the instrument that produces sounds most similar to the human voice."

She pulled a face. "It looks as if it would be extremely difficult to master—all those strings."

"I believe experienced sarangi players are decidedly thin on the ground, at least in this country."

She chuckled, and his stiffness dissipating, they strolled on.

They continued through the various rooms, ultimately returning to the head of the stairs. Wiggs hovered there; Stacie got the distinct impression he was waiting with bated breath for Frederick's verdict.

Somewhat to her relief, Frederick paused and commended Wiggs on the exhibition, adding several complimentary comments, and Wiggs visibly relaxed.

"Good-oh!" Wiggs said. "So it seems I've got the scholars satisfied—Jordan said it was worth his time as well, as did Brougham. With any luck, the general populace will find enough of interest to chat about and keep the governors happy."

Frederick glanced at Stacie. "Lady Eustacia has shown no sign of being bored."

She responded to his unvoiced appeal. "No, indeed!" she assured Wiggs. "You have something sufficiently unusual or ornate in every room to engage the ladies' interest."

"Thank you, my lady." Beaming, Wiggs bowed. "It's good of you to say so."

They left Wiggs happier and distinctly more confident than he had been when they'd arrived.

Frederick gave her his arm, and she took it and allowed him to steady her down the stairs. She was still getting used to the somewhat unnerving dance her senses indulged in whenever he loomed that close.

Hopefully, the effect would fade with time—with continued exposure.

They reached the foyer, and Frederick glanced at Stacie's face. "Thank you for encouraging Wiggs. He gets quite nervous over these exhibitions of his, yet they are always comprehensive and well received, and not just by us scholarly types."

"I spoke nothing but the truth," she returned. "His displays were arranged with the right sort of eye."

He smiled and held the main door open for her. "Perhaps, but I—and I'm sure my academic peers—would never have thought to mention that."

She grinned, and he steered her down the front steps and across the forecourt toward where her coach stood waiting. As the gravel crunched beneath their boots, he reflected that, other than the brief and unavoidable exchange with Brougham, he'd enjoyed the exhibition far more than he'd expected—indeed, in a way he'd enjoyed few such excursions in the past.

He slanted a glance at the lady whose hand lay lightly on his arm. He was honest enough to acknowledge—at least to himself—that a large part of his unanticipated enjoyment had arisen through his interaction with her.

Seeing open enjoyment lighting her expressive face, answering her eager, intelligent questions, engaging with her in minor discussions driven purely by intellectual curiosity—until today, all such interactions had been outside his experience.

They neared her carriage, and he waved the footman back, held the carriage door, and helped her to climb inside. Drawing her fingers from his clasp, she sat and looked at him inquiringly.

"I have an appointment at my club," he informed her. "But in light of our earlier discussions, I'll call at your house tomorrow at two o'clock. Before we make any further decisions, I need to check the quality of your piano."

She smiled, and for a second, he felt as if the sun had broken through the light clouds to beam down on him.

"Very well," she said. "You'll find us at Number Five, Green Street. I'll expect you tomorrow at two."

He nodded, closed the carriage door, and signaled to the coachman.

He slid his hands into his pockets and stood and watched the carriage roll away. A full minute ticked past, then he shook himself back to the present, hailed a hackney, and headed into town.

The following afternoon, Stacie found herself pacing her drawing room, waiting for Frederick to arrive.

He wasn't late—it wanted ten minutes to the hour—but she couldn't seem to sit still.

She'd gone over their exchanges of the previous morning, and as far as she could see, she'd managed to gain his agreement to everything she'd actually wanted. She hadn't intended to host six events over the next year—that had been her initial position for negotiation, a negotiation she'd successfully concluded, giving her the four events per year she'd gauged as optimum for her purpose.

She knew the ton; hosting events too frequently risked ladies taking said events for granted. On the other hand, as she and Frederick had ultimately agreed, each of the musicians they selected to introduce to society would need to appear at least twice if not three times in a year to have any chance of gaining the attention of the ton's more influential hostesses.

There was, she was discovering, many competing pressures to weigh up when making even the most mundane decisions; during their discussions, she'd found having Frederick's views to bolster and balance her own exceedingly helpful.

She swung and paced once more across the hearth, conscious of the fluttering of anticipation inside. She told herself it was because she was looking forward to hearing Frederick play again—this time, in her own music room.

The music room had been the deciding factor in her purchasing this particular house. After she'd finally succeeded in convincing Ryder and Mary that, as she wasn't about to marry, continuing to live at Raventhorne House in Mount Street wasn't a viable option in terms of establishing a life of her own, she'd searched Mayfair for the right house. Money hadn't been an issue—she'd inherited all of her mother's estate on top of her portion from the marquessate—but the house had had to be the right sort of house. Not too large but with a music room that would satisfy the requirements of her scheme and suitable reception rooms to host a large ton gathering.

The instant she'd walked into this house, she'd thought it might be the one, then she'd stepped into the white-and-gilt music room and known she'd found the perfect abode for her and her purpose.

From a corner of the chaise, Ernestine—a widowed cousin of some

forty years of age who filled the role of companion and largely unnecessary chaperon—murmured, "You're restless today." Ernestine, who was
quiet calm personified, looked up from her embroidery and smiled.
"Although I must admit I'm quite looking forward to meeting Lord
Albury myself." Ernestine cocked her head. "Do you think he'll play a
piece on your piano? I've never heard him play, but I've heard all the
rumors. Such a romantic...well, tragedy, I suppose one would say."

"Tragedy?" Stacie stared at Ernestine; she tended to forget that Ernestine was extremely well-connected gossip-wise. With her gaze locked on
Ernestine's face, Stacie forgot about pacing and sank into the armchair
opposite. "What tragedy?"

"Why, the tale of when he last played in the ton."

Stacie gestured for Ernestine to continue. "I haven't heard the story."

"Ah, well...you have to understand that he was considered a prodigy
from an early age—a positive virtuoso on the pianoforte. Through his
teenage years, he occasionally played at his mother's and sisters' events
—both his sisters are rather older than he. Then, when he was...not quite
twenty years old, I believe, he composed a piece for the young lady he'd
fallen head over heels in love with. He openly declared it was dedicated
to her and played it at one of his mother's affairs—by all reports, the
piece was so very evocative, so very moving, several ladies swooned."

Stacie frowned. "How is that a tragedy? It all sounds rather lovely."

"Oh, the tragedy lay in what came after. Unsurprisingly, the entire ton
was agog, knocked cock-a-hoop, then the hostesses and the matchmaking
mamas descended on him, all wanting him to compose a piece for them
or for their daughters. And then came the cruelest cut of all. The young
lady for whom he'd written the piece—to whom he had, in musical terms,
openly offered his heart—accepted an offer from an earl's son and turned
her back on him."

Stacie frowned more definitely, even more puzzled. "But he wasn't
even twenty. He couldn't possibly have expected her to marry him."

"I don't know about that, my dear. Who knows what goes on in the
minds of men—young men, especially? Regardless, by all accounts, his
lordship took her public rejection badly—he fled London and has never
composed anything since."

"Oh." Silently aghast, Stacie felt something inside her twist as the
knowledge sank in that, when it came to performing before the ton, Frederick had, indeed, had a real, sound, and rather painful reason for refusing
her request. His reluctance had been based on rather more than a simple

wish to avoid ton events—a tendency shared to a greater or lesser extent by many gentlemen of his class. "When I spoke with his mother about my notion of having Frederick play at my events, she didn't mention any of that."

Her head bent over her stitching, Ernestine murmured, "I daresay she's hoping he's got over the whole episode—it was more than a decade ago, after all."

No one knew better than Stacie that experiences from one's childhood could cast a long shadow—let alone deeply emotional negative experiences suffered before twenty years of age. "I wish I'd known about this before."

Ernestine glanced up. "Why? If he's agreed to perform at your events, presumably he's consigned what happened to his past. You should be happy to have drawn him back into society. I assure you that everyone who hears him play will be grateful to you for returning him to the ton, as it were."

Stacie didn't reply. She suddenly felt very uncertain. She didn't really care what the rest of the ton thought, but she did care what Frederick thought, and the idea that she'd manipulated him into doing something that might cause him emotional pain...

Oh, dear.

From the murky morass of her whirling thoughts, one unarguable conclusion rose, sharp and clear. Having metaphorically dragged Frederick back into the bosom of the ton, any adverse outcome from his playing at her events would be on her head. She'd manipulated him into performing for her without once considering what it might cost him; it was, therefore, her responsibility to protect him from any threat that arose through him being a part of her scheme.

She was mentally staring at that unnerving conclusion when the doorbell rang, the peal chiming through the house.

Ernestine looked up expectantly, then started to pack up her embroidery. "I expect that'll be him, don't you think?"

Stacie glanced at the clock and numbly nodded. He was right on time.

She heard their parlormaid Hettie's light footsteps patter across the tiles of the front hall, then the rumble of Frederick's voice reached her, and she rose as Hettie opened the drawing room door and announced, "Lord Albury to see you, my lady."

"Thank you, Hettie." Stacie thrust aside her troubling thoughts and plastered on a smile. "Lord Albury." She went forward to meet him. "Welcome to my home."

Frederick took the hand she offered and bowed over it. "Lady Eustacia." His gaze went past her to Ernestine, who had risen and now hovered expectantly.

Retrieving her hand, Stacie turned to her cousin. "Lord Albury, allow me to present my cousin, Mrs. Ernestine Thwaites. Ernestine resides here, keeping me company."

Ernestine smiled in obvious delight and curtsied. "It's a pleasure to meet you, my lord."

Frederick nodded, polite yet aloof. "Mrs. Thwaites."

"I've heard so much about you and your wonderful gift, my lord," Ernestine all but gushed. "I was utterly thrilled to hear that you will be playing for us again."

Frederick's expression grew even more distant. "Indeed." With a curt, clearly-intended-to-be-dismissive nod for Ernestine, he turned to Stacie. "Your piano?"

Shy? Or merely made uncomfortable by praise?

Whichever it was, Stacie smiled and waved toward the double doors in the middle of the drawing room's interior side wall. "It's in the music room—through here."

She walked to the doors, opened them wide, then led the way into the large music room. She glanced back and saw Frederick looking around, taking note of the room's arching ceiling and the overall dimensions.

Stacie glimpsed Ernestine, back in the drawing room, shifting to sit in a chair close by the open doors; thankfully, her cousin would be screened from anyone on the piano stool.

Frederick's and her footsteps echoed as they crossed the polished wooden floor.

"The acoustics are good," he murmured, a tinge of surprise in his voice.

"Indeed, they are." She smiled and admitted, "I bought the house for this room."

A brief smile chased the cool reserve from his face. "That doesn't surprise me."

They reached the grand piano, angled in one corner of the room, with the light from the long bow windows falling over the keyboard and music stand.

As he moved to claim the piano stool, Frederick resurveyed the room.

He sat and announced, "This is placed almost perfectly—let's see how it sounds."

He raised the lid and swept aside the felt strip covering the keys, then spread his fingers over the ivory and played a rapid succession of scales.

Stacie held her breath, hoping for any piece of music, however short. She'd heard him play at the school, and that had only whetted her appetite. To hear him play here, in a room and on an instrument she knew, suddenly escalated to a burning desire.

He frowned, then embarked on another, longer set of scales, one that used every section of the keyboard.

Even that, somehow, sounded special; there was something in his touch, in his mastery of the keys, that invested each note with strength and clarity... She couldn't explain it, but she knew what she heard.

On reaching the end of the exercise, he lifted his hands from the keys, and to Stacie's disappointment—and she was sure Ernestine's as well—he picked up the discarded felt and spread it back over the keys. "If it had been just one or two strings, I would have tuned them myself, but most of the notes are just a fraction out. We'll need an expert tuner to restore it to perfection."

He rose, lowered the piano's lid, and met her eyes. "Unless you have someone else you prefer, I'll arrange for my tuner to call."

"By all means." Of course, he had a preferred expert. "It would be best, I suspect, were it tuned to your specifications."

"Indeed." He looked up the room toward the door to the hall. "If at all possible, I'll bring him around tomorrow—most likely in the early afternoon."

"That will suit admirably." She waved toward the second set of double doors, opposite the still-open pair that joined the music room to the drawing room. "While you're here, perhaps I should show you how I believe we'll accommodate our guests at our...we haven't yet decided what to call them. Musical events? Musical soirées? They aren't quite recitals, are they?"

She saw his lips twitch. He rounded the piano and joined her as she walked to the second set of doors. "No—it would be misleading to call such a function a recital. I've always wondered why hostesses don't simply call such events a musical evening."

She arched her brows, then nodded. "Let's call them that, then— musical evenings. That sounds more inviting—more intimate."

"As our aim is to entice the ton's ladies to attend, then such a label is more likely to be successful."

She didn't miss the cynicism in his tone.

They reached the double doors, and he opened them, and she glided through. "This is the morning room." Filling the rear corner of the house, the room boasted long windows that gave onto a small paved terrace, beyond which rolled the manicured rear lawn, bordered by richly planted flower beds. The garden was enclosed by high brick walls.

She halted and, spreading her arms, turned in a circle. "We'll open all three rooms—having both sets of doors open doesn't appreciably alter the acoustics in the music room."

He shot her an approving glance. "You've tried it?"

She nodded. "Again, one of the reasons I settled on this house. I'd already formed the notion of hosting musical events." She tipped her head his way. "Musical evenings."

He glanced back, across the music room to the drawing room. "You'll be able to accommodate quite a crowd in acceptable comfort."

"Indeed. We'll have rows of chairs in the music room, of course, but those who might prefer to remain in the armchairs here and in the drawing room will still be able to hear the performance reasonably well."

He nodded.

"And through here"—she pointed at another door, then walked to it —"is the dining room, where we'll serve supper."

He followed her through that door, idly glanced at the dining table, chairs, and sideboards, then trailed after her through the main dining room door, and so into the rear of the front hall.

When they reached the main body of the hall, she halted in the space before the stairs and arched her brows at him. "What do you think?"

He met her eyes and nodded. "This will do very well—with one addition. We need a room—it doesn't have to be large, but preferably on this level—where our musicians can wait prior to their performances and to which they can retreat afterward."

She widened her eyes. "I hadn't thought of that, but"—she waved him to the corridor leading away from the hall, opposite the music room —"my private parlor might suit."

She led him down the short corridor to the room at the end—an elegant yet comfortable space at the side of the house. She regarded the long, narrow room as her personal retreat.

He paused beside her just inside the room, looked around, and nodded. "This will be perfect. We'll only have at most five musicians, some with instruments, but there's space enough." He glanced up the corridor to the hall and the reception rooms beyond. "And it's sufficiently distant to give nervous musicians some peace."

He turned to her. "I can see our musical evenings will not fail for want of location and amenities. I'll return tomorrow with the tuner—Hellier. He's Swiss and a stickler for exactness."

She smiled. "Excellent."

She fell in beside him as they walked back toward the hall. What she'd learned about him from Ernestine replayed in her mind. They reached the hall, and she halted in its center and, when he paused beside her, swung to face him and raised her eyes to his. "I haven't yet thanked you for agreeing to my request, and I wanted to assure you that I do most sincerely appreciate your willingness to support my scheme and lend your talents and, indeed, your imprimatur to what I hope you will henceforth regard as *our* musical evenings."

His lips twitched slightly, and he gave an acknowledging dip of his head.

She drew a suddenly tight breath and ventured, "I only very recently learned that you might have real cause to eschew the ton—certainly to avoid playing at events in the manner I've proposed—which only increases my indebtedness to you for being willing to overcome your understandable reticence and lend your support to my scheme."

The instant she'd alluded to his past, he'd lowered his eyes; now, he raised them and met her gaze. "Thank you." His eyes narrowed faintly as they searched hers, his gaze significantly more penetrating than it normally appeared. "As I suspect you've already guessed, I abhor the ton's over-avid attention." His lips curved in a smile that held a definite edge. "I therefore have every intention of hiding behind your skirts—I give you fair warning, I will rely on you to act as guard in keeping the importuning hostesses, the matchmaking mamas, and their swooning daughters at bay."

She managed to keep her smile in place and incline her head in easy acceptance—as if he hadn't meant every word.

His gaze still locked with hers, he straightened. "I'll see you tomorrow." With that, he tipped her a salute and strode for the door, where Hettie stood waiting to hand him his hat and see him out.

Stacie stood in her front hall and watched him go, watched the door close behind him while she replayed what he'd said—not just the words that had fallen from his lips but also what his eyes, his expression, had said.

He hadn't been joking, not at all.

She frowned, not entirely certain how she felt about that. On the one hand, now that she'd manipulated him into performing for the ton again, even if, at the time, she hadn't known of his earlier difficulty, it could be argued—he could argue—that she owed him that degree of social protection. However...the damned man was more than capable of taking care of himself. She'd seen him react to others he wished to keep at a distance— admittedly by erecting a wall of reserve, yet still, she'd never seen him at a loss or even seriously challenged.

Her eyes, fixed unseeing on the closed door, narrowed. She rather suspected she'd just been warned. He would, if pressed, hide behind her —but she was convinced his motive wouldn't be self-preservation but, far more likely, a wish to discombobulate her.

"Huh! If so, the laugh will be on him." She'd cut her eyeteeth dealing with and managing the ladies of the ton; to act as his guard held no terrors for her. She returned to her parlor, opened the door, swanned inside, and declared to the empty room, "It won't be me who'll end flustered."

CHAPTER 4

*A*s promised, Frederick returned to Stacie's house with Hellier, his expert piano tuner, at half past two the next day.

While standing by the piano and watching Hellier delving beneath the propped-up lid, tightening pins and tensioning strings, he found his mind reviewing the happenings during his visit the day before, the insights he'd garnered, and his reactions to those.

The eagerness that had lit Stacie's cousin's eyes had forcibly reminded him of the smothering adoration that had, long ago, driven him from the ton. Luckily, Stacie was blessedly free of any tendency to near-worship; she'd always viewed him as a means to an end, and for that, he was grateful. He had never wanted to be placed on a pedestal and would resist as far as he could.

Indeed, seeing her in her home, in the space she'd made her own, and learning that something as fundamental as which house she'd chosen to buy had been dictated by her scheme, the goal of which was to help local musicians, had been…humbling.

As for her gratitude and her careful allusion to his past experience playing for the ton, he wasn't entirely sure what she'd made him feel—cowardly and selfish?

Hellier grunted and straightened.

Frederick thrust his uncertainties to the back of his mind as the elderly tuner turned to him and tipped his head toward the piano's keyboard. "Try it."

Aware of Stacie rising from the chair by the wall where she'd been sitting, out of the way, and drawing nearer, Frederick sat, flexed his fingers, then set them to the ivory keys.

He dutifully played the extensive series of scales he knew Hellier used to judge tone and tuning.

Hellier waved. "Wait." When Frederick lifted his hands, Hellier dived beneath the lid, fiddled with something, then retreated and nodded to Frederick. "Again."

Frederick started from the beginning and rolled through the lengthy series. As he finished the final set, he looked at Hellier to see the old Swiss tuner with a beatific smile on his face.

Hellier caught his eye and nodded. "Aye—that is now perfect. The tone is very good, and the tuning could not be better. You think the same?"

Frederick nodded. "I do." He looked at the keys. "Let's see."

He launched into Chopin's "Ballade Number 3." Within seconds, the music caught him, and he gave himself up to the flow.

Stacie stood behind and to the side of the piano stool and watched Frederick make her piano sing. His hands traveled over the keys with confidence and a mastery all the more notable for its effortlessness.

He coaxed, and the piano answered; he demanded, and the music swelled.

Her music room had never heard the like, and despite her years of concerts and performances, she hadn't, either. He possessed the ability to make the music manifest, to transform it into a palpable living, pulsing entity that could reach into people's minds, into their hearts and souls.

She managed to spare a glance for the tuner, Hellier, and discovered that he looked as enraptured as she felt, with a dazed smile on his face and his head nodding in time.

She glimpsed Ernestine peeking around the door from the drawing room, the expression on her face one of utter reverence.

Looking back at Frederick, feeling the power of his music surge and swell around her, Stacie had to admit that, when it came to the quality of his playing, every whisper of gossip had been true.

Indeed, the truth—the reality—was utterly stunning. Utterly confounding. Not even hearing him play at the music school had prepared her for this—for the precision of his touch, his mastery of tone, and the evocative totality of his performance.

He truly was a maestro.

Small wonder the other scholars treated him with respect. He didn't just study music, he could bring it to life.

When the final chord sounded and he rested his hands on his thighs as silence reclaimed them, she felt almost bereft.

In that instant, she realized that, courtesy of his talent, having him play at her musical evenings and introducing young musicians, on his coattails as it were, was guaranteed to work.

Frederick drew in a breath and swung to face Hellier. "I can't fault it. You?"

Hellier shook his head. "As always, it is a joy to hear you play. Would I was blessed more often. But you are right—there is nothing more for me to do here. The piano is in perfect tune and, now, worthy of the player."

Frederick smiled. "Thank you. As usual, send your account to me."

Hellier bent to pack his various tools back into his canvas bag. "Aye —I will do that. And"—he glanced curiously at Stacie—"next time this fine instrument needs tuning, do not wait so long."

Stacie smiled. "Rest assured, Mr. Hellier, I won't." She tugged the bellpull, and all but instantly, Hettie appeared.

With a bow to them both, Hellier hefted his bag and left with the maid.

Frederick rose from the piano stool and finally turned to Stacie, noting as he did the door to the drawing room silently closing; Stacie's cousin, no doubt.

As for Stacie, she met his eyes with her usual candor, with pleasure, delight, and a certain eager excitement investing her expression, but no sign that he could see of the overwhelming, idolizing veneration that his playing all too often inspired in ladies of the ton.

Thank Heaven for that.

A weight he hadn't known he was carrying slid from his shoulders.

"Well, my lord"—she smiled in the way of one sharing an adventure —"now we know we have an instrument sufficient to our task, might I suggest we pay another visit to the music school and consult with Mr. Protheroe as to which of his graduates we should invite to play at our first musical evening?"

He arched his brows. "An excellent idea." As he waved her to the door, he accepted that, somehow, he'd grown to be as committed to her scheme as she.

~

Stacie led the way into the music school, her heels clicking purposefully on the worn wooden floor.

Mrs. Withers looked up from her station behind the counter and smiled welcomingly.

Aware of Frederick at her back and sharing the impatience she sensed in him, Stacie blithely said, "Good morning, Mrs. Withers. Would you please inquire of Mr. Protheroe if he has time to discuss which particular graduates would be most suitable to play at my upcoming event?"

Mrs. Withers brightened. "It would be a pleasure, my lady."

Less than a minute later, Stacie and Frederick were seated in the master's room, and Protheroe was flicking through a stack of papers on his desk. "I know I have a list of them here somewhere... Ah!" He drew out a sheet, scanned it, then set it triumphantly on his blotter. "Now we have a place to start." He looked inquiringly at Stacie, then Frederick. "What particular music or instruments did you have in mind?"

Frederick looked at Stacie. She responded by outlining what she felt were their options—any and all types of soloists plus ensembles ranging from two to five or even six in number.

Protheroe confirmed he could recommend ex-graduates suitable to provide any of her suggestions.

Both Stacie and Protheroe looked at Frederick.

Stacie watched Frederick's gaze turn inward. He spent several moments in internal debate, then refocused on her. A second later, he glanced at Protheroe. "Brandon Miller—is he on your list?"

"He is," Protheroe confirmed. "He's one of our most talented ex-students."

"We stumbled on him practicing the other day," Frederick said. "Unless you have another pianist of higher caliber...?" When Protheroe shook his head, Frederick nodded. "Miller, then, to open proceedings."

He met Stacie's eyes. "I suggest we have him play first—we can discuss which pieces with him and select something he's confident with that will run for ten to fifteen minutes. That's long enough for the ton—if he holds their attention that long, he'll have done well."

She nodded. "And then?"

Frederick looked at Protheroe. "For her ladyship's first evening, I'd suggest a smaller group—perhaps just two. And as I'll be playing the piano to end the evening, then stringed instruments would be preferable."

Protheroe nodded and consulted his list. After a moment, he said, "We have Phillip Carpenter, an accomplished violinist, and George Goodes, who's an excellent cellist. They're friends and often play and practice together." Protheroe glanced up, his gaze shifting from Frederick to Stacie. "They work not far away in Goodes's father's printing shop. I could send a boy to ask them to come in for an audition—I would feel happier if you both heard them before you made a decision."

Stacie exchanged a swift glance with Frederick. "And Miller? Can we call him in as well?"

Protheroe nodded. "Brandon is playing harpsichord at one of the smaller theaters in the evenings. He'll be at home—if he's not already somewhere here, practicing. He often slips in. Our graduates are free to use any of our rooms and the larger instruments when they're not being used for lessons." Protheroe rose. "I'll send messengers to summon those three, and meanwhile, may I invite you to take tea with me?"

Stacie smiled and declared that they would be delighted.

The following half hour passed in comfortable conversation over the teacups; given their shared interests in music, engaging topics were easy to come by. By the time Mrs. Withers looked in to say the messengers had returned along with all three musicians, Frederick had gained a deeper appreciation of Protheroe's work and the man's devotion to the cause of fostering musical talent.

With Stacie, Frederick followed Protheroe to the room in which they'd previously come upon Brandon Miller. Inside, the three young men stood waiting in a group beside the piano; all three were patently eager but, unsurprisingly, nervous as well.

Protheroe smiled reassuringly at his erstwhile students, introduced Stacie and Frederick—this time as the Marquess of Albury—and outlined the reason for which they'd been summoned.

The three men exchanged glances that plainly said they could barely believe their luck.

"So"—Protheroe clasped his hands together and turned to Frederick and Stacie—"how would you like to proceed?"

Frederick touched a hand to the back of Stacie's waist. "The string duo first, I think." The young men had brought their instruments, which lay in cases at their feet.

She nodded and smiled at Carpenter and Goodes. "If you could play for us, gentlemen? Ultimately, we'll be looking for a piece or pieces that will run for ten or so minutes."

"I would suggest," Frederick said, "that for this exercise, you choose a piece you personally like and are confident of playing perfectly."

While Carpenter and Goodes unpacked their instruments and, in hushed whispers, debated which piece to play, with Miller adding his opinion when appealed to, Frederick and Protheroe fetched straight-backed chairs from one end of the room and set them in a short row at a spot Frederick indicated, several yards from where Carpenter and Goodes were setting themselves up, Goodes seated on a chair with his lovingly polished cello between his knees and Carpenter standing, thin and tall, by his side.

Frederick sat beside Stacie, and Protheroe sat on her other side.

Frederick noted with approval that neither Carpenter nor Goodes rushed their tuning or preparation. Finally, when they were ready, Carpenter straightened and said, "We've elected to perform J. S. Bach's 'Duet in A Minor.'"

Frederick nodded approvingly. "An excellent choice." He glanced at Stacie and Protheroe, then looked back at Carpenter and Goodes. "When you're ready, gentlemen."

The young men exchanged a wordless look, then Goodes drew in a breath, set bow to string, and commenced.

The sound was pure and mellow, then the violin came in, and Bach's melody unfurled, eventually skipping into counterpoint that was expertly and crisply executed.

Frederick sat back, folded his arms across his chest, and listened.

When it came to musical performances, he was far more critical than the average listener, yet there was little fault to find in Carpenter's and Goodes's efforts. Protheroe hadn't exaggerated their abilities; by the time the pair lifted their bows from their strings and Frederick, along with Stacie, burst into spontaneous applause, Frederick was convinced Carpenter and Goodes, along with Miller, were more than worthy of his and Stacie's support. Once properly introduced to the ton, with him and Stacie as patrons and mentors, the three would do well.

Both Goodes and Carpenter flushed with pleasure.

Frederick gave them a moment, then asked, "What other duets do you know?"

An animated exchange followed, to which everyone, including Stacie and Miller—who plainly knew the other two well—contributed.

Eventually, Frederick was satisfied that Carpenter and Goodes had revealed the full extent of their repertoire. When Stacie, understanding why he'd asked the original question, shot him an inquiring glance, he said, "I think the Beethoven in C Major will work best for our purposes. It has the right ambiance and duration."

Stacie nodded and turned to the young men, who had pricked up their ears at the mention of a purpose and looked hopefully intrigued.

Frederick hid a smile as she explained their notion of introducing local musicians, hailing from music schools other than the Royal Academy, to the notice of the haut ton via musical evenings.

Observing the uncertain expressions on the young men's faces and guessing something of the questions crowding their minds, Frederick added, "Lady Eustacia is extremely well-connected within the ton—her guests will be a select group and will include all the major hostesses and those who might be encouraged to become patronesses of talented musicians of the sort who could play at their events."

Brandon Miller exchanged a faintly troubled glance with Carpenter and Goodes, then, transparently steeling himself, looked at Stacie and Frederick and said, "A chance such as that—to play before the hostesses, lords, and ladies—is...well, a dream to us. But others have tried something similar and got nowhere. If it's just us playing, why would the top-of-the-trees come to listen?"

Frederick caught the look Stacie sent his way and elected to reply himself. "Firstly, because those others weren't Lady Eustacia Cavanaugh, daughter of a marquess and sister of another and connected to many of the haut ton's most influential families, and secondly, because it won't be just you three playing."

He paused, then decided it would be easier to allay their fears using the medium they understood best. He rose and walked to the piano; guessing his intention, Brandon raised the lid and whipped the felt away.

Frederick sat, set his fingers to the keys, and launched into his current favorite exercise—the third part from Mendelssohn's fourth book of "Songs Without Words." As always, he let the music consume him; he opened himself to it, and it flowed like a river through him.

When he played the last chord and lifted his hands, silence reigned. He raised his head and looked at the three young musicians and beheld them struck speechless, their expressions ones of utter awe. He suppressed a cynical smile. "I haven't played before the ton, not at any event, however small, for over ten years. I'll be appearing as the last act of the evening. With my name on the program, I believe we can be certain that not one of those invited will stay away."

Hope washed across the young men's faces as belief in their good fortune—that this opportunity might be real—sank in.

Miller shifted. "Do you want me to play for you as well?"

Frederick nodded, rose from the piano stool, and with a wave, indicated that Miller should take his place. "The Beethoven sonata again, just the first movement, if you please."

Miller sat, drew breath, and played.

His head cocked, Frederick listened; the young man had clearly worked diligently over the days since he'd advised him to *feel* the music and had all but perfected the piece.

When the final chord rang out, Frederick nodded. "Excellent. That is, indeed, impressive and will do well with our particular audience."

Miller looked positively giddy with delight.

Frederick glanced at Stacie and Protheroe, then continued, "You will, of course, be paid according to the usual hire agreement, with a bonus of fifty percent to be added if all goes well." He would be paying them, no matter what Stacie thought or said.

Returning his gaze to the three young musicians, in his mind's eye picturing their appearance before the ton, he smoothly went on, "And given you'll be appearing more or less as my protégés, I will arrange for the three of you to be outfitted as befits that station. I will expect you at Albury House in Upper Grosvenor Street at eleven o'clock tomorrow—don't be late."

"No, my lord," the three chorused, their eyes round.

Frederick looked at Stacie and arched a brow. "Have I forgotten anything?"

Stacie was immeasurably grateful that he'd thought of appropriate clothes for the young men and, even more, that he'd volunteered to arrange to acquire them; she wouldn't have known where to start. "We should mention that we've yet to set a date for our first event, but I would hope to hold it shortly—within the next fortnight, if possible."

Frederick added, "We'll need to consider what other entertainments the ton has scheduled in order to ensure we make the biggest splash."

"Indeed." Stacie rose and smiled at Protheroe as he came to his feet alongside her. "But we'll contact you through the office here, through Mr. Protheroe, as soon as the date is fixed."

Protheroe beamed. "We'll be delighted to act as go-between."

Sensing hers and Frederick's intention to leave, all three musicians broke into effusive thanks that, while disjointed, were patently heartfelt.

Although she accepted those thanks gracefully, Stacie seconded Frederick's observation that, in fact, the shoe was on the other foot, and the three were doing them a favor by consenting to be the first three local musicians to be featured at her musical evenings under Frederick's aegis.

While the three young men pondered the rights of that, Stacie, with Frederick, took her leave of them and Protheroe.

As she stepped into the mild sunshine and felt it touch her face, she found she was smiling in quiet triumph. She glanced at the gentleman— the nobleman—beside her; with him working hand in glove with her, her ultimate goal of launching the careers of local musicians was within reach.

At eleven-thirty the following morning, Frederick sat in the wing chair by the window in his dressing room and watched his tailor, the highly respected Moreton of Savile Row, measure the breadth of Brandon Miller's shoulders.

Phillip Carpenter and George Goodes stood just inside the door from the corridor, somewhat nervously awaiting their turn. Moreton and Brandon occupied the center of the narrow room, which was lined with shelves, cupboards, two armoires, and in the middle of one wall, a gentleman's dressing bench flanked by two long mirrors. Standing nearer to Frederick, Moreton's elderly assistant, Thomas, jotted down the figures Moreton barked as the tailor—an intimidating figure with his precise and severe attire and his wealth of silver-gray hair—wielded his tape measure with grim zeal.

On being summoned by Frederick and informed that he was to prepare a full complement of attire suitable for a concert appearance— coats in black superfine, ivory linen, and sober charcoal waistcoats and trousers—for the three younger men by Monday evening at the latest, Moreton had drawn in a breath and considered protesting the waste of his talents, but Frederick had glibly explained that the three were scheduled to appear before the cream of the haut ton at a private function within the next few weeks, and Moreton had swallowed his pride, pulled out his measure, and suggested repairing to the dressing room.

Noting just how rigidly Brandon was holding himself, Frederick said, "Try to relax—it makes Moreton's task easier."

The tailor grunted in agreement.

Frederick hid a smile and went on, "That's something you three should learn, to help with your public appearances. Create a small ritual, whether it be taking three deep breaths or twitching your sleeves straight—an unobtrusive action that works to focus your mind—and connect that with consciously relaxing, letting all tension flow from you. Then perform that ritual just before you walk on to perform."

George—Frederick was starting to think of the three by their first names—frowned slightly. "Something like checking each button on your waistcoat is done up?"

Frederick nodded. "Just so. Something that looks natural, but means something to you. Almost all experienced performers have some little ritual they use."

Brandon, still standing before Moreton, asked, "What do you do?"

Frederick raised his hands and opened them wide, spreading his fingers as far as they would go, then curled them to his palms, then opened them again, repeating the cycle three times.

"That looks like you're limbering up your fingers," Phillip observed.

Frederick nodded. "Exactly. You don't want your ritual to be anything anyone else notices—its true purpose isn't something others need to know."

He watched them take that in, then George asked, "Is there anything else we should know about performing for Lady Eustacia's guests?"

Frederick thought, then said, "Possibly the most useful advice I can impart is to ignore the audience when you walk in. Don't look at them, and shut your ears to their whispering, because they will whisper, and titter, and sigh, and make every other noise imaginable. They will not be a well-behaved audience. Once you've completed your piece and take your bow, if you wish, you may look at them then, although I will admit, I don't. I keep my gaze just above their heads, nod politely, and walk off."

Brandon had been dismissed and replaced by Phillip. After joining George by the door, his expression puzzled, Brandon asked Frederick, "But isn't the audience why we perform? Don't we need to gauge how they respond to our performance?"

"Oh, you'll know," Frederick assured him. "All you'll need to do to assess their reaction is to use your ears. Even before they applaud, you'll know if you've hit the mark—the first clue is in that instant of silence that follows the end of the last note. The more profound that silence, the longer that instant stretches, the more captive your audience was. If your playing held them and captured them, you'll know it then. In addition to that, there's the quality of the applause—is it enthusiastic and heartfelt or merely polite? Worse, is it stiff or reluctant? And that's quite apart from any calls of bravo or comments that carry to your ears."

The expressions of the three young musicians had eased. Brandon and George were nodding; Phillip had his chin tipped up as Moreton measured his neck.

When, finally satisfied, Moreton released him, Phillip said, "While earning money enough to live on is nice, ultimately, our success is that, isn't it? What we bring to our audience and how successful we are in delivering the joy of the music to them."

George took Phillip's place. "That's the moment that's most uplifting —that instant you spoke of when you realize that, yes, you've done your job and shared the music with those listening."

Phillip looked down the room and caught Frederick's eyes. "We were talking on our way here, and we want to thank you—you and her ladyship —for giving us this opportunity to perform before a more exacting audi-ence. If we succeed in this sphere...well, it's what we've been training for all these years. To share our God-given talents and what those can make of the music with an audience who appreciates that."

The other two murmured their agreement.

Frederick inclined his head in acknowledgment of their words, even while he pondered the fact that, in the matter of playing before any audi-ence, he'd taken the exact opposite stance.

He'd been hiding his talent, hoarding it away, for more than a decade.

From the mouths of babes...

It was somewhat chastening to realize that, in reaction to the ton's over-avid interest, instead of confronting it and overcoming the hurdle, he'd instead run away and withdrawn his talent from the world.

Moreton was finally finished. He dismissed George, rolled up his tape measure, consulted with Thomas, then faced Frederick. "I believe we'll be able to deliver within the specified time frame, my lord. Where do you wish the garments to be sent?"

Frederick glanced at the three young men, then said, "Package each set separately, address each to the relevant gentleman, and send all three packages to the Music School at St Martin-in-the-Fields, Trafalgar Square."

George nodded. "We can pick them up easily from there."

"Indeed. I'm sure the good Mrs. Withers will keep them safe until you do." Frederick turned to Moreton. "Thank you for rising to the occasion, Moreton. You may send the account to me."

"My lord." Moreton bowed. "And can I say that while this commission is somewhat different, we at Moreton and Sons will be happy to execute any such commissions in the future."

Frederick dipped his head. "Thank you, Moreton. I believe you and Thomas know the way out."

With a nod to his three new clients, Moreton quit the room, followed by Thomas.

Frederick waved the three younger men to the door; they filed out, and he joined them. As they walked slowly along the upper gallery and down the main stairs, the three asked, and Frederick explained the rationale behind his choice of pieces; in doing so, he realized he'd brought his knowledge of the ton very much to bear.

After seeing the three men on their way, he retreated to his study. Slumping into his favorite chair by the fireplace, he reviewed the insights generated during the past hour courtesy of his interaction with the youthful trio.

With the benefit of hindsight, he could admit that his reaction to the ton's fawning had been driven more by selfish self-interest than any other cause. He might abhor the over-avid lauding and the smothering attention to the point of outright rejection of the activity that gave rise to it, yet he doubted any serious musician—like the three he'd taken under his wing —would regard his abraded sensitivities as sufficient cause to withhold his, as they'd termed it, God-given talent from the world.

He sat and considered that proposition—contrasted his life and its lack of meaningful hurdles with those of the three young musicians.

All in all, it was difficult to avoid the charge that, in the matter of sharing his talent, he'd been acting in a cowardly manner.

From that, it was a short step to a newfound appreciation of the impact of Stacie on his life. She hadn't accepted his initial lack of interest but had held to her purpose and convinced him to put his talent to good use in introducing worthy musicians to the ton. But en route to gaining her objective, she'd succeeded in persuading him to, once again, accept the responsibility that came with a talent such as his—namely, to sit before an audience and let the music he truly revered speak through his fingers.

～

That afternoon, Frederick called on Stacie in Green Street. On being welcomed into Stacie's private parlor—a cozier room than the formal drawing room—he greeted Stacie and her cousin Ernestine, then moved to the armchair Stacie waved him to, opposite hers and angled toward the chaise where Ernestine sat stitching.

He sat and said, "Now that we have our first three protégés selected and the music they should play at our first event decided and have arranged for appropriate raiment"—he met Stacie's eyes—"is there anything else we need to determine before we decide on a date?"

After the revelations of the morning, he felt re-energized, with his commitment to Stacie's enterprise reinforced. A certain impatience prodded him; he was eager to see how the musical evening would pan out, for himself as much as for their protégés.

Stacie lightly frowned, her expression suggesting she was consulting some mental list, then she shook her head. "Nothing I can think of." She refocused on his face. "But of course, in deciding on a date, we need to consider who we wish to invite and what other entertainments are slated for the same night."

Frederick drew a list from his pocket. "These are the events during the next three weeks for which I've seen invitations. Not that I've accepted any, but the events are scheduled." Glancing at the list, he added, "The coming week isn't crowded, but the week after that is already event-heavy, and the week after that looks ridiculously crammed."

Ernestine looked up from her embroidery. "The week after next is considered the first week of the Season, these days. And by the following week, the social whirl is in full swing."

Frederick caught Stacie's gaze. "If you want to host more than one musical evening during this Season, then for my money, we need to move quickly and decide on a night in the coming week. The major hostesses—most likely all those you'll wish to invite—will already be in town, and the academics and aficionados I believe we should invite will also likely be here—some bury themselves during the height of the Season."

Stacie had to acknowledge his point, yet... "Choosing a date in the upcoming week—with less than a week's notice—"

"Will pique people's curiosity," Ernestine interjected. When both Stacie and Frederick looked at her, she smiled and said, "Such an invitation would certainly pique mine. Every hostess worth her salt knows that less than a week's notice for an evening event at this time of year is virtually guaranteed to ensure a poor showing. Yet the invitation will be coming from you, Stacie, and all the ton's ladies know you've grown up in the very heart of the ton, so why would you do such a thing? If it's not a novice's mistake but a deliberate act...?"

Nonplussed, Stacie widened her eyes, inviting an answer.

Ernestine's smile deepened. "Obviously, it must be because you're absolutely assured of a full house, and you're not concerned that some might not answer the call." Ernestine looked down at her stitchery. "It has always seemed to me that, within the ton, confidence in a certain outcome —or at least giving the appearance of such—is the best guarantee that that outcome will, in fact, be achieved."

Frederick nodded. "A shrewd observation. So"—he looked at Stacie —"the only question is which night will suit us best."

Stacie rose and walked to her writing desk. She picked up the stack of invitations resting on one corner, extracted those pertaining to the coming week, left the others on the desk, and returned to her chair. Holding out her hand for Frederick's list, she sat and compared his list with her invitations. Eventually, she said, "I have a few additional invitations for those evenings, but it looks like Wednesday will be our best option. Almack's, such as it is, won't hold its first ball until the week after." She tipped her head, considering the spread of invitations before her. "Quite possibly out of habit, most hostesses have avoided scheduling their evening events on Wednesday."

Frederick nodded decisively. "Wednesday will work. Our three protégés will have their clothes and, I'm sure, their pieces polished to perfection by then."

"If you write your invitations today and send them via footmen rather than the post," Ernestine said, "then I see no reason the majority of your invitees won't attend. Curiosity alone will draw them to the door."

Stacie bit her lip. "How many do you think we can fit?"

A discussion ensued, resulting in Frederick finally agreeing to a limit of one hundred and fifty guests. "We can seat close to a hundred in the music room alone," Stacie pointed out. "And although we'll invite one hundred and fifty, I doubt all will come."

"Oh, I think you should err on the side of caution, dear," Ernestine said. "Especially in the catering. If you invite one hundred and fifty, then assume all will cross the threshold. Yet I do take your point—if we seat ninety in the music room, others will remain seated in the drawing room and morning room, and still others will stand around the walls, which creates a feeling of earnestness, don't you think?"

She had to agree. "Very well—one hundred and fifty guests. So who should they be?"

They all had people to suggest, for varying reasons. Stacie moved to her desk, sat, assembled paper and pen, and duly noted all the names and addresses.

It took nearly an hour to settle on their guest list, one including the most influential hostesses as well as the majority of the recognized grandes dames and, at Stacie and Ernestine's insistence, several families they knew who were hoping to puff off young ladies that Season. "They," Stacie maintained, "the mamas and young ladies all, chatter so much to each other that, as a group, they are the most likely to spread word of our evening as an event—as well as enthusing over the caliber of our young musicians—far and wide throughout the ton."

Frederick reacted to that comment with a sour look, but made no protest. As he'd rattled off a string of names of gentlemen influential in the world of music, all of whom Stacie had put on the list, he had no grounds for complaint.

She had also included Protheroe and the governors of St Martin-in-the-Fields. "To make sure they know we appreciate the quality of the graduates the music school produces."

With Stacie's family and close connections, including the powerful Cynster ladies, all on the list, they had had to cull some of the lesser hostesses to trim the numbers to the desired one hundred and fifty.

Finally, she declared, "With our guest list agreed, we need to decide on the wording of the invitation." She arched a brow at Frederick. "Do you wish to be listed as co-host or...?"

He shook his head. "Not co-host." He tapped his fingers on the chair's arm, then suggested, "List the program on the reverse of the card."

She envisioned that, then, lips curving, nodded and reached for a fresh sheet of paper. Frederick recited the program as agreed with their three protégés, then paused.

Pen poised, Stacie looked at him.

But it was Ernestine who said, "We should list you with your formal title—Frederick, Marquess of Albury. Anything less will be...well, underplaying your hand, so to speak."

Stacie tried to read what was going on behind Frederick's impassive countenance, but failed.

However, after a moment, he met her eyes and inclined his head in agreement. "And I'll be playing Robert Schumann's 'Fantasie in C Major. Opus Seventeen.' That will fill half an hour, which is the longest we should stretch our guests' patience and their ability to sit still."

She hid a smile; given the quality of his playing, she doubted they would hear a pin drop, let alone a rustle.

He went on, "So timewise, we start with Brandon, and he'll play for about fifteen minutes. Be sure to list a short interval between his performance and that of the string duo, but it should stretch to no more than three minutes. Then Phillip and Brandon will take a few minutes to settle their instruments, plus another ten or so minutes of playing. After that, list another short interval—that one should be a full five minutes to give the audience time to exchange views on our three protégés' performances—"

"And build expectation and anticipation for your performance," Ernestine put in.

Glancing at Frederick, Stacie glimpsed a hint of resistance, but after a second, he nodded. "Quite." He met Stacie's eyes. "So from beginning to end, your program will last just over an hour, which should be ideal."

She looked down at her notes. "So if we invite people to arrive at eight, start our program at nine-thirty, then at the conclusion, just after ten-thirty, pause for, say, ten minutes before serving supper, we'll have a nicely rounded evening, with all our guests away by sometime shortly after midnight."

"That sounds perfect, dear," Ernestine said. "Now"—she set her embroidery in her lap—"do you want help with those invitations?"

In the end, even Frederick helped, penning the invitations to his peers and colleagues in the music world. As many of the invitations were for couples, if not families, there were sixty-seven actual invitations to scribe, then blot, fold into envelopes, and address.

When the last invitation was done, it was nearly time to dress for dinner. Frederick had divided the stack of envelopes into two roughly equal piles, one to be dispatched from Mount Street, carried to the various residences by Raventhorne footmen, and the other to be delivered by the Albury House staff. The latter pile included not just the invitations for Frederick's scholarly peers but also those for his mother, his sisters, and several acquaintances, as well as a large group of the more general invitations to ton families. As he tied the stack of envelopes with a ribbon Ernestine had found, he observed, "It won't hurt for some invitations to be delivered by a footman in the Albury livery."

Stacie agreed; despite the short notice, the news of Frederick's involvement would definitely get around town and feed expectations.

Finally, Frederick rose and picked up his stack of invitations. After taking his leave of Ernestine, he turned to Stacie, and she waved him to the door.

In the front hall, she gave him her hand. "Thank you. Between us, I believe we've organized a musical evening the ton will remember." Her lips curving, she couldn't resist adding, "And with your name on the program, I predict our first event is destined to be an outright crush."

The expression in his eyes as he held her hand was one of resigned cynicism, but all he said as he released her was, "I suspect you'll be proved correct."

With an arrogant lift to one eyebrow, he turned and went out of the door Hettie was holding open.

Stacie watched him descend, all languid grace, to the pavement, then turn for Park Street. He might not appreciate the ton's adoration, but in reality, she doubted he had a humble bone to his name.

⁓

Frederick reached Albury House with just enough time to hand over the stack of invitations to Fortingale, then hurry upstairs and change before joining his mother and Emily in the drawing room.

"Well!" his mother exclaimed as he walked into the room. "I'd almost given up hope." She waved her invitation—already opened—at him. "I take my hat off to Stacie—she is clearly a miracle worker."

"Don't overdo it, Mama." Frederick bent and kissed her check, then nodded a greeting to Emily, who grinned, understanding his mood and not the least bit inclined to pander to it.

"So tell me," the marchioness commanded, "how on earth did Stacie manage it?" Immediately she held up a hand. "No—wait. Perhaps you'd better leave the mystery intact."

Frederick lounged in one of the armchairs. "If you must know, she shamelessly appealed to my sense of noblesse oblige."

"Oh?" Emily looked fascinated; she'd known him since birth. "How on earth did she manage that?"

He sighed and gave them a condensed description of the music school and the difficulties faced by its English graduates. "They're merchants' sons and can't afford to attend the Royal Academy, yet from all I've seen, their artistry would compare favorably with that of the best of the Academy's alumni. The three Stacie and I have chosen to introduce at this event are well and truly worthy of the ton's attention—as you'll see next Wednesday."

"I have to say that choosing the last free Wednesday is a stroke of genius," Emily stated.

"And giving such short notice," his mother added. "Nothing like a subliminal suggestion that something's afoot to bring the ton flocking." She arched her brows at him. "So who has been invited?"

He rattled off all the names he could remember. Fortingale interrupted him, and they adjourned to the dining room, yet even once they'd settled at the table, his mother continued her inquisition. He bore with her questions with what grace he could muster, knowing he could rely on her support, and that said support would be instrumental in ensuring the evening was a social success.

Sure enough, before she and Emily left him to enjoy a quiet brandy, his mother declared, "You and Stacie can rest assured that Emily and I, and your sisters, too, will all do our part in planting the right seeds in the right minds to escalate interest in your joint enterprise."

"And with such an exclusive guest list," Emily said, "you can be assured there will be plenty of interest in what transpires on Wednesday night."

They left him debating whether that last prediction would be a good thing or not.

～

The marchioness led Emily into the drawing room, and the pair settled comfortably to one side of the fireplace.

"You know, my dear Emily, I cannot help but note that Frederick's association with Stacie has brought about a change in him. Never have I known him to be so patient and accommodating in answering my questions."

Emily nodded. "Indeed. And I know you won't take this observation wrongly, dear Philippa, but it did strike me that while Frederick has always done his duty regarding all those dependent on the estate, I cannot recall him being moved—by noblesse oblige or, indeed, anything else— to bestir himself on behalf of someone entirely unknown to him."

The marchioness was nodding. "Exactly so. And in this case, he's not just bestirring himself but has agreed to do something he's trenchantly avoided for well-nigh the past decade." The marchioness arched her brows consideringly. After several moments, she glanced at the door and lowered her voice to say, "I have to admit, Emily dear, that regarding Frederick's interaction with Stacie, I feel more hopeful of an *interesting* outcome than I have in years."

CHAPTER 5

*W*ednesday dawned cool and cloudy and only grew more dismal as the day progressed. By eight o'clock in the evening, as the first of Stacie's guests trod the red carpet leading from the curb to her front door, a fine mizzle was falling.

Nothing, however, could dampen the spirits of those invited to attend the exclusive event that had flung the entire haut ton into rabid speculation over the past four days.

Stacie stood in the middle of her front hall, greeting her guests and directing them into the drawing room, where the earliest arrivals were milling. While, outwardly, she maintained her customary polished façade, inside, she was on tenterhooks.

When she'd sent out the invitations, she'd had no idea the ton would respond with this much avidity. She'd expected Frederick's name to capture attention and draw the required crowd, but she'd assumed the members of that crowd would display the usual level of ton curiosity, not…this! This hugely amplified anticipation, as if each guest had been invited to witness some major, possibly shocking, certainly tantalizing happening.

To her mind, the extreme interest bordered on the bizarre. She could only hope the entertainment they'd planned would satisfy such elevated expectations.

Frederick had arrived early, bringing the three younger musicians with him. The four had taken refuge in her parlor, with Frederick declaring he had no intention of appearing until it was time for him to play.

Stacie had been somewhat surprised at that, but had accepted his decision without quibble.

Those guests she'd most wanted to attend arrived within the first half hour—a telling success. By the time the clocks struck nine o'clock, her rooms were packed, and she felt justified in quitting her position in favor of moving among the guests, stopping here and there to chat, and fielding inquisitive questions on all sides, most of which pertained to Frederick, but some bright-eyed young ladies—who, she suspected, viewed Frederick as far too old to be of interest to them—inquired as to the three younger musicians.

She halted beside Ryder and Mary in an attempt to catch her breath.

"This," Mary informed her with a smile, "is what wild success looks like."

Ryder arched his brows cynically. "It's amazing what tweaking the gossipmongers' noses will do. One could almost believe people were here to listen to the music."

Stacie pulled a laughing face at her half brother, then turned as her brother Rand and his wife, Felicia, who was expecting the couple's first child, joined them. Her other brothers, Kit and Godfrey, as well as Kit's wife, Sylvia, were chatting nearby.

Felicia squeezed Stacie's arm. "This is an amazing turnout. You must be thrilled."

"I am," Stacie assured her. Thrilled and increasingly nervous. To Mary, she said, "Thank you for getting all the Cynster ladies here. Even Helena and Lady Osbaldestone have come out."

"I couldn't have kept them away." Mary nodded at the crowd. "Given the incentive to attend, I can't imagine anyone you favored with an invitation wouldn't have made every effort to be here."

Another thrill of nervousness skittered through Stacie. "I think I'd better check on the performers."

"To make sure they don't bolt?" Rand grinned at her. "I know how persuasive you can be when you set your mind to it, but even I was shocked that you'd managed to get Albury to agree to a performance. His resistance is legendary."

"Yes, well—I'd better go and check that he hasn't changed his mind."

Stacie laughed as she said the words, but as she wended her way through the crowd, leaving hostess duties to Ernestine, ably seconded by Mary, she found herself wondering just how deeply entrenched Frederick's refusal to play before the ton truly was—and whether it might throw up last-minute hurdles.

She reached the front hall, nodded to Pemberly—Ryder's butler on loan for the evening, who was stationed there—then slipped into the corridor that led to the parlor.

As she approached the door, she heard the plucking of strings and the rumble of male voices. She opened the door, whisked inside and shut it, and met the arrested, questioning glances directed her way.

Frederick was lounging in one of the armchairs, while the three younger musicians were standing in a group by the fireplace, Phillip and George with their instruments in hand.

"From the noise out there," Frederick observed, "I take it we have an audience."

"The music room is going to be packed," she confirmed. "I wouldn't be surprised if we have rather more bodies than the one hundred and fifty we invited." She'd been so right in choosing to pursue Frederick as her principal performer; he was the attraction that was going to make the evening an even bigger success than she'd imagined.

She studied the three younger men. They looked a touch pale, unsure and distinctly nervous.

In contrast, Frederick appeared almost preternaturally calm. When she glanced his way, he waved a languid hand. "Don't worry about them—or me. All of us are ready and will perform in exemplary fashion."

She found a smile and directed it toward the three young musicians. "I have to say, you all look the part." And they did. Frederick had seen to that; in their severe black coats, charcoal waistcoats and trousers, and ivory linen, with their hair neatly groomed and shoes polished to a high gloss, the three looked entirely worthy of being his protégés, sartorially as well as musically.

She glanced at the clock on the mantelpiece. "It's almost nine-thirty. Pemberly, who you've met, will come and fetch each of you at the appropriate time and lead you through the dining room and morning room to the music room. His presence will ensure no one tries to distract you."

"Which," Frederick added, "some will otherwise try to do, just when you want to remain focused on your music. So stick with Pemberly and don't lag behind."

The clock struck nine-thirty, and Stacie's nerves jangled. "I need to get out there—Ernestine and the staff should have everyone seated by now." She turned toward the door, but flung a last, bracing smile at the three young men. "Good luck!"

Frederick had risen and followed her to the door; she opened it and glanced at him. He grasped the doorknob. "Stop fretting. You've done your part—now, it's our turn." His smile was cynically amused. "Go and introduce us, then sit back and relax."

She threw him a faintly exasperated look—what hostess relaxed while guests were in her house?—and went.

As per her instructions, led by Ernestine, the staff had guided the majority of guests into the music room, where they had settled like so many richly plumed chickens in the rows of straight-backed chairs. As Stacie made her way through the morning room, she looked through the double doorways and noted that, as expected, several of the older ladies had remained in the drawing room, with chairs and chaises angled so they could hear and partially see into the music room, while others, mostly gentlemen and younger ladies, stood in groups about the open doorways to the music room and lined the walls of the room itself. The morning room also contained several groups of older ladies, plus a smattering of younger ones and more gentlemen.

A steady thrum of chatter blanketed the scene, while eager anticipation and suppressed excitement rippled over all.

Stacie pressed her palms together at her waist, drew in a deep breath, then glided forward. She'd chosen to wear a new silk evening gown in her favorite shade of cherry red to bolster her courage; as she halted to one side of the grand piano, with her back to the long bow windows at the apex of the music room, she was glad she had—in that instant, she needed every tiny degree of support she could muster.

This was it. If this evening wasn't a success, her project—her purpose —would be doomed.

She looked out over her guests, and the chatter faded. An expectant hush took its place. A few ladies shifted, then even the rustling of gowns ceased.

Stacie smiled, and somewhat to her surprise, the gesture was entirely genuine. She spread her hands, palms out. "Welcome to what I hope will be the first of many such evenings. As most of you gathered here will know, I have long harbored a fascination for classical music, and I recently discovered the talents of the graduates of the music school attached to St

Martin-in-the-Fields. Although of high quality, such local musicians rarely have the chance to feature as solo performers. In particular, it seemed a shame—indeed, a travesty—that such talented Englishmen were so rarely seen within the ton, that venues at which we"—her gesture included all those assembled—"might enjoy their gifts simply did not exist. Subsequently, I recruited the Marquess of Albury, one of our own highly talented musicians, to the cause, and with Mr. Protheroe, the Master of Music at the school"—she inclined her head to Protheroe, who was standing against the wall to her right—"Albury and I chose the three performers who will appear before you tonight, prior to Albury himself playing."

She swiftly scanned the faces of her guests; all were listening, all were drinking in her words. At the edge of her vision, she saw that, right on cue, Pemberly had arrived in the morning room with Brandon in tow. "The first to play is Mr. Brandon Miller, on the pianoforte, and he will perform the first movement, the allegro con brio, from Ludwig van Beethoven's 'Piano Sonata Number Twenty-one.'"

With a smile, she turned toward the morning room's doorway and led her guests in politely applauding as Brandon—looking tense and pale but determined—walked forward. He crossed before the piano, halted beside her, and bowed to the audience, then straightened, turned, circled the piano, and took his seat.

Stacie stepped back toward the windows—metaphorically speaking, into the shadows—from where she could survey the audience's reactions.

Brandon's neat and rather handsome appearance had already caused several ladies, young and old, to pass whispered comments in archly complimentary vein. Then he set his hands to the keys, and the first chords rang out, and the whispers abruptly cut off.

His concentration absolute, Brandon performed flawlessly. As the movement unfurled, Stacie noted several of the gentlemen Frederick had invited—scholars and others from the Royal Academy—exchange impressed looks, then sit straighter and pay more focused attention.

Also exchanging pointed, transparently impressed looks were the hostesses Stacie considered her competitors in the musical-events-within-the-ton sphere, but it was too early to feel vindicated; Carpenter and Goodes had to impress as well for her point to be made.

For the following minutes, the audience remained utterly still and silent, trapped in the web of the great composer's music that Brandon brought to vibrant life.

Finally, his fingers flying faultlessly through the runs and trills, Brandon brought the piece to its triumphant conclusion; the final chords rang out, and he lifted his hands from the piano—and a second of silence passed as the audience caught its collective breath—then applause rang out, unrestrained and spontaneously joyous. Sincere.

Brandon flushed, glanced briefly at the audience, then looked around for Stacie.

Smiling delightedly and clapping, she walked forward as several calls of "Bravo!" rang out. She waved Brandon forward, and he rose and joined her and bowed deeply to the audience, who continued to clap and call.

By the wall, Protheroe looked beyond delighted.

Brandon turned to Stacie and half bowed. "Thank you," he mumbled, his voice thick. "I will never forget this."

Stacie touched his arm briefly as unexpected tears formed in her eyes. "You did wonderfully well—all of us thank you."

He stared at her for a second, then turned and bowed again to the audience before walking to where Pemberly stood waiting to escort Brandon back to the parlor and fetch Carpenter and Goodes to replace him.

Stacie gave the assembled company a few minutes—a short interval as per their program—to exchange opinions, comments, and observations; it seemed plain that despite her describing the music school's graduates as "high quality" and "talented," most hadn't truly appreciated the degree of musical ability that had, until now, passed unnoticed, essentially beneath their noses.

Eventually, Pemberly returned and hovered in the parlor, far enough back to be out of sight of those in the music room, with Carpenter and Goodes, carrying their instruments and looking even more pale and tense than Brandon had, close behind him. Stacie saw them and motioned to a waiting footman to place two chairs before the long bow windows, as they'd previously arranged, while she moved once again to her mistress-of-ceremonies position a yard before that spot.

Facing those assembled in the music room, she lightly clapped her hands.

Instantly, all chatter faded, and all eyes fastened on her. "Our second performance of the evening will also come from graduates of the music school of St Martin-in-the-Fields. Mr. Phillip Carpenter, on violin, and

Mr. George Goodes, on cello, will perform for us the 'Duet for Violin and Cello in C Major,' also by Ludwig van Beethoven."

She raised her hands, and the audience clapped with her as she stepped back and nodded to Carpenter and Goodes, and they drew in deep breaths and walked toward her. They halted before the chairs, turned to the audience, and bowed low, then straightened and took their seats.

They glanced at each other. Phillip tweaked a string, then ran his bow across, and George responded. Both appeared satisfied with the outcome; bows poised, they exchanged another long look.

In perfect accord, the pair launched into the lilting piece, quickly bringing approving smiles to several faces. Soon, many heads were nodding in time; the light, smooth, and airy piece was the perfect composition to keep this audience's attention, requiring sufficient skill and subtlety to satisfy the more critical, yet consistently pleasant on the ear of the less-demanding, more-intuitive listener.

Stacie scanned those present for any signs of negativity and found none. Everyone was…simply enjoying the wonderful music.

The final notes sounded, the strings singing in blissful harmony— concluded in perfect unison as both musicians raised their bows.

This time, the applause was even more eager, more enthused. Stacie saw keen calculation in many matrons' faces; string performers of the likes of Carpenter and Goodes could perform at many ton functions—at soirées, parties, routs, and balls—and the ton was always hungry for fresh faces, preferably handsome, and above all, appreciated exactly the sort of skill Carpenter and Goodes had displayed.

Unaware of the speculation running rife through the audience, the pair exchanged a hugely relieved look, then rose and came forward to take their bows.

As the audience continued to clap and call, Carpenter and Goodes turned to Stacie and half bowed, then, as Brandon had done, with a last bow to the audience, returned to Pemberly in the morning room and, under his protection, retreated to the safety of the parlor.

Stacie heaved a huge, ecstatically happy sigh. They'd done it— achieved what they'd needed to achieve. It might be only a first step—a first event—but if they'd failed at this hurdle, the way forward would have been strewn with difficulties. Instead, even before Frederick played to cap off the evening, on the basis of the young musicians' performances alone, they'd caught and fixed the attention of her guests—arguably the most critical and discerning of the ton's lovers of music, especially given the number of Frederick's academic peers present. Indeed, most of the latter group were now chattering with each other in much the same excited vein as the matrons with events later in the Season.

With Frederick's help, she'd succeeded in bringing three local musicians to the attention of the ton.

Unable to stop smiling, she glanced at Protheroe. He was beaming as well and, transparently delighted, bowed to her.

After nodding back, Stacie returned to her survey of the ladies arrayed before her, and Mary caught her eye and smiled in congratulatory encouragement—then Mary was tapped on the shoulder by Honoria, Duchess of St. Ives, and turned to answer what was plainly an inquiry regarding the three musicians.

Stacie glanced toward the morning room—and caught sight of Frederick, standing as far back in the shadows as possible.

For her audience, his performance would be the crowning glory of the night.

She faintly arched a brow at him, and he nodded curtly.

She walked forward—and the immediate hush that fell was startling in its intensity.

On reaching her mistress-of-ceremonies spot, she halted, raised her head, ran her gaze over the audience, and stated, "Our third and final performance of the evening will be Robert Schumann's 'Fantasie in C Major, Opus Seventeen,' performed by Frederick, Marquess of Albury."

The welcoming applause was loud, avid, and eager.

Frederick entered the music room and, without glancing at the audience, walked to Stacie's side. He turned and bowed to the assembled horde, then straightened, circled the piano, sat, and set his fingers to the keys.

By then, an expectant, almost-quivering silence had fallen. He didn't hesitate, and the first series of trills, the building first sequence, fell into and claimed that silence.

It was easy to surrender to the music, to lose himself in it, to let it roll and fall and spill out of the piano, forming a wall of constantly shifting sound between him and those listening.

He'd forgotten how easy that was, forgotten how completely the music shielded him from his audience—from the world. As his hands confidently swept and skipped over the keys, he gloried in that forgotten freedom and allowed his ability full rein.

As the notes built and sang and the chords compounded, he might as well have been alone...except for the presence standing closest to the piano, a little way to his right.

Curiously, he could sense her; in the swirl that was his music, his imagination saw her as a bright soul, a burning beacon his music sought to draw to him...

He was almost at the end of the piece before he realized he was playing to her. For her.

That it was she whom he sought to impress—no one else.

Then the concluding passage commanded his full attention, yet even then, he didn't lose mental sight of her. Under his fingers, the final lilting chords built cleanly, tripping quickly upward, only to slow, to fall quiet, to musically sigh and, finally, close.

The silence when he raised his hands from the keyboard was profound. From its quality—from the absolute stillness that gripped the audience—he cynically surmised he hadn't lost his touch.

That spellbound pause stretched for a long, protracted moment, then applause erupted, thunderous and ecstatic; unmoving, he let the wave roll over him, then he glanced at Stacie—and read her verdict in her shining eyes. She was clapping furiously and smiling giddily, and he had to fight to hold back his answering smile.

But he couldn't forget where they were. Now the music had ended, the audience was back.

However much elation and satisfaction he felt, he wasn't going to show it; he needed to hold this audience at a rigid distance.

Keeping his features locked in the impenetrable and uninformative expression he'd long ago perfected for moments such as this, he rose and walked around the piano to Stacie's side, turned, and without actually focusing on the audience's faces, bowed—not as deeply as generally prescribed, but then, he was a marquess.

He straightened, and the audience continued clapping and calling bravos, then someone thought to stand, and in a surging wave, the entire seated company came to their feet, still clapping and calling. He glanced at Stacie.

She stepped nearer, still clapping herself, and eyes bright with appreciation, said, "That was a tour de force."

A deeper satisfaction gripped him; for one instant, he stared into her periwinkle-blue eyes, then he returned his attention to the audience, swept them with his gaze, and held up a hand.

They quieted somewhat eagerly; he suspected they hoped he would play another piece. Instead, he announced, "Like most of you, I had no idea of the supremely talented musicians this city has spawned and continues to produce. As a group, in our search for performers of musical excellence, we've been guilty of falling into unquestioning habit and assuming that all those worthy of our attention must, necessarily, come from the great music schools of the Continent. Given what you've heard tonight, given the thousands of venues that put on musical performances every night these days, our decades-old assumption is patently absurd. When next you think to host an event with musicians, I urge you to consider the graduates of local music schools, whether the one attached to St Martin-in-the-Fields or the other known music schools in the city. Those schools exist for a reason, namely to foster and train musicians worthy of our notice. I commend their graduates to your attention."

When he dipped his head and ceased speaking, applause once again broke out, but ladies and gentlemen both also turned to their companions and commented, many falling into eager conversations; Frederick hoped those conversations were more about Miller, Carpenter, Goodes, and their ilk than him.

Stacie touched his arm. "That was very well done."

Frederick turned to her as Protheroe came up.

"On behalf of our graduates, I cannot thank you enough, my lord," Protheroe declared. "Your words, your support—and Miller's, Carpenter's, and Goodes's experiences here today—will give all of them heart."

Frederick stopped himself from shrugging. "They deserve every advantage that comes their way—I merely drew this audience's attention to the quality that your graduates have achieved through their own devotion."

"Nevertheless, on their behalf, I thank you." Protheroe bowed, then was forced to give way as a surging tide of ladies and quite a few gentlemen pressed forward to laud Frederick—which he considered entirely unnecessary—and also to congratulate Stacie as well. As Stacie deserved every accolade—it had been her idea after all—Frederick reined in his instinctive dismissiveness and directed the gushing ladies and over-congratulatory men toward her as deftly and quickly as he could.

Within a minute, he and she were besieged; in many ways, this was his worst nightmare. He didn't possess a shy bone in his body, yet he hated—*hated*—the cloying effusiveness and the over-enthusiastic, sometimes even rhapsodic praise his playing incited from people who were normally as coldblooded as he.

He'd never understood why people's responses got under his skin and itched so horrendously, yet they always had. Inevitably, he would start to feel smothered, and his lungs would slowly seize...

Thankfully, Stacie proved an unexpected rock, and as he'd warned her, he wasn't above clinging to her skirts. She knew everyone and, as if she sensed him pokering up in the face of the worst of the gushing, was quick to step in with a distracting question and divert attention from him.

With her beside him, he weathered the first rush, after which his mother, Emily, his sisters and their husbands, and various connections vied with Stacie's brothers and their wives, and her even more varied and more scarifying connections to offer their congratulations.

Then came a stream of his more scholarly acquaintances, including Brougham and his wife; in this instance, Frederick found Brougham's stiff reserve a welcome breath of fresh air.

On the Broughams' heels came the second wave of those who didn't know better than to overenthuse. Frederick gritted his teeth and prayed that supper would soon be announced.

The press of those seeking his attention and Stacie's split their focus. He was pretending to listen to Lady Morecombe, who seemed to think he needed to be made aware of her nephew's "quite exceptional" playing, when he heard old Lady Lannigan, who was rather deaf, assure Stacie, "Your mother would have been so very proud of you, my dear."

He would have paid the comment no heed except, with him and Stacie standing close, hemmed in on all sides, he sensed her stiffen. He glanced at her face—making Lady Morecombe lose track of her recitation—but could see nothing in the calm set of Stacie's features to give him a clue as to the cause of her reaction.

An even older lady, one Frederick didn't know, jostled Lady Lannigan on and declared, "Your mother would have killed for success such as this, my dear Stacie, and what with you being her spitting image, it does take us back, you know."

Although Stacie's answering smile remained bright and relaxed, Frederick glimpsed something more like recoil or rejection in her eyes. It was such a change to the joy that had been there before—that he and his fellow musicians had put there—that he wanted to step in and chase the darkness away, but Lady Morecombe had the temerity to poke his arm and recall him to her account of her nephew's dubious talents.

Another surge of impatient ladies made him step back; in short order, he found himself behind the piano, surrounded on all sides. He raised his head and looked for Stacie, but she'd been surrounded and pushed the other way.

That unnerving feeling of not being able to breathe rose inexorably.

He held against it, but the sensation of people standing too close built until he fixed the nearest ladies with a steely eye and said, "If you'll excuse me, I must see to our other performers."

Without waiting for even an acknowledgment, he pushed through the circling crowd and escaped around the piano and into the morning room. It was less crowded there, but there were still ladies wanting to waylay him; he pretended not to see and strode for the door into the hall.

Speaking of those other performers, they'd followed him when he'd left the parlor and had listened to his performance from the morning room, but at its end, had slipped away.

He found them sitting and quietly talking in the parlor. They turned to him with wide, shining eyes. He nodded and shut the door. "Now you know what awaits you if you're of a mind to pursue musical performances for the ton."

"But none of us are of your caliber," Brandon said.

"Yet." Frederick dropped into a vacant armchair. "All three of you have the potential to command similar respect from those who truly know music. As for the others, they are more fickle, but they will spread your name, and that's what builds fame."

Frederick looked at the three faces turned his way, then frowned. "Have they fed you yet?"

Phillip blinked, and George said, "They're going to feed us as well?"

Frederick snorted, rose, crossed to the bellpull, and tugged it. He'd slumped back in the armchair by the time a harassed-looking footman in the Raventhorne livery arrived.

The footman's demeanor abruptly changed when he saw Frederick. He snapped to attention. "Yes, my lord?"

"They must be serving supper by now."

"Indeed, my lord. About to be called any minute now."

"In that case, please ask the cook to prepare a platter of her best selections for our three musicians here." He waved at Brandon, Phillip, and George. "They performed superbly and should be appropriately rewarded."

"And for you, my lord?"

"No—I'll eat later." Most likely after he'd returned home; unlike many other musicians, he was rarely hungry immediately after a performance.

"Yes, my lord." The footman retreated and shut the door.

Frederick looked at his three protégés and smiled. "You did very well. And speaking of rewards..." He reached into his coat and withdrew three envelopes. He checked the names inscribed on each and handed them to the younger men. "Your fees." He waited until they'd opened the envelopes and looked inside. "And any performance of similar duration you give for any ton hostess in the future should net you at least ten pounds more."

He grinned at the young men's stunned expressions. "Welcome to the world of ton events—courtesy of Lady Eustacia, you now have a position within it, and it's one you would be wise to maintain and build upon. If, in the future, you have any questions—about the wisdom of accepting any particular offer of an engagement, or which pieces to play at an event, or regarding the sum offered, by all means, call on me, and we'll discuss it—you know where Albury House is, and my people will recognize you."

Brandon was the first to find his voice. "Th-thank you, my lord."

The other two gabbled their thanks as well, then Phillip wonderingly said, "It's a little like a dream come true—I'm half thinking I'll wake up, and it won't be real."

A tap on the door heralded two maids each ferrying a platter; the cook had clearly correctly interpreted Frederick's instruction, and the platters were piled with delicacies.

The maids set down the platters and drew plates and napkins and forks from their apron pockets. After laying everything down—all the while casting admiring glances at the three younger men, all of whom blushed, much to Frederick's amusement—the maids bobbed and departed.

The three young musicians' gazes had fixed on the succulent tidbits stacked on the platters, but none of them moved.

Frederick grinned and waved at the food. "Have at it."

The trio needed no further urging.

Frederick waited, comfortable and far more relaxed than he had been, and when the platters held nothing but crumbs, he summoned another footman and sent his three protégés, now wilting but still smiling, out to his carriage with instructions to his coachman to ferry the three to their homes, then return to pick him up; his mother and Emily had traveled separately in the larger Albury carriage.

Once the door shut behind Goodes, Frederick lay back in the armchair, stretched his legs out before him, and looked up at the ceiling. Now his excuse for hiding in the parlor had departed, he should return to the reception rooms and circulate. He knew his mother and Emily would think so, and most likely, so would Stacie.

He considered the melee that would surround him if he reappeared and pulled a face. "There's *should*...and then there's *will*."

He clasped his hands on his chest and remained where he was.

Stacie had lost sight of Frederick some minutes before Pemberly found her, and she gave the order for supper to be announced. Although she kept her eyes peeled, she didn't spot Frederick's dark head anywhere among the crowd, and then she was too busy assisting some of the older grandes dames into the supper room or ferrying other's choices out to where they remained in the drawing room to have time to search.

Supper was in full swing when Mary popped up at her elbow and caught her hand. "Frederick—where is he?"

"I don't know." Stacie glanced around again. "He must be here somewhere."

"He isn't—Felicia, Sylvia, and I have quartered the rooms. He's vanished." Mary caught her eye. "Would he have left the house without telling you?"

"I doubt it. Once he agreed to perform, he's been nothing but supportive. He might be with his three protégés."

"Pemberly said they left."

"Oh yes—Frederick was going to send them home in his carriage. That must be where he went..." Stacie looked at the door to the front hall. "I think I know where he must be."

"Well"—Mary prodded her—"go and winkle him back out. While I can appreciate that a gushing crowd isn't to his liking, to gain the most from this event with respect to ensuring the success of the next and the next, he needs to be swanning around, available for those you enticed to attend with the promise of hearing him play and, subsequently, meeting him."

Stacie hadn't promised anyone the latter but refrained from saying so; she understood Mary's point well enough. The ton's more influential ladies and the senior hostesses had come with the expectation of not only hearing the elusive marquess play but speaking with him as well. If Stacie wanted to ensure those ladies' attendance at her next event, she had to fulfill their expectations no matter that those extended beyond what she'd offered.

Mary went on, "If he needs you to hold his hand, do so. If you get him back out here, I'll help, and so will the others."

Stacie nodded. "If you and Ernestine will hold the fort here, I'll see what I can do."

She made her way into the front hall. After smiling and farewelling two of the older ladies, before anyone else appeared, she hurried down the corridor to the parlor. She didn't knock but opened the door and whisked inside, closed the door, and turned—and was unsurprised to find Frederick slouched in an armchair and arching his brows at her.

"Have you come to take refuge, too?"

"No." She marched across, halted beside his outstretched legs, and looked down at him. "I've come to inveigle you back out."

Frederick raised his brows higher. "Have they all left?"

"Thus far, only a few have gone."

"In that case, I prefer to remain here."

He heard her sigh.

"It's not a question of preferring but of what's needed to ensure the major hostesses, especially, continue to support our events in the future." When he glanced up, she trapped his gaze. "You committed to this enterprise—as Mary pointed out, having dangled the lure before the beast, we need to deliver what they expect, or the ladies will be miffed."

"They can remain miffed for all I care. Regardless, when I play again, they will come."

Her lips tightened. "You don't know how difficult some of the major hostesses can be." Her gaze locked with his, she drew breath and said, "I don't know what's behind your obvious aversion to the ton, but we need you to set it aside and show those who've attended tonight that if they come to future events, you will be approachable—available to speak with —at least for a little while."

Before he could respond, she clasped her hands before her and went on, "If you need help dealing with the grandes dames, the hostesses, and others, I'll gladly stick by your side throughout, but we can't risk allowing the hostesses and the grandes dames to leave feeling short-changed."

He stared up at her. He wasn't actually afraid of crowds. He disliked —*intensely* disliked—the cloying, smothering attention, but if he truly wished, he could endure it. Possibly cuttingly, but ignoring the aggravation and dealing with anyone who wished to speak with him...that really wasn't all that hard.

And if she promised to remain by his side...

It hit him then, the real reason he'd quit the music room and the crowds. He'd put up with the guests well enough while she'd been beside him, but once they'd become separated, he'd lost interest in being guest-prey and had seized on the excuse of dealing with his protégés to retreat —and he'd stayed in the parlor because he'd known that at some point, she would come looking for him...

He was there and had remained there precisely to engineer this moment.

This interlude alone with her, because he preferred talking to her rather than to anyone else, even his peers.

He'd allowed his gaze to unfocus while his thoughts streamed through his mind; he refocused on her and saw the genuine worry in her fine eyes, noted the way she was unconsciously gripping—not quite wringing—her fingers, and was appalled by his silly intransigence, his selfishness. He'd left her to shoulder the social weight of the evening, and now, on top of deserting her, he'd dragged her away from her guests.

He should have come to his feet when she'd entered. Where were his manners?

Abruptly, he drew in his legs and stood.

Only to realize, too late, that she'd been standing too close; instinctively, she stepped back, trod on her hem, and with a smothered squeak, arms flailing, toppled backward.

He lunged and grabbed her about her waist, but his feet got tangled in her multilayered skirts, and he tripped, then he was falling, too.

With a massive effort, he flung them sideways, toward the chaise.

At the last second, he twisted and landed stretched full length on his back, with her on top of him.

Her elbow rammed into his chest, and his breath left him, just as the sensations of her body impacting on his—her lush breasts squashed to his chest, her hips and thighs cradling his—slammed into his awareness, and a ravenous desire he'd been endeavoring to suppress roared to full-blown life.

He froze.

So did she. She wasn't breathing any more than he was.

Her gaze locked with his; he saw the change in her wide blue eyes as she registered that the softness of her stomach was cradling that part of his anatomy the state of which he couldn't control.

He steeled himself to deal with fluster, rejection, and retreat.

Instead...

Her eyes widened even more.

She stared at him—and he stared at her as the realization dawned that they were *both* struck dumb and rendered immobile by the most searing desire he'd ever experienced.

The doorlatch clicked. "You can rest in here."

He and Stacie turned their heads to see Ernestine looking down as she and another middle-aged matron guided two elderly ladies, both leaning heavily on canes, into the room.

"You can lie on the chaise, Lady Hernshaw, and recoup before attempting your carriage—oh!" Glancing at the chaise, Ernestine came to a jarring halt. Her free hand rose to her throat. "Oh—oh, dear!"

Frederick managed not to roll his eyes. *Oh, dear?* The situation was far worse than that.

A multitude of gasps and shocked exclamations confirmed his fears; not only had the two elderly biddies and the other lady seen him and Stacie lying together on the chaise, but apparently, a small cavalcade of ladies had trailed them to the parlor door and got an eyeful as well.

Stifling a sigh, he smiled reassuringly at Stacie and whispered, "Follow my lead," then helped her to scramble off him. The instant she was on her feet, he swung his legs around and rose to stand beside her.

With blithely arrogant unconcern, he directed a smug smile at the assembled ladies. "It seems you ladies will be the first to know. Lady Eustacia has just done me the honor of agreeing to be my marchioness."

He'd kept her hand locked in his; he felt the jolt of her shock and pressed her fingers in warning, then smoothly, smiling with the full force of his ready charm, he raised her hand to his lips and kissed the back of her knuckles.

The impulse to follow that innocent kiss with one far less innocent almost floored him. *What the hell?*

He wrestled his desire back into its cage as Stacie, her features rather blank for a lady who had supposedly just landed one of the biggest and certainly the most elusive catch on the marriage mart, shifted to face him.

Wearing the smile of a nobleman who'd seized a prize he'd wanted, he met her eyes as she endeavored to assemble the correct expression; her lips curved, and her features softened into a believable mask of happiness.

Thankfully, only he was close enough to see the horror that swam in the depths of her eyes.

CHAPTER 6

$\mathcal{I}$t was almost two hours later before the house finally fell silent, the guests all gone and Stacie's sisters-in-law packed off to their own homes with a promise to reveal all tomorrow—meaning today, for it was now long past midnight.

Frederick could only give thanks that her brothers—including her half brother, Raventhorne—had left earlier, before Frederick had been discovered not quite in flagrante delicto with their only sister.

Later today would be soon enough to deal with the Cavanaughs.

The other Cavanaughs. First, he had to calm Stacie.

He sat in the armchair he'd earlier occupied in her parlor and sipped the large brandy Ernestine had happily handed him before taking herself off. Being affianced meant that he and Stacie no longer required a chaperon, which, given the subject they had to discuss, was just as well.

Stacie, meanwhile, was wearing a track in the carpet before the fireplace. "You don't understand!" Dramatically, she flung out a hand. "I can't marry you!"

He'd intended to swiftly and simply explain how and when their supposed engagement would come to an unproductive end, but her vehemence struck a nerve. Didn't she know what a catch he was? Just thinking that might be atrociously arrogant, yet it was undeniably true. Shouldn't she at least have paused to consider the prospect before insisting it could never be?

Stacie halted, hauled in a huge breath, then walked to the chaise and collapsed on its end. From the moment they'd fallen on the wretched piece of furniture and she'd realized that not only was Frederick attracted to her but she was equally attracted to him, her mind had felt fractured, her wits in utter disarray.

That he desired her was one thing; over the years, many gentlemen had. What had rocked her—blindsided her—was her response; apparently, she desired him—or desired him to desire her or...

Never having dealt with such a situation before, she wasn't certain she was interpreting any of it correctly, not least her own reactions.

Subsequent to that moment and his utterly stunning but necessary declaration, she'd been forced to keep her entire focus on not panicking and, instead, presenting the right façade—that of a lady thrilled at having secured an offer from one of the ton's most eligible noblemen. Indeed, given the success of his musical performance, at that moment, he was arguably the ton's *most* eligible gentleman—wealthy, well-born, titled, handsome, and talented. From the ton's perspective, he was an enormous catch.

But she wasn't going to marry. For her, marrying was far too dangerous and not just for her.

Not that she could explain that, certainly not to him.

She eyed him where he sat, sipping brandy and silently regarding her —as if she was a puzzle he wanted to solve. Given the desire that had erupted between them, that, courtesy of that moment on the chaise, had manifested and remained simmering in the air, him wanting to know more might prove dangerous, too.

But the time for mindless panic was over; she had to face what was and sort it out. "It was neither my fault nor yours that I fell and we landed"—she waved at the velvet expanse beside her—"as we did. I understand perfectly why you declared we were engaged—Lady Hernshaw might be old, but even overcome with faintness, she has all her wits about her."

"I noted that her attack of faintness evaporated on learning our news."

"Be that as it may, I don't wish to marry, and neither do you." She studied him. "You're what? Thirty? You have years yet before you need to marry."

He tipped his head. "Thirty-two, but otherwise, you're correct. I was planning on enjoying my bachelor existence for quite a few more years."

"There you are, then. So!" She blew out a breath and tried to focus her slowly reassembling wits. "At this moment, only you and I know our engagement is a sham, made necessary by unavoidable circumstances."

"Indeed." He took another sip of brandy, watching her over the rim of the glass.

"But neither of us wishes to marry, so what's the best way of resolving this…situation?"

He lowered the glass, studied her for a moment, then said, "Us stepping back from the altar won't be easy to explain. I'm a marquess possessed of significant wealth and estates, in excellent health, and passably handsome. In ton terms, I'm the definition of a highly eligible parti."

She made a derisive sound. "You're ridiculously handsome and an excellent catch."

His lips twitched, and he inclined his head. "As you say. And you're a marquess's daughter, sister of another, have a certain level of independent wealth, and are considered a great beauty. All the ton's ladies will envy you while all the ton's gentlemen will envy me. By every criterion imaginable, we are the definition of a well-nigh perfect match—no one is going to readily understand us suddenly changing our minds and calling it off.

"Compounding that, you have, until now, avoided all matrimonial entanglements, I presume despite the active encouragement of your female relatives and connections, many of whom rank as grandes dames." He pointed a finger at her. "That, more than anything else, is going to make backing away from our necessary declaration an exceedingly delicate task. You must have noticed how incredibly thrilled and relieved your ladies were on learning you'd finally taken the plunge."

She grimaced. He was more observant than she'd given him credit for; the female members of her family had been in alt. But… "They'll come around."

Frederick nodded. "In time. Which is my point." He continued to watch Stacie closely. "There is a relatively simple and straightforward way out of the snare that circumstances have forced us into, but it can't happen overnight."

She fixed her eyes on his. "What way?"

He inwardly smiled, careful not to allow his satisfaction to reach his eyes. Neither he nor she had planned any of this; it hadn't been some trap one had devised and the other fallen into. Neither had wanted to become engaged, yet now they were, her resistance, perversely, had provoked a contrary reaction in him. He didn't understand it, didn't entirely trust it, yet the impulse to carefully consider the benefits of their new situation before ending it was too strong, too powerful, for him to deny.

And underneath all else, he was curious—about so very many things.

"It's easy enough." He held her gaze. "No one will believe us innocent of wrongdoing if we break our engagement off now, so we'll behave as if we are, in fact, a newly affianced couple, and we'll continue to play that part until summer. Then, in July, when the ton has quit the capital and is busy doing other things, we'll quietly let it be known that we have, after all, decided we don't suit."

A frown slowly formed in her eyes as she imagined that.

Smoothly, he continued, "Given our respective ages—that we are both beyond the years of mindless frivolity and are regarded as sensible adults —no one will question such a plainly well-considered decision. However, for the very same reason of our ages, which also place us in the liable-to-be-indulging-in-liaisons class, we can't call off the engagement too quickly, say within the next few weeks, because then everyone will assume we invented the engagement to conceal a potentially scandalous interaction."

Her gaze grew distant, her frown manifesting and drawing her fine brows down.

After a moment, he murmured, "We have a simple choice—end our engagement soon and find ourselves the scandalmongers' favorite target, a fate neither of us deserves, or take our time, pretend our engagement is real, and ultimately, step free without any repercussions."

She refocused on his face. "You're willing to do that—to pretend we're engaged for the next four months?"

He lightly shrugged. "We've managed to work together in successfully organizing our first musical evening." It had been only a week since he'd agreed to the venture, yet... "We've rubbed along well enough." He drained the brandy, watching her all the while. Lowering the glass, he murmured, "Of course, once the ton gets over its excitement and moves onto the next happening, we won't need to be quite so assiduous in keeping up our façade."

"That's true." After a moment, she straightened, and her chin firmed. "I'll need to tell my family the truth."

He thought quickly and countered, "Just your sisters-in-law and

Ernestine. If your sisters-in-law tell your brothers, well and good, but I'll speak with them directly."

Her frown returned. "The Cynsters—"

"No. And I won't be revealing the truth to my mother and Emily, either." He caught her gaze and willed her to accept the condition, one his instincts insisted was necessary. "The more people who know our engagement is, as you termed it, a sham, the harder it will be to maintain a believable façade for the wider ton and the more likely someone will let our secret slip, and we'll be plunged into scandal for no good reason."

She grimaced. "You're right, but this seems so unfair—it wasn't as if we were actually indulging."

More's the pity. He promptly buried the thought.

The clock on the mantelpiece whirred, then chimed three times. He set aside the glass and got to his feet. "I should leave—we'll both have meetings with others to weather later today. I'll send a notice to the *Gazette*, but it won't run until tomorrow's edition."

She rose and fell in beside him as he walked to the door. "Not that the ton will need a notice in a newspaper—I predict our engagement will be the principal topic of conversation over the breakfast cups throughout Mayfair and surrounds."

He grunted and walked with her along the short corridor to the dimly lit front hall. She'd sent her staff to their beds before he and she had sought refuge in the parlor; the two of them were the only ones awake and about in the house.

They halted before the front door, and he faced her, caught her hand, and gently squeezed. "So we're agreed—we behave as if our engagement is real, at least until July?"

She hesitated, then nodded.

He scanned her face, but the shadows cloaked her expression and made reading her eyes impossible. They were standing quite close; on impulse, he raised the hand he held to his lips and, more slowly this time, brushed a lingering kiss to her knuckles.

Because he was watching her like a hawk, he detected the slight hitch in her breathing and the way her lips fractionally parted. He definitely wasn't the only one who felt the prod of that flaring attraction, wasn't the only one susceptible to it.

For a second, he battled an impulse to lean closer and taste her lips, but he wasn't sure either of them was yet ready for that—ready for what such a caress might reveal. Instead, he forced himself to smile easily and release her hand. "I'll call later in the day."

She nodded again. "Until later."

She opened the door, and with a last tip of his head, he walked out. He paused on the porch and heard the door softly shut behind him. His carriage waited by the curb, his coachman nodding on the box.

He started down the steps, his mind toying with a novel notion. She'd inveigled him into performing for the ton again; she hadn't accepted his initial dismissal and had persisted until he'd agreed.

If pushed, he might now admit that him returning to playing within the ton might, indeed, be a good thing—something that was meant to be.

So why shouldn't he return the favor?

He had no idea why she was so set against marrying—given her age and unmarried state, it didn't appear to be marriage to him but marriage in general she'd taken against.

She'd boldly challenged his stance of not playing for the ton—and had been proved correct.

Perhaps it was time someone—him—challenged her attitude to marrying.

He reached the carriage and opened the door, startling his coachman awake. "Home, Jenkins," he ordered and climbed aboard and sat.

As the coach quietly rattled off, he leaned back in the shadows and pondered a fact even more unexpected than their engagement, namely, that a large part of his mind was insisting that convincing Stacie to allow their unintentional engagement to stand was not just a good but an excellent idea.

∿

Stacie stood in the shadows of the front hall and stared at the door she'd closed and locked. Her senses were not entirely steady; the back of her knuckles, where Frederick's lips had brushed, still felt entrancingly warm.

She hauled in a constricted breath and slowly let it out. She wasn't at all sure that agreeing to a four-month-long sham engagement was the wisest course, but his arguments had made sense. And he hadn't even thought to blame her for treading on her hem and landing them in this ludicrous predicament; some gentlemen would have.

After a moment, she looked around her—recalling all the people who had been there that night, the unalloyed success of her long-anticipated first musical evening, ultimately trumped by what the ton would consider the highest triumph of all, namely her engagement to Albury.

Success upon success—and behind it lurked potential disaster.

Still, he had thought of a safe way out for both of them; despite what her panicked mind had thought, they hadn't been trapped into unavoidable matrimony.

Her thoughts, she realized, were going around and around.

She was utterly wrung out; she needed sleep. With a sigh, she turned and started up the stairs.

Today was already a new day.

After the eventful night, Frederick breakfasted later than usual. He was still at the breakfast table, sipping coffee and glancing through *The Times*, when his mother, trailed by Emily, swept into the room.

"Good morning, Frederick," his mother said as she continued to the sideboard.

Slowly, Frederick inclined his head. "Mama. Emily." Despite his mother's even tone, he could only view her appearance with deep suspicion; she and Emily usually breakfasted in his mother's apartments.

When his mother turned from the sideboard, a plate bearing a single slice of ham and a piece of cheese in her hand, Fortingale leapt to draw out a chair at the round table. Emily followed and accepted the seat alongside.

The instant Fortingale stepped back, both ladies fixed their gazes inquiringly on Frederick's face.

He studied them, then lowered his coffee cup. "Yes?" They'd been at the house when the news of his engagement to Stacie had broken, so it wasn't merely that fact that was exercising his mother.

She heaved a put-upon sigh. "Would it have been too much to ask to have been informed of your intention to ask Stacie to marry you? Not that I'm against the move at all—indeed, I applaud it—but a little warning would have been nice. As it was, I was as stunned as everyone else." She threw her hands in the air, then reached for the toast rack.

He weighed his options and replied, "As I hadn't made up my mind to it before the moment, issuing a warning wasn't possible. I am, however, pleased that you approve of my choice."

"Of course, I approve of her—how could I not? She's a marquess's daughter, extremely well-connected among the ton, of a sensible age and of pleasant disposition, is attractive enough to have captured your eye"—his mother wagged her butter knife at him—"enough to hold her own against music and your books!—and she even shares something of your passion for music. At least, she understands your passion for music, which is more than most young ladies would."

Frederick idly listened as his mother rattled on, enumerating Stacie's many qualifications to be his wife, most of which he already knew.

When the marchioness paused to take a bite of her toast, now slathered with butter and jam, in a pensive tone, Emily said, "Of course, there is the shadow of her mother, which the poor girl has had to contend with all these many years."

Frederick focused on Emily. "What about her mother?" When, instead of immediately answering, Emily exchanged a glance with his mother, Frederick said, "I've heard several older ladies mention that Stacie is the image of her mother, and last night, speaking of the evening's entertainment, some lady said that had Stacie's mother been alive, she would have been proud of Stacie's success."

His words had brought both his mother's and Emily's gazes back to him. He met his mother's eyes and arched an interrogatory eyebrow. "So what don't I know about her mother?"

His mother sighed. "Her mother, Lavinia, was her father's second wife. She was as well-born as you or I, entirely haut ton, and was, as you can guess via the references to Stacie, very beautiful. Stacie is, indeed, almost identical in looks. Thankfully, she has shown no sign whatsoever of being identical in character—in that, I strongly suspect she takes after her father, and he was a delightful man."

"What was it about her mother's character that was...less than perfect?"

His mother looked at Emily. "You mentioned her—you can explain. I'm not sure I can—not without giving him the wrong impression." She tipped her head. "And failing to give him the right one as well."

Emily frowned, then looked across the table. "Lavinia wasn't the sort of lady one admired. Or trusted. Not with anything. Not that she was a thief. Rather, she used people's secrets and their weaknesses against them—she was like that from a young girl. Manipulative—extremely so."

"You knew her." It wasn't a question.

Emily was the gentlest person he knew, yet her features set stonily. "Unfortunately, yes. She was a few years older, but as young ladies, we moved in the same circles. She was a viscount's daughter and intent on moving up the social ladder. She set her sights on Raventhorne. He'd been recently widowed, and as Philippa said, he was a kind man—truly one of the old school who prided himself on his manners and his care of others. Lavinia snared him in her net—she was one of those ladies who used their physical assets shamelessly—and so she became his second marchioness."

His mother waved her crust to get his attention. "That, in itself, was not particularly remarkable or reprehensible. It was what came later that ensured that, while courtesy of her birth and station Lavinia continued to have the entree to our circles, she could count no friends among us."

Not knowing what questions to ask, he waited, with his gaze on the two women on the opposite side of the table, and hoped one of them would explain.

Eventually, Emily obliged. "At first, Lavinia played the dutiful wife—she bore Raventhorne four children, but soon after the last was born, she and he went their separate ways, although it was patently obvious to all who knew them that he remained besotted with her. Lavinia, however, proceeded to take a succession of lovers."

"None of which," his mother interjected, "made the ton blink. Not at first and not really by the fact of it, either."

"It was the number of lovers she took and the…tone, I suppose one might say," Emily explained. "Over the years, Lavinia became more and more brazen—and what lovers she was known to take, more and more questionable. Ultimately, it seemed as if the stench of scandal permanently engulfed her, although nothing ever got to the point of being something one couldn't ignore."

"For Raventhorne's sake and that of his children," his mother said, "the ton largely turned a blind eye—he was besotted with her until he died, but she was a viper of the first degree, and her questionable exploits and her excesses stung him repeatedly and took their toll."

Emily nodded. "Then Raventhorne died, and Ryder—who was his son by his first marriage and who Lavinia always hated—acceded to the title, and after that, the ton had little time for Lavinia."

"Not that she didn't still receive invitations and attend the major functions," his mother put in. "She was still the Marchioness of Raventhorne, after all, but we increasingly viewed her as beneath our notice, so to speak."

"And then," Emily said, "some months after Ryder married Mary Cynster, Lavinia died in some accident at Raventhorne Abbey."

"Few have ever heard the details of what happened," his mother informed him, "but of course, the ton as a whole heaved a collective sigh of relief—Lavinia's behavior had become increasingly difficult to overlook."

When both Emily and his mother fell silent, their expressions suggesting they were reliving the past, Frederick reviewed what they'd revealed, then asked, "How does—how did—her mother's behavior affect Stacie?"

His mother cast a tight-lipped look at Emily, who, after a moment, volunteered, "Stacie was still in the schoolroom when her father died and Ryder inherited. Lavinia refused to remain at Raventhorne House—I suspect Ryder would have been able to exercise more control over her if she had, and there was never any love lost there—and insisted, instead, that the estate buy her a town house, and she moved there, taking Stacie and her younger brother, Godfrey, with her. For the next six or so years, Stacie lived in her mother's house, and Lavinia kept her close, very firmly under her wing."

"Indeed." The marchioness nodded. "That is arguably the only good thing one can say of Lavinia—regardless of what scandals she herself courted, she was absolutely rigid in ensuring that no hint of untoward behavior, much less scandal, ever touched Stacie."

Emily reached for her teacup. "Stacie was reared quite strictly by modern ton standards. As far as the ton saw, while with Lavinia, she lived a structured, tightly controlled, and utterly blameless life. And since Lavinia's death, she's lived rather quietly under her half brother Ryder's, and of course that means Mary's, wing."

"Which is to say," his mother declared, "that despite her advanced age and her years living with Lavinia, Stacie enjoys an utterly unblemished reputation within the ton."

"Indeed." Emily nodded decisively. "So one can safely state that despite anything you might hear regarding her mother's indiscretions, Stacie herself is considered by all as above reproach."

Frederick studied the ladies' faces, then slowly nodded. "Thank you for telling me."

"Well!" His mother folded her arms, leaned them on the table, and looked at him expectantly. "Now we have that settled, and we've all agreed that Stacie is the perfect bride for you, when is the engagement ball to be?"

He stared at her, then, thinking furiously, refolded *The Times* and set it aside. "As you might guess, our announcement was...brought forward by circumstance. Neither Stacie nor I have had time to decide what we wish to do regarding such things—our inclination, at this point, is to proceed slowly."

"Slowly?" His mother sat up. "But you're already thirty-two!"

"Precisely my point." Frederick edged back his chair and rose. "We are both beyond the age of impetuosity, and I won't have Stacie harassed. There is to be no talk of engagement balls or any similar event until we've had a chance to decide what we wish."

With a brief nod to his mother and another to Emily, he beat a hasty retreat and took refuge in his study.

After tossing the newspaper on his desk, he dropped into the chair behind it. "An engagement ball—good Lord!"

He stared unseeing across the room while he reviewed all his mother and Emily had revealed of Stacie's life. Nothing in anything he'd heard to that point answered the question of why his supposed-bride-to-be was so set against marrying.

He couldn't ignore the increasing compulsion to view learning the truth as a personal challenge—a gauntlet she had unwittingly flung at his feet. He was determined to learn what she had against marriage and, once he had, if she still featured as the perfect wife for him, to persuade her to change her mind.

~

By eleven o'clock on the morning following her first musical evening, Stacie was deeply regretting not having asked Pemberly to stay behind; poor Hettie wasn't up to the task of repelling the horde of determined ladies who had started to ply the knocker and present their cards shortly after ten-thirty.

And when one breached their defenses, the others followed.

Even with Ernestine assisting as best she could, Stacie felt she was slowly sinking beneath the tide of eager and often-arch questions. All the ladies were keen to learn every detail regarding her unheralded engagement to a gentleman who, Stacie now realized, featured as one of the ton's greatest enigmas.

For these ladies, the pinnacle of her musical evening's success had been the announcement of her and Frederick's engagement.

"So terribly romantic," old Lady Culpepper declared.

"You can rest assured, my dear," Lady Holbrook said, "that all those who were not present will be kicking themselves."

"I, for one," Mrs. Wyshwilson stated, "will never forget the evening. The music—so sublime!—and then the announcement!"

Lady Moreton, a music lover, assured Stacie, "The entire ton will be talking of your musical evening, which will, at least, ensure that your next musical event will be as well attended as you might wish."

There was that, Stacie supposed—a single hint of silver lining in what was otherwise stormy gray.

While she dealt with the countless queries as to the engagement, determinedly turning aside the many that bordered on the impertinent, she felt her face setting into a strained smile. And then there were the inevitable comparisons to her mother, and the repeated refrain of how very proud Lavinia would have been had she lived to see her only daughter snaffle a marquess, just as she had.

Despite the way those comments grated on her nerves, Stacie had to admit they were true. Had she been alive, her mother would have been in her element, manipulating and orchestrating the entire event to her own benefit.

Thankfully, her mother was dead.

Ernestine was visibly flagging and Stacie was wilting when, at a quarter to twelve, Hettie walked into the drawing room with a genuinely bright smile on her face and announced, "The Marchioness of Raventhorne, my lady. Mrs. Randolph Cavanaugh and Mrs. Christopher Cavanaugh."

"Thank God," Stacie breathed. Reinforcements had arrived.

Mary walked in, surveyed the room, took note of Stacie's harried state, and smiled. "Ladies. In the circumstances, I'm sure you understand that I and Lady Eustacia's sisters-in-law have much to discuss with Lady Eustacia and Mrs. Thwaites."

"Oh, of course, my dear Lady Mary."

"Perfectly understandable."

"We'll just be on our way."

"Such delightful news—we had to drop by and congratulate Lady Eustacia, but now we really should get on."

Stacie could only marvel. Mary didn't have to say or do anything more to prompt the ladies to set down their teacups and beat a path to the door.

As the last straggler bustled out into the hall, Stacie collapsed into an armchair. She looked at Mary. "I don't know how you do that, but I want to learn."

Mary smiled, patted her arm, and moved to sit on the chaise opposite. "You'll learn the knack soon enough. But I should have realized how it would be and come earlier."

"I'm grovelingly glad you came when you did," Stacie assured her. "If it had gone on for much longer, I might have screamed."

Hettie appeared in the drawing room doorway. "That's the last of them gone, my lady." She glanced at the tea trays scattered about the room. "Would you like me to bring a fresh tray?"

"Please." Stacie gestured to the other trays. "Have Rosie help and take these trays away. I haven't actually managed to have a cup myself yet."

"Nor I." Ernestine had claimed one of the other armchairs. "That was…an experience. And not an altogether pleasant one."

"Oh?" Mary looked her question.

Ernestine waved. "Nothing truly nasty—just a great deal of over-inquisitiveness."

Felicia and Sylvia had sunk onto the chaise alongside Mary.

Stacie regarded the three ladies. Along with Ernestine, they were her closest friends. She drew in a breath and let it out with, "There's something I have to tell you all—to explain—but let's wait until the tea tray arrives."

All four regarded her sober expression, which stated very clearly that her news wasn't something they were going to be happy to hear, then Felicia nodded and said, "While we're waiting, I can report that Rand had quite a conversation with the master of the music school, Mr. Protheroe. There were several gentlemen present last night who invest with Rand, and as a group, they were so impressed with the quality of the young musicians' performances that they floated the notion of starting a series of musical scholarships to be administered through the school."

"So," Sylvia said, with an encouraging smile, "that's one unlooked-for benefit that has come from your very first musical evening."

"Even Ryder, who I regret to say is not terribly musically inclined, was impressed," Mary said.

"Kit, too," Sylvia added. "He said to tell you that hearing the performances last night made all the evenings he spent sneaking you out of your mother's house to attend concerts worthwhile."

Stacie had to smile. "I'm glad he enjoyed the evening."

"Everyone who attended enjoyed the evening," Mary informed her. "Although your culminating announcement might have drawn attention from your principal purpose, absolutely everyone present was captivated by the music—they might be temporarily distracted, but they won't forget the experience."

Stacie sighed. "I hope not." She sat up as Hettie appeared, bearing a fresh tea tray. Rosie, the younger parlormaid, slipped into the room in Hettie's wake. After Hettie set the fresh tea tray on the low table before Stacie, the maids made short work of collecting the other trays.

When the door closed behind them, Stacie looked at the teapot, wondering where to start.

"Tea first," Mary said, not unkindly. "Here—I'll pour."

Stacie sat back and let Mary do the honors.

When all five of them had teacups in their hands and had taken their first sips, Stacie began, "There's no easy way to say this. The engagement Frederick and I announced last night is a sham—one forced on us by a totally innocent circumstance."

"Oh!" Ernestine put her fingers to her lips. "I knew you wouldn't have been doing what you were doing in the parlor like that. His lordship has been so very correct in all other respects—it seemed so odd."

"It was odd," Stacie said. "It was an accident, but then Lady Hernshaw and Mrs. Meethe saw us, well, grappling like that, and there was nothing Frederick could do other than declare we'd become engaged."

Mary, Felicia, and Sylvia looked puzzled.

"What exactly happened?" Mary asked. "All we heard was that Ernestine, Lady Hernshaw, Mrs. Meethe, and several other ladies walked into the parlor and surprised you and Frederick in an embrace consequent on you having accepted his suit."

Stacie arched her brows. "How very restrained of them all. The truth was rather more gossipworthy. As you know"—she tipped her head at Mary—"I went in search of Frederick to convince him to rejoin the guests. He was in the parlor, biding his time, I assume until everyone left. He wasn't terribly thrilled at the notion of coming back out, but then something I said struck the right note, and he came to his feet—I believe to return to the fray with me. Only I was standing too close, and I stepped back too quickly and caught my heel in my hem. I started to fall, but he caught me, but that put him off balance, and both of us fell—thanks to his efforts, we landed on the chaise, with me on top of him."

"Oh," Felicia said.

"Indeed. That was when the door opened and Ernestine brought in Lady Hernshaw and Mrs. Meethe. They were inside the room before they looked up and saw us." Stacie gestured weakly. "So Frederick helped me up and told them all—the other ladies were about the door, looking in— that I'd just accepted his offer of marriage. After that, of course, everyone was all smiles."

"Oh, dear." Ernestine had raised both hands to her cheeks. "It's all my fault—I shouldn't have taken Lady Hernshaw to your private parlor."

"Nonsense," Stacie chided. "It wasn't your fault—or anyone else's, either. My private parlor was the obvious place to take an older lady needing to lie down."

"Hmm." Mary was frowning into her teacup. After a moment, she looked up and met Stacie's eyes. "Is there any chance of you and Frederick converting the sham into a reality?"

Stacie couldn't stop herself from exclaiming, "Good God, no!"

Sylvia tipped her head and regarded her assessingly. "Why not? You both seem to get along well with each other. You could do a lot worse."

"Does he have a preference for someone else?" Felicia asked.

"Or do you?" Mary put in.

Stacie frowned. "We haven't discussed it, but I suspect he doesn't— and I certainly don't."

"Well, then," Mary said. "There's no reason to dismiss the notion out of hand." When Stacie opened her mouth to disagree, Mary held up a staying hand. "You have to admit that he's eligible—well, beyond eligible given the potential bride we're discussing is you. He's not only of suitable rank but possessed of wealth, standing, and charm, is as handsome as they come, and he's a renowned pianist." She arched her brows. "If I was constructing a gentleman to suit you, I doubt I could do better."

This was what Stacie had feared. She was going to have to put her foot down without actually explaining. "Whether we suit or not isn't the point."

Mary looked faintly stunned. "It isn't?"

"No. In my case, the most important point is that I have no interest in marrying at all—not Frederick or anyone else." She paused, seeing a lack of comprehension in the eyes of all three of her sisters-in-law, and reached for the one argument that might hold them off. "I understand that all three of you have found untold happiness with my brothers, and I'm happy for you—happy for that. How could I not be? But I hope that, in return, you can accept that marriage wouldn't suit me—it's not something I want, it's not something I need."

She paused for several seconds, then less stridently, went on, "So the arrangement between Frederick and me will not be progressing, as most will suppose, to the altar."

Mary's gaze hadn't left Stacie's face. Although plainly puzzled, Mary slowly nodded. "Very well. If that's your decision, then, quite obviously"—she glanced at Felicia and Sylvia, and then at Ernestine, then returned her gaze to Stacie—"we'll support you in whatever way we can."

Stacie knew a moment of utter relief. In such a situation, the support of her sisters-in-law would count for a great deal. She tipped her head to them. "Thank you."

Mary straightened. "So have you and Frederick any idea of how to bring your engagement to an acceptable end?"

Stacie nodded. "We discussed it last night, after everyone else had left. His suggestion is that we behave exactly as the ton would expect of an engaged couple of our rank and that we keep up that façade until July. Then, while the ton is busy in the country, we'll quietly let it be known that, sadly, we've decided we don't suit." She studied Mary's face. "Do you think that will do?"

Mary arched her brows. "That's...really quite ingenious." A second later, she met Stacie's eyes. "It's simple, yet effective. And yes, that will work. It's hardly an unheard-of progression of events—engagements announced early in the Season have occasionally been rescinded come summer."

It was Felicia who asked, "As part of the charade, as it were, do you want Mary and Ryder to host an engagement ball?"

"Good heavens, no!" Stacie couldn't think of anything worse. She looked again at Mary. "Surely we can say that, given my age, Frederick and I would rather simply go on quietly?"

Mary grimaced. "We can try that line. If he can restrain his family from pushing too hard, we might even be able to hold to it."

"I'll speak with him, but he's as much an unwilling captive to this situation as I am," Stacie said. "Neither of us intended this situation to come to be—it was an unforeseeable accident that landed us in a compromising position just as others happened upon us." She shrugged.

"Announcing our engagement was the only viable way to avoid a scandal, but neither of us actually wishes to marry the other."

Mary considered her for several moments, then nodded. "Very well." She glanced at the clock, then rose. "If you need support or help, send for us, and we'll come running. But for now, I think we three should hie home and break the news to our other halves—before they get too carried away with the idea of your upcoming wedding."

"Thank you." Stacie hadn't been looking forward to telling Ryder, Rand, and Kit that her supposed engagement was a sham. "And you will make it clear to them that this is not in any way Frederick's fault—that, in fact, it was the only way he could protect my reputation?"

Mary grinned. "We will—I suspect that will be the most interesting part of our discussions."

Felicia and Sylvia rose as well, and with Ernestine, Stacie accompanied her sisters-in-law to the door, beyond which the larger Raventhorne town carriage sat waiting.

When the horses clopped away, Stacie shut the door and turned.

Ernestine was waiting to catch her eyes. "Are you sure you don't blame me for bringing the ladies in and"—she gestured with both hands —"instigating this dreadful situation?"

Stacie smiled, and for the first time that day, the gesture felt genuine. She grasped Ernestine's hand and pressed her fingers. "It wasn't your fault—it wasn't you who made me fall, and you didn't make Frederick try to catch me." When Ernestine continued to look uncertain, Stacie added, "Neither I, nor Frederick, nor you, nor Lady Hernshaw, nor Mrs. Meethe intended any of this to happen. It was just..." She gestured.

Ernestine nodded. "Fate. It was Fate. Yes, I see." She paused, then added, "I believe I'll lie down for a short nap before luncheon."

Stacie tipped her head. "I'll see you at the table."

Leaving Ernestine climbing the stairs, Stacie made her way down the corridor to her private parlor. She paused on the threshold, eyeing the chaise, then closed the door, crossed the room, and dropped into one of the armchairs.

She felt significantly more confident than she had earlier that morning.

Her gaze shifted to the armchair Frederick had occupied. It didn't take much imagination to conjure the image of him sitting there. The longer she studied the mental image, the more her resolution—her resolve never to marry and especially not him—hardened.

Having come to know something of the man behind the mask—the pianist, the scholar, the nobleman prepared to arrange clothing for three young musicians not of his class—the very last thing she would ever wish to do was to set the stage for him to be harmed. Hurt. Emotionally tortured.

Because no matter the situation, regardless of whatever happened, at base, nothing had changed—and nothing ever would. She was her mother's daughter, after all.

CHAPTER 7

That afternoon at precisely three o'clock, Frederick halted his curricle with its team of matched bays outside Stacie's house.

He tossed the reins to his tiger, Timson, leapt down to the pavement, strode up the steps, and plied the knocker. He suspected he was in for a fight, but he was well-armed with arguments and felt confident he would prevail.

The parlormaid recognized him and showed him into the drawing room. Too restless to sit, he stood by the window, watching his horses and the passing traffic.

Stacie joined him moments later. "What is it?" she asked.

He glanced at the door she'd left open, then walked across and shut it. He turned back to her and caught her eye. "Engaged, remember?"

She pulled a face. "That will take some getting used to."

He nodded. "I'm aware. Apropos of that, I'm here so we can go driving in the park, that being one of those things that affianced couples are expected to do."

She looked pained. "Must we? We had twenty and more ladies call here this morning—we've only just caught our breaths."

He spread his hands in a what-would-you gesture. "You know the ropes better than I, and we need to keep in mind that in order to make our eventual crying-off believable—meaning unremarkable and, therefore, unscandalous—we need to do everything required to signal to the ton that we are, indeed, happily engaged. We can't afford to miss a beat and raise eyebrows and, ultimately, suspicions."

She pulled a face and sighed. "I know you're right, but this seems an awfully steep price for both you and I to pay, all because of an innocent fall."

The result of which hadn't been quite so innocent. He held back that observation and waited, his eyes on her.

Eventually, she sighed even more deeply and turned toward the door. "Let me fetch my bonnet and cape."

He nodded and swung back to the window; he didn't allow his lips to curve until she'd left the room.

She returned several minutes later. By then, he was waiting in the front hall, the better to admire the teal carriage gown she'd donned; he wasn't so enamored of her fashionable bonnet, the brim of which would interrupt his view of her face.

She was carrying a military-style cape in a slightly darker shade of teal. When she stepped down to the hall tiles, he reached for the cape and held it for her. "Did you have any trouble with the ladies this morning?"

"In truth, it was a trifle overwhelming—their curiosity was boundless. Indeed, I don't know that Ernestine and I would have coped if it hadn't been for Mary, Felicia, and Sylvia—they arrived and rescued us." After tying the cape's gold cords at her throat, she met his eyes and arched her brows. "Shall we?"

He gave her his arm and escorted her out to his curricle.

She took his hand and gathered her skirts, ready to climb in, then met his eyes. "Incidentally, as I intimated I would, I've told Ernestine, Mary, Felicia, and Sylvia the truth, and while we can be sure they won't spread the news to all and sundry, I suspect my brothers will have heard by now."

"Duly noted." He helped her into the curricle, then rounded the horses' heads and took the reins from Timson. "Wait here until we return."

Timson saluted. "Yes, m'lord."

Frederick climbed to the seat, flicked the reins, and set the bays trotting.

Stacie sat beside Frederick, and as they rattled along the cobbles toward the park, which lay beyond the end of the street, she complimented him on his horses and the comfort of the carriage, which even she recognized as being of the latest design.

"I do like good horses and carriages," he admitted with a half smile.

She'd noted that little, private smile before; it was oddly endearing, imparting a hint of wistfulness to a face otherwise reminiscent of chiseled stone.

They turned in to Park Lane and entered the park via the Grosvenor Gate.

If she'd had a choice, she would have happily hidden away for the rest of the Season until summer rolled around and they could end their sham engagement, but he'd been right; they had to be seen doing the expected things, and if he could make the sacrifice, then she could do no less. It was, after all, her reputation he was seeking to protect with the fiction of their engagement.

He set his horses trotting along the avenue and glanced her way. "I thought the evening went well. Our three protégés performed brilliantly—my peers were even more impressed than I had hoped they would be. I believe Protheroe will find himself dealing with inquiries of all sorts in the coming weeks."

Amid all the personal drama, the musical side of the evening had all but slipped from her mind. She recalled Felicia's report and told Frederick about Rand and his investors intending to offer musical scholarships via the school.

He nodded. "An excellent idea. I'll speak to Rand when next I see him."

A hail reached them. A group of ladies and several gentlemen were standing by the verge; one of the gentlemen flagged them down.

"And so it begins," Frederick murmured and angled his horses to halt beside the group.

Unsurprisingly, they were the principal cynosure of attention in the park that afternoon. They remained in the carriage, which Frederick moved along every now and then, and consequently, the crowd ebbed and flowed around them, with older ladies drawing up alongside in their landaus and barouches, while the younger crowd walked up to stand on the verge and chat.

Having been born and raised within the ton, Stacie had no real difficulty dealing with the congratulations, comments—even the arch ones—and the many leading inquiries, primarily as to when the wedding would take place. To her relief, she realized that, despite what she'd interpreted as his liking for country solitude, Frederick, too, could hold his own in this sphere; she didn't need to monitor his conversations with a view to rescuing him from some grande dame's inquisition.

What surprised her far more was that, after the predictable questions relating to their unexpected engagement, many—young, old, male, and female—moved on to comment on the musical aspect of the evening. Indeed, although many had not been present, their names not having been on the highly select guest list, with their eagerness to engage on the subject, they blatantly signaled a wish that they might be invited to attend her next musical evening.

Despite the distraction of their shock engagement—or perhaps because of it—her musical evening had raised awareness of the existence of highly talented local musicians far more effectively than she'd thought possible.

When Frederick steered his horses on to the next knot of well-wishers, she mused, "Given the many angling for invitations to my next musical evening, I might have to stage it at Raventhorne House—the reception rooms are much larger there."

Or you could hold it at Albury House, which has the best and largest music room in Mayfair. Frederick bit back the words; for her to stage an event in his house...even given her age and their now established partnership, even given their engagement, that could only happen if she was formally his hostess—ergo, his wife.

As he drew the curricle up to the verge, he couldn't resist asking, "Is the Raventhorne House music room up to scratch?"

"Hmm. For most, I would say yes, but you...? You'll have to play the piano there and see."

Another bevy of well-wishers converged on the carriage, and with appropriately bright smiles on their faces, he and she gave themselves over to accepting the breathless or hearty congratulations—he'd noticed congratulations seemed to come primarily in those two styles—and answering the usual questions.

Because he was seated on the avenue side of the curricle, conversing with the older ladies who drew up alongside in their open carriages largely fell to him.

Of course, many of those ladies, after grilling him, insisted on commanding Stacie's attention as well. Several of those exchanges, conducted across him, contained what he now recognized as repeating refrains—of how much like her mother Stacie was, how her mother would have crowed at her success, how her mother must surely be spinning in her grave over not being present to exploit such a triumph.

As the triumph referred to was Stacie having successfully—in ton terms—snared him, and the comments were, of necessity, exchanged across him, when he and Stacie allowed their eyes to meet, they were hard-pressed not to laugh.

After one such blithely delivered comment, Frederick was forced to look down to hide his desperately compressed lips; he disguised the movement by drawing out his fob watch and checking the time.

When Lady Foster finally instructed her coachman to drive on, Frederick met Stacie's laughing eyes. "This outing has gone far better than I'd hoped, and we've been here for forty minutes—I suggest we cut and run while we're ahead."

Her smile reached her lips and curved them, and she nodded. "Yes. Let's call this a success, too, and leave."

He flicked the reins and steered the curricle on and out of the fashionable stretch.

His compulsion to learn what lay behind her resistance to marriage grew stronger with every hour he spent in her company. He waited until they'd reached the straight section of carriageway running parallel to the Oxford road, then, with his gaze on his horses' heads, quietly asked, "Purely for my edification, is it marriage in general or specifically marriage to me that you're so adamantly set against?"

He'd intended the query to be light, almost flippant, yet even to his ears, a hint of uncertainty—a vulnerability he hadn't until that moment known he possessed—shone through.

She turned her bonneted head to look at him; he felt her gaze briefly search his face. Then she said, "My stance has nothing to do with you," and he was shocked by the relief that slid through his veins.

What have I got myself into?

She drew breath and faced forward. "I've been set against marriage since before I left the schoolroom, so to answer your question, it's marriage in general, the institution, that I've decided is not for me."

He debated the wisdom of probing, but eventually said, "Can I ask why?" A swift glance at her face showed her chin firming, and in an even, unthreatening tone, he went on, "It would help to ensure that I don't tread on your toes during the coming months."

A frown formed on her face, and she didn't immediately reply.

He didn't press but steered his horses out of the Cumberland Gate and around into Park Lane. She would answer, or she wouldn't.

They'd just made the turn into Green Street when she glanced at his face. "My reasons are...wretchedly complicated and highly personal and not readily explainable to others. However, I can assure you that I won't change my mind."

He drew his horses to a halt outside her house and met her eyes.

The expression in those stunning eyes was serious, even somber, but she put out a hand and lightly gripped his arm, and her lips curved up in an easy smile. "I appreciate that you are quite the catch, but you don't need to worry that I'll suddenly be seized by a desire to be a marchioness and press to make our engagement a real one."

I wasn't worried about that.

The words burned his tongue, yet as much as she couldn't explain her stance, he couldn't explain his, either—indeed, in that moment, he wasn't even sure what his ultimate goal was.

He'd lived his entire life operating more or less on impulse, by trusting his instincts; if they'd ever led him wrongly, he couldn't remember it.

Now, those instincts decreed that he needed to do whatever was required to gain her trust. He couldn't recall ever wanting to secure anyone else's trust before, yet with her, for some reason, his instincts insisted that was paramount.

So he returned her easy smile with one several degrees more reassuringly charming, tossed the reins to the waiting Timson, then descended, rounded the curricle, and helped her down.

As they climbed the steps to her door, she said, "After the excitements of last night, I doubt any of the hostesses will expect to see us tonight, although I'm sure they'll hope."

He imagined it and nodded. "Indeed. Tonight's events will be best avoided." He met her eyes and smiled. "There's only so much interrogation I can bear with in one day."

She chuckled, and on impulse, he caught her hand and drew her nearer. Close enough that her skirts pressed against his legs.

Her laughter died. Anticipation leapt to life between them, a palpable thrill running down their nerves. He felt it and knew she did, too. An expression he couldn't define filled her eyes. Keeping his gaze locked with hers, slowly, he raised her hand and pressed his lips to her gloved knuckles, then, greatly daring, he turned her hand and pressed a gentle kiss to the skin at her wrist bared by the slit in her glove.

He heard her breath catch. Slowly raising his head, he leaned close—close enough to, if he dared, brush his lips to her cheek. Instead, he hovered there and breathed, "My tiger is watching, and so are the biddies who live across the road."

She exhaled. "Oh. I see."

Hiding a smile at how breathless she'd sounded, he straightened, briefly met her now wide eyes, and as the door beside them opened, released her, stepped back, tipped his head in a salute, and strolled down the steps. Without looking back, he called, "I'll come around tomorrow morning, and we can make our plans."

Stacie watched him leap into his curricle, take up the reins, and with a flourishing wave, drive off.

She stood and watched until the curricle turned the corner, then she looked down at the tiles beneath her feet. After a moment, she shook her head, straightened, and walked inside.

～

Frederick strolled into his front hall to find Fortingale hovering.

Relieving Frederick of his driving gloves, Fortingale informed him, "A message just arrived, my lord. From Raventhorne House. I placed the missive on your desk. The footman who brought it said nothing about a reply."

"Thank you, Fortingale." Frederick had been expecting the summons. "I'll deal with it now, and I expect I'll be going out again shortly."

"Indeed, my lord. Will you require the carriage?"

Raventhorne House was in Mount Street, only a few blocks away. "No—I'll walk."

He strolled into his study and found the letter bearing the seal of the Marquess of Raventhorne in the middle of his blotter. After sitting in the chair behind the desk, Frederick picked up his letter knife, broke the seal, and spread open the parchment.

As he'd anticipated, the Marquess of Raventhorne requested his presence at his earliest convenience to discuss a matter of mutual importance. Frederick grinned at Ryder's formal—yet plainly terse—phrasing. He could imagine the eldest Cavanaugh hadn't been thrilled to have his only sister's engagement sprung on him.

Sitting back in his chair, Frederick considered what would await him at Raventhorne House. He was acquainted with Ryder, who was actually Stacie's half brother; he and Ryder occasionally met in the House of Lords, although neither were deeply immersed in politics.

Ryder was several years older than Rand, whom Frederick knew from schooldays and, more recently, through investing circles. As Frederick was about eighteen months older than Rand, in age, he fell between Stacie's two older siblings. Frederick had crossed paths with Rand at Eton, but Ryder had already left the school before Frederick had arrived —suggesting that Ryder was at least five years older than Frederick.

As for Stacie's other brothers—Christopher, who was known as Kit, and Godfrey, the only one of her siblings younger than she—Frederick knew little beyond the fact that Kit had recently found a wife.

"So," he murmured, eyes narrowing. He tapped a finger on the edge of his desk. "Three are married, and the youngest is not."

That might prove telling.

A few moments later, he roused himself, rose, and headed for Mount Street. Doubtless, Stacie's brothers had questions for him, and he had questions he wanted answered, too.

He arrived at Mount Street and was promptly shown into what proved to be Ryder's study.

He'd expected to face Ryder and, possibly, Rand; instead, he discovered all four Cavanaugh brothers lounging about the room. Ryder sat behind his desk, which was set before the bow window, which left Ryder's face poorly lit.

Rand was seated in one of the two large armchairs angled before the desk, while Kit sat propped on the wide sill of the bow window, behind and to Ryder's left.

Godfrey had been drifting down the room, perusing the books on the shelves; he'd halted and whirled to stare at Frederick when he'd stepped into the room.

Frederick had paused for a split second, sweeping his gaze over the room, taking in the brothers' strictly impassive faces. Brows faintly arching, he walked on into their midst; he heard the door click shut behind him and had to battle an urge to grin.

Rand rose, as did Ryder, and Kit pushed to his feet. Ryder nodded. "Albury."

There was not the slightest intonation in Ryder's voice to give Frederick a clue as to the brothers' thoughts. In urbane fashion, he nodded back. "Raventhorne." With his gaze, he acknowledged the other three men, noting that Godfrey had shifted to take up a position by the window, opposite Kit and flanking Ryder.

Ryder waved Frederick to the armchair opposite the one Rand sank back into. Frederick sat, crossed his legs, rested his hands, relaxed, on the chair's arms, and gave his attention to Ryder.

Ryder sat, clasped his hands before him, and fixed his hazel gaze on Frederick. "It came as...something of a surprise to learn that you and our sister have formed a tendre and decided to marry—indeed, coming out of the blue as it did, to say the news came as a shock would be an understatement."

Very real surprise, aggravation at being caught unawares, yet acceptance rather than rejection—Frederick noted all three emotions emanating in varying degrees from each of the brothers.

He blinked. Clearly, contrary to Stacie's belief, her sisters-in-law had failed to alert their husbands to the true state of affairs. He rapidly revised his assumption of how much the four male Cavanaughs knew. "First," he said, in reply to the implied question of what the hell he'd been thinking springing such an event on them, "I take it none of you have met with your ladies this afternoon."

Ryder frowned and glanced at Rand, who shook his head, then at Kit, who, looking mystified, shook his head as well. Ryder turned back to Frederick. "We were all out at lunches and meetings. We convened here less than half an hour ago. So no, we haven't spoken to our wives since breakfast."

Frederick inclined his head. "In that case, there's rather a lot you need to hear. However, before we go further, allow me to point out that I have two sisters of my own, so I fully appreciate your position." He hadn't come with any definite plan of what to say, but instinct prodded, and he smoothly continued, "It is, therefore, imperative that you understand the true situation between myself and Stacie."

He proceeded to describe the fateful events that had taken place in Stacie's private parlor toward the end of her musical evening. "After everyone else had left, I remained behind, and we discussed the situation and decided on our way forward—specifically, that we will continue as if engaged until July and, once the ton has scattered, will quietly let it be known that we have, in the end, decided we don't suit."

All four brothers had listened to his tale without interrupting. As the full meaning sank in, he could almost see them deflating.

It was Godfrey who put their disappointment into words. "So it's not real?"

Frederick considered, then replied, "It might be a necessary fiction, but in execution, it's real enough, and we must never forget that, in order for Stacie and, indeed, myself to emerge from this situation without the slightest whiff of scandal attaching to our names, the engagement must, to all intents and purposes, *be* real."

Ryder's eyes had narrowed. "Until you—together—end it."

Frederick met Ryder's hard gaze, inclined his head, and allowed his gaze to fall. Assessing the atmosphere in the room, he let a heartbeat pass, then added, "That said"—he raised his gaze to Ryder's face—"in working alongside Stacie over the past weeks, through her endeavors to convince me to support her enterprise and through the preparations contingent on putting on last night's entertainment, I've come to value your sister for her unique qualities, for herself. In short, I would not oppose the notion of converting what has commenced as, in her words, a sham into a reality— provided, of course, that Stacie herself agreed."

Until that moment, he hadn't known he would say that—admit that— yet now he had, he knew without question that it was the right step.

The change in atmosphere was marked, the brothers shifting from being cast down to considering what they plainly viewed as an acceptable and hopeful possibility.

Ryder's thinning lips told Frederick that his subtle manipulations weren't going unremarked, yet judging by Ryder's carefully controlled yet considering expression, not even he was immune to the tug of Frederick's lure.

After a long moment of regarding each other, Frederick arched a brow in silent question.

Ryder's lips thinned even more, then he shifted his gaze to Rand, then turned to look at Kit, then Godfrey.

Finally, Ryder swiveled to face Frederick again, stared at him assessingly for several heartbeats, then said, "Rand has already informed me that, financially speaking, you and the estate are in excellent shape."

Frederick cut an amused glance at Rand and saw faint color tinge Rand's cheeks.

Returning his gaze to Ryder, Frederick tipped his head in confirmation.

"As for all the rest," Ryder went on, "if you were sitting on this side of the desk and the lady in question was one of your sisters, is there anything—any point at all—that you, as her guardian, would wish to know, prior to giving your agreement to this suit?"

Frederick's brows arched spontaneously. "That's a shrewd and cleverly phrased question. Regardless, there is nothing that comes to mind about my current life that in any way impinges on my suitability to offer for Stacie's hand." He met Ryder's eyes. "Is that what you wished to know?"

"It is." Ryder paused, then nodded. "If you can persuade Stacie to accept your suit, you'll have our blessing, our backing, and should you need it, our active support."

Frederick nearly allowed his surprise to show; a promise of backing and active support was far more than he'd expected.

"I take it," Ryder said, "that I should place an announcement in the *Gazette.*"

Frederick agreed. "Better it comes from you than me."

Ryder nodded. "I'll do it today."

Frederick hesitated, but they had offered to help. "Accepting that we are all in favor of the same end goal, what can you tell me about Stacie's reasons for holding so firmly against marriage?"

Ryder glanced at his brothers. "I know she's avoided encouraging any gentleman, but is she truly set against it?"

"More to the point," Kit said, "is it marriage per se or marriage to *you* that she's so set against?"

"I've asked," Frederick returned, "and she insists it's the former. She's adamant that marriage, the institution, is not for her. And yes, I've asked why she believes that—her reply was that her reasons were too difficult to explain."

Ryder grimaced. "Mary, and more recently Felicia and Sylvia, have started to suspect that there's something"—he gestured—"more profound behind Stacie's avowed disinterest in matrimony. But as for what that might be?" He shook his head. "I have no clue."

Frederick arched his brows challengingly. "So guess."

After a moment, Kit said, "We've always known she was dismissive of marriage in relation to herself, but it seems she's hardened her stance into outright refusal."

"Or perhaps," Rand said, meeting Kit's eyes, "she was always of that mind, but found it easier simply to avoid the subject rather than state—and argue—her case." He looked at Frederick. "You and this engagement—sham or not—has forced her to state her position plainly."

Godfrey shifted. "I doubt any of us have ever asked her directly whether she wished to marry or not."

Ryder grunted. "Few would have, and even so, she's adept at skirting around the subject."

"Remember," Kit said, "when Stacie caught Sylvia's bouquet at our wedding breakfast? Sylvia was up on a chair and had the best view. She said that when the bouquet landed in Stacie's hands, she looked more horrified than delighted."

"God, yes! She nearly bit off my nose when I mentioned it later." Godfrey paused, then added, "She was upset and even angry over having caught the bouquet."

Frederick waited, but when the brothers appeared sunk in thought and volunteered nothing more, he prompted, "It seems we're all agreed that the Stacie I'm now dealing with has a deeply entrenched aversion to marrying. It's not some whim assumed to make herself interesting or in pursuit of the label of eccentric but a sincerely and deeply held belief. Do you have any insights into how long she's held that view?"

The question clearly made the brothers uncomfortable. They exchanged looks, and eventually, it seemed to fall to Rand to reply. He appeared to gather his thoughts, then, reluctantly, met Frederick's eyes. "We can only guess, but I think all of us suspect that any...adverse view of marriage Stacie holds would have been formed during the years she spent under our mother Lavinia's wing."

Frederick held up a hand and looked at Ryder. "She wasn't your mother."

Ryder shook his head. "Lavinia was our father's second wife. However, the pater and she had gone their separate ways long before he died—at Lavinia's insistence. For her part, Lavinia attached herself to the most racy and ramshackle set—she took great delight in sailing as close as she could to the line the ton would tolerate."

"Our father died when Stacie was thirteen," Rand said, "and thereafter, she lived with Lavinia."

"When I came into the title," Ryder explained, "Lavinia insisted on moving out of this house. She demanded the estate buy her a town house, essentially as her dower house in Mayfair, and to keep her quiet, I did."

"At first," Kit said, "we four all theoretically lived with her, again, at her insistence, but of course, the three of us—Rand, me, and Godfrey—spent most of our time away at school."

"And later," Rand said, "as soon as we were old enough, Kit and I moved out and shared rooms." He paused, then said, "Lavinia openly consorted with a small horde of lovers in those years."

After a moment of silence, Godfrey said, "Stacie was with Mama virtually all the time. Mama kept her close. But how much she knew of Mama's...activities, that I don't know." He looked at Rand, then at Ryder, and grimaced. "I'm not sure I want to—or could—guess what she might have seen."

"Or heard." Kit's tone was harsh. He looked at Ryder, then at Rand. "Mama, I'm sure, had plans for Stacie—matrimonial plans. I do know that Mama would never countenance Stacie attending concerts—I once heard her refusing Stacie on the grounds that it wouldn't do for anyone to start imagining her a blue stocking." Kit shifted his gaze to Frederick. "When a concert Stacie particularly wanted to attend was on, she would plead illness and remain in her room, and with the staff's help, I would smuggle her out and take her to the concert. That was the only way she could indulge her love of music."

Frederick noted the exchange of looks—the silent discussion—that was going on between Ryder and Rand. Clearly, there was something more. Thinking to ease any reluctance on their parts to speak of it, he volunteered, "If it's any help, my mother and her companion, Mrs. Weston, gave me the benefit of all they knew of Stacie, including their view that Lavinia was assiduous in ensuring that no hint of scandal ever touched Stacie. If Mrs. Weston, who is not prone to gossip but is, nevertheless, one of those to whom others appear to whisper all their secrets, says Lavinia was strongly protective of Stacie, then she was."

Ryder arched his brows and looked at Rand. "Your choice."

Rand studied his hands for a moment, then raised his gaze to Frederick's face. "Lavinia was a fiend. She had plans for all her children's futures—if she'd lived long enough, she would have attempted to sell our names and hands to the highest bidders. That was her attitude to us—it was always based on our potential use to her." He paused, then went on, "Being the eldest of her children, I was the one she sought to exploit first, but she realized that my matrimonial value would be greatly increased if I was the marquess rather than Ryder's heir. She concocted a scheme to murder Ryder, and Mary as well, thus installing me as the marquess."

Frederick blinked.

Rand continued, "Her plan, obviously, came to naught. You've no doubt heard that Lavinia died in an accident on the Raventhorne Abbey estate. She fell to her death from an upper-story window while attempting to flee justice. We were all there that evening, Stacie included. She was there earlier, too, and saw Lavinia kill one of her henchmen in cold blood by ramming a hatpin through the man's eye—that was the sort of person Lavinia was."

After a moment, Rand said, "Prior to our father's death, he and Stacie were particularly close—she was his only daughter. And as Godfrey and Kit said, we have no way of knowing what Stacie saw and heard while she lived under Lavinia's wing. But that she might have, through all that, and most especially through Lavinia's abiding view that marriage among our class was nothing more than a transaction, formed an adverse view of marriage is, perhaps, not to be wondered at."

Frederick considered all he'd heard, then ventured, "What you've told me explains why Stacie would have a poor view of her parents' marriage, specifically her mother's role in that. But as far as I can see, none of that explains why she should so trenchantly recoil from marriage for herself." He cut his gaze to Ryder. "If nothing else, she's had the example of your marriage to Mary, and also the Cynster marriages in general, to counter the view her experience of her mother might have instilled in her."

Ryder met his eyes, then grimaced. "I have to agree, but the problem is, we're guessing at what's in Stacie's mind." He raised his hands, palms out. "I'll admit I'm less than confident over that."

Both Rand and Kit humphed in agreement.

Godfrey stirred. "Actually"—he met Ryder's gaze, then looked at Frederick—"there's one aspect of what happened back then on which none of us have touched. That said, I can't see how it would impinge on Stacie's thoughts of marriage for herself, as it's patently something that was peculiar to Mama."

Frederick arched his brows. "What aspect?"

Godfrey looked at Rand, and when Rand, faintly puzzled, nodded in encouragement, returned his gaze to Frederick. "While Papa was still alive, Mama didn't just take great delight in being scandalous, she took even more delight, derived even more real joy, from knowing her exploits were reported—in full detail—to Papa." Godfrey's features hardened. "Malicious isn't a strong enough word to describe her—she took pleasure in, reveled in, hurting people. Not us, her children, but literally anyone else was fair game, and Papa was her favorite target."

He paused, then went on, "I don't know why—as far as I know, he never did anything to even curb her excesses. Where she was concerned, he was weak—always trying to appease her, she who was never either grateful or satisfied." Godfrey glanced at Rand and Kit.

Frederick followed his gaze and saw that Godfrey's older brothers looked shocked.

Godfrey went on, "Stacie and I saw it, but while Rand, Kit, and Ryder knew of Mama's excesses, she largely kept her maliciously malevolent side from them. Probably because she knew how they would react if they learned she was attacking Papa like that."

"Why," Ryder asked, his expression appalled, "didn't you say something? To any of us?"

Godfrey gave his powerful eldest brother a don't-be-silly look. "You forget—I was ten when Papa died. Yes, I'd seen what was happening, but back then, I had nothing to compare it with. I saw and understood what Mama was doing, but I didn't know, then, that marriages weren't supposed to be like that. I can remember events from the last few years of Papa's life quite vividly, but it's only been in recent years, since you married and I've seen how a marriage is supposed to be, that I've come to understand how truly horrendous Mama's behavior was."

Godfrey's gaze passed from Ryder, to Kit, to Rand. "I saw what happened, but only now do I understand what was actually happening." He briefly shrugged. "That's why I never said anything. But"—he shifted his gaze to Frederick—"the relevant point is that whatever I saw, Stacie—three years older—saw much more, especially as Mama made a point of keeping her close. That said"—Godfrey glanced at his brothers—"and speaking as the one of us who has spent most time with her over the last decade, Stacie is absolutely nothing like Mama, and while I can see that her experience of Mama's actions might make her tentative over marrying, I can't see why it would make her swear off marriage altogether."

Frederick studied Godfrey's face, then looked at Ryder, then at Kit and Rand. "There's…an enormous amount to digest in all that. The reason behind Stacie's aversion to marriage might well lie buried somewhere in it, yet correctly guessing the way a lady's mind works is…not something our sex excels at."

Several minutes passed in silence, then Ryder warned, "Changing Stacie's mind about marriage won't be easy—especially without knowing what her objection is based on."

Frederick met Ryder's gaze, then rose. "Luckily," he said, "I enjoy challenges."

On returning to Albury House, Frederick went straight to his study, rang for a footman, and dispatched the man to the City with a message.

Frederick spent the next half hour dealing with his correspondence and reports sent up from Brampton Hall.

A tap on the door heralded Fortingale. "Mr. Camber has arrived in response to your summons, my lord."

Frederick nodded. "Show him in."

Fortingale bowed and withdrew. Frederick set aside the papers he'd been working on, then William Camber walked in.

"Good afternoon, Camber." Frederick waved the private inquiry agent to his usual chair before the desk. "Take a seat—I have an assignment for you that's somewhat different from the norm."

Camber was a middle-aged, neatly dressed, and entirely unremarkable man, all qualities that played well in his line of work. Of heavier than average build, he wore steel-rimmed spectacles, and his gray hair was thinning, but still covered his large head. Camber sat. "I'm always pleased to take commissions from you, my lord. Never a dull moment."

Frederick usually used Camber to track down old manuscripts on music and the occasional ancient score. "In this case, while the results might well be eye-opening, they might also be distasteful. I give you fair warning."

Unperturbed, Camber simply nodded and waited.

Frederick leaned back and steepled his fingers before his face. "I want you to unearth absolutely everything you can about the late Marchioness of Raventhorne. *Not* the current one—don't go near her or, indeed, any of the family. The lady I'm referring to died several years ago in an accident —but I have no interest in that accident. I already know all I need to about that. What I want you to find out is all you can learn about the late marchioness's behavior, habits—all aspects of the way she lived—over, say, the last five to ten years of her life."

Camber's gaze had grown distant as he took in Frederick's instructions. "Did she live in London?"

"As I understand it, for the most part, yes. Initially at Raventhorne House in Mount Street and, later, in a town house in Mayfair—I'm not sure where."

Camber refocused on Frederick's face. "Quite a bit different from chasing old books and papers."

"Indeed. One other point." Frederick had been tossing up how much to reveal to Camber, but without telling the agent of his interest, he risked not gaining the critical information he was seeking. "The focus of my interest is the late marchioness's only daughter. I'm particularly interested in how and in what way the late marchioness might have influenced and affected her daughter's view of the world."

Slowly, Camber nodded. "Very well. The usual rates?"

"Yes. And also as usual, discretion is paramount."

"Naturally, my lord. How quickly do you need this information?"

Frederick lowered his hands and grimaced. "The sooner the better."

Camber nodded again and rose. "I'll get back with a report as soon as I can."

Frederick half smiled. "And once you do, I expect to have another commission waiting—but it'll be back to music, I fear."

Camber returned Frederick's smile. "I'll look forward to it, my lord." With a bow, Camber turned and left.

Frederick stared after him and inwardly acknowledged that, at some point during that day, he'd made one of his impulsive decisions—one that looked set to change his life.

CHAPTER 8

The following morning, after perusing the notice announcing Lady Eustacia Cavanaugh's engagement to the Marquess of Albury in his morning edition of the *Gazette*, Frederick strolled around to Green Street and discovered the Raventhorne carriage, the Raventhorne coat of arms blazoned on the doors, drawn up before Stacie's house. He halted on the pavement, then decided that Stacie's sister-in-law was a preferable audience to a group of gossipmongers and continued up the steps to Stacie's door.

He was shown into the drawing room to find not only Mary but also Kit's wife, Sylvia, to whom Frederick had been introduced at Stacie's event, seated on the chaise.

Stacie came forward to greet him with a smile that declared she wasn't entirely certain of how the next moments would go.

He smiled urbanely. "Good morning, my dear." He took the hand she offered and raised it briefly to his lips. "I'm delighted to see you're not inundated with callers this morning."

"No, indeed—it's been something of a relief. Perhaps something else has happened to capture the ton's attention."

He heard a soft snort from the direction of the chaise. Presumably, Stacie hadn't realized her sister-in-law's carriage stood guard outside. Or perhaps she didn't register the discouraging effect Mary's presence would have on the overly curious.

Regardless, he followed her down the room and exchanged greetings with Mary and Sylvia. From behind their pleasant smiles, both ladies viewed him with quiet assessment; he assumed they'd heard from their husbands of his quest to persuade Stacie to the altar and were still weighing whether or not to support his effort.

After greeting Ernestine, rather than sit, Frederick swung to face Stacie, still standing beside him; the movement put them closer than was customary, but he didn't step away, and she couldn't, not without appearing flustered. He smiled understandingly—conspiratorially. "I'm due at a meeting in the City shortly, but I hoped to inveigle you and Mrs. Thwaites to join me in my box for the performance at Drury Lane tonight —Charles Kean is reprising his Hamlet for one night only."

"Oh!" Ernestine raised her fingers to her lips. When the others all looked at her, face alight, she confided, "I've always wanted to see Kean in that role."

His smile faintly triumphant, Frederick arched a brow at Stacie.

She frowned. "I'm not sure…"

Frederick's smile faded; he trapped her gaze. "Many who attended your event two nights ago will be present. As your intention is to hold more such events, introducing more of the worthy graduates of the music school to the ton—an aim I wholeheartedly support—then consolidating and maintaining your social position is as essential to your goal and the future of those graduates as me practicing on a piano is."

Stacie understood the real message in his words. The ton would expect to see them behaving as an engaged couple; if she wanted to establish her musical evenings as she'd planned, she couldn't afford not to satisfy society's expectations.

But just being as close to him as she was now was playing havoc with her nerves. Spending hours in a dimly lit box with him seated close beside her…

She glanced at Mary.

Mary met her eyes and arched her brows. "Have you seen Kean play Hamlet?"

"No."

"In that case," Mary said, "you should go—his performance is definitely worth experiencing."

No help from that quarter, yet Kean's brilliance notwithstanding, she doubted she would be able to concentrate on the stage. Raising her gaze to meet Frederick's—he hadn't shifted, and with an armchair behind her, she couldn't ease away—she said, "Thank you, my lord—Ernestine and I would be happy to accept your invitation."

He smiled—and despite not being all that happy over being jockeyed into another public appearance, she found herself charmed; when he wished, the man could be diabolical.

"Excellent." He glanced at Mary and Sylvia and half bowed. "I'll leave you ladies to your morning." To Ernestine and Stacie, he said, "I'll pick you up in my carriage at eight."

Delighted, Ernestine assured him they would be ready and waiting.

"I'll see you out." Stacie waved toward the door—and he finally consented to move.

She noted that he didn't try to hide his satisfaction as, side by side, they walked into the front hall. When she paused before the door and he turned to her, reaching for and taking her hand, she fixed him with a level look. "Do you always get what you want?"

He met her gaze as he raised her hand. "Almost always." He held her gaze and pressed a kiss to her knuckles.

For a moment, she felt captured, trapped in his mesmerizing eyes—then his smile deepened a fraction, and he released her hand and stepped toward the door, which a round-eyed Hettie promptly opened.

He still held Stacie's gaze, then with a dip of his head, he turned away. "I'll see you this evening."

He walked out of the door and left her wondering what that odd moment of strange connection had been about.

~

As the curtain of the Drury Lane theater parted on the first act, and the lights dimmed and the patrons quietened, with Ernestine, Frederick's mother, and her companion, Mrs. Weston, on one side and Frederick on the other, Stacie sat at the front of the Albury box and heaved a silent sigh of relief.

Both Mary and Sylvia had urged her to make the best of the situation and enjoy the benefits of having a handsome nobleman squire her about, yet a niggling reluctance still plagued her. As a rule, she tried not to lie or manipulate others, and what she and Frederick were presently doing amounted to lying and manipulating on a grand scale.

Countering that, she sternly told herself that their actions were all in a good—if not excellent—cause, specifically in ensuring her continued ability to introduce worthy musicians to the ton's notice. And as Mary had pointed out, as Frederick was more than doing his part, Stacie needed to step up and keep him company.

That hadn't been quite so easily done as said; just getting through the foyer had been an ordeal. But Frederick had held close to her side and guided her through the crush; she'd glimpsed a certain steely ruthlessness behind his ineffably sophisticated mask as he'd arrogantly ignored most who'd sought to detain them, acknowledging only those whose station made them impossible to avoid, all the while relentlessly forging a path through the melee.

Despite her leaping nerves and the near-constant abrasion of her senses whenever he was close, she'd been grateful.

She slanted a glance at him as he sat, apparently relaxed, beside her. Although his face was wreathed in shadows, she noted his gaze was not on the stage. He was scanning the boxes on the other side of the theater; she glanced that way and realized that many of the occupants, both male and female, were surreptitiously staring at the Albury box.

Of course. She shifted her gaze back to the stage and determinedly kept it there. Much of her reluctance to go about in public stemmed from her aversion of being stared at, of being the focus of that sort of attention. It was inevitable, she knew, and indeed, Frederick had probably been wise to engineer this outing; at least in the theater, unlike in a drawing room, all people could do was stare from a distance.

Over time, the ton's avid interest would fade; some new scandal would occur, and all attention would deflect to that.

She tried to concentrate on the performance, but too many of her senses preferred to focus on a distraction nearer to hand. She'd circulated within the ton for over eight years; she'd met countless gentlemen, many as handsome and even a few as physically commanding as Frederick, yet none had ever drawn her attention as he did. Why he should possess such an apparently effortless ability to snare her senses, she had no idea.

Yet he did.

She could only pray that, as with the ton's interest, the effect would fade with time and constant exposure.

Before she knew it, the curtains swept in, the lights flared, and the first intermission began.

As always, that signaled the emptying of some boxes and the consequent filling of others. Naturally, the Albury box was one of those soon full to bursting.

Having anticipated that, she steeled herself to play her part, standing to one side of the box with Frederick, who appropriated her arm and looped it with his. Clamping down hard on her wayward senses, she exchanged the usual pleasantries and observations with those who made it into their orbit.

Apparently as shrewd as her son, his mother held court on the opposite side of the box, thereby forcing those crowding inside to face one way or the other.

Among the first to appear were two gentlemen whom Frederick introduced as his closest friends—George, Lord Farleigh, and Percy, Viscount Piper. Both were elegant, charming, and proved surprisingly capable; after making their bows to Stacie and Ernestine, and to the marchioness and Mrs. Weston, the pair retreated to hover just inside the door of the box, effectively acting as guards and directing questioning glances at Frederick over whether those seeking entrance should be admitted.

Even with their help, it proved something of a crush, but a manageable one. Several times, Stacie had to bite her lip to hold back a chuckle occasioned by Frederick's glib exercise of a sharp and acerbic wit she hadn't, until then, realized he possessed.

Finally, the theater's bells rang, sending people scurrying back to their seats for the commencement of the second act.

As their box emptied, Frederick invited George and Percy to remain; he suspected they'd come purely because he'd mentioned over luncheon that he would be attending with Stacie, and they'd helped by keeping the worst of the horde at bay. Smiling, they accepted, taking seats in the second row of chairs, behind him and Stacie.

He and she reclaimed their seats, and as the lights dimmed, Frederick settled back to watch Kean and his players and think of other things.

From his perspective, socially, matters were progressing well. Between them, he and Stacie were projecting exactly the picture he wished—that of a more mature, recently engaged couple. Thus far, he'd managed to keep his instincts—or rather, the impulses they incited—from pushing him into stepping over any line, into doing anything that might alert her to his revised direction. That said, he was conscious of having to hold himself back from behaving overly protectively. That wasn't a battle he'd ever had to fight before; presumably, his new view of Stacie as his perfect bride had recast something inside him so that any even-vague threat to her peace provoked a forceful response from him.

He would have to work to keep that muted, at least for now.

His mind skated over the recent exchanges and snagged on a comment from Lady Hendrickson, who had once again raised the specter of Stacie's mother, Lavinia, expounding in a rather pointed way over how Lavinia would have wallowed in the attention occasioned by their engagement, then capping the exchange with the so-oft-repeated mantra of how very like Lavinia Stacie was.

Something in the comment struck Frederick as odd—as wrong. While Kean dominated the stage, Frederick mentally stepped back to the conversation at Raventhorne House…

Stacie is absolutely nothing like Mama.

So Godfrey had stated, and he was arguably the person who knew Stacie best and viewed her most clearly.

Yet how many times had Frederick heard the refrain *You are exactly like your mother* directed at Stacie, just in the few weeks he'd known her?

The comments, of course, referred to different things. Godfrey had sought to assure him that Stacie's character was nothing like that of her mother's, while all the ladies' comments referred to what he gathered was a remarkable physical likeness. By all accounts, Lavinia had been a great beauty; the ladies' comments were intended as compliments.

Frederick's instincts jabbed. *That* was what was wrong. The comments were compliments, yet Stacie didn't like receiving them. It was her reaction that was nagging at him; every time a comment along those lines was leveled her way, she stiffened—just a fraction—and her smile turned false.

While Kean declaimed before him, Frederick tried to negotiate the subtleties of Stacie's mind. All he could conclude was that she didn't like being told that she was like her mother—not in any way.

Given what he'd learned of the woman, no one could wonder at that.

The second act had rolled straight on into the third, which now came to an end, and the curtains swished closed, and the lights came up for the main intermission.

Frederick had arranged for a champagne supper to be served in the box; as the door opened to admit the servers with their trolley, and George and Percy moved chairs out of the way, Frederick glanced at Stacie as she rose and stood beside him.

She was a stunning sight, gowned in violet-blue silk with pearls looped about her slender throat and pearl-encrusted combs anchoring her fabulous hair, yet it had never been her beauty that had impressed him; he was far too jaded for that. Instead, by her focus on her project, she'd reached past all his long-standing defenses and engaged his interest; that alone made her unique in his eyes.

All that had followed over the past weeks had only drawn him deeper —deeper into a type of fascination he had heretofore reserved for music and old books.

That, he supposed, was why she inspired the same acquisitive, possessive, protective urges he normally associated with his collection of ancient tomes and old scores.

The servers passed around flutes of champagne and platters of delicacies. They barely had a chance to sample and sip before the first of the visitors arrived.

Stacie faced the fresh onslaught with unexpected confidence; with Frederick beside her, she felt surprisingly assured that she could weather the curious tide. Lord Farleigh and Viscount Piper were doing sterling service at the door, admitting only those of high rank or influence or those connected with Albury or herself and denying the merely curious, all with invincible charm.

Midway through the intermission, Mary and Sylvia appeared. "It's bedlam in the gallery outside this box," Mary reported. "I'm almost sorry I didn't insist on Ryder and Kit escorting us."

Sylvia laughed and glanced around at the crowded box. "But where would they have fitted?"

"True," Mary returned with a smile, then said to Stacie, "Felicia sent her best. She's feeling too bloated to appear in public and swears the baby can't come soon enough."

Stacie and Sylvia smiled. Everyone in the family was looking forward to the birth of Rand and Felicia's first child, although the blessed event was still some months away.

Mary glanced around, her gaze sharp and shrewd, then lowered her voice to say, "We just dropped by to see how you were faring—clearly you have everything in hand." Mary's gaze slid approvingly to Frederick, currently chatting with old Lady Faubert. "This was well done. Appearing here will stand you and Frederick in good stead."

"I've realized he was right," Stacie murmured back. "If I want to pursue my dream of establishing myself as a hostess of select musical evenings and advance the careers of our local musicians, then making the most of the opportunities arising from our engagement is the only sensible course."

"Exactly!" Mary gave one of her approving nods.

"My father has always maintained," Sylvia said, "that having a goal is only a beginning, and that one's efforts to overcome hurdles and cling to that goal and not turn aside from it are what, ultimately, make the goal worthwhile." She paused, then added, "He usually ends that homily by saying that nothing worthwhile in life is ever easy, and while the saying might be trite, I suspect it's also true."

Stacie inclined her head.

Mary touched her arm. "You've clearly found your feet, so we'll leave you to it and return to our box. I must say hello to Frederick's mother before we leave."

Stacie smiled and let them go, then with a calm serenity that had previously escaped her, turned to the lady Frederick brought to meet her.

Frederick sensed Stacie's increasing steadiness as she answered Lady Conway's questions about the music school. With his eyes, he tracked Mary and Sylvia as they made their way through the still-considerable crowd to speak with his mother and Emily.

Mary had patted his arm as she'd passed him, and Sylvia had given him an obviously encouraging nod. Combined with their assessing behavior earlier in the day, he could only conclude that, not only did they know of his true intentions regarding Stacie, but they approved and, like their husbands, were willing to actively support his campaign.

That was excellent news. Heartening news. Of all Stacie's many connections, Mary's opinion was unquestionably the one that would carry most weight—not only with Stacie but also with everyone else. Yet from all he'd seen, Stacie was close to Felicia and Sylvia as well; their opinions would matter to her, too.

Well and good; it appeared he had their backing.

He returned his attention to Stacie; seeing her still engrossed with Lady Conway, he allowed himself to drink in the vision she presented— and marvel that, in the space of a day, he'd not only made up his mind whom he would marry but had succeeded in gaining the support of her family in wooing her to his side.

~

The next morning, after a lengthy internal debate, Frederick called at Mount Street at precisely eleven o'clock. After sending in his card, he was conducted to a family parlour at the rear of the mansion, where he found Mary, Felicia, and Sylvia reclining in relaxed fashion in comfortable armchairs.

Mary studied him as he walked in. "Good morning, Albury."

Frederick managed not to wince. He inclined his head to her. "Frederick, please."

Mary smiled. "As I understand your ambition is to become one of this family, then first names are probably appropriate at this juncture."

She waited while he exchanged nods with Felicia and Sylvia.

When he looked back at Mary, she arched her brows. "I assume this isn't a social call." She waved him to an armchair opposite hers. "How can we help?"

Frederick seized the moment of sitting to review the wisdom of what he was about to do, but it still seemed the obvious way forward. He settled, looked first at Mary, then at Felicia and Sylvia. "I'll take it as read that you are all aware that I wish to convert Stacie's and my sham engagement into the real thing. However, as I believe you are also aware, Stacie harbors a very strong antipathy toward the married state."

All three ladies were nodding.

He went on, "I have yet to learn what it is that compels her to reject the notion of marriage, especially with such adamantine resolve, but from all her brothers have told me and all I've otherwise learned, it seems certain her reasoning derives—in some way, manner, or form—from the years she spent under her mother's wing, her years of being exposed to her mother's notions of marriage and wifely behavior."

Mary stared at him, then nodded. "I would have to agree. I can't think of anything else that might have engendered such a strong and lasting aversion to marriage. One really needs to look no further than Lavinia's influence."

He tipped his head in acknowledgment. "Sadly, understanding that tells me nothing of the specific root cause, leaving me unable to directly counter it."

Mary grimaced. "I take your point." She looked at Felicia and Sylvia. "I've never had the slightest inkling as to why Stacie feels as she does, only that she is, indeed, set against marriage. Do either of you have any insights?"

Both Felicia and Sylvia shook their heads. "Although I do agree," Felicia said, "that her aversion to marrying runs deep." She looked at Sylvia. "Her reaction when she unintentionally caught your bouquet made that abundantly plain."

Sylvia nodded, eyes wide. "Indeed."

When the three said nothing more, but simply looked at him expectantly, Frederick went on, "So that's where we all stand in the matter of getting Stacie to marry—me or anyone else. Given I can see no reasonable way of learning what the foundation of her aversion is—I have asked directly, and she maintains her reasons are too complicated to explain—the only way forward I can see is to set the matter of her aversion to matrimony to one side and, rather than attacking it directly, hope to find a way around it—namely, by demonstrating in the most effective way possible the benefits of becoming the Marchioness of Albury."

Mary blinked, then sat back in her chair, her gaze growing distant as she thought, then she refocused on him and nodded. "That's a potentially viable approach, especially now that she's committed to this vision of hers of creating musical evenings and has settled on you as an essential part of her plans."

"Yes," Frederick said, "but we need to be subtle. The last thing I would wish is to have her think that marrying me is a condition to succeeding in her aims."

"Good God, no." Felicia wrinkled her nose. "That sort of coercion is hardly a prescription for wedded bliss."

"What I need," Frederick said, deeming it wise to be specific, "is a campaign of events that will demonstrate the advantages that will accrue to Stacie on marrying me, not in the sense of pressuring her to shift her stance but rather...for want of a better word, seducing her into changing it. The decision needs to be hers alone. All I can do—all we can do—is cast the position of my marchioness in the most appealing light."

Mary narrowed her eyes at him in considering fashion. "That's a very clever way forward and might just work."

Frederick felt a soupçon of relief. He'd come there in the hope of recruiting all three ladies, but Mary especially. Of all the ladies in the ton, few would understand better than she the advantages of being a marchioness, and as she was close to Stacie, Mary was also best placed to know how those advantages would appeal to Stacie—a necessary requirement for the successful formulation of his campaign. He inclined his head to Mary. "I came here hoping that you would advise me as to the most useful avenues and events through which I might advance my cause with Stacie."

Mary studied him. "What you're proposing is essentially an old-fashioned wooing."

He blinked. "I suppose I am."

"It's really rather simple." Felicia shifted her bulk in the chair as if she'd grown uncomfortable. "You need to convince Stacie that marrying you is better than not marrying you."

"Better for her," Sylvia put in, "which, in her circumstances, translates to a brighter and better future for her musical evenings."

"That's a pertinent point," Mary said. "Stacie wants for nothing. The only thing she actively wants of life—at least that we're aware of—is to succeed in becoming a major hostess of musical events. We should bear that in mind in framing your wooing."

Frederick quashed the impulse to wince at the word. "Another point we need to bear in mind is that Stacie isn't blind. The longer my campaign to change her mind"—he much preferred that description —"lasts, the more likely it will be that I'll cross some invisible line, and she'll sense my true intentions before I've progressed my case with her sufficiently well for any rescripting of her attitude to override her ire."

"Hmm." He found himself the subject of Mary's blue gaze. After a moment, she said, in the tone of one making an interesting observation, "You do know that Stacie is a dab hand at manipulation, don't you? I know, because I am, too. Yet from what I've seen of you, Frederick, you could give both me and Stacie a run for our money in that sphere."

He held Mary's gaze, not entirely sure what to say. In the end, he ventured, "I've been aware of Stacie's attempts to sway me from the first —when she so artfully endeavored to persuade me to her cause. She was remarkably open about her machinations. In return, I've not, to date, sought to hide my attempts to influence her. She recognized what I was doing yesterday morning in convincing her to accept my invitation to the theater and didn't seem overly exercised. Whether she's consciously aware of my more-subtle manipulations or not, I can't say, but I'm certain that, at some point, she'll realize."

Mary considered, then tipped her head in acknowledgment. "If she knows that manipulation is a habit of yours..." She shrugged. "Ryder's even worse than you, yet between him and me, that hasn't been a problem." She smiled rather foxily. "Essentially, we expect it of each other and so are never surprised."

He stifled a laugh.

"So!" Mary sat up. "Let's put our minds to devising your campaign."

Frederick kept his lips shut and his expression hopeful.

Felicia stirred. "Why not make a list of all the possible events and select those most useful?"

Mary rang for paper and pen.

Frederick sat back and let the ladies have free rein, occasionally commenting and suggesting events such as a visit to the Royal Academy's private museum. He watched Mary create a reassuringly long list of events, each with its possible connection to music noted alongside.

Eventually, Mary sat back and, with Sylvia, who had moved to sit on the arm of Mary's chair, reviewed the list. Then Mary looked at Frederick, eyes narrowed in a considering fashion he'd already learned to be wary of. "We've basically created a concerted campaign that should cover the spectrum of advantages that might help in swaying Stacie to accept your suit. However, none of this will work unless your desire to woo her is genuine—unless you're willing to let her see that, possibly not immediately but at some point."

He comprehended, none better, what Mary was alluding to—that essential conviction, the genuine passion required to persuade another to one's cause; indeed, it had been Stacie's passion for her musical evenings and the potential benefit to local musicians that had drawn him to support her. He also understood Mary's underlying query—her doubt. When the time came, would he willingly face what he felt for Stacie and own to it?

I will if I have to—if there's no other way.

Holding Mary's gaze, he replied, "Speak to anyone who knows me, and they will tell you that I am relentless in pursuing anything I decide I want. I've decided I wish to have Stacie as my marchioness, ergo, I will do whatever is necessary to secure her hand in marriage."

Mary searched his eyes, then nodded. "Good. Because I warn you, 'whatever is necessary' might, indeed, be what it takes to achieve our now-shared goal." With a flourish, she held out the list.

Frederick leaned forward and took it, then sat back and ran his eyes down the page.

"Obviously, some events occur on specific dates, but others can be arranged to suit," Mary said. "I suggest you leave Stacie as little time to think and dwell on things as possible—essentially, you need to sweep her off her feet and keep her twirling until her resistance weakens, you seize the moment and lay your revised proposition before her, and she—we all hope—agrees."

Frederick quashed an urge to make an arrogant retort; he knew exactly what he needed to do. However, with their list, Stacie's sisters-in-law had, indeed, helped, so with becoming meekness, he nodded and tucked the list into his coat pocket. "Thank you, ladies." He rose and took his leave of them; as he walked out of the parlor, he wondered what they would say of him after he'd gone.

Mary watched Frederick depart. Only after his footsteps had faded did she allow a slow smile to curve her lips.

"What?" Sylvia asked as she returned to the armchair she'd previously occupied.

Mary tilted her head. "It occurs to me that Albury—Frederick—coming to see us as he just did is, to put it mildly, a distinctly notable move. I can't think of many gentlemen, finding themselves in his shoes, who would have even thought to make it. But he did. That suggests he's truly focused his mind on how to win Stacie—which, in my view, is exactly what she needs. Given her dogged stance against marriage, the only happening that might shift her from it is being pursued—relentlessly —by a determined man."

Felicia arched her brows. "One willing to do 'whatever is necessary' to win her?"

"Precisely." After a moment, Mary added, "I have to say that I'm now feeling a great deal more hopeful that this might prove to be a truly excellent match."

Sylvia sighed. "All we can do is keep our fingers crossed that Frederick can convince Stacie of that."

CHAPTER 9

*T*he next day was Sunday. Frederick consulted Mary's list, then sent a footman to Green Street and, subsequently, drove his curricle around to fetch Stacie for a drive to Richmond Park.

The day was fine, with light fluffy clouds chased across a blue sky by a flirtatious breeze. They passed the journey chatting about, of all things, family—swapping anecdotes of their elder siblings, Frederick being the youngest on his side and Stacie being the youngest bar Godfrey on hers, with Frederick having older sisters while she had older brothers.

They arrived in Richmond in a lighthearted mood and discovered that the park wasn't overly crowded; it proved an easy matter to find a suitable spot to spread a rug and enjoy the contents of the picnic basket Frederick's cook had provided.

Stacie found herself relaxing far more than she'd anticipated—far more than she had in...she honestly couldn't say how long. Being out of London, and although not precisely out of sight of the ton—there were other ladies and gentlemen about—certainly no longer under unremitting scrutiny, combined with Frederick's unexpectedly charming and undemanding company made it easy to close her eyes, tip her face up to the gentle sun, and simply enjoy the moment.

And if she was aware that Frederick watched her closely, he didn't seem exercised by anything he saw.

Frederick was, in fact, entranced by the glimpses he was catching of a less-serious Stacie. Over their previous encounters, she'd been focused, intent, passionate, and committed—driven. Or more recently, agitated, upset, and tense.

Now, when a pair of young fawns came investigating, wanting to snuffle up the crumbs of their repast, and he rose and waved his arms to shoo them off, Stacie dissolved into gales of laughter—ringing peals that fell on his ears like the music of angels.

He turned and stared at her—and found himself smiling, then laughing with her.

As he returned to the rug and slumped beside her in the sunshine, he felt something in his chest shift. He let his fingers brush her hand, felt an answering tremble in her slender digits before she stilled them, and smiled to himself and closed his eyes, content.

Later, he seized the moment of repacking the basket and folding the rug, then handing Stacie back into the curricle to touch her fingers, hold her hand, brush her back—taking advantage of all the little touches that were allowable between an engaged couple.

By the time he handed her down in Green Street and, retaining possession of her hand, walked her to her door, her nerves no longer leapt at his touch. Quietly satisfied with the day's advances, he paused on the porch, raised her hand to his lips, and kissed her knuckles. "Thank you for your company and for a very pleasant day."

Her answering smile was soft and sincere. "And thank you, my lord, for a delightful picnic. It was a lovely idea."

He smiled, leaned closer, brushed his lips to her cheek, and whispered, "That's for the old biddy across the street."

He straightened, tipped her a salute, and left her with a smile on her lips and laughter in her eyes.

～

The following morning, Stacie found herself on foot in Hyde Park, amongst a good-natured crowd all jostling for the best position from which to watch the launching of the huge, yellow-and-red-striped-silk balloon that was slowly inflating in a roped-off square around which the crowd had gathered.

Courtesy of the three gentlemen ranged at her back, she suspected that she, in fact, had the very best position from which to view the balloon ascension. Frederick, having been alerted to the event by Percy and George, had arrived at her door with the pair and insisted she join them.

When she'd admitted she'd never attended a balloon ascension before, nothing would do for them but that she don her bonnet and cape and accompany them into the park.

The stroll from Green Street to the clearing that the balloonists had selected for their exploit hadn't taken long. They'd arrived just as the ropes to keep back the gathering crowd were being strung up, and George and Percy—apparently veteran balloon watchers—had leapt to secure what they'd informed her was a prime position. "We'll be able to see all the preparations from here," Percy had earnestly assured her.

Somewhat to her surprise, she'd found those preparations quite fascinating—and they were made even more so by Frederick's deep-voiced murmurs in her ear, explaining the significance of what she was seeing. George and Percy also freely shared their knowledge, and she found herself relaxing in their undemanding company.

Eventually, with the balloon rising level with the treetops, the two balloonists paced back and forth, directing their assistants as they slowed the hot-air machine. Growing expectant, the crowd quietened, then everyone, the balloonists included, looked up, watching as the balloon swelled the last little bit, its rippling silk pulling taut until, finally, the wicker basket slung beneath the balloon lifted from the grass, and the balloon bobbed and tugged against the four thick ropes anchoring it to the ground.

That, apparently, was a signal of sorts. The machine cut off completely, and the balloonists rushed for the rope ladder hanging from the basket, while the assistants raced to and crouched beside the four mooring points of the ropes that, now, were all that was holding the balloon to earth.

The balloonists pulled in the rope ladder, shut and latched the gate into the basket, then peered over the sides.

"Release!" the elder balloonist roared, and the assistants furiously worked toggles, and the until-then-taut ropes eased, then ran free as the balloon slowly, majestically, rose.

A collective "Oh" of wonder wafted from the crowd.

"Wish us luck!" the younger balloonist yelled, and the crowd cheered and waved their hats.

Stacie held on to her bonnet as she tipped back her head and marveled at the sight of the gaily striped balloon rising slowly into the blue sky.

As she followed the balloon's flight, she tipped farther back, then felt hands—Frederick's hands with their long, strong fingers—close gently about her waist, steadying her.

Her senses no longer skittered at his touch; instead, they all but purred.

She told herself not to imagine that, on his part, the action meant anything at all—he was merely being protective—but she wasn't sure she believed that.

She wasn't sure she cared.

Caught up in the moment, oh-so-aware of Frederick immediately behind her, his long legs just behind hers, her skirts brushing against his trousers, his chest mere inches behind her shoulders, the warmth of his body a caress down her back, she felt that his hands and his hold were anchoring her not to the ground but to this moment of simple pleasure.

Simple happiness. Yesterday, today—he seemed to know just what outings would deliver that blessing to her.

～

Later that afternoon, Stacie found Frederick in her front hall again, this time to join her in an outing she had suggested on their way back from the park. They'd strolled to Green Street, trailing George and Percy, and had parted outside her house; while she'd gone inside to lunch with Ernestine, Frederick had headed to the Athenaeum with his friends.

As she emerged from the corridor leading to her parlor, he arched a brow at her. "Ready?"

She nodded and accepted her cape, which he held for her, then allowed him to escort her out of the door to his waiting carriage. He handed her in, then called to his coachman, "St Martin-in-the-Fields," then climbed inside and shut the door.

They spent the minutes to their destination reviewing what they wished to say, then over the next hour, they met with Protheroe and the three young men they now termed their initial protégés. Frederick favored all three with a critical assessment of their performance, a paean that nevertheless carried suggestions for improvement, minor though those were. His report reduced Brandon, Phillip, and George to a blushing and tongue-tied state; the three stammered out their thanks, patently valuing Frederick's critiques and thrilled to have earned his approbation.

Stacie then reported on the social aspect—how the ton had taken not just to their performances and presentation but also to the notion of such musical evenings introducing unknown local musicians. "As well as numerous inquiries about hiring you for individual events, several hostesses have asked if there is a need for more opportunities for musicians such as yourselves, and I've encouraged them to consider hosting similar events."

Smiling delightedly, Protheroe nodded. "We've already had several inquiries from ladies wishing to hire Brandon, Phillip and George, or other young musicians of similar caliber." He glanced approvingly at the three young men. "The lads suggested, and I agreed, that we should wait to discuss such requests with you before accepting. You will know if the ladies' events will be...well, suitable in the sense of advancing your protégés' reputations."

Stacie exchanged a glance with Frederick. "That was very wise. There may well be some events that would be less than suitable when assessed in those terms."

Frederick agreed, and he and she spent a good fifteen minutes poring over the list of inquiries received to date and explaining to Protheroe and the three musicians why some of the proposed events would be excellent venues at which to show off their skills, while others would be better avoided.

"Never, ever, accept an invitation to play out of doors." Wielding a pencil he'd pulled from his pocket, Frederick put a line through one inquiry. "The lack of acoustics will frustrate you and, ultimately, defeat you. So any request with the words alfresco, picnic, summer party, or the like is to be avoided."

"And when a lady says 'conservatory,' she generally means one filled with plants, not a musical one," Stacie added. "That said, some conservatories will function perfectly adequately as venues for musical performances, but those packed with plants won't." She pointed to another entry on the list. "You would need to see the space before you could safely accept."

Frederick nodded. "Dense foliage eats sound."

Protheroe received the winnowed list Frederick handed him with obvious gratitude. "Thank you—your explanations will help us enormously."

Stacie listened as Frederick reiterated an invitation she gathered he'd already issued to the three young musicians to call on him for advice whenever they felt in need of it.

She gave a similar assurance to Protheroe, that she would always be available for consultation on any question regarding musical events in the ton.

"Speaking of musical events"—Protheroe looked at her hopefully —"have you given any thought to hosting another of your own?"

Stacie glanced at Frederick. "I originally planned on four events spread throughout the year, which would mean at least one if not two more during the Season."

Frederick plainly thought, then offered, "I would suggest we hold off for a time before scheduling another event." He met Stacie's eyes. "Your first event garnered a great deal of attention, both before and after, purely because of its exclusivity. Holding events too close together makes them seem...not so special. Perhaps look to hold another late in the Season, then assess how the ton receives that before settling on the timing and structure of more events to be held later in the year."

She arched her brows, weighing the obvious merits of his argument, then met his eyes. "My only concern is that other hostesses will copy the pattern and dilute the very exclusivity you mentioned."

He held her gaze, his golden-brown eyes twinkling. "As I have no plans to play for any other hostess, I have difficulty imagining how any other lady is going to steal your thunder."

The others chuckled, and she had to battle a grin; he was too charmingly arrogant for words. "There is that, I suppose." She inclined her head in acceptance. "Very well. Shall we assume we'll be holding another musical evening later in the Season—perhaps toward the end of May— and leave any further organizing for later?"

Protheroe and the three young men nodded in agreement.

Frederick stirred. "Now we have some idea of our audience's capacity for sitting still and listening, I believe we can add a third introductory act. Either another soloist or a small group. We can leave any decisions until later, but"—he looked at Protheroe—"that's something to bear in mind."

Stacie and Frederick left the master and the three musicians happily revisiting the list of inquiries for their services.

On the pavement outside St. Martin's colonnaded façade, as he handed Stacie into his carriage, Frederick said, "I daresay you have a small mountain of invitations for the rest of the week, as do I." He patted a bulge in his pocket. "I brought them with me, thinking it might be helpful for us to compare the summonses and prioritize those events at which we feel most inclined to show our faces."

His near-disgusted tone made Stacie laugh. "All right." She settled on the seat, and he followed her into the carriage. "Let's repair to Green Street and plot out our schedule over tea."

~

They'd agreed to attend two balls that evening.

The first, at Lady Horowich's house, was also the first ton event they'd attended since the announcement of their engagement; as Stacie climbed her ladyship's staircase on Frederick's arm, she fully expected the next hour to be akin to a trial by fire.

Lady Horowich embraced them warmly, welcoming them with barely concealed delight. Given Stacie and Frederick had chosen her event for their first ton appearance, that was, perhaps, unsurprising.

Far more unexpected was the acceptance displayed by her ladyship's guests; as, with Frederick, Stacie passed through the crowd, exchanging greetings and chatting here and there, she detected not the slightest hint of aloofness, disapprobation, suspicion, or even plain old jealousy.

The last she viewed as decidedly odd; Frederick was—had been—a significant catch. At least, she assumed so, and she couldn't see how it would be otherwise. A wealthy marquess, handsome to boot, not given to gaming or any other major vice? He was a matchmaker's dream, yet she sensed nothing but approval, even from those ladies intent on securing titled husbands for their daughters.

It seemed that her and Frederick's unconventionally announced engagement had been embraced as if it were merely the natural order of things.

Of course, many remained terribly curious, but with Frederick by her side, and him perfectly prepared to be charmingly yet ruthlessly cutting if provoked, she had no real difficulty navigating the waters of her ladyship's ballroom.

Then the musicians struck up—and she realized she had no idea whether her supposed fiancé could waltz at least creditably. Yet when she turned to him, he smiled, tilted his head toward the clearing dance floor, and arched his brows, and when she smiled back and nodded, he tightened his hold on her hand and drew her onto the floor and, with a graceful flourish, turned her in to his arms.

Their first circuit of the ballroom was a revelation.

"You're an expert dancer," she accused.

He widened his eyes at her. "I thought you would have guessed. Musician from birth. A natural flair for rhythm and movement, especially as pertains to orchestral music."

She laughed. "When you put it like that, I fail to see how I missed the point myself."

He smiled in reply and whirled her through the turn, leaving her breathless. With an "Indeed," he set them revolving back up the room.

She was still breathless and not a little giddy when, at the end of the dance, he led her from the floor.

Other gentlemen were eyeing her hopefully, but Frederick steered her toward two couples who had recently arrived. "My sisters," he murmured, his breath tickling her ear, "will probably fall on your neck."

His sisters—Lady Candice and Lady Marjorie—didn't go quite that far but warmly embraced Stacie. While their husbands, Henry, Lord Harbury, and Douglas, Lord Rawton, pumped Frederick's hand and slapped his shoulder, Lady Marjorie confided that she, Lady Candice, their mother, and Mrs. Weston had all but given up hope of Frederick bestirring himself to select a suitable wife.

"At least," Lady Candice added, "not in the next decade."

Stacie recalled Frederick mentioning that Lady Horowich was a connection of sorts, and the scales fell from her eyes. It was likely, if not certain, that many of those gathered in the ballroom were connections—perhaps distant, but connections nonetheless—and from his sisters' comments, it seemed the Brampton family as a whole was delighted that Frederick had chosen her—a marquess's daughter, sister to another, well-dowered and long-established within the ton and, therefore, a paragon of suitability—as his bride.

She'd assumed the ton's reactions would center on her having succeeded in securing Frederick as her future husband. She hadn't, until then, realized that a good proportion of the ton would view their engagement from the opposing viewpoint—that of Frederick having secured her as his future wife.

As she'd assiduously avoided everything to do with the marriage mart, she hadn't previously listed her qualifications as a nobleman's bride. Now...she had to admit she was exceedingly well-qualified, and she hadn't even included their shared interest in music.

After Frederick deflected all inquiries as to their plans with a deft touch Stacie had to admire, they parted from his sisters and brothers-in-law on excellent terms, with promises of gathering for a family dinner in due course.

Once again moving through the crowd on Frederick's arm, Stacie

glanced around and no longer felt the slightest surprise at the ready acceptance of their engagement.

Frederick squeezed the hand she'd placed on his sleeve and lowered
his head to say, "We need to stop and chat with the couple just ahead.
Brampton is a cousin a few times removed and currently my heir."

That was all the warning he gave her before introducing her to a
genial gentleman of early middle years—Mr. Carlisle Brampton—and his
wife, who proved to be one connection of Frederick's who was not
thrilled to meet Frederick's recently acquired fiancée.

Yet Aurelia Brampton exchanged nods and accorded Stacie a curtsy
perfectly gauged for her rank. Carlisle's wife was a lady best described as
severely handsome; her contributions to the ensuing exchanges were cold
and stilted, and she remained as stiff as a poker throughout.

In contrast, her husband was of the bluff and easygoing sort; if he was
bothered that Frederick's proposed marriage would threaten his position
as Frederick's heir, Stacie saw no evidence of it, and she truly didn't think
Carlisle, as he insisted she call him, was capable of acting at all.

After only a few minutes, Frederick made their excuses on the
grounds they had another engagement to attend, and they set off through
the crowd toward the ballroom door.

Frederick dipped his head closer to Stacie's. "Aurelia is always rigidly
stiff—I've never seen her otherwise—and she tries to make Carlisle the
same. In her presence, I'm always tempted to drop something she values
in front of her, to see if her stays will snap when she bends."

Stacie pressed her lips together to hold back a laugh, then asked, "Is
there a reason for her being so starchy?"

"I've heard her parents described as the ultimate in high-sticklers.
They are rarely in London, and I've only met them once, at Carlisle's
wedding years ago. For what it's worth, my sisters are of the opinion that
Aurelia was brought up to live in fear of scandal of any sort whatsoever—
of even a hint of it touching her hems."

"Hmm," Stacie replied. "In that case, you and I are, ultimately, not
going to feature among Aurelia's favorite people, even if, in calling off
our engagement, we restore to her a direct pathway to becoming a future
marchioness."

"Bite your tongue," Frederick murmured, which Stacie interpreted as
an understandable reprimand over alluding to their future plans in public.

Yet his expression remained confident, relaxed and smiling, as he said, "Trust me, there won't be any scandal over us." He glanced down and met her eyes. "Society will just shrug and go merrily on."

The following afternoon, Frederick called at Green Street and took Stacie for a drive in the park, a pleasant interlude that demonstrated that the curious horde had started to lose interest in their romance and look elsewhere for more gossipworthy news.

After driving through the fashionable stretch of the avenue, Frederick drew into the verge and, leaving Timson holding the horses, helped Stacie down, and they ambled across the lawns to the banks of the Serpentine and watched, smiling, as three little girls threw bread crumbs to a gaggle of swans and noisy ducks.

Frederick thought he saw the shadow of a pleasant memory pass fleetingly over Stacie's face. When they started back to the curricle and he asked what had made her smile so fondly, she admitted that her father used to bring her and her brother Godfrey to the Serpentine, where she would feed the ducks and swans while Godfrey sailed his toy yacht.

Then she turned the tables on him, forcing him to admit that his major interest, even as a boy, had been music, music, and more music. "Papa soon gave up trying to instill other interests in me. In retrospect, I feel for him—I was his only son, yet at that age, all I wanted to do was play the piano."

She slanted him a glance. "I take it the riding and driving came later, along with the dancing?"

He smiled. "Indeed."

They couldn't expect to keep to themselves for long, and several groups took advantage of their stroll back to the curricle to approach and exchange the usual pleasantries, along with the expected subtle inquiries, but none were overly pushy, and they reached the carriage without him needing to cut anyone off.

He helped Stacie to the seat, joined her and took up the reins, and tooled them back to Green Street.

When he took his leave of her in the front hall—kissing her hand but, as they weren't on the porch and he therefore had no excuse, abstaining from kissing her cheek—she was still smiling. When he returned down the steps to the pavement, he was smiling, too.

~

The dinner at Albury House that evening, arranged by his mother several weeks before, wasn't an event he could legitimately avoid, no matter how much he wished to, and as his recently acquired fiancée, Stacie had to sit through it, too.

The other guests were his mother's friends, those still alive and able to get about, and included his godparents. Predictably, the entire company was delighted to learn of his engagement and even more delighted to meet Stacie.

"Knew your father quite well," Lord Hardacre boomed. "Excellent sort!" He opened his mouth to say something else, but abruptly shut it, then mumbled, "Pity he died when you were still so young. Good man. Good man."

To Frederick's relief, all the others steered clear of the topic of Stacie's parents, even though all members of the company were of the haut ton and of an age that guaranteed they would have heard a great deal about the late Marchioness of Raventhorne.

As he'd expected, the conversation took a turn toward the stultifying all too soon. The exchanges around the dining table revolved about the various guests' health, or lack of it, and the deaths of acquaintances and relatives, followed by reminiscences of the exploits of those who had passed on.

Luckily, to a man and woman, the company valued their sleep, and all departed relatively early, freeing Frederick to insist on accompanying Stacie in her carriage on the drive home.

For him, sitting in the comfortable darkness close beside her and breathing in the subtle perfume that rose from her skin and hair was the best part of the evening. He'd taken her hand to help her into the carriage and had followed closely behind her, allowing him to retain his hold on her fingers; when he dared to link his fingers with hers and she didn't tug hers free, he looked ahead and smiled to himself.

The distance to her house was too short to attempt anything more.

Her gaze apparently on the streetscape slipping past the window, she murmured, "Did you notice Lady Constance fell asleep at the table?"

"At one point, I thought she would topple forward and land with her face in her plate. I signaled to Fortingale, and he jogged her elbow while pretending to refill her glass."

"I wondered if he'd had a hand in waking her up." After a moment, she said, "That was well done of you. She would have hated it if she'd slumped onto the table."

He lightly shrugged. "She's a good old thing—she used to bring me sweets and insist that I play for her. Consequently, of my mother's friends, she was a favorite."

The carriage drew up, and he leaned forward and opened the door, then descended to the pavement and steadied Stacie as she climbed down. She looked up and told her coachman he could drive on to the mews, as Frederick had elected to walk home. When the man glanced his way, Frederick nodded a confirmation, and the coachman flicked his reins, and the carriage rolled away.

Still holding Stacie's hand, Frederick strolled with her up the steps to the porch and to her front door. With her free hand, she reached for the bell chain. Before she could tug, he raised the hand he held and pressed a lingering kiss to the inside of her wrist.

Her eyes, wide, flew to his face. He met her gaze, then, slowly, giving her plenty of time to draw back if she would, he shifted closer, bent his head, and pressed a soft kiss—not just a brush of the lips but a true kiss—to the corner of her lips.

She'd tensed. As he slowly straightened, she watched him intently. In the faint light that fell through the transom above the door, he could see her pulse beating—too fast, too hard—in her throat.

To his senses, she was like a cornered fawn, ready to leap away at the slightest sign of threat.

He smiled gently. "No biddy across the street tonight—that simply felt right."

She blinked; her eyes were very blue, the pupils dark and fathomless.

Allowing his smile to deepen a fraction, he reached out, closed his hand around hers where it had frozen on the bell chain, and gave the chain a tug.

Then he lowered his hand and stepped back. His gaze on her, he waited until her sleepy maid opened the door, then he saluted Stacie, turned, and walked down the steps. He glanced back to see the door closing behind her.

Smiling, he thrust his hands into his pockets, turned toward Park Street, and lengthened his stride.

≈

They'd arranged to meet at the eastern end of Rotten Row at eight o'clock the next morning.

Stacie wouldn't have been surprised if, in the wake of that odd almost-kiss Frederick had claimed, she'd had difficulty falling asleep. Instead, the instant her head had hit the pillow, she'd lost touch with the world and had woken with the first birdcalls, refreshed and looking forward to getting out and feeling the wind in her face.

She decided that the only way to deal with that almost-kiss was to ignore it. Why he'd done it was a mystery, but given his character, which she was coming to realize was impulsive—he was an inherently adventurous spirit to whom very few people had ever said no—perhaps, as he'd said, to him it had simply fitted the moment.

Regardless, she wasn't of a mind to allow such a minor incident to mar her enjoyment of the ride. With her groom trailing behind, she rode into the park and turned south to Rotten Row.

She saw Frederick waiting, mounted today on a raw-boned gray and watching the other riders as they thundered off down the tan.

Then he turned his head and saw her and smiled—and her silly heart flipped, flopped, and turned over.

Ignoring the sudden constriction about her lungs, she smiled back, irrationally pleased she'd chosen to wear her new peacock-blue riding habit, with its matching cap sporting a jaunty peacock feather curling up and over her head.

She drew her mare in alongside the larger gray. "Good morning, my lord."

Still smiling, he inclined his head to her. "A very fetching outfit." His warm gaze said he approved. "You cast us drab gentlemen into the shade."

Her smile widened.

The gray shifted, powerful and restless.

Feeling increasingly breathless, she waved at the track. "Shall we?"

He nodded, and they walked their horses forward to take their place in the queue at the head of the track, and in short order, it was their turn to tap their heels to their horses' flanks and fly down the tan.

It was exhilarating and satisfying, thundering down the track with Frederick holding the gray back just enough for her mare to keep pace. The wind of their passing blew Stacie's curls from her face and tugged at the feather in her cap. Excitement sang in her veins, familiar yet with an undercurrent of heightened awareness, of additional subtle pleasure.

They reached the end of the tan and reluctantly slowed, then wheeled to the right, onto the grass, slowing to a trot as they headed back toward the starting point.

Stacie glanced at Frederick, and he met her gaze and grinned.

His eyes reflected the same unalloyed pleasure and joy that was buoying her. "Shall we do that again?" he asked.

She laughed. "Yes—let's." In that moment, she felt more carefree and lighter of heart than she had in a very long time.

They both looked ahead and urged their horses into a faster trot, eager to experience the thrill of galloping—galloping together—again.

As they wheeled to rejoin the queue, the word "liberated" sprang to her mind. She hadn't realized that being an engaged lady, even a faux-engaged lady, would make her feel this unfettered—this free.

That evening saw them attending Lady Kilpatrick's ball. Her ladyship was one of the major hostesses, and an invitation from her equated to a command.

Unfortunately, because of that, her ladyship's events were always unmitigated crushes, a condition neither Frederick nor Stacie appreciated. By mutual accord, they sought refuge on the dance floor.

Frederick claimed the first two dances, then surrendered Stacie's hand to Percy and himself moved on to partner Mrs. Forsythe, a young matron he introduced to Stacie as a distant connection.

Stacie found Percy to be almost as good a dancer as Frederick. When she remarked on their shared skill, Percy revealed that when he, George, and Frederick had first come on the town, they'd decided that dancing was an activity at which it would pay to excel, so had hired a dance master to polish their steps.

Percy grinned. "An excellent investment in time and expense—all three of us can attest that ladies definitely appreciate a gentleman who can dance."

Stacie chuckled and nodded. "That's certainly true."

When, eventually, they swirled to a halt at the end of the measure and straightened from their curtsy and bow, a gentleman approached them.

Smiling, he bowed to Stacie. "Lady Eustacia." The gentleman exchanged nods with Percy. "Do introduce us, Piper."

Stacie didn't know Percy well enough to decide if his impassive demeanor meant he disapproved of the gentleman or simply had little time for him, but nevertheless, Percy obliged. "Lady Eustacia, allow me to present Mr. Hadley Barkshaw."

Barkshaw smiled, a touch ingratiatingly. "You've met my sister, Aurelia—Carlisle Brampton's wife."

"Ah." Understanding dawned, and Stacie smiled and extended her hand. "You're a connection of Frederick's."

"Indeed." Taking her hand, Hadley bowed over it. "And if I may, might I beg the honor of this dance?"

The musicians chose that moment to start up again—a country-dance, this time. Stacie saw no reason not to incline her head and, with a parting smile for Percy, allowed Barkshaw to lead her into the nearest set.

The dance was one that kept partners together, close enough to converse; while they turned and twirled, Barkshaw chatted—in a self-absorbed vein touching on subjects that confirmed Stacie's assessment that he was some years younger than Frederick and his friends, possibly of similar age to herself. Eventually, Barkshaw congratulated her on her and Frederick's engagement and capped his comment by brightly asking when they expected to wed.

Stacie countered by asking if Barkshaw had yet had a chance to congratulate Frederick. Barkshaw admitted he hadn't yet crossed Frederick's path, underscoring that he and Frederick did not move in the same circles; Stacie sensed that Barkshaw almost said as much but, at the last moment, held the words back.

Instead, he recommenced his steady patter of comments and observations, some of which were entertaining. However, he returned twice more to the question of when she and Frederick planned to marry, leaving Stacie wondering if Barkshaw was one of those gentlemen who sought to curry favor with the hostesses by always knowing the latest ton news; there was no denying that the date of her and Frederick's wedding was currently a topic of considerable speculation.

She was more than experienced enough to fob Barkshaw off; indeed, they might be of similar age, but in terms of managing within the ton, she sensed she was his senior by several years.

Regardless, when the lengthy country-dance eventually ended, she was pleased to find Frederick waiting and promptly reclaimed his arm.

Frederick greeted Barkshaw with his usual cool aloofness. For his part, Barkshaw promptly congratulated Frederick on his and Stacie's engagement, then with a bow and polite thanks to Stacie for the dance, Barkshaw took himself off.

Frederick eyed Barkshaw's departing back. "Aurelia must have dragged him here. I expect she's trying to encourage him to settle down."

Stacie made a disparaging sound. "Judging from the general tone of his comments, that's going to be a hard row for her to hoe, at least at present."

"Oh?" Twining her arm more definitely with his, Frederick steered her around the edge of the dance floor. "I've had enough—can we go?"

She looked ahead. "The door is at the far end—by the time we reach it, we'll have more than done our duty and can legitimately escape."

As she'd foreseen, they were constantly stopped by this lady or that gentleman, all wanting to offer congratulations and glean whatever news they were willing to share. She was growing adept at sliding around the leading questions, and Frederick more than held his own with his coolly arrogant aloofness and sometimes cutting wit.

At one point, when they were momentarily free of others, Frederick tapped Stacie's wrist and asked, "What did you mean by implying that Aurelia had her work cut out for her with Hadley?"

Stacie lightly shrugged. "Just that he struck me as an inexperienced rakehell—one who is yet a junior in the field, but seeking to find his way down that path." She paused, then added, "Actually, when you think about it, he seems an odd sort of brother for Aurelia to have. I would have expected someone more like Carlisle—indeed, someone more serious and less genial than Carlisle."

Frederick tipped his head. "True." He considered the point, then conceded, "I hadn't thought of that before, but you're right. As I mentioned earlier, Aurelia's parents are as rigidly correct as she is, if not more so. Perhaps Hadley's going through a delayed and prolonged rebellious phase."

Stacie chuckled. "That might explain it."

Frederick lowered his head and whispered, "There's a side door just ahead which gives access to the foyer—dare we take it?"

She glanced up and met his eyes. "I would love to, but we can't. We have to take our leave of Lady Kilpatrick—and luckily for us, she's just over there."

Frederick looked, heaved a put-upon sigh that made Stacie smile, and led her to their hostess's side.

~

The next morning, Frederick called for Stacie before any callers had had a chance to descend, and they hailed a hackney, traveled to Leicester Square, and took refuge with Mr. Griggs.

"It feels like sneaking away," Stacie had confessed as they'd jolted over the cobbles.

Frederick had grinned. "That's because it is."

Griggs had received the book Stacie had ordered, *Courvoisier's Arrangements for Harp*. She fell on it, eagerly turning the pages.

Along with Griggs, Frederick indulgently watched the joy and delight in her face.

When she finally looked up, blue eyes shining, and shut the book, Frederick reached for it. "May I?"

She smiled and slid the book to him, then turned to Griggs, exclaiming over the excellence of his contacts on the Continent and arranging for him to send her his bill, before settling to discuss another book.

Frederick studied her new tome. When, eventually, Stacie and Griggs glanced his way, Frederick looked up and met Stacie's eyes. "If you would like, from this"—he lifted the book—"I could create piano accompaniments to these songs."

Her eyes widened. "You could?" When he nodded, her face lit again. "Thank you—that would be wonderful!"

Smiling, Frederick set the book by her elbow and joined her and Griggs in a lengthy discussion of their shared obsession.

~

Thursday evening saw them at yet another major ball. The Season had commenced in earnest, and Lady Cartwright's ballroom was packed. It seemed to be a night where many of those who had been present at Stacie's musical evening just a week before sought out her and Frederick, to offer their congratulations in person and also to inquire as to their plans.

As many of those inquiring had every reason to expect to be invited to a wedding that would link two marquessates, Stacie and Frederick had to grin and bear with the incessant questions with what civility they could muster.

After one such encounter, Frederick met Stacie's eyes and laconically arched an eyebrow. "I've said the same thing so often in recent days, the phrases just roll off my tongue."

She pulled an expressive face. "Sadly, it's only to be expected. As we effectively sprang the initial event on them, now, no one wants to be behindhand with our news."

They continued to play their parts and circulated through the milling throng, occasionally being separated by the crowd and by connections of Frederick's or Stacie's wanting to privately bend their ears.

While both of them were experienced in ton ways and, however reluctantly, at home in this sphere, and both had grown sufficiently at ease with their situation to deal with any and all interrogations, Frederick noted that, when separated, more or less instinctively they gravitated back to the other's side.

Not because either needed the support of the other but simply because they preferred each other's company.

That was a somewhat surprising and rather refreshing realization.

Tonight, Stacie looked ravishing in a draped silk gown in a particular hue of magenta that rendered her dark hair and dramatic features even more eye-catching than usual, while the silk lovingly caressed her generous curves, in Frederick's opinion drawing far too many male eyes.

Just how aware he was of that was another telltale realization.

Among the compliments showered upon her, he again heard the apparently perennial comment comparing her to her mother. Alert, he watched her exceedingly closely and, from the faint tightening about her eyes and luscious lips, judged his earlier supposition that she viewed such compliments in a negative light to be correct.

She hid her reaction, doubtless understanding that the ladies who so gushingly pressed the comparison on her intended to be kind. As they parted from the latest unintentionally offending lady and moved on through the crowd, he tried to put a name to the emotion he sensed such comments evoked in Stacie. It wasn't offense, not really; it wasn't resentment, either. She wasn't angry or annoyed or sad.

He felt her reaction—understanding it—was important, that it might hold a clue to her stance on marriage, although he couldn't see why being told she was "just like her mother" in a comparison based solely on physical resemblance should cause her to reject the married state.

While Stacie was aware that Frederick was studying her, she didn't feel she had to shield herself from him; like her brothers, he was one of those men in whose company she felt entirely relaxed. At base, it came down to the fact that she trusted him. Indeed, she had from the first.

They continued to play the game they'd embarked on, deliberately deceiving the ton, and as they passed from one group of her ladyship's guests to the next, Stacie inwardly and rather guiltily admitted she was actually enjoying her role.

Being Frederick's fiancée... Essentially, she was savoring an experience she'd never thought to have, being the affianced bride of a thoroughly eligible nobleman. It was another piece of the silver lining of their situation; courtesy of Fate's interference in their lives, she could experience this, and all in complete safety, both hers and Frederick's.

I might as well enjoy it to the full.

She could see no reason why she shouldn't, so she lowered her guard another inch and actively embraced the moment.

She'd slipped into the withdrawing room and was behind one of the screens when she heard several ladies—at least three—gossiping about her. About the engagement. Unable to help herself, she paused where she was and listened.

"Ah, but the source of tension won't be the Cavanaughs or the Bramptons, my dear. I note Lady Halbertson hasn't shown her face tonight. Understandable, but telling, don't you think?"

Stacie frowned. *Lady Halbertson?*

"I met her yesterday at Mrs. Phillips's luncheon," a second lady put in, "and she certainly put on an excellent show of not being concerned in the least by the announcement."

"I'd heard she and he had parted some months ago," a third lady said.

"Be that as it may," the first speaker intoned, "it must have been particularly galling for her ladyship to see him going from her bed to Lady Eustacia's, so to speak, and all within a few months. I find it difficult to credit that a widow in her situation wouldn't have entertained some degree of hope of snaring a catch like Albury."

"I daresay you're right," the second speaker said. "She must at least have had her nose put out of joint."

"No matter how well she's hiding that," the first speaker stated.

The ladies' voices shifted and grew slightly muffled. Stacie held her breath and peered around the edge of the screen. Five other screens were erected around the room, but the center of the room presently held only a maid.

Stacie walked quickly to the door and let herself out.

In the corridor, she paused. Was she surprised that Frederick had had a mistress? Hardly. And it seemed they'd broken off the liaison months ago—long before she'd approached Frederick. And according to his mother, he'd been hiding in Surrey for months before that.

Of course, if he drove up to town to visit his mistress, he was hardly likely to inform his mother.

Not that Frederick's love life, past or future, was any real concern of hers, yet she had to admit to being curious about what sort of woman Lady Halbertson was—about what sort of lady had caught Frederick's eye.

According to the three anonymous ladies, Stacie wasn't going to find out that night. She returned to Frederick's side just as the musicians started the prelude to a waltz. Smiling, she reached for his hand. "Come, my lord, and sweep me off my feet again."

He arched his brows at her, but readily acquiesced. He twisted his hand, and his fingers closed firmly about hers, and he led her onto the floor.

She sighed and smiled up at him as she turned in to his arms and he set them elegantly twirling. "This," she announced, "is one definite benefit to being engaged—being able to waltz with you many more times than twice without creating a scandal."

His answering smile was pleased, arrogantly proud, but cloaked an underlying intensity she hadn't expected.

In an attempt to tease out his thoughts, she tilted her head and said, "I confess I'm enjoying the role of your fiancée far more than I'd anticipated."

The sense of him considering something—weighing something—only grew.

When he said nothing, she finally arched a brow at him. "What is it?"

He searched her eyes, her face, then, still smiling, said, "I'm glad that being my fiancée isn't beyond your skills."

She almost snorted. "When it comes to being arrogant—and do remember I have Ryder with whom to compare you—I hereby declare that you take the cake."

He laughed and swept her into a vigorous, perfectly gauged turn, reducing her to laughter, too.

CHAPTER 10

The following day, they'd agreed to attend an alfresco luncheon at Lady Waltham's estate by the river at Twickenham.

Frederick drove them down in his curricle. Most of the other guests were there before them; they walked onto her ladyship's lawns and, as they'd expected, found only the crème de la crème of the haut ton present —one of the reasons they'd chosen that event after two evenings enduring ton crushes, and with two balls to attend that evening, neither of which they could avoid.

As they paused to chat to the first group of guests they came upon, Frederick glanced at Stacie; lips curved, eyes bright, features dramatically alive, she truly had relaxed into the role of his fiancée. His campaign was progressing very much as he wished, and this outing—recommended by Mary—held the promise of allowing them to ease just that little bit closer. Despite the select guest list, the lawns were a trifle crowded, encouraging couples to wander between beds and borders that, in this season, were bountiful and lush, creating avenues that, along some stretches, were effectively private.

Having attained the status of acceptably engaged couple, he and Stacie were able to wander freely, with no need to remain within sight of any others. They were some way from the lawns when they turned down a long avenue with deep borders on either side. Prompted by he knew not what, nonchalantly, he reached out and twined the fingers of one hand with hers—and she accepted the touch without protest, as if she found nothing overly remarkable in him claiming her hand.

As if she'd grown accustomed to feeling his fingers around hers. He looked ahead and fought to keep a too-wide smile from his face.

Surveying the colorful flowers, she paused to examine the nodding heads, then, as they strolled on, without prompting, launched into a tale of the exploits of her brothers in disrupting a long-ago garden party.

He listened to her words and watched her face, tracing the changing expressions that flowed across her vivid features. Warmth of a sort he'd never felt before bloomed in his chest and spread. Under its heady influence, he was tempted—*so* tempted—to use his hold on her hand to draw her to a halt and claim a kiss—a proper kiss—there, in the privacy of the colorful avenue.

But he didn't dare.

Not yet. She was not at all blind and, intellectually at least, nowhere near innocent. Stealing a real kiss without some sound external reason to act as an excuse would alert her to his change of direction, and like an untamed filly, she would spook and shy away.

Despite the subtle yet real changes between them—in the ballrooms as well as in venues such as this—and, he hoped, in her view of them and, thus, in the potential for making their engagement real, he seriously doubted she was yet ready to hear the proposition he was determined to lay before her.

He had to play a careful game, advancing step by inexorable step without her noticing how close he was getting, and how much closer she was getting to him, physically as well as emotionally. Unfortunately, as they ambled down the avenue, with the sunshine warm upon them and the bucolic surroundings creating a landscape of color and movement, she responded to that, her pleasure clear in her expression, and forcing himself to toe the line he knew he must grew more difficult with every step.

On reaching the end of the avenue, he turned them onto the path that would lead them back to the lawns and the other guests.

Stacie glanced at him, faintly surprised, for she'd realized some time ago that he liked crowds even less than she did. But then the lawns opened before them, and the first person her eyes fell on was a tall, willowy, blond-haired lady, stylishly gowned and exuding an aura of self-confidence that, combined with her cool beauty, was arresting. Facing to their right, the lady was standing with a circle of others with whom she was conversing.

The group were the nearest knot of guests; Stacie sensed Frederick hesitate and looked up to see him contemplating the group, as if taking stock, then smoothly, he looped her arm in his, and together, he and she strolled toward the group.

Several in the circle saw them coming; their faces lit, and they eagerly shuffled to make space for Stacie and Frederick to join them.

The lovely lady turned, saw Frederick, and smiled.

The quality of that smile warned Stacie as to whom, exactly, the willowy lady was. She also realized she'd met the woman previously, over the years at various ton functions.

At his urbane best, Frederick nodded to the group, all of whom were known to Stacie. He and she exchanged the usual greetings until, at last, they reached the beautiful blonde.

Stacie smiled easily. "I believe we've met before."

The lady returned her smile with what appeared to be genuine interest and dipped in a regulation curtsy. "Indeed, Lady Eustacia, but it was years ago. I'm Lady Halbertson. I'm delighted to meet you."

"And I you, Lady Halbertson." Politely, Stacie held out her hand.

Frances Halbertson lightly touched fingers, and Stacie told herself not to leap to judgment.

She shot a swift glance at Frederick, but detected not the slightest sign of any anticipation of awkwardness in his perennially coolly arrogant demeanor. If she hadn't grown up in her mother's household, keeping her own awareness of the erstwhile connection between him and Lady Halbertson from her expression would have been impossible. As it was, she pretended to listen to the chatter of the others in the group, noting that none seemed aware of any source of potential friction.

Then one of the group made a comment about Kean's performance as Hamlet at Drury Lane.

"Magnificent!" Lord Jeffries boomed in reply. "I would say his Hamlet outstrips even his father's." His lordship focused on Stacie. "Saw you in Albury's box that night, Lady Eustacia—what did you think of Kean, heh?"

She could hardly say that she'd been too caught up in thinking of other things and had barely noticed the great actor. "I expect his delivery might best be described as outstanding. It patently satisfied the audience."

"I'm not at all certain," Mrs. Jellicoe sapiently remarked, "that the majority of the audience were watching the stage."

Others chimed in with their views, some chiding, others agreeing, and a lengthy discussion on the true role of the theater in the lives of the haut ton ensued.

Throughout, Stacie kept a surreptitious eye on Lady Halbertson, but although her ladyship stood on Frederick's other side, she never once attempted to capture his gaze or even his attention.

Yet the pair had been lovers; of that, Stacie was now absolutely certain.

Eventually, she and Frederick moved on; again, Stacie watched like a hawk, but Frederick didn't so much as glance back at her ladyship, and Lady Halbertson's gaze didn't follow him.

Instead, her ladyship watched Stacie as she and Frederick strolled about the knots of guests.

That, Stacie had to admit, was a trifle unsettling, even if she'd sensed no overt jealousy or, indeed, any negative sentiment from Lady Halbertson. To be observed in that manner by one's intended's recently retired mistress was off-putting; she couldn't imagine what was going through Frances Halbertson's head.

Clearly, from Frederick's perspective—and apparently, that of the members of the ton who knew of it—the affair was over and done with. Given both he and her ladyship belonged to the very upper strata of society, as did Stacie, crossing each other's paths at events such as this was impossible to avoid.

Stacie told herself that what lay—or had lain—between her ladyship and Frederick was none of her business, yet she couldn't help thinking that if she was standing in Lady Halbertson's pumps, she might just resent the lady, not that much younger and of similar birth, who, shortly after Frederick had broken off their liaison—and she had little doubt it had been he who had ended it—had caught his eye to the point of him offering marriage.

She cut a glance at Frederick's face, but his debonair mask was firmly in place, and nothing of his thoughts, much less his feelings, showed.

Shortly after that, luncheon was announced. Lady Waltham's notion of a picnic was to serve food designed to be eaten with one's fingers, served on silver platters her footmen ferried between the guests, who sat at wrought-iron tables and chairs scattered about the south lawn. Couples tended to play musical tables, moving from one table to another as others did the same and openings appeared.

Stacie happily followed Frederick's direction, and by availing themselves of the option of constantly moving, they managed to keep their tempers from being frayed by the many older ladies who remained intent on interrogating them.

She had to admit it was extremely handy to be on the arm of a nobleman who, when moved to it, could look down his nose and turn cool aloofness into chilly dismissal in less time than it took to blink.

Even the older grandes dames took note and—albeit reluctantly—drew in their horns.

She and Frederick remained a part of the larger company until the copious quantities of champagne served with the meal had their inevitable effect, and many of the older guests grew somnolent and inattentive.

Then Frederick seized a moment while they were moving between groups to tug her sideways, onto another of the gently twisting garden paths.

This one, she soon discovered, led to the ornamental lake. Although several other couples were strolling the path around the lake's shore, all were sufficiently distant to allow her and Frederick to converse without fear of being overheard.

She couldn't resist seizing the moment to say, "Earlier, you asked me what my reasons for rejecting marriage were in order not to step on my toes unnecessarily." She caught his gaze as it swung, sharp and intent, to her face. "Mentioning that Lady Halbertson had, until recently, been your mistress could be said to fall under the same category, albeit in reverse."

His eyes searched hers, then he looked ahead. "Frances and I broke things off a few months ago." He frowned. She sensed nothing beyond earnestness when he asked, "Should I have mentioned it?"

She twined her arm more tightly with his and leaned closer to say, "Obviously, I've already heard the whispers, and today, I saw the proof. Had I truly been your fiancée, I might have been...concerned."

He looked genuinely puzzled. "I can't see why. It's over and done and firmly in my past."

"Yours, perhaps. But tell me—who broke the liaison off? You or her?"

He hesitated for several moments, during which they neared and passed another couple going in the opposite direction; Stacie noted he'd wiped his face of all expression before the other couple got close.

Once the others were well past, he replied, "I *thought* she and I had both decided to end our association."

"I hear a 'but.'"

He tipped his head. "I'm only as good as the next man in comprehending what goes on in ladies' heads. I can't speak for Frances, but she seemed to accept my suggestion readily—with good grace."

Stacie could have told him that accepting a situation gracefully when there was no real choice simply demonstrated that Lady Halbertson was intelligent enough not to try to hold him when he didn't want to be held.

If the implications of the comments she'd overheard at Lady Kilpatrick's were correct, then Lady Halbertson might have hoped for more from the association. As her ladyship's presence at Lady Waltham's attested, she was of sufficiently high birth to aspire to being Frederick's wife—and she was certainly beautiful enough. Frederick wasn't just handsome and titled, he was also significantly wealthy, and while that wealth meant nothing to Stacie, wealthy herself, she knew the pursuit of funds played a much larger role in the lives of many others, including—and sometimes especially—those of the haut ton.

Frederick watched the flow of thoughts flit across Stacie's expressive face; now she'd relaxed completely in his company, she didn't bother screening her feelings from him, which was proving a great help. Also a source of encouragement; even though their engagement was a sham, she'd taken very real note of Frances and his past relationship with her—that was, he felt, significant. As his faux fiancée, if Stacie had felt nothing at all for him, surely she would have just shrugged aside the issue as irrelevant, at least to her.

He was still debating that conclusion when she abruptly halted.

"Look!" She pointed to a narrow path that wended up the heavily treed rise that overlooked the end of the lake, tracing the line of the path upward to where sections of white columns and a domed roof could be glimpsed between the leafy canopies. "There's a folly—a Grecian temple—up there." She tightened her hold on his arm and towed him onto the minor path. "Let's climb up and take in the view."

The path was only wide enough for a single person and rose in long flights of stone steps. Frederick gallantly urged Stacie ahead, then had to bear with the intoxicating sight of her silk-clad hips and derriere sifting side to side before his face, which, given the avenue his thoughts were all too ready to go rampaging down, did nothing for his comfort.

They finally reached the folly, which did, indeed, provide an expansive view of the lake. Branches bursting into leaf obscured the view of the path directly below, but the farther reaches of the lake spread before them, with sunlight dancing across the surface set rippling by the light breeze.

Stacie immediately crossed to the edge of the marble floor. Spreading one palm on one of the columns, she stretched up on her toes and peered between the branches, which were sorely in need of pruning.

Frederick followed in more leisurely fashion, his gaze dwelling on a different sight.

"I can't quite see the house." Stacie leaned forward.

Her palm slipped on the smooth marble, and she started to tip. "Oh!"

Frederick swooped, looped an arm about her waist, and hauled her back to safety.

Hauled her against himself.

Not safe.

Before he could do more than suck in a breath and tense every muscle he possessed, she wriggled around until she faced him and looked into his eyes. "Thank you."

Then she stretched up, set her lips to his, and kissed him.

It wasn't a thank-you peck but a full-blown kiss—lips to lips, alluring pressure, more than a whisper of heat and hunger.

He was far more experienced than she could possibly know; he understood—with a leap of intuition that he knew in his bones was accurate—just why she'd kissed him.

Why she was still kissing him, her lips exploring his, even as his arms slowly tightened around her and, equally slowly, he angled his head.

Then he took over—took charge—and kissed her back. And answered her questions. The ones that had prompted her to act so impulsively—to kiss him and seek answers.

Curiosity was the principal cause, but simple curiosity had been prodded by her meeting with Frances Halbertson into transforming into something more.

Something he wanted and was more than willing to stoke.

Something wildly ingenuous, innocent yet not.

An inquisitive desire, a need to experience, to sensually know.

There was no possible way to answer such demands other than through an actual kiss. She'd given him the opportunity, and he seized it with both hands.

Seized her, one hand at her back holding her flush against him, the other cradling her head as he artfully parted her lips and slid his tongue between and steered them both into deeper waters.

She didn't resist but followed; he sensed she wasn't a complete novice—she'd definitely been kissed before—but that only heightened the challenge. He lured her on; their tongues tangled as he traced the contours of her mouth and, with assured arrogance, claimed.

Her hands had, until then, rested splayed against his chest, their warmth and delicate pressure another, subtler goad; now she sent her palms skating upward, feathering over his shoulders, then rising to clamp about his head and hold him. Then she kissed him back.

She opened some door inside her, and passion poured forth. Hungry and greedy and wanting. Desire ignited, hers and his, and what had started as an exploratory kiss turned voracious.

Heat flowed between them. They traded kiss for achingly needy kiss, then dived into the next.

The tide rose, and he couldn't step away, couldn't hold back, couldn't not answer her siren's call; he fell into the exchange, and she fell with him, and desire and passion reared in a wave and dragged them under.

Through a thickening fog of desire, distant voices reached his ears.

Self-preservation spiked; desperate, he seized its reins and wrenched back from the surging swell of a passion more powerful than any he'd previously known.

He raised his head and looked into Stacie's face, at her lips, swollen from his kisses.

Her lashes rose, and her eyes—wide and very blue—met his. She blinked, then blinked again, then searched his eyes, his face. He had no idea what she saw there—whether the stunning revelation that had rocked him to his bedrock showed.

His pulse still hammered in his ears. He wanted her, desired her— how much, he hadn't realized. Until that moment, he hadn't understood how hungry for a woman he could be.

Still-surging passion kept him anchored where he was; if he moved, toward her or away from her, it might break free.

Stacie couldn't help but stare; her entire awareness was consumed by what she'd just learned, what she'd just experienced, and most of all, by the feelings that had risen and were still spilling through her—a yearning for more, for an even closer connection with a man... No, with *this* man. Others had kissed her, and she'd never felt like this, as if she needed so much more—more kisses, more contact, more of him.

It was a shock to realize she'd never felt desire before.

And if this was it, she needed more.

But they weren't actually engaged. They couldn't, shouldn't...

The very fact she was thinking along such lines shook her to her core.

Others were nearing, coming up the steps.

He didn't say anything; neither did she.

What could she say? She had instigated the kiss, and it had happened. And it had spiraled out of control.

Perhaps she should apologize, but she'd be lying. She wasn't sorry at all.

Two young ladies preceded two gentlemen into the folly.

Stacie stepped away from Frederick and turned to face the newcomers.

Smoothly, he captured her hand and set it on his sleeve. "Come," he said, and his voice held its usual even tone. "We should head back to town. We have those two balls to attend this evening."

A reminder that, notwithstanding the drama of the last minutes, their charade had to go on.

She gripped his arm, signaling her agreement, then, after exchanging politely distant nods with the four who had invaded the folly, she allowed Frederick to guide her back to the steps and followed him down.

The following day—after they'd weathered two horrendous crushes that had been bad enough to have Frederick seriously question how long he could continue his campaign to win Stacie—he called in Green Street to find her in the front hall, preparing to leave the house.

He looked at her. "I came to ask if you would like to go for a drive in the park." That had been Mary's suggested activity for this morning—a quiet breather after the two balls last night.

"Oh." Stacie blinked, then said, "I need to go shopping for gloves." She waggled her gloved fingers at him. "These have worn too thin."

He rapidly rejigged his plans. "Where are you headed?"

"My glover's shop is on the corner of Bruton and Old Bond Streets."

He smiled. "My curricle's outside. I'll drive you there."

She eyed him suspiciously. "And then?"

He shrugged. "I'll escort you around, then drive you back here. Who knows? I might buy myself a pair of gloves, too."

Stacie studied him, then nodded. "Very well." She took his arm and allowed him to escort her to his curricle and help her up to the seat.

She couldn't broach any sensitive subject while they were in the open carriage, not with his tiger on the box behind. But they hadn't yet spoken of the heated moments in Lady Waltham's folly; during the previous evening—through the balls they'd attended, both of which had been unbearably crowded and packed with many who knew them well and far too many who had been watching them like hawks—a suitably private and appropriate moment hadn't presented itself. Indeed, their only private moments had been in the shadowed dimness of the carriage as they'd traveled around Mayfair's streets, and she hadn't been game to mention that subject in such close and potentially intimate confines.

But she was determined to raise and address the incident and, hopefully, lay it to some sort of rest.

She'd expected to toss and turn last night, but instead, had instantly fallen asleep—and dreamed of that kiss. And of him. Given they weren't truly engaged and really shouldn't pursue what had flared between them, that he'd invaded her dreams—the first man ever to do so—seemed particularly unhelpful.

He drove them to Bruton Street. Leaving the curricle in the tiger's care, they set off along the pavement.

Now was her moment; they might be surrounded by the fashionable, but no one ever listened to comments exchanged by others walking past. "About what occurred in Lady Waltham's folly." She shot a glance at his face. "That wasn't supposed to happen."

His expression was, as usual, unreadable, but he dipped his head her way. "No, it wasn't." Then, almost as if he couldn't hold back the words, he added, "But I'm not sorry it did." He caught her eyes. "Are you?"

She felt compelled to answer truthfully. "No."

He smiled—a surprisingly sweet and charming smile. "Good." He looked forward. "In that case, there's nothing more to be said."

She wasn't sure what she'd expected but... As they'd reached the corner of Bruton Street and Old Bond Street and the door to her glover's shop, she inclined her head in tacit agreement and let the matter drop.

Frederick escorted her into the shop, then ambled in her wake as she looked over the merchandise and the little glover scurried around, showing her this pair and that.

For his part, Frederick was in a good—nay, excellent—mood. The revelations of the previous day had left him even more convinced that his instincts had steered him correctly, yet again, in prompting him to pursue Stacie. Her confession that she wasn't sorry about that eye-opening outburst of unrestrained passion set the seal on his satisfaction; his campaign was proceeding even better than he'd hoped. They'd cleared a hurdle he hadn't known how to approach; she as well as he now knew with a certainty that they were compatible in that highly pertinent sphere, in much the same way as they were in others.

Victory was possible, if not yet assured; for today, that was enough.

The balls they'd attended the previous evening, while a shared torture in terms of the crowds, hadn't otherwise tested them; he and Stacie had fallen into the pattern of easy interaction they'd established over the past week—that of an acknowledged couple. As his goal was to make their supposedly temporary charade permanent, knowing that under pressure, Stacie defaulted to that role—indeed, had sought refuge in it—underscored his belief that he was making real and steady progress.

He'd expected her to say something about the moments in the folly and had waited—on tenterhooks, to some degree—to see what tack she would take. Would she recoil and insist on keeping him at a distance henceforth? He'd been fairly certain she hadn't succumbed to any missish panic, but given it had been such an unexpectedly intense exchange, he hadn't felt confident in predicting what tack she might take.

Her straightforward acceptance—that the eruption of passion had occurred, that the connection between them was there—and her admission that she wasn't sorry to have learned that had been music to his ears.

He waited patiently while she purchased two pairs of gloves, then, feeling in charity with the world, bought a pair for himself. She stuffed her purchases into her reticule, he slipped his pair into his pocket, and they left the little glover smiling.

Stepping onto the pavement, he caught her hand, wound her arm in his, and started them walking down Old Bond Street. When she looked up at him, faint suspicion in her eyes, he smiled easily. "Have you anywhere else you need to visit?"

Somewhat warily, she admitted, "No."

His smile deepened. "In that case, now we're here, we might as well be seen doing those things engaged couples do."

She arched her brows and looked at the shops lining the street ahead. "What did you have in mind?"

He paused as if considering the options before them. "Jewelers," he announced. "Engaged couples visit jewelers, don't they?"

"I suppose they do."

They stopped at two smaller establishments before he opened the door of Aspreys Emporium and ushered her inside.

They gravitated to the jewelry section. A clerk waiting behind the counter saw them and came forward to greet them. Stacie smiled and told the young man, "We're just looking."

Frederick caught the clerk's eyes and, with his head, indicated the cases of more valuable pieces located farther into the shop.

The clerk perked up and looked at Stacie. "Of course, my lady—I rather fancy the pieces that will interest a discerning lady such as yourself will be found in the cases over here."

Stacie followed the clerk to the cases in question and instantly became absorbed. Frederick hid a grin and watched her, drinking in the delight she didn't try to hide—even if she thought this was a charade, what woman didn't enjoy looking at good jewelry? Assured that his latest impulsive idea would work, he scanned the contents of the cases himself.

It didn't take long for him to guess what would appeal to her most. A lovely ruby ring, with a matching bracelet, earrings, and necklace in a delicate gold setting lay displayed on a bed of black velvet toward the rear of the case. Eventually, Stacie's eyes found the set. He leaned a hip against the case, then bent his head to hers; following her gaze, he suggested, "Why don't you try them on?"

She turned her head and, at close quarters, met his eyes.

He held her gaze in barely veiled challenge, then lightly raised one shoulder. "Why not?"

The clerk bustled to the rear of the case and opened it. "The ruby parure? An excellent choice, my lady. It will look exceptionally well on you."

The man wasn't spouting nonsense; the gems looked utterly perfect on Stacie, as if they'd been created specifically for her.

And she liked them; Frederick could tell by the way her countenance lit as she preened before the oval mirror the clerk fetched. Despite believing this was all for show, she couldn't resist the rich color of the gems or their fabulous fire. The clerk fussed and insisted she don the entire set, and despite the high neckline of her walking dress, the result was truly stunning. If she wore the set with one of her ball gowns, she would draw every eye—female as well as male.

Frederick took due note that, despite her slender fingers, the ring sat well and wasn't too loose.

Eventually, with a reluctance she couldn't hide, Stacie removed the jewels and returned them to the black-velvet-lined case. "Thank you." She pushed the case toward the clerk. "They are lovely, but we'll need to consider others before deciding."

The clerk's face fell.

Frederick waited until Stacie turned toward the door to catch the clerk's eye, flip a calling card his way, look pointedly at the case in his hands, and fractionally nod. The man's eyes widened. Frederick didn't wait to see more; he trailed Stacie to the door, opened it for her, and followed her outside.

On the pavement, she retook his arm and sighed. "Those rubies were lovely, but I feel for that poor clerk. He was so disappointed."

Frederick patted her hand and led her on. "I'm sure he'll recover."

In planning his campaign, Frederick had gambled that, by Saturday evening, he would have advanced his cause sufficiently that a visit to a performance of the Royal Opera Company at Covent Garden would be not only a viable outing but also a productive one.

Productive in the sense of consolidating all the advances he'd made to that point.

As matters transpired, he couldn't have planned better. He sat in the dimness of the Albury box, located directly opposite the stage in the middle of the second tier, and for once, the music emanating from the orchestra, the superbly delivered vocal histrionics, and the drama unfolding on the stage failed to capture and hold his attention.

His usual fascination couldn't compete with the lure of the lady beside him.

Another revelation, one he felt he didn't need to dwell on.

The important thing was that Stacie was enjoying herself hugely. She sat upright in the chair beside him, her features lit by the backwash from the powerful limelights illuminating the stage, on which the dramatic flair of Pacini's celebrated "Maria, regina d'Inghilterra" held sway.

Stacie's absorption was complete; she was utterly captivated by Tarantini's words, his characters' dramatic actions, and swept away by Pacini's glorious music, brought to life by the talented orchestra.

While making their way to the box, threading through the inevitable crowd in the foyer, she'd instinctively clutched his arm tighter and leaned into him, seeking—inviting—his protection. Unwilling to be trapped in conversation, they'd both done their part in glibly deflecting various attempts by members of the ton to detain them, ultimately taking refuge in the box and happily relaxing in their own company.

Now, watching her face, tracking her responses to the soaring music, he not only accepted but embraced the obvious—they were made for each other. No lady he'd ever met came anywhere close to her in terms of shared interest or in terms of his interest in her.

Her family, his mother—the entire ton—would be thrilled if he could convince her to make their faux engagement real and face an altar by his side.

The only person who remained to be convinced of the rightness of a marriage between them was her.

Despite all his advances, he wasn't sure he was even close to succeeding; he still didn't know what it would take to change her mind.

The opera came to an end. They didn't dally but escaped from the box and down a side stair, avoiding any who might have thought to waylay them.

"You do know your way about, my lord," she remarked as he ushered her through a side door, and they walked through the shadows to the front of the building.

He settled her arm in his and scanned the way ahead. "I wasn't of a mind to exchange pleasantries."

"Oh, I'm not complaining." She leaned on his arm and directed a playful glance at his face. "As you're very well aware, your dislike of the ton's jabbering is entirely matched by mine."

Just as they were well matched in so many other ways. "Jabbering?" he mused. "An excellent word for it." He looked down into her dancing eyes. "I take it you enjoyed the performance."

She inclined her head and faced forward. "I did, indeed. It was wonderful! Thank you for arranging the outing."

He smiled as they reached his carriage. "It was, indeed, my pleasure."

He opened the carriage door, helped her in, and followed.

As the carriage rattled toward Mayfair and they sat enveloped in soft darkness, he debated whether it was time to speak—to carefully suggest that perhaps they should consider making their engagement real.

But I don't yet know what's driving her aversion to marriage.

The same instincts that made him impulsive were currently advocating caution; as he usually did, he listened to them and didn't speak.

Yet as the carriage rolled on and they both remained silent, unease wormed through him. It was distinctly unnerving to realize that, in this, he, who cared little about anyone else's opinion and rarely entertained the slightest self-doubt, wasn't yet confident enough in his ability to carry this particular argument. More, that she now figured so critically in his view of his future that he wasn't willing to risk proposing to her—laying his proposition before her—while there was the slightest chance she might refuse and, worse, retreat.

Another revelation slid into his mind, one more fundamentally disturbing than all those before it.

In setting himself to win Stacie, he'd embraced the vision of what she and he could be together. He'd envisaged the gamut of what a life shared with her would be like, how satisfying it would be, and in doing so, he'd opened himself to the threat of not succeeding. To the threat of losing her and all that vision promised.

In seeking to win her, he'd made himself vulnerable in a way he hadn't foreseen.

When she made a comment about the cellist's performance, he was grateful for the reprieve from his unsettling thoughts and glibly spun out the conversation as the carriage ferried them to her door.

In Green Street, he saw her into the house, thereby ensuring that, with her parlormaid present, he had no chance of bestowing any further inexcusable attention on Stacie. He left her with a bow and a crooked smile.

That smile had faded by the time he reached his carriage, ordered his coachman to drive home, and climbed inside.

CHAPTER 11

On Monday morning, with no shared outing scheduled until a soirée that evening, Frederick took refuge in his study. Apparently, Mary was hosting some family event at which Stacie would be present; slumped in the chair behind his desk, he decided it behooved him to seize the period of enforced inaction to review where he and Stacie now stood.

He'd been pursuing her, carefully if doggedly, for over a week. Yesterday being Sunday, as per Mary's instructions, he'd taken Stacie for a drive through the park in the afternoon. According to Mary, that should have been their only engagement for the day, but Stacie had suggested he dine with her and Ernestine that evening—a quiet, private dinner with just the three of them for company. Inwardly, he'd leapt at the chance; outwardly, he'd concealed his eagerness and accepted the invitation and had passed a pleasant evening with the two ladies. At their urging, he'd told them of his travels. Stacie's eyes had lit when he'd described the great opera houses of the Continent, and she'd later admitted that visiting such places in Vienna, Strasbourg, Venice, Milan, and Rome was an abiding dream.

He'd taken due note, then—to his own considerable surprise—had suggested that he repay the ladies' generosity by playing for them. Stacie and Ernestine had eagerly accepted; Stacie had opened the doors between the drawing room and music room, and while Ernestine had remained in her armchair in the drawing room, listening to the gentle sonata he chose to play, Stacie had come and leaned against the piano and listened; in reality, he'd played for her.

Never before had he voluntarily offered to play for a lady. Never before had he watched a lady's face as he played—and felt such a connection he'd almost been afraid.

That moment still lived in his mind.

He hadn't previously spent much if any time thinking about marriage; he had imagined waiting until he was closer to forty before biting the bullet and engaging with the marriage mart and, through a tedious process, acquiring a suitable bride.

Then Stacie had pushed her way into his life and caught, first, his attention, and then, his eye.

And then had come that moment when they'd fallen on the chaise, and his physical, visceral reaction to her had been stunningly intense.

He should have paid more attention to that—to what such a powerful reaction presaged—but in the circumstances, seizing the opportunity and securing Stacie as his bride had seemed the easiest way forward. No dealing with the marriage mart, and a lady with whom he shared more than he'd imagined possible.

In hindsight, he should also have been wary of that feeling of taking the easy way out; Fate had a habit of presenting her lures as attractively simple and straightforward.

There was, he now knew, nothing simple and straightforward about securing Stacie as his bride.

And of course, in drawing her inch by inch closer to him, he'd inevitably drawn closer to her, leaving him determined to succeed—for the truly simple reason that there was no longer any alternative, at least none acceptable to him.

He studied that conclusion for several minutes, then blew out a breath. "So—what's my next step?"

He was debating his options when Fortingale tapped and entered.

"Mr. Camber is here to see you, my lord."

Frederick sat up. "Excellent. Show him in."

Camber duly appeared; Frederick waved him to an armchair before the desk.

The inquiry agent came forward, bowed, and sat. As soon as the door clicked shut, Camber said, "Regarding your latest commission, my lord, I've managed to compile a fairly detailed report."

Frederick sat back and gestured for Camber to continue.

"I tracked down a gentleman who, for the last five or so years of her life, was known to be the late marchioness's close confidante—he was referred to by many as her cicisbeo and was reputed to know all her secrets."

Frederick wondered if Ryder and Rand knew of the man's existence. "His name?"

"The Honorable Mr. Claude Potherby, my lord. He currently lives a lonely life in a tiny village outside Leeds. When I called, Potherby was quite happy to talk to me—I got the impression he rarely has company and welcomed even mine."

"I see." Frederick made a mental note to tell Ryder and Rand of Potherby. If they'd bought the man's silence, as Frederick would have assuredly done had he been in their shoes, then Potherby seemed to have forgotten. Or perhaps they'd forgotten Potherby? In either case, they needed to know. "I assume Potherby was a font of information?"

Camber nodded soberly. "He was, indeed, my lord." Camber paused, then said, "It was almost as if being able to speak about the subject was... well, cathartic. I got the impression he hadn't been asked about the late marchioness by anyone, and so all he knew was bottled up in his head. If I was asked to swear to it, I'd say he spoke honestly—he was relieved to be able to let it all out."

"And what did he say with regard to my particular interest?"

"First, that the daughter is the spitting image of her mother, but very different in character. It seems the late marchioness was a particularly nasty sort, a past master at manipulation and, specifically, at using it to cause her husband pain of the emotional sort. According to Potherby—who apparently had known the late marchioness from childhood—she had always been cruel, but she was very beautiful and also very clever at hiding her true colors. In his words, people saw the beauty and not the rotten core. He admitted to being devoted to her in his way, but he wasn't blind to her faults. Apparently, while her husband was alive, he was her principal target, but she was always very ready to wield her manipulative skills to hurt others. Potherby said that, in his view, she gloried in causing others pain."

Camber paused to draw breath. "But to pass on to the late marchioness's children, apparently, she possessed no maternal feelings for any of them but viewed them as her chattels to eventually be sold on the marriage mart. Potherby insisted that was her principal focus in the years prior to her death—how to make the most by essentially selling her children in marriage."

Camber fought to hide his disgust; Frederick hoped he himself was more successful.

"Anyway," Camber went on, "it seems one good thing about her having that aim is that she took great care of her children's reputations and especially that of the daughter. However, Potherby believes that the young lady inherited her mother's talent for manipulating people, along with her looks. Quite what that actually means about the daughter, he swore he couldn't say, but he was certain the girl was appalled by her mother's vicious behavior and, he suspects, would have done something to counter it if she'd been able. As it was, with the late marchioness keeping her daughter very close, the girl was forced to witness many acts of outright cruelty perpetrated by her mother, both on her father and on others."

Frederick inwardly swore.

"Further to that"—Camber paused to draw in a breath before continuing—"Potherby recalled a specific instance when the girl tried to protest the late marchioness's actions toward the girl's father, and the marchioness lectured her daughter that the marchioness's actions and those like it were the only way to deal with a husband—that it was necessary to make his heart bleed to keep him in line."

Frederick simply stared; even swearing was beyond him.

After several long moments of staring back, Camber, his stoic expression unrevealing, said, "That's the sum of what Potherby told me. Nothing I learned from any other source contradicted anything Potherby said, and regarding those matters more widely known, other sources confirmed the man's stories."

Cold fury raged through Frederick, but he had no outlet for it; Stacie's unnatural mother was long dead. He steepled his fingers before his face and forced himself to replay all Camber had told him to make sure he would remember every word.

Eventually, he lowered his hands and refocused on Camber, who had remained silent and still. "Thank you. As always, your service has been exemplary. Send in your account—I'll be doubling the rate as you've delivered so quickly and so thoroughly."

Camber inclined his head. "Thank you, my lord."

"Now"—Frederick reached out, lifted a sheet from a stack to the side of the desk, glanced at it, and held it out to Camber—"returning to matters musical, for your next foray, I would like you to attend this auction in Glasgow and bid for me on the circled item."

Camber took the sheet, scanned it, then nodded. "What sort of price should I expect, and what's your upper limit?"

Frederick settled to discuss the details of the auction of an old gentleman's library that contained a very old and rare text on Egyptian music that Frederick was determined to add to his collection.

Camber jotted notes on the auction notice. "What competition might I have?"

"I can't say—that sheet was all the auctioneers put out. An acquaintance in Scotland noticed the item and sent it on to me. How many other collectors might have learned of that volume being amongst what is otherwise dross, I can't even guess, but there's always the possibility someone else has heard of it."

Someone like Brougham, who no doubt also had acquaintances around the country who knew of his passion.

Camber met Frederick's gaze. "You didn't say how high I should go."

After a second of debating, Frederick replied, "I don't care how high —I'll leave that in your hands—but I want that book."

"Aye, my lord." Camber rose. "I'll make sure you get it."

With a nod, Frederick dismissed Camber and watched the man leave. When the door shut behind his heavy frame, Frederick leaned back in his chair and let his mind return to what Camber had said of Stacie's mother.

As he juggled the various insights Potherby had shared and set them against his own observations, several aspects stood out.

Manipulation was one such recurring note. In their initial interactions, before he'd agreed to play for her event, Stacie had, he felt certain, thought she was manipulating him. He'd seen through her ploys from the first, not that she had attempted to conceal them—indeed, for someone skilled in the art, she'd been remarkably forthright regarding her machinations; she hadn't cared that he'd noticed.

She hadn't been trying to pull the wool over his eyes but rather to open them. A telling difference, that.

As it transpired, he was considered to be an arch-manipulator. His mother, his sisters, and even his close friends would all happily testify as to how easy he found it to nudge people into doing what he wished.

That skill was one of the reasons he was widely acknowledged as someone who always got his own way.

But being a manipulator meant one tended to recognize the trait in others—as he had in Stacie and also in Ryder and in Mary, and they had in him. More, it was generally accepted that manipulating a manipulator wasn't easy and, often, was well-nigh impossible; they knew all the tricks.

Consequently, while he'd recognized what Stacie was doing, he'd gone along with her promptings for his own reasons, not because she'd succeeded in steering him along.

He stared unseeing across the room. "But does she know that?"

Thinking back, he couldn't be sure that she did, that she'd realized he'd seen through her efforts completely; at the time, if anything, he'd hidden the extent of his awareness from her. It was, therefore, perfectly possible that she thought she had and could manipulate him.

The more he turned over the pieces of the puzzle Camber had laid before him, he felt increasingly sure that a large part of the reason for Stacie's aversion to marriage lay in the combination or concatenation of three things: her constantly lauded physical similarity to her mother, the ability to manipulate that she'd inherited from her mother, and her mother's use of manipulation to harm others, especially her husband.

Make his heart bleed to keep him in line.

Just the thought of the impact that concept would have had on a girl as given to caring for others as Stacie made Frederick feel physically ill.

Regardless, that much, he felt was now clear. Much less clear was how, exactly, those three factors came together in Stacie's mind to set her so adamantly against marriage.

She couldn't possibly believe that she would act as her mother had. Both Godfrey and Mary had stated what Frederick had had confirmed from countless sources, including his own observations: In character, Stacie was nothing like her mother. Instead, she was a naturally caring and nurturing soul—a person inherently kind, who consciously tried to do good, even when manipulating others, which she would only do if she was convinced it was for those others' own good.

He sat and, in light of what he now knew, tried to make sense of her stance—and as with all such things female, found that a wasted exercise. He simply couldn't see what lay at the root of her resistance to marriage.

He shook his head and sat up. "I'm still missing a piece of the puzzle. The central piece, what's more."

He still couldn't see the picture clearly.

As he studied the landscape of their interactions, a whimsical thought bloomed in his mind—that Stacie was like a fairy-tale princess whose evil mother had planted a hedge of thorns all around her and trapped her inside, holding her forever in thrall.

He was going to rip up that hedge, eradicate it root and branch; it had held Stacie captive for far too long, and he was determined to free her.

Jaw setting, he nodded. "So I attack the roots."

Imagining that, slowly, he arched his brows. How was he to convince Stacie that she would never be like her mother when she was constantly being informed just how very much like her mother she was?

Stacie sat in the Raventhorne House drawing room and laughed at the antics of Clarissa, her three-year-old niece, who was playing on the terrace outside the open windows. Mary had summoned all the family's female members to welcome a cousin's baby into the fold, and Clarissa was pushing the empty perambulator back and forth along the terrace, apparently pretending to be a nursemaid.

Felicia lowered herself into the armchair beside Stacie's. "This is such a lovely idea—getting all the ladies together to meet the new addition."

Stacie smiled. "Yours will be next." Felicia and Rand's baby was due to be born in late May or perhaps June.

"And after that will come Sylvia and Kit's little one in September." Felicia directed a fond look across the room at Sylvia, a childhood friend and now her sister-in-law. "She's certainly got that telltale glow."

"Auntie Stacie!" Having spotted Stacie, Clarissa had abandoned the pram and come pelting indoors. She skidded to a stop before Stacie and slapped her little hands on Stacie's knees. Beaming at Stacie, the little girl, with curls the same tawny blond as her father's and her mother's blue eyes, jigged up and down. "Up! Up!"

Stacie laughed, leaned forward, scooped the little girl into her arms, and deposited her in her lap. Clarissa wriggled around to face the room, then leaned back, making herself comfortable against Stacie.

Smiling, Stacie settled her arms loosely around Clarissa's warm little body. "And how's my poppet?"

Clarissa raised her chin. "I'm Daddy's poppet, too."

"Indeed, you are. But you can be my poppet as well," Stacie said.

Clarissa nodded seriously. "Good." Turning her head, she shot a mischievous look at Stacie. "I like being your poppet." Lowering her voice, she confided, "It's best that Daddy doesn't think I'm only his."

Felicia struggled to mute her laugh.

When Clarissa solemnly faced the room again, Stacie arched a brow at her sister-in-law. "From the mouth of babes."

Felicia smiled and nodded. "Indeed."

Mary and Ryder's boys—Julian, now six, and Arthur, five—were out with their tutor, but three other youngsters—a boy and two girls, children of other Cavanaugh cousins, who had been playing a game in a corner—had heard Clarissa's squeal, seen Stacie, and after some debate, abandoned their game in favor of begging Stacie for a story.

Clarissa—entrenched in pride of place in Stacie's lap—added her voice, distinctly more dominant, to the plea.

"All right," Stacie said. "But you must all sit quietly while I tell it."

The three promptly settled on the rug before her feet, and Clarissa wriggled down to join them so she could watch Stacie's face as she told the tale with all the histrionic flair at her command.

"Are you ready?" Stacie asked.

Eyes big, the children nodded.

"Very well—today, I'll tell you the tale of Little Red Riding Hood." Stacie proceeded to deliver the fairy tale, much as if she'd been on a stage and the four children her audience. They oohed and aahed and clapped in delight as she told them of the little girl who set out to take her grandmother some buns.

When Julian, Ryder and Mary's eldest son, had turned one year old, Stacie had bought a copy of *Perrault's Mother Goose Tales* and, gradually, over the ensuing years, had familiarized herself with most of the stories. To the children, she was now the storyteller of the family, and she delighted in the role.

Her one real regret over her refusal to consider marriage was that she would, therefore, never have children of her own. She'd always loved children; watching them evolve from infants through childhood and their teenage years to their adult selves had always fascinated her, and she possessed an innate knack of engaging with youngsters of any age.

But not even for the chance of having a child of her own would she rethink her refusal to marry; what good would her love for a child be if she meanwhile destroyed its father?

More, while she felt like this about children now, when it came to children of her own, how could she be certain that she wouldn't turn into her mother?

Courting such a risk was potentially too damaging for everyone involved, so she determinedly made do with her nieces, nephews, and cousins' children. When she reached the triumphant end of Little Red Riding Hood's story, she had the four at her feet cheering.

Cradling the new baby, Mary appeared beside Stacie. "I believe you're the most appropriate person to introduce this little one to our younger family members." Leaning down, Mary handed the infant to Stacie. Spontaneously smiling, Stacie accepted the warmly wrapped bundle and settled the baby in her arms.

She drew back the fine muslin so she could look down into the tiny, round, pudgy face. The other four children scrambled to their feet and pressed close about Stacie's legs, the better to peer at the baby.

"Not too close," she warned. "This is Rex Maximillian. He's come to join our family."

"Why isn't he opening his eyes?"

"Can he play with us?"

"Can I push him in his pram?"

Stacie fielded the questions with gentle authority, aware of Mary's too-understanding gaze trained on her face.

The children eventually convinced themselves that Rex in his current form was unlikely to actively engage with them and drifted back to their previously discarded game.

By then, Rex's warm weight had sunk through Stacie's gown, and when he stirred and turned toward her, the urge to cuddle him close was nearly overpowering. She resettled his wrap, rose, and carried him back to his mother.

After handing over the infant, she remained for a few more minutes, long enough for several of her relatives to comment on the subdued nature of her engagement celebrations. Her explanation that Frederick was a rather private individual rang true and was accepted, however grudgingly, by all.

Intending to slip away, Stacie turned to the door, only to have Clarissa bound up and clutch her hand.

"Come and play, Auntie Stacie!" The blond angel bounced up and down.

Stacie looked into Clarissa's bright eyes and reflected that no child would ever have approached Stacie's mother in that way. Stacie smiled and crouched down so her face and Clarissa's were closer to level. "I have to go now, and you have your cousins to play with."

Clarissa pouted. "But they're not you! And they can't tell stories!"

Stacie laughed and rose. "Be that as it may, poppet"—she ruffled Clarissa's curls—"I need to be on my way."

Clarissa's eyes searched hers, assessing her determination, then the little girl's expression eased into reluctant acceptance. "All right." She flung her arms around Stacie's legs, pressed her face into Stacie's gown, and hugged tight. "I'll be good and say goodbye." The words were muffled, then Clarissa released her, danced back, and waved. "Goodbye!"

Stacie laughed, waved, and before anyone else could catch her, found Mary, whispered that she was off, briefly squeezed Mary's arm, and determinedly made for the drawing room door.

She paused in the doorway and looked back on a scene that spoke of family and the central role of women in establishing and nurturing that— a role that called to her, that she yearned for, yet had accepted could never be hers.

Stacie turned and left. Her inner yearning would have to be satisfied with what came her way via the safer role of spinster aunt.

～

The next morning, bright and early, Stacie rode out to meet Frederick in the park, with, as usual, her groom trailing behind. As she trotted her mare out of Green Street and into Park Lane, her mind drifted over the events of the previous evening. She and Frederick had elected to attend a soirée at Lord and Lady Manning's house; the conversation had revolved about politics, business, and investments rather than the usual superficial ton topics, which had been a welcome change.

The difference had kept her on her mental toes and prevented her from thinking of other things, which had been all to the good. Would that that state had extended to the rest of her night. Instead, once in her bed, she'd spent hours restless and wakeful, unable to find sleep—which she blamed wholly on the aftereffects of Mary's morning gathering.

Stirring those yearnings she normally kept deeply suppressed always left her feeling…empty. Unfulfilled and unhappy when there really was no reason to feel that way.

These days, her life was one many would be delighted to have.

Sternly telling herself that, she turned her mare in at the Grosvenor Gate and saw Frederick mounted on his gray, waiting a little way ahead.

She summoned a suitably bright smile and trotted over to join him. "Good morning, my lord."

With a slow, appreciative smile, he gracefully inclined his head. "My lady." The gray shifted, and Frederick looked southward, then, gathering his reins, arched a brow at her. "Shall we?"

With a dip of her head, she turned her mare toward the beginning of Rotten Row.

They cantered beneath the trees, and she told herself to concentrate on the moment—on riding with Frederick and the associated simple pleasures—and not let any other thoughts intrude.

While she was reasonably successful in directing her thoughts, her feelings were less easy to corral.

Frederick sensed her distance, her distraction. After they'd galloped down the tan and turned their horses to walk back for a second run, he studied her face more closely and realized she was pensive.

Instinct prodded. He'd been waiting, watching for just the right moment to broach the sensitive topic that, at least in his mind, hovered between them.

He would have to speak soon, and his manipulator's instincts were insisting that this moment was propitious.

Should he speak? Or risk waiting for some even better time?

And if no other good chance came his way?

Yet something in him still balked at the prospect of rolling the dice—she might refuse him, and then what?

He glanced around. There was no one within hearing distance. Before he could think any further, he drew breath and, in an even but quiet—private—tone said, "It seems to me that, since announcing our engagement, we've rubbed along very well." When she glanced at him, he caught her eyes, arched a brow, and gently smiled. "For instance, I haven't previously shared my morning rides with any lady, yet I enjoy our gallops."

She dipped her head. "I do, too. I love to ride, and given my brothers are rarely available these days, I haven't recently been able to indulge in the pastime. As you know, a single lady galloping down Rotten Row is frowned upon and not just by the grandes dames."

He nodded. "There's our shared appreciation of good music, too, which reaches deeper than most of our peers."

Her lips quirked upward. "It's not easy to find someone willing to sit through an opera a second time just because there's a new first violin."

He chuckled. "Indeed. I have to admit that, on occasions such as that, I usually end up going alone."

Their gazes met and held as the obvious extension—that she would always readily accompany him—hovered between them.

He couldn't risk the moment stretching too thin. "Even last night," he smoothly went on, "I gathered from the discussions that your views on politics and business largely align with mine."

"Given our families, that's probably not surprising."

"Indeed—and then there are our families and, more, our views of society." He didn't have to fabricate his wryness as he said, "Despite our station, it seems you and I both prefer to live quietly, outside the glare of the ton."

"Definitely." After a moment, she added, "We are remarkably well matched."

He could never hope for a better moment. They were almost back to the head of the track. He edged his horse higher on the verge and drew rein, and obligingly, she halted her mare alongside.

When she looked his way, her brows arching in question, he met her eyes. "In light of all the above, I can't help but wonder if us actually marrying each other wouldn't be the answer to both our prayers."

Stacie held Frederick's gaze and waited for her instinctive, violent aversion to marriage to leap to the front of her mind. But that habitual reaction didn't materialize—at least not as her first thought. Instead, she found herself tilting her head, regarding him steadily, and with wary curiosity, asking, "How so?"

"Well, in my case"—his gaze remained on her face—"marrying you will rank as me very satisfactorily doing my duty to the title, which will mean my mother, sisters, and older relatives will cease badgering me over doing just that, and I will no longer be hounded to distraction during those times I choose to appear within the ton—for instance, at your musical evenings or at the theater or opera. You have no idea what a relief these last few evenings have been, now that the ton has accepted our engagement and I'm no longer viewed as an unclaimed eligible nobleman."

She couldn't help gently smiling; she knew the ways of their world.

He continued, "And in my eyes, best and most important of all is your understanding and appreciation of music. That's something I could never hope to find in any other." His gaze held hers. "You are unique—I have never come across a lady who would fit the position of my marchioness as perfectly as you."

He paused, then went on, "That our engagement was initially proposed as temporary protection shouldn't blind us to the fact that us marrying could well be in the best interests of us both, nor is there anything in our current situation that should discourage us from changing our minds and making our faux engagement real."

The mare shifted, and Stacie glanced at the horse and patted its neck. She knew—in her mind, in her heart—that all he'd said was true. Yet even though her usual aversion had yet to strike with full force, she knew the picture he was painting simply could not be.

Regardless, most strangely—and she had no idea why—curiosity was still trumping, still holding back her usual panic, her invariable recoil from and denial of any suggestion of her marrying.

Perhaps because he was being so utterly reasonable and...unpushy. She sensed no pressure from him at all, no threat; this was just another discussion between them, albeit one of potentially life-changing consequence. She raised her head, met his eyes, and rather challengingly asked, "What do you see as the benefits for me?"

Frederick held tight to his purpose and fought to hit the right note—one of cataloging the obvious. "Quite aside from consolidating your position in wider society and bestowing all the benefits and freedoms accruing to a married lady, marrying me will reassure your family as nothing else will—despite their outward acceptance of your decision not to wed, they worry about you and your future. Deep down, all would prefer to see you suitably married, and you marrying me will come as a relief."

He paused to see if she might feel prompted to volunteer something of the reason behind her decision not to wed, but when she remained silent, one dark brow slowly arching as if to inquire if that was all he had to say, he went on, "Most importantly, however, you becoming my marchioness will give you all the position you could wish for and all the clout you might need to engage with the ton in support of worthy local musicians.

"The goal you've embraced as your life's work is to introduce local musicians to the ton—to create an avenue whereby they get the right sort of exposure so they gain patrons who can advance their careers. That, I've discovered, is important to me as well, and I will continue to support you regardless of any formal connection between us." He clung to her gaze. "However, you know, as do I, that the best—the most effective and certain—route to achieving your goal, which I now share, is to become my marchioness—to throw in your lot with mine and work with me to convert our sham engagement into a real one."

Pensiveness had returned to her eyes and brought a frown along with it. Frederick braced to hear her reject the notion out of hand.

Instead, after a moment that seemed to stretch forever, she blinked, refocused on him, studied his face, then glanced around.

More riders had arrived, and the queue for the track was lengthy.

"I believe I'll return to Green Street." She shook her reins and turned her mare.

Frederick swallowed his temper along with his impatience and, lips thinning, nudged the gray to pace alongside.

He held his tongue—there was nothing more he wanted to say—and waited as they trotted their mounts back up the park, then slowed and walked through the gate back into Park Lane.

By then, he was growing curious. She hadn't reiterated her refusal to even consider marriage. Presumably, that meant she was considering it— or at least, considering what he'd said. If so, the last thing he should do was prod her.

They reached the cobbles outside her front door, and still, she'd said not a word. He dismounted, handed his reins to her groom, and went to lift her down. He closed his hands about her waist and, for once, sensed no real reaction to his touch; admittedly, over the course of the past week, she'd grown much more accustomed to it. Searching her face as he lifted her to the pavement, he saw that, if anything, her pensiveness had deep- ened, and so had her frown; the latter now knitted her fine brows.

With her feet on the ground, she finally looked up at him.

He held himself unmoving as, her lips tight, she studied his face and his eyes. Finally, unable to hold back the words, he arched a brow at her. "What do you think of my suggestion?" In effect, his proposal.

Her lips compressed even more, then eased. "I feel that I should be telling you—again—that marriage is not for me." She held his gaze. "Not even marriage to you." She paused, then drew breath and said, "As it is…" Her frown deepened still further, then she reached out and lightly squeezed his arm. "I don't know what to say to you other than I'll think about it."

He couldn't whoop in triumph—and that was hardly an acceptance.

With his features schooled to utter impassivity, he inclined his head, then waved her to her door.

He followed her up the steps and, when the door opened, bowed over her hand, straightened, then leaned close and touched his lips to her cheek before releasing her and, with a final salute, walking down the steps to where her groom held the horses.

CHAPTER 12

That evening, Stacie and Frederick attended a dinner that had the potential to prove significant in garnering support for local musicians via a connection to the respective music schools of both Oxford and Cambridge Universities.

Stacie had learned that, while Frederick was a graduate of Christchurch College in Oxford, that university's premier school for musicians and musical historians, Lord Brougham, after leaving Eton at the same time as Frederick, had taken his degree at Kings College, Cambridge. She'd been given to understand, from others as well as from the men themselves, that no greater rivalry existed in the annals of music than that between those two university colleges.

Yet in the matter of the quality of the three young musicians who had performed at her musical evening, Frederick had made an effort to elicit Brougham's opinion, and for his part, Brougham had been genuinely supportive, albeit in his rather stiff way.

Although in ton terms, the dinner was restrained and relatively quiet, intellectually, the conversation was stimulating, intense, and demanding. Quite exhausting, in its way.

By the time Stacie climbed the stairs and opened her bedroom door, she was flagging—and immeasurably glad that Frederick hadn't pressed her to discuss his suggestion of the morning further, either on the way to Grosvenor Square or during the return journey.

Kitty, Stacie's maid, was waiting to help her out of her gown and brush out her hair. "So was the dinner worthwhile, my lady?"

While dressing for the evening, she'd explained to Kitty what she and Frederick had hoped to achieve at the dinner. Stacie stretched her neck by tipping her head from side to side. "I think so. At the very least, there's now considerably more awareness of the potential quality of our locally trained musicians, and that's all to the good."

Kitty chattered on, filling Stacie in on how Ernestine had spent her evening and how things were going below stairs; Kitty had long acted as Stacie's eyes and ears within her household.

Reassured that no domestic issue required her attention, Stacie allowed Kitty to drop her nightgown over her head, then shooed the maid away to her rest and headed for her own.

Kitty grinned and bobbed a curtsy. "Goodnight, my lady." She slipped out of the door and pulled it shut behind her.

Stacie climbed between the cool sheets, laid her head on the pillow, and sighed. After a moment, she reached out and turned down the lamp on her nightstand.

Darkness enveloped her. She closed her eyes and willed herself to sleep.

Only to find, as she'd feared would be the case, that her mind, finally free of all other distractions, promptly returned to Frederick's suggestion.

It would undoubtedly be easier to pretend he'd never made it, that she'd never heard the words, but her mind wasn't having that. She had heard, and entirely contrary to her expectations, the greater part of her conscious self wanted to—as she'd informed him—*think* about it.

On the one hand, that seemed absurd; she knew perfectly well why she didn't dare accept any man's proposal. It was safer for everyone that way.

On the other hand...there was equally no question as to the genuine value of the benefits Frederick had described; indeed, many of those had been on show throughout the evening. Being the partner of Lord Frederick Brampton, Marquess of Albury, musical scholar and renowned pianist, had elevated her to a position where everything she'd said that had touched on music had been listened to carefully and treated with respect.

As Lady Eustacia Cavanaugh, she was accorded the respect due her rank, but as Frederick's partner, she was instantly transformed into someone whose opinions on music mattered to the musical world and, indeed, to the world at large.

The same opinions, just advanced from a different stage.

She might have thought he'd planned it—making his suggestion in the morning, knowing the advantages would be amply demonstrated that evening. "Except *I* was the one who insisted we attend the dinner." He'd been reluctant, but had allowed himself to be talked around.

Sleep, clearly, wasn't going to be hers anytime soon. She opened her eyes and stared at the underside of her tester bed's canopy.

She should have told him no. Categorically no. She still didn't understand why she hadn't.

Instead, she'd told him she would think about his suggestion, implying an evaluation of sorts. To her mind, it was, therefore, incumbent on her to undertake at least a review. "At the bare minimum, I'm going to have to come up with understandable, explainable, and preferably irrefutable reasons for refusing him."

She'd learned enough of him to be certain that, this time, he wouldn't accept a single-word dismissal.

"So, to the pros and cons. The pros are obvious—he listed most of them. The ones he didn't mention"—such as that marriage to him might enable her to have children of her own, satisfying a yearning that had only grown stronger over the past year of seeing Rand and Kit marry and set up their nurseries—"I'm already aware of, and I don't need to add any further weight to his list."

For instance, by enumerating his personal attributes—his temperament, his relative unflappability and natural decisiveness, his intelligence, his musical talent, that he danced like a dream and was handsome enough to turn her head and set her pulse racing. On top of that, he'd shown an unexpected ability to understand her, and he'd never expected her to be anyone other than herself. More, he seemed to actually *see* her, clearly and without the veneer of his own expectations, and was confident enough in himself to deal with her openly and directly...

She frowned at the canopy, then, in a whisper, admitted, "The pros are substantial."

Indeed, with no other gentleman had she even bothered considering advantages, let alone felt...as if she should allow herself to be tempted.

"Dangerous," she murmured. Lord Frederick Brampton, Marquess of Albury, had proved to be more so than she'd imagined he could be.

"That brings me to the cons." To the tangle of her fears that she hadn't truly examined for years.

She paused, vacillating, then accepted that she wouldn't be able to look Frederick in the eye and refuse him if she didn't take the lid off what, for her, loomed as Pandora's box and examine what lay inside, before setting the lid firmly back in place.

Because nothing would have changed; the basis of her fear of marriage was immutable, and time had no power to erode it.

She forced herself to do it—to lift the tangled skein of her memories from the mental box in which she'd locked it, tease out the strands, and critically study each one. She hadn't ever done that, but in light of the challenge of Frederick's suggestion, it was, she supposed, time she did. Not that she held out any hope that the total weight of her cons would have miraculously lightened enough for the pros to tip the scales Frederick's way, but she had to at least keep faith with him and properly assess both sides.

So she let herself remember—vividly remember—her father and his love, the true and utterly unconditional love he had borne for her mother. How her mother had exploited that love, the existence of it, as the chink in her father's self-armor and inflicted cruelty upon cruelty, devastating attacks that would simply not have been possible if her father hadn't possessed such a weakness—if he hadn't carried the vulnerability caused by his love for her mother. If it hadn't been for his abiding, forgiving, enduring love.

None of her three brothers, not even Godfrey, had seen the truth; sent away to school, they'd seen and known very little of the worst incidents, but Stacie had been there, always there, and she'd heard, seen, and understood.

Her heart had bled for her father, while his had been broken again and again, until, at the last, he'd closed his eyes and died.

If anyone had ever died of a broken heart, it was he.

Since that time, she'd held to one overriding, unflinching, unshakeable purpose—to the silent vow she'd made on her father's grave: that she would never, ever, become like her mother.

The surest way to guard against that had been—and arguably still was—never to marry.

In the nearly fourteen years since she'd first made that vow, nothing had occurred to make her reassess her chosen way of fulfilling it.

But now, there was Frederick and the unexpected situation in which they found themselves—all through no fault of their own.

She paused as, on one level, her mind cleared.

Here she was, against all expectations, actually considering the pros and cons of marrying him...because he and all his pros had made her want enough, desire enough, to hope there might be some way...

"Really?"

Yes, really—why else am I putting myself through this?

She blew out a breath. "Yes, all right." Now she was talking to herself, but perhaps speaking the words aloud might help.

Honesty would help, too. She closed her eyes and said, "Becoming Frederick's marchioness...is tempting."

More than tempting—the position fits me so remarkably well that it lures me with the intensity of a siren's song.

Eyes still closed, she grimaced. "That's why I didn't—couldn't bring myself to—immediately say no."

She'd actually wanted to force herself to reassess—to see if there was some way she might claim what he was offering.

And if she was going to deal honestly, then one point she'd omitted on the pro side was a corollary of having children—that being Frederick's wife would give her the chance to explore and enjoy the delights of the marriage bed, legitimately and with a partner whose touch set her nerves leaping and her senses slavering without him even meaning to. She, after all, had been the one to initiate that reckless kiss in Lady Waltham's folly —all because she hadn't been able to resist the compulsion to learn if his kiss would be different from her previous experiences, and it had been.

Startlingly so. Passionately so.

She couldn't pretend, even to herself, that she didn't desire him.

"As for having children..." If, with Frederick, she brought children into this world, it would be into the embrace of a large and supportive family, as witnessed by Mary's event of yesterday. Her mother had refused to allow let alone encourage any such familial interaction. "She wanted to keep us dependent on her, tied to her apron strings until she consented to cut us loose—for a price." Any children she had with Frederick would have a very different life from the isolation she and Godfrey especially, kept tight under her mother's wing, had endured. "Our children would be safe—I don't need to refuse him out of concern on that score."

Indeed, now she'd matured enough to understand the tug she felt over children, she'd realized she possessed the full gamut of maternal instincts, something her mother had never demonstrated in even the smallest degree. That had been a critical and glaring lack in her mother's psyche, one she now felt confident she didn't share.

Well and good—I've just convinced myself that no amount of concern over children or the marriage bed should stand in the way of me accepting Frederick.

She frowned, but couldn't deny that conclusion or the one to which it ultimately led. "I could be happy being his wife. I would no longer be alone within the ton, I would have a household to manage and, with luck, children to love." Those were her long-ago girlish aspirations, before she'd set aside all thought of marriage. "On top of that, I would have a husband I already respect, a gentleman who shares many of my own interests, and who is amenable to helping me achieve my chosen purpose of helping local musicians."

What more could I possibly want?

She huffed, then admitted, "Nothing." After a moment, she added, "So why am I dithering?"

The answer to that was a lot longer in coming, but eventually, she dredged it up from the depths of her box of fears. "I don't want to hurt him." Like her mother had hurt her father.

That was the lynchpin, the crux of it all.

She firmed her lips, then opened them and confessed, "I am like her— I know I am. I manipulate people exactly as she did—sometimes without even thinking." She paused, then went on, "Others manipulate—Mary and Ryder both often do—but they aren't like me. They aren't *her* daughter—they don't carry her blood. I do, and I can never escape that. I might not want to hurt Frederick, not at first, but there's no guarantee that, over time, knowing I can, knowing exactly how to do it, the temptation to strike at him in that way won't prove irresistible. And once I start...I know how it will end."

That was her greatest fear—the fear that had made her vow never to marry.

"I couldn't bear to become like Mama and use a man's love, his love for me, to hurt and ultimately kill him. I would rather die an old maid."

That was indisputable.

Then she blinked and replayed what she'd just said—the simplest statement of her fundamental fear—and this time, paid attention to the words. In a wondering tone, she stated, "Hurting Frederick will only be possible if he loves me."

I don't think he does.

Rapidly—almost desperately—she replayed every moment she'd spent in his company. They got along, he and she, and yes, desire was undeniably there, but that was another lesson she'd learned at her mother's knee—lust and love weren't the same thing. One didn't equate to the other, didn't imply the existence of the other.

Eyes wide, she stared up at the canopy and battled to contain a sense of rising hope enough to continue to think.

Could she risk it?

Would she? Did she have the courage to grasp Frederick's proffered hand and make a bid for a happy life?

Did she truly believe she could? That such a much-desired outcome was possible without her falling prey to the unthinkable?

Or should she pander to her fear, retreat from taking such a risk-laden step, and continue on her path into a lonely future?

Those and similar questions circled around and around in her head and, ultimately, followed her into her dreams.

~

Stacie called at Albury House at half past ten, the earliest possible hour at which she could risk being seen treading up the steps of her fiancé's house.

Fortingale, Frederick's extremely correct butler, opened the door to her knock and masked his surprise well. He bowed her inside. "Lady Eustacia. I fear the marchioness has yet to leave her chamber."

"That's entirely all right, Fortingale." Looking down, she tugged off her gloves. "I haven't—"

"Stacie?"

She looked up and saw Frederick descending the long sweep of the grand staircase. Forgetting Fortingale even as the butler lifted her cape from her shoulders, she went forward to meet her supposed intended. "Good morning, my lord."

"Good morning, my lady." He stepped down to the hall tiles.

She stuffed her gloves into her reticule, pulled the strings tight, and halted before him.

With his gaze, sharp and searching, locked on her face, he grasped the hand she offered and smoothly raised it to his lips. "As always, I'm delighted to see you."

She ignored the frisson of awareness that raced over her skin at the brush of his lips over her bare knuckles. She'd ransacked her wardrobe to find the perfect gown to strike just the right note for this encounter and had settled on a severe creation in sapphire blue, trimmed with silver ribbon. Retrieving her hand, she raised her chin and met his gaze. "Might I claim a few minutes of your time?"

"Of course." He stepped back and waved her down a corridor. "My study might be more comfortable than the drawing room."

She acquiesced with a nod and allowed him to usher her down the corridor and into an elegantly proportioned room that, courtesy of the mahogany paneling and the bookshelves lining the walls, felt surprisingly cozy. A large desk stood in pride of place with two armchairs facing it, and a pair of wing chairs sat angled before the hearth, but Frederick led her to two comfortable leather armchairs that faced each other across a shallow alcove formed by three long windows that looked out on a small terrace. Trees bordered the terrace, and a small fountain spilled its waters in the center, creating a cool, green oasis that seemed far removed from the bustle of London's streets.

Her gaze on the greenery, she sank onto the leather and took a moment to steady her over-tense nerves. But the momentous moment wouldn't be denied; she drew in a long breath, refocused her wits, marshaled her courage and her determination, and shifted her gaze to Frederick as he sat in the chair opposite.

His expression remained impassive, but his eyes said he was watchful, waiting to learn what this was about.

She'd resolved to be honest, open, and direct; he deserved nothing less. Her head erect, her hands clasped tightly in her lap, she drew breath and plunged in. "Yesterday, you floated the idea of us making our engagement real." She met his eyes. "Were you serious?"

Hope surged through Frederick; instantly, he suppressed it and evenly replied, "Entirely. And I haven't changed my mind." When she didn't immediately go on, he prompted, "You said you would think about it."

She gave a tiny nod. "I've carefully considered the prospect—all the various aspects of it—and I have...certain reservations."

He would have been stunned had she simply agreed. "Such as?" He kept his tone as undemanding as he could.

Yet rather than answer the straightforward question, she continued,

"My reservations arise from the considerations that I've previously noted are too complicated to explain, which is something that hasn't changed. However"—she paused to draw in a tense breath before continuing—"my reservations can be overcome if you will agree to a stipulation—an agreed condition."

He masked his surprise. "One stipulation—one condition?"

Her nod was decisive and definite; from her expression, from her eyes, he could tell that she'd thought this through, and whatever her condition was, it was critically important to her.

He inclined his head. "And that condition is?"

Her gaze turned inward, and she hesitated, he sensed to gather her courage as well as her words, then she refocused on his eyes and said, "I need you to promise—on your honor—that you will never, ever, fall in love with me."

He stared at her and didn't move so much as an eyelash. He'd heard her words, had absorbed them, but for a long moment, he couldn't make sense of them.

Then he did.

His gaze was locked with hers and hers with his; he looked deep into her eyes—and felt as if the earth shifted beneath his feet.

Understanding slammed into him. He felt like sucking in a sharp breath, but controlled the urge and, more slowly, expanded his chest. To gain time—to give him a chance to regain his balance—he arched a noncommittal brow. "That's it?"

The tension gripping her was palpable. Without shifting her gaze from his, she nodded. "That's all I need to be certain of."

His wits were still reeling. How many gentlemen of his age and ilk would be thrilled to have such an ultimatum placed before them? He didn't doubt that her condition was, indeed, an ultimatum; if he didn't grant her stipulation, she wouldn't agree to be his wife.

He couldn't resist asking, "Doesn't it strike you that, in this day and age, your stipulation is a rather odd demand for a lady to make of her would-be husband?"

Her eyes narrowed, and her chin tipped up a notch. "Regardless, that's the promise I require before I will feel free to accept your proposal."

Free of what? "Why such a condition? Are you already in love with someone else? Or is some other gentleman in love with you? In the circumstances, those are highly pertinent questions."

Temper glimmered in her fine eyes and overrode the tension that until then had bound her. "No, I am not in love with any gentleman. Nor is any gentleman in love with me. I believe I can assure you on both those counts with absolute certainty. As for the reasons behind my stipulation, as I've already stated, those are too complex to explain."

He hadn't expected her to capitulate and reveal all, but it had been worth a try.

He studied her—the now-stubborn set of her delicate chin, the vibrant life he'd managed to spark in her eyes—and tried to piece together what her stipulation said of her and her reasons for avoiding matrimony... Why did she fear love? What danger did she see in him loving her? What threat did she perceive?

Given the personal reality he'd only just fully grasped, those were, arguably, the most pertinent questions.

But she was waiting, and he could delay giving her his answer for only so long. Yet...

Gentling his tone to one of supplication, he asked, "Can I ask why—why you feel the need for such a stipulation?"

He could almost see the answer forming in her eyes: *Because I...*

Yet after a long moment of studying him, she said, "Perhaps one day I'll be able to explain it to you, but at this point, my stipulation is the assurance I require in order to see my way clear to agreeing to your proposal." She paused, then added, "I need that promise, and I need to believe you will adhere to it."

He couldn't claim she wasn't being clear. And regardless of the oddity of her request, courtesy of the startling epiphany her making that request had brought crashing down on him, he was in a position to give her an answer he prayed she would accept, although the devil was in the phrasing. Holding her gaze, keeping his own rock-steady, he said, "On my honor, I promise that, should we wed, I will not, thereafter, fall in love with you."

As he understood it, falling in love was one of those acts that, once committed, had to be reversed before it could be repeated.

When she continued to stare at him, a frown forming in her eyes, he arched a brow at her. "Will that do?"

Stacie wasn't sure how to answer. He'd given her what she'd asked for, and she certainly didn't doubt his honor, yet for some reason, she was...not as assured as she needed to be. She studied his—as ever, uninformative—face, fleetingly compressed her lips, then replied, "I would feel a lot more comfortable—a lot more assured—if you will further agree that, if in some benighted future you do unintentionally fall in love with me, you will agree to a divorce."

He snorted dismissively. "In our circles? You know that's not going to happen."

She wasn't surprised by his refusal. She grimaced and shifted in the chair. She felt restless, on edge—on the cusp of seizing something she only now realized she truly and quite desperately wanted. It hung there, the ultimate prize, almost within her grasp, yet there was just one tiny, quibbling hurdle…

Abruptly, she flung her hands in the air and met his eyes. "Suggest something, then—some penalty that will convince me beyond all doubt, reasonable or otherwise, that you will exercise all your considerable willpower and take any and every step necessary to avoid breaking your promise not to fall in love with me."

His eyes narrowed on her face. After a tense moment, he nodded. "Very well. I swear that if, once we are wed, I break my promise and fall in love with you, I will donate my entire collection of musical texts to whomever you wish." His words were clipped, carrying a definite edge. He almost glared as he pointedly arched his brows at her. "Good enough?"

She glanced at the shelves lining the room.

As if reading her mind, he stated, "This isn't my collection—it's at Brampton Hall."

"I see." She replayed his words. She knew how much his collection meant to him; it embodied his chosen life-purpose. He would never willingly give that up or even put it at risk, not for any price. She couldn't ask for a more cast-iron guarantee.

His promise was enough to vanquish her lingering fears.

Before she'd left her room that morning, she'd made a pact with Fate, that if he gave her the promise she needed, she would accept his assurance, take his proffered hand, and marry him.

Her heart broke free of the shackles she'd placed upon it and soared.

She met his eyes and let him see her burgeoning happiness. "Thank you." Formally, she inclined her head to him. "Given your agreement to my stipulation and your promise, I would be honored to accept your suggestion to make our engagement real."

"And subsequently, marry me." His gaze steady on her eyes, he waited.

Smiling now, she nodded. "Yes." When he still waited, she parroted, "And subsequently, marry you."

Although apparently satisfied, he raised a staying hand. "Having reached that point, I find that I, too, have a stipulation to make."

She widened her eyes at him. "What?"

"That we marry as soon as possible—by special license."

Something like panic fluttered in her chest; she'd assumed they'd have an engagement that ran for months. "Why?"

Because I want my ring on your finger before you have a chance to change your mind. Frederick knew better than to utter those words. Instead, he advanced another equally valid reason. "Because once the ton —let alone our families—hear of us setting a date, we won't be allowed a moment's peace."

CHAPTER 13

$\mathcal{S}$ ix days later, Frederick stood facing the altar in St. George's Church in Hanover Square, praying that Stacie hadn't changed her mind and wishing the ceremony, at least, was over.

Unfortunately, it had yet to start. To his right stood Percy, with George beyond him, and at his back were ranged the select few who had been invited to witness this most restricted of ton events.

The wedding of Lady Eustacia Cavanaugh and Frederick, Marquess of Albury, was destined to set a new record for the smallest of haut ton weddings, much to the relief of both principal participants.

Six days of what Frederick mentally termed "fuss" were about to reach their culmination. Impatience of an unfamiliar sort pricked and prodded; he accepted the absolute necessity of the event, yet wanted it over and done with.

From the moment Stacie had walked into his mother's drawing room and into his life, she'd flung challenges his way, intentionally or otherwise. First, it had been luring him into performing once again before the ton, then she herself had become the source of subsequent challenges—to protect her reputation after they'd been discovered in a compromising situation, then to learn the secret of why she refused to marry, and ultimately, to persuade her to accept that they were a well-nigh perfect match and agree to marry him.

Now, to cap it all, she'd presented him with the challenge to beat all challenges—to overcome her irrational fear of him loving her before she realized he already did.

When she'd demanded he promise not to fall in love with her, it had been impossible to ignore the reality that, at some point over the previous weeks, he'd fallen victim to Cupid's bow. Without a whimper, without any real resistance; Stacie had woven a web of enthrallment, and he'd willingly succumbed.

At least, courtesy of her stipulation, he now had what he suspected was a reasonably accurate understanding of the root cause of her resistance to marriage, and to his mind, the implications weren't all bad.

Once he'd had a chance to reflect on her apparent aversion to him loving her, it hadn't required any huge deductive leap to guess that her father had loved her mother and that her mother had betrayed that love, causing her father untold pain. He'd confirmed with Ryder and Rand that Stacie had been devoted to her father, that he and she had been especially close. Put that together with the constant refrain that most likely had filled Stacie's ears ever since she could comprehend speech, namely that she was an exact replica of her mother, and the demand Stacie had made of him no longer seemed so strange.

The aspect of that which had given him most heart was that making such a demand of him was the equivalent of seeking to protect him. Stacie cared for him at least that much—enough to take steps to ensure that, by her reasoning, she wouldn't be able to cause him the same hurt her mother had visited on her father.

To his mind, that was a very large step in a positive direction—one he could work with and build upon. Now all he had to do was untangle her thinking and convince her that, despite the physical similarity, inside, in her character and in her heart, she wasn't and never would become a reincarnation of her mother.

Even if he loved her.

If he'd read what Stacie had revealed correctly, she saw him loving her as some sort of catalyst that would draw forth and feed the darkness of spirit that had characterized her mother. It would, therefore, be necessary to hide the true nature of his feelings until he'd convinced her that there was no danger in him loving her—until he'd overwritten and erased her mistaken belief that she would ever transform into a malignant harpy.

Luckily, hiding all softer emotions—more or less pretending not to love—was virtually a stock-in-trade for gentlemen like him. Indeed, in that regard, his late father had provided an exemplary role model; Frederick had never doubted his father had loved his mother, and his mother hadn't, either, yet no one viewing Frederick's father in public would have described his feelings toward his marchioness as noticeably warm.

Beside Frederick, Percy shifted, then whispered, "I haven't forgotten the ring."

Frederick nodded. It was the second time Percy had told him that; his friends were more nervous than he was. He was the first of their number to marry; no more than he had they played these roles before, and the last days had been enough to make anyone's head whirl.

It had been Wednesday morning when Stacie had come to see him, and after she'd agreed to marry him, they'd gone straight to Raventhorne House, where their news had been greeted with great elation and with very pointed congratulations directed his way. He'd left Stacie surrounded by her family and gone to the Old Deanery in the City to call on his distant connection, Charles Blomfield, currently the Bishop of London. Subsequently, armed with a special license, he and Stacie had visited the Rector of St. George's, Reverend Hodgson, and settled on the date and time. After that, they'd returned to Albury House and broken the news of their impending nuptials to his mother—who hadn't known whether to be thrilled that he would be married so soon or miffed for the same reason.

Thereafter, the family matriarchs—his mother and Mary—had taken over proceedings and dictated how things would be. He'd left Stacie to her sisters-in-law's devices, called on Percy and George and enlisted their support, then gone on to Moreton in Savile Row. The tailor had been quietly thrilled to receive Frederick's order of a new dove-gray morning suit and had assured him it would be delivered on Monday.

Frederick's next stop had been Aspreys; after finalizing his purchases there—the ruby parure and a worked gold band the same size as the ruby ring—he'd deemed his preparations complete and had retreated to his study at Albury House.

He felt sure Stacie's preparations had been a great deal more complex and harried—he'd known better than to inquire about her gown—yet although his mother and Mary had insisted on celebratory family dinners on Friday and Saturday evenings, those had merely replaced the events he and Stacie had had scheduled. That had suited him and Stacie both, and with Sunday being a day of rest even among the ton, and no one expecting them to attend events yesterday, the lead-up to the wedding had been not just swift but also largely out of sight of society.

Given that Stacie had specifically requested a small, intimate, family wedding, and Frederick had wanted the knot tied as quickly as possible, they had both managed to get what they'd wanted.

Frederick had been idly listening to the organ, critically noting the organist's shortcomings, when the music paused, then resumed with the opening chords of Mendelssohn's wedding march. Frederick had chosen the piece; he'd felt it fitting to have Stacie walk down the nave to him to the music of one of his favorite composers.

The change in tune meant that she was on her way. A sudden sense of teetering on some precipice seized him. He hauled in a slow breath, steeled himself, and turned.

All he could see was her—a slender yet curvaceous vision in ivory, pearls, and lace, with the finest of lace veils draped over her face and her glossy dark hair. Tiny seed pearls were liberally sprinkled over her bodice and gleamed from the folds of her skirt, while larger pearls circled her throat, bobbed at her ear lobes, and anchored the veil in her hair.

She was Venus-Aphrodite translated to the here and now, and she stole what little breath he'd managed to draw in and left him giddy.

He was vaguely aware of a young girl-child—presumably Ryder and Mary's daughter—cavorting ahead of Stacie and scattering white rose petals with gay abandon. Stacie was leaning on the arm of some man— Ryder, Frederick supposed—but he couldn't shift his attention from her enough to be sure.

As the music played and Stacie drew nearer and he could finally make out her eyes, large and shining behind the fine veil, the only thought that surfaced through the fog of his entrancement was that hiding his feelings for her had just become much harder.

Through her fine veil, Stacie studied Frederick as he watched her slow approach, and sensed more than saw that she'd succeeded in claiming every last iota of his attention. Sylvia, Felicia, and Mary had been right; all the hours she'd spent at the modiste's in pursuit of garnering just that reaction had been worth it.

She'd asked Ryder to walk her down the aisle, while Rand had accompanied her in the carriage to the church. Clarissa was dancing ahead of her, dispensing rose petals with unrestrained alacrity, while Mary walked a yard to the right to ensure her daughter adhered to their script.

Her nephews, Julian and Arthur, were acting as trainbearers, and Felicia and Sylvia, her matrons of honor, were following the pair.

This was the wedding she'd never thought to have, and in her eyes, it was perfect. Small, intimate, undemanding—an event she could enjoy without worrying who might think what. Only thirty guests, gathered in knots to either side, had been invited; all were either her family or Frederick's.

This was one journey she'd never thought to take, pacing down the center of St. George's nave to where Frederick waited, his eyes on hers, his hand rising and extending toward her as Ryder lifted her fingers from his sleeve and placed them in Frederick's outstretched hand.

Ryder stepped back, and she stepped forward.

Out of one life and into another—and not a hint of panic stirred.

Frederick's lips lifted in his slow, sensual smile as his fingers closed firmly around hers, then he turned, and she turned with him to face the altar and the Bishop of London, who, beaming, came forward to conduct the service.

She listened in a daze of awe and wonder as the familiar phrases rolled resonantly off the bishop's tongue, and she and Frederick made their responses and their vows in clear, confident voices. Then came the moment when Frederick raised her left hand and slipped a delicately worked gold band onto her third finger.

And he and she were married. The bishop declared it was so, and she looked up and saw relief, expectation, hope, and happiness in Frederick's hazel eyes and felt the same emotions bloom inside her.

This felt right—so very right. She'd made the correct decision.

Then, still smiling, Frederick tipped up her chin and bent his head, and his lips found hers in a kiss that spoke of promises—all those promises they hadn't discussed but which were there, nonetheless, intrinsic parts of their bargain.

When he raised his head, she felt giddy. He searched her eyes and grinned—a very male expression.

Then he took her hand and turned her to meet their well-wishers, and the crowd, gay, happy, and delighted, swamped them.

For several minutes, a melee of congratulations, kisses, and slapping of shoulders held sway. The bishop joined them, as did the rector and the organist, but eventually, the group found their way onto the porch and into the line of carriages waiting to ferry them to Mount Street and the wedding breakfast.

Frederick and Stacie traveled in the first landau. As the top was down, several ladies walking along the fashionable pavements of Grosvenor

Street spotted them, took in the profusion of her ivory lace veil and the pearl diadem anchoring it in her hair—saw Frederick in his morning suit sitting beside her—and halted, gasping, then, as they passed, immediately fell into rabid conversation.

She glanced at Frederick, and he arched a laconic brow. "I expect," she said, "that our secret wedding will be the talk of the ton this evening."

He lightly shrugged. "I don't care. By then, we'll have quit town."

She blinked her eyes wide. She hadn't thought to ask... "Where are we going?"

The curve of his lips deepened. Looking ahead, he raised her hand, the one he hadn't yet let go, pressed a kiss to her fingers, then lowered their linked hands to rest on his thigh. "I thought we should go to Brampton Hall. It's only just over two hours away, and it's quiet there, and as I spend most of the year there, I thought you would like to get to know the place."

She smiled and faced forward. "I would like that."

Now she'd taken the plunge and they'd married, she found that she was eager to get on—to learn more about him, about his households and estates. Not just so that she could be the most perfect wife but also because she was curious as to what those places would reveal of him.

Their wedding breakfast proved all she'd hoped it would be—a warm, joyous, family affair. Even Aurelia Brampton unbent enough to smile, and she seemed surprisingly uncensorious over the antics of Julian and Arthur, let alone Clarissa's insistence on depositing rose petals on every lady's lap.

With just over forty sitting down to dine, the company was easily accommodated in the formal dining room at Raventhorne House—the house Stacie considered her childhood home. A portrait of her father looked down the length of the table; once the formal toasts were completed, Stacie seized a moment to turn to the portrait and raise her glass in a silent salute to her sire.

As she turned back to the table, Frederick arched a brow at her. "Your father?"

She nodded and leaned her shoulder briefly against his. "He would have approved of you—he would be very happy that I've married you."

He met her eyes, then closed his hand over hers and lightly squeezed. "I'm glad."

Later, a string quartet from the music school played a collection of waltzes, and they danced.

She had refused point-blank to throw her bouquet; aside from her lack of enthusiasm, as she'd pointed out, there'd been no unmarried young lady of suitable age present to catch it. "Not unless you count Clarissa."

As she'd made that comment in Ryder's hearing, she'd immediately had his support, and consequently, there was to be no tossing of her bouquet.

"Thank God for that," Godfrey had said when she'd mentioned it. "Given the recent spate of results—Sylvia catching Felicia's bouquet, and you then catching Sylvia's, and both of you ending up married within months—I would have felt forced to leave the room, just in case."

She'd laughed and told him he wouldn't escape forever, and cited herself as proof of that, which had only made Godfrey look even more wary.

Frederick spent his wedding breakfast never far from his bride—something he discovered was no hardship. She captured and held his attention in a way no other lady ever had; he tried to tell himself it was because she was now his wife, but knew it was simply because she was Stacie.

She'd caught his attention from the first moment he'd laid eyes on her and, now, had fixed it for all time.

While riding to Mount Street in the carriage beside her, he'd imagined that having to rein in his desire, stoked to fresh and eager heights by the knowledge that she was now his, would be his principal distraction over the hours of the extended luncheon; instead, his overriding impulse was to ensure nothing—but nothing—disturbed his new wife's peace. He hovered close enough to ensure that no one said anything to upset her in any way and, especially, that no one referred to her likeness to her mother. Luckily, doubtless because everyone present was close family and had already made such comments often in the past, no one raised the specter of the late marchioness; had any done so, it might have tested his resolve not to react overly protectively—possessively protectively.

Indeed, managing to appease his instincts where Stacie was concerned without triggering her suspicions over why he was reacting in such a way loomed as his biggest hurdle going forward. He could only hope that her expectations of what constituted normal behavior in husbands had been gleaned primarily from observations of her married brothers' reactions, and that she wouldn't dwell on the emotion that gave rise to such actions.

Yet while they were surrounded by others, especially other males, he felt as if he were walking on eggshells. The sooner he could whisk her away to Brampton Hall, where they would be effectively alone, the better.

Until then, he had to grin and bear with the constant pricking and flaring of his instincts.

By the time she stopped beside him and, with a laughing smile, informed him she was about to go and change out of her delicate wedding gown into a dress more suitable for driving into Surrey, he was more than ready to depart.

Twenty minutes later, he handed her up into his curricle, joined her on the seat, and with her waving madly to the crowd clustered on the Raventhorne House steps, he flourished his whip and gave his bays the office, and finally, they were away.

As he tooled the carriage out of Mayfair, through Kensington, and out along the road to Guildford, he felt all tensions ease, then slide away.

He glanced at the lady beside him—his wife. His marchioness.

She'd settled on the seat and was looking about her with evident interest, apparently intent on noting the landmarks they passed.

He smiled and gave his attention to his horses.

Brampton Hall and their wedding night lay ahead, and that was one challenge he was more than ready to meet.

Twilight was falling by the time Frederick turned his horses between the stately gateposts that flanked the winding gravel drive that, Stacie assumed, would lead them to his home—the marquessate's principal seat of Brampton Hall.

She sat straighter on the seat and looked around, surveying all she could see in the gathering dusk.

Frederick glanced her way. "The ornamental lake is behind the house —you can't see it from here."

"Is this area all lawns and trees?" She waved to both sides of the drive.

He nodded. "The formal gardens are clustered around the house—if anything, they extend more to the other side, the west."

Everything she could see was well-tended, the lawns neatly clipped, the trees mature but trimmed.

She suddenly thought to ask, "Did you send word you were marrying today—that we would be coming to stay?"

He chuckled. "I did—they're expecting us."

"Oh, good." She told herself that was better than them arriving without warning and throwing the household into utter chaos. Still, the notion of formally meeting a full household of staff as their new mistress was distinctly daunting.

Frederick reached across, closed his hand about one of hers, and squeezed reassuringly. "Most here have known me all my life. They'll be relieved I've married someone like you—someone who will deal with them reasonably and whom they can respect—they'll welcome you with open arms." He paused, then added, "Figuratively speaking, at least."

She smiled and turned her hand in his and gripped lightly, then released her hold so he could steer the horses around the next curve. How had he known that she was having a minor panic and specifically over that? Such moments made her increasingly grateful to Fate for having steered her his way.

The horses trotted around a corner, and the house rose before them. It was a surprise—not a Palladian mansion but an older hall that sprawled in all directions, two stories high in a composite style that was neither this nor that. Constructed primarily from honey-colored sandstone with a sound slate roof, the central block faced an oval forecourt, while the wings extending to both sides rambled into leafy gardens. Roses climbed walls and wreathed around balconies in several locations.

Most windows sported shutters, although none were closed, and warm lamplight spilled through the gleaming ground-floor windows as Frederick halted the curricle before the shallow front steps that led up to a wide porch and a pair of arched oak doors.

Wide-eyed, Stacie stared, drinking in all she could see. All she could feel. The place was old enough to have developed an aura—one of peace and tranquility.

Frederick turned to her; she felt his gaze roam her face, then from the corner of her eye, she saw his features ease, and his lips curved, and he said, "Welcome to Brampton Hall, my lady."

She drew her eyes from the house and met his gaze. "It's lovely."

His smile deepened. "I'm glad you approve."

A groom had come running to take the reins; the lad bobbed and beamed at Stacie, and she smiled and nodded in reply. Frederick descended, rounded the curricle, and handed her down, and with her arm in his, she walked up the steps and across the porch.

The double doors were pulled open before they reached them. Lamplight filled the high-ceilinged hall, illuminating the staff drawn up in two rows forming a path to the bottom of the stairs.

She didn't have time to be nervous before Frederick was introducing her to the butler, Hughes, and the housekeeper, Mrs. Hughes. To Stacie, the couple seemed a reflection of the house—eminently capable yet comfortable. Hughes was of average height and solid girth and exuded an air of competence, while Mrs. Hughes was a touch shorter—not much taller than Stacie—with apple cheeks, a round, cushiony figure, and steel-gray hair drawn back in a bun.

As Frederick had intimated, the Hugheses appeared very happy to welcome Stacie and seemed genuinely delighted at the prospect of having her as their mistress. They accompanied her down the lines of staff, not just introducing each member but giving her a snippet of information as to that member's duties and also how long they'd been connected with the estate; Stacie noted that, for many, the latter was all of their lives.

Eventually, they reached the stairs, and Frederick reclaimed her hand, led her up two steps, then turned and addressed the staff, thanking them for their congratulations and felicitations.

Stacie gripped his hand and, smiling on the small crowd, added, "Thank you for your welcome." She let her gaze sweep the hall, with the family's richly colored baronial pennants and shields decorating the walls. "This is a lovely house, and I can already tell I'm going to enjoy living here. I look forward to working with you in the days, months, and years to come."

Faces lit, and a cheer went up.

Smiling still, she let Frederick tow her on up the stairs.

When they stepped into the gallery, he looked at her. "Did you mean that? That you like the place and think you'll enjoy living here?"

"Yes." As he drew her along, she swung the hand she held and looked at the portraits and pictures and through the long windows they passed. "If you must know, I felt at home the instant I stepped over the threshold —it felt as if I was stepping into a community living inside an old oak tree that has sunk its roots deep into the soil and grown strong enough to weather anything that comes its way." She paused, then added, "Some houses have an atmosphere so strong you can feel it. When I stepped into the hall...it felt as if the house embraced me." She caught his eye and smiled self-deprecatingly. "Silly, I know, but there it is."

He shook his head. "I don't think that's silly at all." He met her eyes and returned her smile. "I prefer to live here for a reason."

He'd led her down a long corridor. He stopped before the doors at its end, then glanced at her, a slight frown on his face. "That door"—he tipped his head at the door to their left—"leads to the marchioness's apartments, but I honestly don't know what state they'll be in. I didn't specifically tell the Hugheses to prepare those rooms, and of course, everything in there hails from my mother's time."

She drew in a suddenly tight breath. "Where are your rooms?"

He nodded to the double doors before them.

With a boldness that was entirely feigned, she stepped forward. "Let's use those."

Her maid, Kitty, was still on the road, following them down from London in a carriage, with Stacie's trunks and boxes and Frederick's valet for company. There was no lady's maid to assist her to undress and no nightgown for her to don.

She doubted she would need either.

Frederick opened one of the double doors and ushered her into what was obviously his domain; the decor was a blend of golden browns that instantly brought his eyes to mind.

The large room spread across the end of the wing, with wide windows overlooking the lawns that led down to the lake. A huge four-poster bed, hung with brocades and satin in shades of gold and rich browns, dominated the left half of the room. The smaller windows flanking its head gave a view of the gardens on that side; in the last of the fading light, Stacie could just make out the pale blooms of roses bobbing on the canes of massive, old bushes.

The other half of the room contained a comfortable grouping of two armchairs and a table set before the fireplace, which was flanked by windows framing views of mature trees.

Nearer to hand, chests of drawers sat to either side of the main door, their tops strewn with an assortment of music sheets, loosely stacked, while across the room, beneath one end of the wide windows, sat a desk with several large books piled upon it.

Frederick shut the door. Stacie barely had time to catch her breath before his arm slid around her and he turned her to face him.

She looked up, into his eyes—eyes that, from the first, had truly seen her. Her gaze locked with his, and she felt warmth bloom, swell, and spread beneath her skin, not a blush but a more elemental heat.

He arched both brows at her, the faintly amused expression on his face contradicted by the intentness in his eyes. Then slowly, he drew her closer—and she went, setting her palms against his chest and letting him draw her fully against him as he bent his head.

Warmth wrapped around her, lapped at her senses, and tempted.

She wanted this.

She stretched up and offered her lips—invited his kiss—and his lips settled on hers, warm and persuasive, and she mentally sighed and let go.

She set herself free to follow his lead into passion, into intimacy, into whatever lay in store for them in this marriage of bodies and minds.

Until the moment Stacie surrendered her mouth, surrendered herself fully to his embrace, Frederick hadn't had any plan in mind, but now instinct rose and prodded, prompted, and he recognized its wisdom and followed that path.

He needed her, but she needed him more. Reining in all inclination to rush, he took his time savoring her lips, her mouth, let the minutes spin out as their tongues tangled and played and her breath grew shorter and shorter.

Her hands slid upward, palms sliding over his shoulders, then her fingers tunneled into his hair. He deepened the kiss, edging the exchange into more deeply evocative, provocative territory; only when she was well-nigh desperate and her hands clenched tight in his hair did he send his hands roaming over the swollen mounds of her breasts, caressing and possessing, before tracing the indentation of her waist, neat and taut beneath her carriage dress and light stays, then sending his hands sliding still lower to explore the luscious curves of her derriere, screened by layers of skirt and petticoats.

He hid a smile when she wrenched back from the kiss, gasped, "Too many clothes!" and fell on the buttons of his shirt and waistcoat. Inwardly grinning, he set his fingers to the long line of tiny buttons running down her spine.

He had her gown gaping and loose by the time she opened his coat, waistcoat, and shirt and tried to push the garments off his shoulders.

He stepped back and stripped off coat, waistcoat, and shirt in one fell swoop. He had to look down to free his hands from the cuffs, then let the garments fall to the floor.

He looked up—to find her staring at his bared chest, a strange expression on her face and something like wonder in her eyes. Then she reached out and trailed her fingertips across his bare skin, and he closed his eyes and clenched his jaw to hold back a shudder.

She stepped closer, splayed her palms, warm and soft, on his chest, and stroked, explored. Caressed.

He gritted his teeth and let her have the moment. When he was sure he could move without losing control, he raised his hands to her shoulders and peeled the bodice of her gown down. It was her turn to lower her hands and slip her arms free of her sleeves. The instant she had, he stepped into her, one hand at the back of her waist urging her against him, eliminating the gap between their bodies as he bent his head and found her lips and kissed her—this time, he let desire rise and slip free, let hunger raise its head and enter the fray, let passion begin the slow, inexorable build that could find surcease in only one way.

Stacie was beyond giddy—she'd lost touch with the world and didn't care. She needed this—all he could show her of passion and desire and this addictive heat.

The taut skin of his chest, stretched over firm flesh and bone, the tempting sweep of muscles banding the expanse, and the crinkly dark hair adorning it were all elements within her greater fascination with his body and the passion she sensed—had always sensed—thrumming never far beneath his skin.

It was passion that made him such a consummate musician, that allowed him to imbue his playing with an unparalleled touch, with an almost ruthless evocation of emotion. As she'd hoped and suspected he would, he was bringing that same skill to this endeavor; his concentration was absolute, his attention focused, and his determination, clear in his kiss, in the power inherent in his touch as he divested her of her clothes, testified to his intent to wring every last drop of evocative emotion from this engagement, too.

Her skirts susurrated as they slid to the floor; her petticoats followed, and then she was locked in his embrace, with only the fine silk of her chemise between his heated skin and her swollen breasts.

She didn't need to exercise any degree of will; all she had to do was follow his lead and wallow in the glory.

Their kiss heated even more, escalating into a conflagration that reduced any lingering missish reservations to ash.

Passion rose, and hunger became a tangible entity.

Her lips melded with his, her desire equal to and aligned with his. She slid her hands upward, twined her arms about his neck, and pressed into him, against him, the softness of her stomach cushioning the hard ridge of his erection, and kissed him back in blatant, flagrant invitation.

More, she said with that kiss. *I want more.*

Frederick couldn't mistake her meaning; she pressed it on him with lips that burned and an unrestrained ardor that set his own alight.

She might have been innocent in the technical sense, yet age and knowledge had honed her expectations, and as ever, those expectations mirrored his.

It was another challenge—to deliver to those expectations while maintaining some degree of control.

He picked up the gauntlet she'd flung, angled his head, took control of the kiss, and with one arm around her waist, held her hips flush against him while he closed his other hand about her breast. The silk of her chemise shifted under his fingers, a tantalizing sensory addition he used to advantage, to heighten the sensations of his caresses. He closed his hand and gently kneaded, and she moaned softly into the kiss. His fingertips found, trapped, and plucked at her furled nipple, until she shifted restlessly in his arms.

Ruthlessly, he played on her senses, until she broke from the kiss, tipped her head back, and breasts heaving, hauled in a shuddering breath.

He didn't give her time to find her mental feet; he'd already undone the tiny buttons that ran down the front of the chemise and seized the moment of her disorientation to ease the garment off her shoulders. It slithered down to her waist, then slowly slid lower.

She raised her head, eyes widening as cool air washed over her heated flesh. She would have instinctively grabbed the chemise and held it to her, but he raised his hands, framed her face, and kissed her.

And waltzed them both into desire's flames.

Stacie couldn't think. At all. Sensation consumed her as his tongue tangled with hers and his hands slid from her face only to fasten about her waist and pull her flush against him.

Her nerves leapt and sparked at the contact—at the feel of his hard chest pressing against her breasts, the raspy hair laced across his hard muscles subtly abrading her almost-painfully tight nipples.

His hands—his lean, strong pianist's hands—explored, caressed, stroked, claimed, and with a touch of arrogance that was all him, possessed. Her breasts, the globes of her bottom, the curves of her upper thighs—he made them all his. He relentlessly stoked fires beneath her skin, until she was burning.

And all she wanted was more—yet more. A wild, wanton, passionate side of her had been buried by her refusal to marry—her effective denial of this—but now the gates had been opened, and in his arms, that passionate side sought the light.

Sought satisfaction.

Marriage had set her free. Free to embrace even this side of her—so long denied, so hungry.

So ravenous.

She sent her hands skating over his hot skin, gripping, tensing her fingers into the muscle bands, exploring and delighting when muscles rippled under her trailing fingertips.

He was still half clothed, which seemed unfair. Emboldened, she experimented. Eventually, she pressed into him and sinuously shifted, caressing his chest with her breasts, and sensed her moment—a fractional hiatus when she finally succeeded in fracturing his focus and turning it inward—and reached for his waistband and the buttons closing the flap of his trousers.

In seconds, she had the buttons undone, but he realized, caught her hands, pulled back from the kiss, hesitated for a second—she thought he swore softly, but couldn't be sure through the haze clouding her senses—then he released her, swooped, swept her up into his arms, and carried her to the bed.

At last was her only thought as he juggled her, tossed back the coverlet, then laid her on the silken sheets. She'd linked her arms around his neck and drew him down with her, and he came readily, stretching out alongside her.

She boldly tugged, wanting him to cover her, only to discover he had other ideas. That he wanted to explore every inch of her body as if she were the rarest of pianos and he had to note and then worship every single key, every taut wire.

He made her arch. He made her gasp and moan and, ultimately, writhe.

She'd thought she'd reached the wanting stage already, but he made her ache with heightened need.

Then his clever fingers delved between her thighs, breaching and penetrating, and her body convulsed as it never had before in an eruption of pleasure so intense, stars danced before her eyes.

He reduced her to panting limpness, then seized the moment to slip from her side and dispense with his trousers and stockings.

Then, finally gloriously nude—a sight that made her breathing suspend and her eyes feel like saucers—he returned to her.

To her arms as she welcomed him to her, her muscles functioning once again as the effect of her passionate release faded, to her lips as he claimed them anew, to her body as he came down atop her, spread her thighs with his, and settled heavily between.

Glorious! Her senses sang as they absorbed the full impact of his weight, his naked form, pressing her into the bed. Her awareness fractured as she tried to take in every tiny nuance of the moment.

Then he reached down and touched her, traced his long fingers through the slick folds of her entrance, and heat flooded her again. Passion laid its hand on her anew, and she welcomed its heady flame.

He continued to kiss her as he shifted his hips, and the broad head of his erection nudged between her folds, then eased deeper into her body.

Novel sensations swamped her, the thickness of him stretching her channel. The intrusion of his body into hers was startling and, more than anything else, embodied the term intimacy.

He paused, every muscle in his lean frame tensed to the point of quivering—and she thought he was waiting for some sign from her. She tightened her arms about him, tipped her head back to better return his kiss, and raised her legs, wrapped them about his hips, and drew him to her.

She sensed his breath hitch, then he flexed his spine and, with one powerful thrust, drove all the way home.

Filling her and nudging her core.

She yelped, but before the sound had fully dissipated, the pinching pain had eased.

He raised his head and, breathing harshly, looked into her face. "Are you all right?"

She could only just make out the gravelly words. In answer, she smiled beatifically.

He grunted, and she realized the tremors rippling through his taut muscles were proof of how much effort he was expending to give her those moments.

She stretched up and pressed her lips to his, tightened her arms and her legs about him, and urged him on.

He eased out a breath, then drew fractionally back before thrusting home again. Soon, she was rising to his increasingly forceful tempo, then the crescendo caught them, and the world dissolved into a vortex of want, need, passion, and desire, and nothing else mattered but reaching the pinnacle of sensation that steadily rose on their horizon.

Frederick gritted his teeth and clung to control, wanting to—needing to—ensure he didn't reach that rapturous peak before she did. She was new to this, and in some ways, so was he.

He'd always prided himself on being a generous lover, but with all other women, the driving force behind his generosity had largely been academic; he'd behaved so because he'd felt he should. But with her, there was nothing academic about his need to worship her, to accord each and every curve the reverence it was due; the uncontestable reason behind his drive to ensure her pleasure was simply because her pleasure was his.

Braced above her, he looked down at her face, felt the lush curves of her body cradling and caressing his as she shifted beneath him, as she undulated and writhed to the rhythm of his thrusts.

Her skin was so fine, skimming his fingertips over it felt like stroking the most delicately polished porcelain. The sight of desire's rosy tint spread beneath the alabaster white sent possessive satisfaction coursing through him, pushing him on, tempting him to increase his pace and take her more aggressively—something he fought against.

In the end, his instincts took over. He was an experienced composer; he knew what notes to hit and how to string movements into a symphony that swept them both along.

She gasped and seemed to recognize his intent, and she surrendered herself with unfettered abandon, letting him play her like his own sensual instrument, and as with his musical performances, he lost himself in the music they made.

He lost himself wholly in her.

The end, when it came—when the crescendo of their passions exploded in a starburst of pleasure, and their striving tensions snapped, and glory streaked like lightning down their veins—was as much of a revelation to him as it was to her.

For an indefinable instant, they hung suspended, buoyed high on a surge of exquisite, ethereal emotion.

Then oblivion rolled over them, caught them, snared them, and inexorably swept them into its bliss-filled sea.

Later, he stirred and lifted from her.

She remained sunk in slumber. He eased down beside her and drew up the covers, then propped on his elbow and gave in to the impulse to stare.

To catalog every feature, for once devoid of her customary vibrancy, her expression blank in the aftermath of passion.

To him, in that moment, she appeared delicate, vulnerable, and infinitely precious. A lady he would, forevermore, protect against all comers—whether her foe be some person intent on harming her or an idea planted long ago in her head.

He couldn't, and he sensed he would never be able to, back away from that duty. Indeed, in his mind, it didn't register as a duty but rather as a right.

Something he had claimed that night, along with making her his wife.

After long moments of studying her and sorting through the web of feelings she inspired in him, he carefully lay down, raised his arm, reached around her, and gently eased her nearer. She wriggled and snuggled closer, then sighed and sank deeper into sleep.

He relaxed and closed his eyes, only to have his brain decide to examine the new landscape in which he found himself. He hadn't expected the changes; he hadn't known that making love to a woman whom he loved would be a significantly different experience—one that touched and influenced him in very different ways—from making love to a lady for whom he felt nothing more than sexual interest.

Out of that—because of that difference—so much about the engagement had been heightened; it had felt as if every thud of his heartbeat had been more powerful, deeper, more intense.

As for the final moments...they had been the ultimate in rapture.

Luckily, having been a virgin, she had no prior experience with which to compare. She wouldn't see—had no cause to even guess—that what they'd shared had been in any way extraordinary.

He told himself all was well and allowed his lips to curve into an arrogantly smug smile.

Out of today, he'd got all that he wanted—her in his bed with his ring on her finger—and most importantly, his secret remained safe, known only to him and no one else.

CHAPTER 14

*W*hen Stacie woke to her first day of married life, it was to find herself alone in her husband's big bed. The bed curtains had been drawn to protect her from the sight of anyone entering the room, but had been left open on the side facing the wide windows, and weak sunshine streamed in, informing her that it was well and truly morning.

She stretched languorously, feeling delicious aches in places she'd never felt achy before, then, prodded by hunger and curiosity, she slipped from the bed and found and donned her chemise. Having detected no sound or other signs of life, she explored and discovered that the narrow door in the inner wall closer to the fireplace led to a large, obviously male dressing room—thankfully empty, although there were signs that Frederick at least, if not his valet, whom she'd yet to meet, had been there at some point. The corresponding door on the other side of the room led into a large bathing chamber. She was delighted to see a huge claw-footed tub, along with the usual washbasin and commode. A second door to the bathing room, opposite the one through which she'd entered, led to what had to be the marchioness's dressing room; Stacie found her clothes hanging in the two armoires and in neat piles in the drawers of the chests, and her brushes and combs had been placed on the dressing table, along with her jewelry chest—and a red-velvet-covered jewel case she didn't recognize.

The dressing table sat before the window; she padded to it and stared at the unknown case. Her first thought had been that it was a part of the Brampton family jewels, but the case looked new.

And now she was closer, she could see that "Aspreys" was stamped in gold lettering across the top of the case.

"Oh," she breathed. "He didn't."

She picked up the case and, holding her breath, opened it—and found herself staring at the ruby parure she'd so admired. The stones glinted and gleamed. Her first impulse was to don the entire set, but that would be too much for a day about the house. Looking around, she hesitated, then saw the bellpull and crossed to it and tugged.

When Kitty arrived, bearing a pitcher of warm water, Stacie insisted on dressing in one of her ruby-red gowns.

After sitting on the dressing stool to allow Kitty to arrange her hair, she opened the new jewel case and picked up the bracelet.

Kitty's eyes flew wide. "Ooh, my lady! They're so beautiful." She lowered her voice. "Are they from the master?"

Stacie smiled. "Yes. Sadly, I can't wear the whole set during the day —the bracelet and ring will have to suffice." So Frederick would know she treasured his wedding gift.

After directing Kitty to retrieve the rest of her clothes from the marquess's bedchamber, Stacie walked into the marchioness's bedroom. Although the room had clearly been prepared for occupation, as Frederick had intimated, the furniture and fabrics were from decades past.

She looked around, then, having decided that before redecorating, she should wait to ask Frederick's mother, now the dowager marchioness, if she wished to claim any of the pieces or hangings for her rooms, either those she would keep here or those at Albury House, Stacie quit the room in search of her husband.

She found him in the breakfast parlor, having been directed to the pleasant room that looked onto the garden by Kitty, who had put her early-morning hours to good use learning the layout of the house and the ways of the household. Apparently, for those who preferred to dine downstairs, breakfast was available from the sideboard in the breakfast parlor between the hours of seven and nine.

It was a quarter to the latter hour when she walked into the well-lit room and found Frederick perusing a news sheet. On seeing her, he lowered the sheet and, his lips curving, nodded. "Good morning, my dear."

Smiling, she inclined her head. "My lord." That seemed appropriate in multiple ways.

She went to the sideboard and allowed Hughes to hand her a plate and lift the lids of the silver serving platters. Once she'd made her selections, she turned to the round table. Frederick rose, waved back the footman, and drew out the chair beside his.

Pleased, she sat, her bracelet helpfully tapping against the edge of her plate, then as Frederick—who had noticed the sound and its source—leaned over her, easing in her chair, she looked into his face. "Thank you for your very thoughtful gift, my lord. It's beautiful—I'll treasure it forever."

He remained hovering over her as his eyes searched hers; he was transparently gratified that her thanks were obviously genuine. "It was, indeed, my pleasure." His gaze shifted to her hand where the ruby ring glowed. "The stones and design suit you—the set was made for you."

He started to straighten, and suddenly struck, she caught his eye. "I just realized—I haven't given you anything."

The smile that lit his face rendered the austere planes quite beautiful. "You've already given me a treasure beyond price."

She tilted her head, staring at him as she tried to imagine...

His smile deepened, and he whispered, "You." Then he straightened and returned to his chair.

She decided his unexpected answer was simply that of a sophisticated gentleman seeking to put his new bride at ease. While she ate, he questioned her as to what she wished to do that day, and she admitted she felt a strong need to learn her way around the large house and the immediate grounds.

He readily offered to escort her—another thing she hadn't expected—but he seemed infinitely more relaxed here, in the country, than he had in London. And she quickly realized he knew Brampton Hall better than anyone else.

Rather than guide her, he encouraged her to explore as she would, while he adopted the role of "font of local knowledge." He had tales, most funny and many self-deprecating, about the places he followed her into.

By the time the bell for luncheon rang over the gardens and he caught her hand and unerringly led her out of the hedge maze in the shrubbery, she'd learned a great deal—not just about her new home but also about the man she would share it with.

~

On the fourth night they'd spent at the Hall, Frederick lay on his back in the center of his decidedly rumpled bed, one arm bent with his hand behind his head, the other looped around his pleasurably exhausted and now-sleeping wife, and marveled at the changes she'd brought into his life.

Through showing her over his home—the house, gardens, and estate —he'd found himself viewing each aspect through her eyes, seeing those aspects anew, appreciating them all the more.

As for the contentment he felt in moments such as this, bone-deep and abiding, a sense of home that extended so much further than simply place, he had no words with which to do it justice. He dwelled on the feeling, on the peace and calm certainty it brought, then turned his head and, through the shadows, studied what he could see of her face.

All in all, in securing Stacie as his bride, he was inclined to feel not just lucky but blessed.

The resolution he'd made on the night of their wedding to protect her from all harm had expanded and taken on a broader scope; he no longer wanted only to protect her, he wanted to set her free.

He wanted to lift the shadows from her mind, wanted to erase them so she no longer feared love.

More, he wanted to give her the choice to love if she wished—if she dared.

If, like him, she came to count the subtle and immutable joys of loving as worth every iota of the concomitant vulnerability.

Quite how he had got to his present state, he didn't know and honestly didn't care. Living his life beside her felt so right, it was impossible to question that he and she were where they needed to be.

Together.

Feeling her soft, warm weight against his side, he closed his eyes— and consigned the question of how to vanquish her fears to the morrow.

~

On the afternoon of the following day—the fourth after they had arrived at Brampton Hall—they sustained their first bride visit.

"That's Lady Cormanby's carriage." Frederick narrowed his eyes on the old-fashioned equipage as it lumbered around the curve of the drive, heading for the forecourt. "And I'll wager she's brought her son and daughter with her—she'll want to foist them on your acquaintance."

He and Stacie were mounted; after luncheon, they'd gone out riding over the estate's lands to the west, purely to familiarize her with them. She was eager to learn about the estate and those who worked on it; his tenant farmers had been delighted to welcome her and, he'd judged, they'd all been thrilled that, so early in her tenure, she'd come riding out to meet them. He and she had been on their way back when he'd spotted the carriage and drawn rein in the trees off the drive, effectively screened from the forecourt and the porch.

Beside his heavy black, the chestnut mare he'd had saddled for Stacie danced as Stacie craned her head and watched the carriage roll into the forecourt. "We can't ride off and avoid her, you know."

He grunted; that was, in fact, what he'd been about to suggest. "It's only the fourth day after our wedding. Isn't she supposed to give us at least a week?" He knew he sounded as if he was whining; that was because he was. He'd expected not to have to share Stacie with anyone else—much less a nosy neighbor—for at least the regulation seven days.

"Yes, she should have waited, but she's here now." Stacie glanced at him, read his reluctance in his eyes, and smiled commiseratingly. "Come on—let's ride to the stables, then you can introduce me to her and her children. I promise I'll get rid of them after twenty minutes."

His brows rose at that, and he nodded. "All right." Watching Lady Cormanby put to rout would be worth the initial irritation.

Stacie felt very much on her mettle as, still in her riding habit, she preceded Frederick to the formal drawing room where Hughes had deposited Lady Cormanby and her two adult children. A faintly intrigued smile on her lips—one conveying welcome but also surprise—Stacie swept into the room, bringing all three callers to their feet.

Frederick trailed after her, and she aimed her smile at their visitors. "Good afternoon."

"Lady Albury. Lord Albury." Lady Cormanby dipped into a regulation curtsy, one her daughter hurriedly mimicked, while her son bowed deeply. The son was barely in his twenties and looked distinctly uncomfortable, while the daughter, possibly a year or two younger, wore an expression that suggested she wished she were anywhere but there.

In contrast, Lady Cormanby's gaze was sharp and inquisitive; she was a heavy woman trussed into a gown the frills and ruffles of which did her no favors. Rising from her curtsy, she looked pointedly at Frederick.

With languid grace, he stepped forward. "My dear, allow me to introduce Lady Cormanby, Miss Cormanby, and Mr. William Cormanby, of Cormanby Manor, some miles to our south."

Stacie bestowed gracious nods upon the three, then, with a wave, invited them to sit. While Lady Cormanby and her daughter settled on the chaise and the son claimed a straight-backed chair set to one side, Stacie sank gracefully into one of the armchairs angled before the huge fireplace. As Frederick moved past her to take up a position beside her, leaning against the mantelpiece, she sent him an appreciative look. Brief though his introduction had been, he'd told her that Lady Cormanby was a neighbor, but not one with whom they shared a boundary.

"I hope, my lord, my lady," Lady Cormanby said in her rather mannish voice, "that you will overlook our precipitousness in calling, but we are due to travel into Cornwall tomorrow, and I couldn't leave the district without calling in person to offer our family's felicitations on your marriage."

Stacie smiled brightly. "Why, thank you. I do hope it's not any sort of family emergency that compels you to travel to Cornwall?"

Lady Cormanby colored. "Well, no—but I'd thought to visit my sister and her family. Mind you, Cormanby isn't keen, and his chest is bothering him, so it's possible we might have to delay."

"And where in Cornwall does your sister live?"

Lady Cormanby faintly frowned. "In Truro."

"That's a pleasant place—I've visited several times. Tell me—" And Stacie rattled on, leading the conversation down whatever rabbit hole Lady Cormanby, in answering Stacie's incessant questions, alluded to.

She paused only to offer refreshments, which were somewhat gratefully accepted, but even when Hughes had delivered the tea and cakes and she poured, Stacie didn't ease her relentless and rather ruthless interrogation.

To any question Lady Cormanby sought to ask, such as how long they thought to remain in the country, Stacie returned brief, uninformative answers—"I really can't say"—before turning the question back on her ladyship, for instance with "I assume you're based at Cormanby Manor, but you mentioned your sister—do you visit family often? Where?" and so on.

With amused appreciation, Frederick watched and learned, and sure enough, a few minutes past the twenty Stacie had suggested, Lady Cormanby, looking rather dazed, set down her empty cup, gathered her children with a look, and rose. "Thank you for your hospitality, Lady Albury, but we really must be going."

Stacie rose, too, and with every appearance of having enjoyed her ladyship's company, walked with their visitors back into the front hall and onto the porch. Frederick followed and halted beside her. As Lady Cormanby nodded in farewell, Stacie smiled and said, "I hope you enjoy Cornwall."

Her ladyship blinked. "Cornwall?" Then she colored. "Ah—yes, Cornwall. Truro. Indeed." With a last vague nod, she followed her children down the steps.

Smiling with genuine delight, Frederick remained beside Stacie as she waved the Cormanbys off. The rout had been even more comprehensive than he'd imagined possible—and his new marchioness had accomplished it in style.

~

Five halcyon days later, Stacie accompanied Frederick on a visit to the estate's cider mill. As they rode past ripening fields and down lanes that overarching trees had turned into tunnels of dappled shade, she marveled at the simple happiness that seemed, these days, to be her permanent state of being.

Her declared purpose of establishing herself as a hostess of musical evenings for the haut ton—and through that, advancing the careers of worthy local musicians—had been intended to absorb her and give her life a continuing focus; in reality, given the episodic nature of such musical evenings, such a purpose could never have filled her days.

Becoming Frederick's wife—his marchioness—had. The role fitted her so well, it was almost uncanny. Quite aside from the unending delights of the nights spent in his big bed, wrapped in his arms, running a large household and supporting Frederick in managing the estate—being the lady by his side—was all but second nature, and everyone on the estate had welcomed her and, indeed, actively sought to please her.

There had been not a single hiccup or unexpected hitch; she and the staff at Brampton Hall had, within a day, taken each other's measure and had embraced the other with a certain relief.

She was coming to believe that Fate had designed the role of Frederick's wife expressly for her.

He rode beside her on a powerful black gelding, idly looking about him as, having galloped earlier, they walked their horses down a shady lane.

When, apparently sensing her gaze, he turned his head and met her eyes, then, after surveying her expression, arched his brows in gentle question, she smiled and faced forward. "I'm not sure I should tell you this"—*your arrogance needs no encouragement*—"but I believe I owe you a debt of gratitude for suggesting we convert our sham engagement into a real one."

When he made no lighthearted riposte, she glanced at him and discovered he was studying her in a more serious and intent fashion than she'd expected.

After several seconds searching her eyes, he asked, "Does that mean you're happy—and content—being my wife, my marchioness?"

Surprised, she blinked at him. "Do you really need to ask?"

His lips quirked, and he shrugged and looked ahead. "As I've mentioned before, I'm too wise to believe I can read—or even accurately deduce—the state of any female's mind."

"Well," she said, nudging her mare to keep pace with the black, "I am —content and quite happy."

From the corner of her eye, she saw the curve of his lips deepen.

"Good," he returned. "And as for your gratitude..." His glanced at her, and she felt the warmth in his gaze. "I'm sure that, between us, we can negotiate a suitable way in which you might demonstrate it."

Pleasurable anticipation coursed through her; they'd discovered they were both adventurous spirits when it came to their sensual encounters. She grinned and shot him a deliberately provocative glance. "You may be sure I'll put my mind to it."

He laughed, and smiling delightedly, she rode on by his side.

The cider mill proved to be far more absorbing than she'd imagined. The brewer, a Mr. Tranchard, was a keen enthusiast, and when she expressed an interest in learning about the process by which the larger part of the estate's apple crop was converted into a brew well known throughout the local area, he was only too happy to escort her around the mill and explain all the stages from the washing and crushing to the fermenting and eventual bottling into jugs.

A thin, wiry man, Tranchard clapped his hands together and assured her, "We supply the Hall and all the tenant farms and have enough left over to sell to several local inns."

She assured him she'd already sampled his wares. "It was the delightful taste that made me inquire as to the source. I was fascinated to learn it was from the estate."

Although Frederick knew everything there was to know about the cider-making process—the mill had been in existence since he'd been a boy—he'd trailed Stacie and Tranchard through the building, amused by the impact Stacie's genuine and unaffected interest had on Tranchard, who could sometimes be standoffish. During the two weeks since they'd arrived at Brampton Hall as man and wife, he'd come to appreciate her innate ability to interact with anyone regardless of social rank, to know just how to approach people and draw them to her.

She seemed intuitively able to convince people that they all shared the same goal; he recognized her actions as a form of subtle manipulation, yet her intent was entirely benign.

She put people at ease to the extent they wanted to help her in whatever way she needed. Given she was a noblewoman, now a marchioness, that wasn't a skill to be scoffed at.

He waited and watched, and when they finally rode away from the mill, they left Tranchard utterly captivated.

～

A week later, Frederick felt a tug, a compulsion he hadn't experienced for years.

It drew him to the music room, to the grand piano that stood in pride of place by the windows.

Stacie was busy at a meeting with Mrs. Hughes, discussing household matters and expenditures to do with refurbishing several rooms. Other than himself, there was no one around that part of the house.

He contemplated the piano for several minutes, then surrendered. After raising the lid and removing the felt covering, he sat on the stool, stared at the keys, and felt his mind empty, his active thoughts flowing away, then he raised his hands, placed his fingers on the keys, closed his eyes, and played.

Sometime later, he paused, rose, crossed to a side table against the wall, and from the table's drawer, retrieved a bundle of sheets ruled for scoring music and two pencils, already sharpened.

Returning to the piano, he sat and scribbled, then set aside paper and pencil and, now driven, continued refining the lilting melody.

It was nearly an hour later when Stacie walked in. Immediately, he lifted his fingers from the keys.

"There you are!" Smiling, she strolled to the piano. "I haven't heard that piece before—what is it?"

He almost told her—self-preservation caught his tongue just in time. "Just a minor air." He had to assume she'd heard the stories of his past, of his supposed young love and the last piece he'd composed and played; if she had, then learning that he was composing a piece for her would alert her to his feelings for her, and he didn't think he'd yet convinced her that him loving her embodied no threat.

She halted in the curve of the piano; from there, she couldn't see that the music sheets were newly created, in pencil rather than printed.

If she saw, if she asked...

He couldn't explain without giving himself away. In reality, he was quietly amazed; he'd thought the impetus to compose had left him, an outcome of that long-ago public debacle—that the creative spark necessary to ignite the flame had died. Apparently, an ember had lurked beneath the cold ashes, and she—all she was, all she was becoming as his wife—had been enough to coax it back to life.

The musician in him exulted.

The rest of him was focused on keeping the development concealed. Holding her gaze, he reached for the felt to cover the keys and, with a deliberately seductive smile, asked, "Did you have some purpose in mind in hunting me down?"

Her smile deepened. "I did, as it happens. I wondered if you had time to stroll the gardens with me before we change for dinner. Storrocks is of the opinion that we should cut down the old elm on the west lawn and replace it with an oak or a beech."

"Is he?" He closed the lid of the piano and rose. He left the incriminating music sheets facedown on top of the piano; he would hide them later, after she'd gone upstairs. "Did he say why he's taken against the elm?"

Stacie turned, and side by side, they walked toward the door. "He says it's of an age when it's liable to start dropping branches." She slanted a teasing glance up at him. "I believe he imagines that we'll soon have infants and small children resting or racing around on the lawn, so he views the elm as a potential threat better removed."

"Ah—I see." His lips curving, he caught her hand, laced his fingers in hers, and walked beside her into the front hall. "In that case, I suspect we had better examine the tree and then duly agree with Storrocks."

Three days later, Frederick drove Stacie into the nearby town of Guildford so she could experience the town's market day, a once-a-month event.

He drove into the town along Millbrook, the road that followed the river Wey, then turned onto Castle Street so she could view and exclaim over the castle, sitting on its hill above the town. The market was held where the eastern end of North Street widened into a rectangular space that passed for the town square. Frederick left his curricle and horses at an inn in the High Street and, with Stacie on his arm, escorted her around the corner to where a plethora of colorful stalls had been set up, running along either side of North Street. Combined with the shops that lined the street, the stalls created three long avenues of temptation.

There were food stalls of all kinds, offering everything from potatoes and turnips to sweetmeats and pastries. There were glovers and buckle makers and ribbon sellers, haberdashery of every conceivable sort, and fabrics aplenty. The stalls selling animals were restricted to one corner, but the noise from the pens added to the cacophony; everyone in the crowd seemed to be either talking or listening to someone speak, and the raucous calls of sellers blared over the scene.

Despite the noise, despite the throng of people weaving their way along the aisles, the atmosphere was good-natured, and almost everyone was smiling.

They were halfway up the first aisle when Frederick touched Stacie's hand in warning, then drew her to the side, out of the flow of bodies, as an older couple approached.

The gentleman, a bluff, jolly-looking sort, beamed and bobbed a bow. "Lord Albury—a pleasure, my lord." The gentleman turned to Stacie. "And this must be your delightful wife."

"Indeed." In the face of such open enthusiasm, Frederick couldn't help but smile. "My dear, allow me to present Alderman Geary and Mrs. Geary."

"Lady Albury—your devoted servant, ma'am." Geary swept Stacie a much more formal bow.

Mrs. Geary sank into a curtsy. A plain lady with a kind face, as she rose, she inquired, "Is this your first visit to Guildford, ma'am?"

Stacie smiled. "It is, indeed." She glanced at Frederick. "Lord Albury suggested that I would find market day entertaining, and that has, indeed, proved to be the case." With her gaze, she indicated the bright stalls to left and right. "The town hosts a very impressive turnout."

Pleased, Geary puffed out his chest. "We on the town council strive to ensure our market offers both range and competition." He twinkled at Stacie. "Keeps the prices down, and keeps the housewives coming back."

Stacie laughed and added a favorable comment about the neatness and organized arrangement of the stalls, which played to Geary's pride.

Frederick and Stacie remained exchanging comments with the Gearys —including the couple's views on the local sights, which Stacie thought to elicit—before parting company and moving on.

They hadn't got much farther when Lady Fairweather hailed Frederick from the next aisle over. When he looked, her ladyship pointed an imperious finger at him and ordered, "You wait right there, my lord."

When Frederick dutifully stood rooted to the spot, Stacie looked up at him, a startled question in her eyes.

He grinned. "Yes, I know, but she's a local eccentric, rides like the devil on the hunt, and has a heart as large as the county."

"Ah—I see." Stacie subsequently composed herself and waited patiently beside him as Lady Fairweather found a gap between stalls a little farther along and barged through, into the aisle in which they stood. A much younger lady followed rather more timidly, towed along in her ladyship's wake.

As Lady Fairweather, a tall, raw-boned woman with a head of graying brassy-brown curls and features that might generously be described as horse-faced, pushed through the crowd to join them, her gaze remained fixed on Frederick. Only at the last minute, as she halted before them, did her ladyship shift her shrewd hazel gaze to Stacie. "So you're the lady who finally managed to make him see sense, heh? I've been telling him for years that he needs a wife to help him properly oversee the Hall—men always seem to think that paying the bills and making sure the place doesn't fall down is enough, but you look like the sort who knows her way around a household. Are the Hugheses treating you well?"

Stacie smiled. "Exceedingly well, thank you. They are, metaphorically speaking, my left and right hand."

"Just so." Lady Fairweather nodded decisively. "Knew just from looking at you that you had a good head on your shoulders."

Frederick smoothly cut in, "My dear, allow me to present Letitia, Lady Fairweather, of Cannon Grange, and her daughter, Emily."

Stacie extended her hand. "It's a pleasure to make your acquaintance, Lady Fairweather."

Her ladyship engulfed Stacie's hand in her much larger one and shot a disapproving look at Frederick. "No need to stand on ceremony—everyone calls me Letty."

Stacie's smiled broadened, and she retrieved her hand. "And I'm Eustacia, but do call me Stacie." She turned to the young lady, very much cast into her robust mother's shadow, and offered her hand. "And Emily—how do you do?"

Emily touched fingers and bobbed a curtsy. "It's lovely to meet you, ma'am."

Stacie glanced at Lady Fairweather, then asked Emily, "Are you out yet?"

Emily smiled resignedly. "Next year. Mama thought I should wait until I'm nineteen."

"Time to learn a bit more sense, and that will make you stand out from the herd," Letty said.

Stacie arched her brows. "That's...rather a wise notion. Many young ladies are—well, very young and quite silly, which does tend to put the gentlemen off."

"See?" Letty glanced at her daughter. "I told you an extra year won't hurt."

"Indeed." Stacie turned to Letty. "I'm thinking of hosting a dinner party in the next month or so, to introduce myself to the local families, as it were. I do hope you'll consent to Emily attending, too."

Frederick noted the blush and the air of hope that infused Emily's features.

With her sharp eyes, Letty saw it, too. After a second of meeting her daughter's patently pleading gaze, she humphed. "Don't see why not. An invitation to dine at a marchioness's table isn't, I believe, something one needs to be formally presented to accept."

"Exactly." Stacie smiled encouragingly at Emily. "And it will stand you in good stead for attending similar dinners in London next Season."

Letty and Frederick fell into a discussion about a local weir, leaving Stacie and Emily happily discussing the latest fashions.

When, eventually, they parted from the eccentric Lady Fairweather and her rather more conservative daughter, Emily was a good deal happier than when the pair had approached.

Once Frederick and Stacie had moved on into the crowd, he dipped his head and murmured, "Since when have you been considering hosting a dinner?"

Stacie shot him a grin. "Since about ten minutes ago." She settled her arm more comfortably in his. "Yes, I dreamed it up to give Emily something to look forward to, but hosting such a dinner is, in fact, something I ought—we ought—to do."

"If you say so." Although his resigned tone gave no indication of it, Frederick was pleased that she'd reached the stage of claiming the position of his marchioness in a wider, county-circle setting.

Then he noticed another couple approaching and said, "Actually, in terms of the guests we should invite to such an event, Sir Hugh McNab and his lady—the magistrate and his wife—should definitely be on our list."

They halted as the McNabs came up with them. Ignoring the stream of marketgoers swerving around them, Frederick made the introductions and watched as Stacie charmed the magistrate and his wife. Amongst her other comments, Stacie made mention of her intention to host a dinner party "perhaps in early summer," and when the couples parted, Lady McNab was all a-flutter.

As they walked on, Frederick observed, "Mama wasn't one for entertaining the locals—London was always her true home. She held house parties at the Hall, but her guests were her and my father's London friends."

After a moment, Stacie said, "If I had to choose, I would opt for life in the country. Living in the country and visiting town to attend performances, catch up with family, and grace the occasional social event"—she cast a glance up at his face—"that, to me, would be my ideal."

He nodded. "Add in visits to scholarly lectures and events, and that's my ideal as well."

He didn't bother stating how perfectly they were matched; that was obvious. As he continued to walk beside her, protectively steering her through the crowd, pointing out this and that and being amused by the sights that tickled her fancy, he felt contentment settle just a little deeper into his bones.

He couldn't imagine a life more pleasant than this.

All he had to do to ensure it continued for the rest of his life—that, if anything, the peace and joy and happiness only deepened—was to find some way to convince his lovely wife that love developing within their marriage wasn't a reason for ending it.

CHAPTER 15

rederick had still not broached the issue of love within their marriage with his wife—indeed, he had absolutely no idea how to safely do so and, until he found some solution, was relying on his ability to pass off any too-revealing reactions as simply the way a nobleman such as he would react in the circumstances—when, six days later, Camber arrived at the Hall.

On being summoned from the music room where he'd been putting the hour Stacie passed with Mrs. Hughes to good use, Frederick saw the inquiry agent waiting in the front hall with a large, brown-paper-wrapped package under his arm. Frederick couldn't hold back his smile. "You got it!"

Camber grinned. "More accurately, I used your funds to outbid everyone else, my lord."

Frederick approached and held out his hands, and Camber relinquished the package.

Frederick saw the agent's gaze deflect and go past him; he glanced around and found Stacie coming down the stairs. He had no doubt that Camber had heard of his marriage and knew who his wife was, yet discretion on all fronts was Camber's motto. "My dear, this is Mr. Camber—he's the agent I mentioned through whom I acquire rare books."

Stacie smiled and nodded to Camber. "Sir."

"Ma'am." Camber bowed deeply.

Frederick noted that not by so much as a flicker of an eyelash did

Camber betray that he knew rather a lot about Stacie. "Come into the study and tell me about the auction."

With an inclusive smile, Frederick waved Stacie ahead of him, and together, they led Camber into the study.

Over the past weeks, Stacie had often joined Frederick there, discussing the estate and issues pertaining to it. He'd repositioned one of the armchairs to the side of his desk, and she'd made it her own.

As Stacie sank into the chair, she studied the package Frederick had set on his desk and was eagerly unwrapping. "Is that your latest find?"

"Yes. I'd heard it was listed in the library of a deceased gentleman in Glasgow and the heirs were auctioning the library off." Frederick glanced at Camber as the agent settled in the chair facing the desk. "How did it go?"

"The bidding was fast and furious at first. I hadn't expected quite so much interest, so I let the eager ones make the running. I only came in when there was just one gentleman left bidding."

"Oh?" With the book unwrapped and the paper tossed aside, Frederick dropped into his desk chair the better to examine the tome. "Who was that?"

"Your nemesis," Camber replied. "Lord Brougham."

Frederick had opened the book, but looked up at that, a faint frown on his face. "I had hoped he wouldn't get wind of it."

"Well, he had, and he was mightily put out when he realized you were my client."

Frederick blinked. "You told him?"

Camber looked offended. "Of course not—but he went from brow-beating me to brow-beating the auctioneer's clerk, and *he* wasn't up to holding Brougham at bay." Camber paused, then added, "Daresay the staff of a small auction house in Glasgow aren't used to the high dramas generated by rare book auctions in the capital."

"Hmm." Frederick had already gone back to the book. "I daresay you're right, and I suppose it doesn't really matter that Brougham knows I have it."

Camber made no reply.

Stacie watched as Frederick pored over the tome, carefully turning pages using only the very tips of his fingers. After several moments of utter silence, she asked, "Is it really such a find?"

Frederick had, apparently, fallen into the book; it took several seconds for him to look up, replay her words, and comprehend her question. Then he glanced at the book. "Yes, it is." Evidently returned to the land of the living, he reached for a side drawer of the desk, opened it, and extracted a slip of paper. He held it out to Camber. "Your fee and a bonus. Thank you —as always, you've delivered to my satisfaction."

Camber rose and took the bank draft. He glanced at the figure and smiled. "And as always, it's a pleasure doing business with you, my lord."

Stacie rose and went to the bellpull. "Can we offer you some refreshments, Mr. Camber?"

"Thank you, my lady, but I need to be on my way back to town."

She smiled. "Perhaps just a mug of cider while your horse is being watered?"

Camber arched his brows, then nodded. "I wouldn't say no to that, my lady—I'm rather partial to cider."

"In that case, you're in for a treat—our cider is made on the estate." Hughes arrived, and Stacie delegated to the butler the task of providing Camber with a mug of their best cider before seeing him on his way.

"Good day, my lord," Camber said, addressing Frederick, now buried in the book.

Frederick didn't look up, just raised a hand. "Again, my thanks—I'll be in touch when I next have an acquisition that requires your expertise."

Camber tried but failed to hide an indulgent smile, bowed to Stacie, and followed Hughes from the room.

Stacie ambled back to the armchair and sank into it. Smiling indulgently herself, she watched Frederick pore over the old tome; he was completely and utterly engrossed.

The sight reminded her of the promise she'd made when she'd been negotiating with him over his appearances at her musical events. "I'd forgotten I guaranteed you access to my great-grandmother's musical legacy." When he looked up, blinking, she continued, "The old musical texts and folios of music at Raventhorne Abbey—remember?"

"Ah, yes." Renewed interest lit his eyes.

"I'm sure Ryder and Mary won't mind if we borrow the books and folios for a while."

Frederick studied her eyes, then said, "We can call on Ryder and Mary when next we go up to town."

She smiled and nodded. "We'll have to remember."

Yes, they would, because if he had his way, they wouldn't be returning to London for months.

Stacie stretched, then waved a hand at his recently acquired tome. "If you're finished for the moment, can I have a quick perusal?"

He glanced down at the book he'd only just started examining, then closed it and handed it to her. He watched as she took it, laid it in her lap, and carefully opened the cover.

He studied the sight of her poring over the book. The past weeks with her here, just him and her and the staff and estate workers, had been his notion of idyllic. He saw no reason for the interlude to end before it needed to—even in pursuit of rare manuscripts.

It was something of a minor shock to realize that, above all, he wanted to keep Stacie to himself—to hoard her smiles, to greedily capture all her attention, to selfishly wallow in her very presence and exclude every possible distraction.

Selfish, certainly.

In love, indubitably.

Luckily, with respect to his actions and the motives that drove them, his wife appeared to be blissfully blind.

～

Stacie woke in the depths of the night and couldn't get back to sleep. She knew it was deep night from the quality of the silence that blanketed the Hall. Even outside, bar the distant hoot of an owl, all lay quiet under a cloudy and moonless sky.

Frederick lay softly snoring beside her; she didn't want to wake him by tossing and turning, so she lay still and willed herself to sleep.

To no avail.

Finally, she slipped from beneath his arm, flung her robe about her, found her slippers and eased her feet into them, then crept from the room. There was just enough light to see her way as she walked quietly through the gallery, down the stairs, and turned toward the kitchen. A glass of warm milk was a childhood remedy for wakefulness she'd continued to use into adulthood; for her, it was usually effective.

She pushed through the swinging green-baize-covered door, walked down the deeply shadowed corridor beyond, and passed under the archway at its end, into the large kitchen. The servants' hall stretched to her left; she turned right, toward the kitchen proper and the long deal table that ran down its length. A glow emanated from the huge hearth in the wall beyond the table's end, assuring her that the kitchen fire, although banked, still burned. Focusing on the hearth, smiling, she headed for the welcoming glow.

To her right, a shadow shifted.

Startled, she half turned—only to have a man loom before her. Before she could gasp, let alone scream, he locked his hands about her throat.

And squeezed.

She tried to raise her knee, but he shoved her against the table and crowded close, his body pinning hers. Shocked, she stared into a face shadowed by a hat pulled low and a muffler wound about nose and chin; all she could see was a pair of dark eyes gleaming malevolently at her.

Instinctively, her hands had risen to where his fingers cruelly gripped. Desperate, she tried to pry his hands away, but couldn't budge even one finger.

Her lungs heaved and strained. She was starting to choke; her head was swimming.

In a panic, she flung her hands to either side, seeking something with which to strike at her attacker—anything amid the odd things that had been left on the table.

One of her sweeping hands hit a tin saucepan and sent it careening; it landed on the stone floor with an unholy clatter.

"What the devil?"

Frederick!

Her attacker jerked upright, hauling her with him.

In the next instant, he flung her away—at Frederick.

She slammed into him, knocking him off balance. He stumbled, and they fell, but wrapping one arm about her, he juggled her, cushioning her against him as, with his other arm, he broke their fall.

They still landed in a tangle of limbs on the stone flags, but neither was hurt.

Frederick cursed and fought to free himself from Stacie and her clinging robe as several instincts battled for supremacy. After launching Stacie at him, the intruder had turned and fled; Frederick could hear the thud of the man's boots receding along the short corridor leading to the rear door.

He could also hear a thunder of feet coming down the servants' stair, which settled the question of what he should do. The staff could give chase; he would see to his wife.

By the time Hughes and several footmen burst into the room, Frederick had lifted Stacie up, steadying her on her feet as he got to his.

"My lord!" Hughes started toward them.

Frederick pointed down the corridor. "Intruder!" he barked. "He went that way."

Hughes and the footmen raced off.

Stacie was still gasping, with one hand at her throat. Gently, Frederick steered her to a bench beside the hearth. "Sit. I'll get you some water."

He was filling a glass when Mrs. Hughes came rushing in.

The housekeeper looked around wildly. "What's amiss?"

"Some blackguard broke in. Hughes and the others have gone after him." Frederick crouched before Stacie; although the light was poor, he could see she was abnormally pale, and there was a necklace of red marks ringing her throat. The sight sent white-hot rage surging through him, but he ruthlessly clamped down on the impulse to go charging after the man and, instead, gently urged Stacie to take the glass and sip, which she did.

Mrs. Hughes had been followed by several maids, including Stacie's. Exclaiming, the girl rushed up, then patted Stacie's shoulder and hovered solicitously, and Frederick saw Stacie rally.

He rose. Mrs. Hughes and the maids were setting things to rights—picking up the saucepan and rearranging things knocked askew. He turned toward the corridor to the rear door just as Hughes and the footmen returned.

"Anything?" Frederick asked.

"No sign of the blackguard himself, my lord," Hughes reported. "But the scullery window's been forced, and his footprints are there, outside the window, plain as day."

"I couldn't sleep." Stacie's voice was hoarse. Everyone turned to look at her as she went on, "I came downstairs to get some warm milk."

"I know just how you like it," her maid chirped. "I'll get some warming right away."

The maid rushed to the hearth; Mrs. Hughes sent another maid to fetch the milk jug, then went to assist with the fire.

Stacie barely seemed to notice. She pointed to a gap between two of the kitchen cupboards. "He was hiding there, and when I passed on my way to the hearth, he leapt out and seized me."

"Luckily," Frederick said, "I'd followed her ladyship down." He didn't want to think of what might have been the outcome if he hadn't sensed her leaving his side. Hadn't given in to the prod of his instincts that had insisted he get up and go after her. Just in case she'd needed his help—and she had.

The bruises forming around her neck were proof of the intruder's murderous intent.

Feeling consciously more like his warrior-ancestors than he ever had, Frederick looked at Hughes. "Until we find out what this was about—if the blackguard merely thought to try his luck and won't be back, or if he was sent here for some specific reason and might try again—I want two footmen on guard duty overnight."

"Indeed, my lord." Hughes exchanged a glance with the footmen, who all looked determined. "We'll see to it."

Mrs. Hughes, meanwhile, had noticed the bruises marring Stacie's alabaster skin. The housekeeper tutted. "Mercy me! That dastardly man! What is the world coming to? I've an arnica salve, my lady, which will make those come and go much quicker. Just let me fetch it—the sooner it's on, the faster they'll go."

Frederick waited with what patience he could muster while Mrs. Hughes and Stacie's maid fussed and applied the ointment to Stacie's throat, and Hughes and the footmen organized a watch and devised a way to barricade the scullery window until it could be repaired.

Finally, Frederick was able to extricate Stacie. She was plainly still shaken, but had consumed the warm milk she'd come to the kitchen in search of; she rose and, leaning heavily on his arm, thanked the staff for their assistance, then he solicitously ushered her from the kitchen.

In the front hall, at the bottom of the stairs, she paused, drew in a deeper breath, then met his eyes. "Thank God you followed me."

He clenched his jaw and said nothing, just waved her on, and side by side, they started slowly up the stairs. After a moment, he asked, "Does it hurt to speak?"

"Not as much as it did—the milk helped—and Mrs. Hughes's salve is working wonders."

"Good." He hesitated, then asked, "Did you get any hint as to what the man was after?"

She shook her head. "I think I surprised him. I assume he was a burglar, and he didn't want me to scream and raise the alarm." As they reached the gallery, she shot Frederick a glance. "Do you think he was after your new book?"

Frederick's brows rose. He contemplated the possibility.

"The book did arrive just yesterday, and tonight…" She paused, then asked, "Have you ever had someone break in before?"

"No." He had to admit the coincidence was striking, yet… "I can't believe Brougham would send a burglar to steal the book, and he's the most likely culprit if the book was the man's target." After a moment's hesitation, he asked, "Did you see enough of the man's face to be able to identify him?"

She shook her head. "He had his hat pulled low and a muffler about his face." As if remembering, she tilted her head. "That said, I don't think he was a gentleman of any stripe. Not a laborer, but not much higher."

Frederick grunted. He was waging an uphill battle to confine his newly risen protective urges within readily explainable—excusable—bounds. The protective possessiveness he'd felt on seeing the blackguard with his hands wrapped about Stacie's throat had all but blinded him with its ferocity; even now, if he could lay hands on the man...

White-hot fury still burned inside him, yet he had no outlet for it. Suppressing it, pushing it deep, he steered Stacie into their room—his room that they now shared—and guided her to the bed.

Once she was settled beneath the sheets, he joined her.

She seemed exhausted now, as if the energy that had carried her through the ordeal had run out and left her drained. She turned in to his arms and snuggled close, cushioning her head on his shoulder. He held her gently and brushed his lips across her forehead. Soon, her breathing deepened and slowed.

He closed his eyes; a roiling mix of emotions still churned inside him. Considering them, their power, and the effect they were having on him, he realized that love had changed that, too. Apparently, loving didn't only create a gaping emotional vulnerability, it also catapulted all associated emotions onto an entirely new level of intensity.

He lay listening to Stacie's slumberous breathing while his heightened emotions kept him wide-awake.

I should have had a glass of warm milk, too.

❧

The day passed without any further sightings or clues as to the man who had broken into the Hall and left its mistress with a necklace of bruises around her throat.

Frederick dispatched grooms to inquire at the local inns, including those at Guildford, but none had played host to an unknown man the previous night, only their regulars. Given the proximity to London, it was possible, even likely, that the man hadn't dallied but had ridden down, then ridden straight back, leaving no trail to be followed.

Stymied on that front, Frederick told himself the man could have been a would-be burglar who had imagined the newly-wed couple would be off somewhere on a wedding trip, leaving the Hall with a skeleton staff. He'd heard tales of such burglaries, apparently triggered by the wedding announcement in the news sheets.

Regardless, with nothing more to be done, he allowed himself to fall back into what was fast becoming his much-desired married life.

~

On Sunday afternoon, after lunching with Frederick, Stacie left him in his study and, after chatting with the head gardener, Storrocks, about the tree he was planting to replace the now-removed elm, made her way to the stables and asked the head stableman, Bristow, for the gray mare she favored to be harnessed to the gig.

While she enjoyed riding, she'd discovered that for visiting the estate's cottages and the tenant farmers' families, tooling herself around in the gig was preferable; once on the ground, she didn't need to worry about how to get back into her saddle.

After her first round of visits, when Frederick had accompanied her to introduce his workers and explain what each family did, what acres they farmed or what service they performed for the estate, she'd taken to calling at the various cottages on a three-week roster. That didn't seem too intrusive, and she continued to learn a great deal about how the estate functioned, and the people seemed to genuinely welcome her interest. She also hoped that knowing she would visit every third week meant people—the farmwives especially—would have an avenue to alert her to any looming problem. According to Mary, who ran a similar watching brief at Raventhorne Abbey, becoming a conduit for information was one very real way in which to assist one's husband.

While she waited for the gig to be readied, she leaned against the stable yard fence and tilted her face up to the gentle sun. Eyes closed, she smiled; she was increasingly grateful that Frederick had suggested and argued for their marriage. Even had she tried to imagine her perfect life—the one that would best and most deeply satisfy and fulfill her—she could never have designed a position that suited her better than being his marchioness.

When she'd accepted his offer, she hadn't fully appreciated all the benefits, but the past weeks had opened her eyes to what truly mattered to her—having a sense of place, of belonging, of having a role that others looked to her to fill. Having a purpose beyond herself, a larger role that contributed to so many, in so many different ways and on many different planes, and was significantly broader in scope than her desire to advance the cause of worthy English musicians.

Not even the recent incident with the burglar—who surely had to have been just some man trying his luck—could dampen her appreciation. Mrs. Hughes's salve had worked miracles, and the bruises were already fading; she'd concealed the blotchy marks by looping a gauzy scarf about her throat.

The scrunch of steps on the gravel had her opening her eyes to see Frederick—his gaze on her—approaching.

She smiled, letting all she felt at the sight of him infuse her expression. "Hello." She glanced around as the clop of hooves on the cobbles heralded Bristow, the mare, and the gig. She straightened from the fence and waved at the gig. "I was just about to drive out and visit some of the farms."

Frederick returned her smile with a lazy one of his own, then joined her, and together, they walked to where Bristow had halted the gig. "I came hoping to catch you before you left. I've nothing I need to do this afternoon—do you mind if I accompany you?"

He had any number of business and estate matters sitting on his desk, but he was very certain that keeping her within his protective reach ranked much higher in terms of his peace of mind.

Her smile brightened. "I would be delighted to have your company, my lord."

He took her gloved hand and helped her to the seat, then rounded the gig and climbed in beside her.

She'd already picked up the reins and looped them through her fingers. Then she paused and looked at him. "Would you prefer to take the reins?"

Smiling contentedly, he shook his head. "No. I know you're more than competent, and with you driving, I can sit back and admire the view."

As his gaze rested appreciatively on her as he said the words, she read his meaning accurately. She arched a brow in a gesture intended to be quelling, which only made him grin unrepentantly, then, lips lifting, she faced forward, shook the reins and clucked at the mare, and set the horse trotting out of the stable yard and onto the track that wound through the wood at the rear of the Hall, eventually leading to a lane that would take them to three of the estate's farms.

Frederick relaxed against the seat. He stretched out one arm along the seat's back behind her and did as he'd said and watched her as she managed the horse, drinking in the picture she presented in a lightweight, pale-lemon carriage gown with a froth of gauze rising from the upstanding collar. She looked fresh and delightfully summery against the green of the trees and bushes they drove past.

He glanced ahead as she steered the horse around the last bend before they met the lane.

His gaze fell on the rocks strewn across the track.

The mare was going too fast to halt.

He didn't think—he just reacted, gave himself wholly over to his instincts, half rose, seized Stacie, and as the mare danced over the rocks and the gig's wheels hit the first line of small boulders, flung them both out of the carriage onto the rising verge.

He twisted and landed mostly on his back, holding her against him, as a sharp *crack* shattered the bucolic peace, followed by an ominous splintering sound. The landing jarred him, but the bank was inches thick in leaf mold and, thankfully, free of sharp objects.

Stacie lifted her head from Frederick's chest and searched his face. "Are you all right?" The most important thing.

He nodded. As she watched, his lips and the lines of his face settled into a grim mask. His eyes met hers. "You?"

"No damage." She slipped from his hold, sat up, and looked at the gig. "The same cannot be said for the gig."

The small carriage was a wreck. The axle had broken in two, and one wheel had shattered to shards. The seat sat tipped at a skewed, drunken angle, while the other wheel had wedged tight between two rocks.

The mare had halted just beyond the bed of stones and, with the shafts at an odd angle and the harness dragging at her, stood looking about her uncertainly.

Frederick had also sat up and looked. Now, he pushed to his feet. "The mare looks to be unharmed."

He walked to the horse, ran assessing hands down her legs, then rapidly unbuckled the traces.

Stacie got to her feet and stood staring at the remains of the gig. Then she looked at the rocks and frowned. "These have been deliberately placed. They aren't part of a rockslide or anything like that."

"Indeed." Frederick walked the mare around the rocks and the wreckage.

Still frowning, Stacie waved at the rocks. "Who would do such a thing? And why?"

"I don't know." Frederick halted beside her. His only thought was to get her back to the safety of the house; the fear behind the thought grew claws and pricked at him. "Regardless, we need to return to the Hall."

He didn't want to spend even a minute more in the vicinity of a trap that might or might not have killed her; he had no idea if whoever had set it had lingered, waiting to ensure the outcome. To his ears, his voice sounded as if it came from a long way away; his senses were elsewhere, scanning the area around them for the slightest hint of threat. "I'll send out some stable boys to retrieve the wreckage and clear the track."

He'd shortened the traces and offered them to her; the mare couldn't carry them both. "You ride. I'll walk."

Stacie looked at him, then shook her head. "I'd rather walk as well."

He wasn't going to argue. He offered her his free arm, and she looped hers in it, and they set off.

Initially, they walked briskly—he tried to be surreptitious about constantly scanning the woods to either side—but once they left the trees' shade, he eased the pace and turned his mind to assessing possibilities and options.

Stacie withdrew her arm, but promptly laced her fingers with his. Looking ahead, she asked, "Do you think this was about the book?"

He frowned. "I don't see how that could be."

"Well"—she tipped her head in that considering way she had—"if you were killed, then it's possible—indeed, many would see it as likely—that your library would be auctioned off." He met her gaze as she said, "Someone wanting to get their hands on that book might be unscrupulous enough to consider murder as a viable means of gaining access to it."

He blinked and refrained from pointing out that anyone who had watched to see who drove around the lanes in recent weeks would have seen her and not him. He rarely drove about the estate; in fact, he couldn't remember when he'd last done so. And that was the cause of the ice in his gut; the accident had been aimed squarely at her.

Combined with the incident two nights before... He had to accept that the "burglar" might well have been sent to harm her, and entirely unintentionally, she'd walked into the man's arms in the kitchen. If the man had been sent to kill her, he wouldn't have expected to come across her there but to find her asleep in her bed in the marchioness's bedchamber. If whoever was directing the man held to the old and still generally accepted ways of married noble life, that's where he would have directed his henchman to look for her.

Regardless, at that moment, the images dominating his mind were of her flung lifeless from the wrecked gig or possibly crushed beneath its weight...

He shoved the images aside and looked ahead. He felt his jaw firm, and he forced himself to nod. "I suppose that's a possible motive." Not a complete lie; it was just an option both his rational mind and his instincts rejected as unlikely.

Indeed, his rational mind questioned whether he was overreacting and the two incidents were, in fact, entirely unrelated—that the intruder had merely been some non-local chancing his luck in the hope of picking up a few choice valuables, while the rocks had been some idiot-children's prank—but his instincts were having none of it.

As they neared the rear of the house and veered toward the stable yard, he found himself pondering a prospect he'd had no inkling might ever hove on his horizon. Was someone trying to kill Stacie? And if so, who and why?

~

Later that evening, when, after dinner, he and Stacie had retired, as they now usually did, to the room she'd chosen as her private parlor, after they'd spent ten minutes or so reading—he his latest acquisition and she a novel culled from the library shelves—he set his finger on the page to note his place, looked up, and with every indication that he'd just thought of the matter, said, "I've just remembered—I'll need to go up to London tomorrow. I have to attend a meeting of historical scholars at the museum tomorrow afternoon."

She raised her head and opened her eyes wide. "Oh?"

When she appeared to fall into thought and didn't say anything more, he grimaced. "I'll most likely remain there overnight, and given I'll be there, I might as well clear the business that's built up since we've been down here. I might end remaining for a few days—perhaps as long as a week."

He wanted her to accompany him, but didn't want to order her to do so. The meeting was real enough, but regardless of it being very much in his academic bailiwick, too enamored of the contentment he'd found with her at the Hall, he hadn't intended to attend. Now, however, he needed an excuse to return with her to London. Once he had her back in the capital, surrounding her with unobtrusive guards would be easy, in addition to Ernestine, who had moved to Albury House, as well as his mother and Emily, all three of whom he felt sure he could count on to keep Stacie amused and accompanied wherever she went.

His emotions, his instincts, would no longer allow him to countenance her roaming alone, as she'd been doing on the estate, but conversely, the very last thing he wanted to do was to make her feel under constant guard, and in the country, concealing watchers was well-nigh impossible. The only alternative would be to restrict her movements, effectively caging her—and that would be even worse. Consequently, London was his—their—best option.

He also felt reasonably certain that whoever was behind the attacks lived in town and had sent someone into Surrey to do their dirty work. The principal business he expected to pursue while in the capital would be to search out the blackguard behind the deeds and, one way or another, nullify the threat to her.

In that respect, London at present also contained Ryder, Rand, Kit, and Godfrey; Frederick felt confident he would have their unqualified support in hunting down the man who had dared to threaten their sister. They might even have some inkling of who it might be.

Her gaze distant, Stacie remained silent, apparently inwardly debating.

Frederick compressed his lips against an almost-overpowering urge to blurt out that he *needed* her to go with him, that in the circumstances, with her under threat, he couldn't function if they were separated by miles...

But it was too soon—still too early in their marriage. Caution insisted he hold his tongue and do nothing precipitous to give his game away. He needed to wait and let her grow not just comfortable but rooted in the position of his marchioness before he confessed to sliding around the promise he'd given her not to fall in love with her.

Finally—although the wait was probably less than a minute—she refocused on his face and smiled. "If you don't mind, I'll come to town with you."

Don't cheer. Making sure no hint of relief or triumph showed, he inclined his head and returned her smile with an easy one of his own. "In that case, perhaps we can catch up with your brothers and sisters-in-law while we're there."

Stacie nodded eagerly, glad of having a perfectly valid excuse to cling to her husband's company. "Felicia's close to her time, and I'd like to be near—or at least, nearer. And I would also like to check in on Protheroe, our three protégés, and the music school in general. If we're going to hold another musical evening—perhaps at the end of this month, before the ton quits the capital—then it would be wise, I suspect, to give Protheroe and the lads fair warning, especially if we decide to include an additional string performance."

Frederick agreed and declared the matter settled, and they decided to leave after breakfast.

While Frederick crossed to the bellpull and, when Hughes responded, informed him of their intentions, and Hughes assured them all the necessary arrangements would be set in train, Stacie's thoughts returned to her primary concern—protecting her arrogant husband from further harm. Her first step in that regard had to be separating Frederick from the book he currently held in his hands. She was counting on him not taking the tome to London; she'd discovered that there was a hidden room off the Hall's library—probably originally a priest's hole—in which the most prized of Frederick's acquisitions were stored.

If the blasted book was left at the Hall, that would potentially create two targets for whoever was after it, and hopefully, the tome itself would prove the more attractive. Certainly, murdering its owner seemed a less-direct way of laying hands on the book, when a well-planned burglary would achieve a quicker result with, surely, less risk to the villain. Not that any burglar was likely to discover the priest's hole, but if there was another attempted burglary while they were away, then that the book was the villain's objective would be beyond doubt.

The notion that she might be the true target of the attacks had occurred to her, but she couldn't imagine why anyone with the where-withal let alone the knowledge to hire a thug to commit violent deeds would have her in their sights. That she'd walked into the kitchen in the middle of the night and surprised the villain's henchman had to have been mere accident, and she doubted the sort of thug a villainous would-be thief hired would know that sometimes ladies drove gigs and not just gentlemen.

While Frederick gave orders as to which team of horses he wanted harnessed to his curricle the following day, and that Elliot and Kitty should follow with their luggage in the larger carriage as before, Stacie studied Frederick's face.

Whoever the villain was, he most likely resided in London. Finding and exposing the blackguard would undoubtedly be their surest way forward, and in terms of ferreting out the villain, Frederick would have access to greater resources in town. Eyes narrowing fractionally, she scanned his—as always—uninformative countenance. Despite the lack of any evidence therein, she strongly suspected that, on his list of "business to be accomplished while in town," the top spot was taken by: *Find the blackguard and deal with him.*

Or words to that effect.

CHAPTER 16

*T*hey arrived at Albury House an hour before luncheon. At Frederick's order, Hughes had sent a rider up to town at daybreak to advise the household of their anticipated arrival. Amid all the unexpected drama, Stacie had forgotten that this would be her first visit to Albury House as its new mistress, a fact borne in on her as, bowed in with a flourish by Fortingale, she set foot on the hall tiles and found the staff lined up to greet her.

She smiled and stepped up to the task. When she reached the end of the line, just enough time remained to refresh themselves and shake the dust of the journey from their clothes before luncheon would be announced.

With a subtly expectant smile flirting about his lips, Frederick led her to the marquess's apartments, which dominated one corner of the first floor. He opened the door, glanced inside, then stepped back and waved her in.

She stepped over the threshold—and laughed. Delighted, she looked all around the large room, then glanced over her shoulder at her remarkably clever husband. "I take it red wasn't previously your preferred color?"

With an acknowledging dip of his head, he closed the door and joined her. "Until now, red hasn't featured in my color choices." His long fingers found her hand; gently gripping, he raised it to his lips and lightly kissed her knuckles. "But it's your favorite color, so in that sense, it's now mine as well."

The room had been redecorated in garnet red; rich, sumptuous velvets and heavy brocades toned wonderfully with the dark walnut of the furniture. Indeed, the room was both masculine and feminine; she could easily see him lounging in the bed or in one of the comfortable chairs, but she also felt entirely at home—that this room encompassed the meaning of the word.

She met his eyes. "It's lovely." Her lips lifted in a deliberately seductive smile. "I feel I should reward such thoughtfulness."

He appeared to consider it, then sighed. "Sadly, with Mama, Emily, and Ernestine eagerly awaiting us downstairs, I regretfully suggest all demonstrations of your gratitude would best be delayed until tonight."

She laughed. "Very well, my lord. Tonight it is." She turned toward the minor door he waved her toward. "For now, we'll have to be content with making ourselves presentable."

They did and, subsequently, descended to the dining room and weathered a luncheon that had patently been designed by the cook and Mrs. Macaffrey to rival anything Mrs. Hughes and her team had placed before them.

After growing used to sharing meals with Frederick alone, Stacie found it a trifle disconcerting to have to actively make conversation. She managed to avoid giving any undertakings regarding possible activities for her afternoon, but allowed the other three ladies to indulge in as much speculation as they wished.

When they rose from the table, Frederick made his excuses and departed for his meeting at the museum.

Stacie accompanied the other three ladies to her mother-in-law's private drawing room.

Halfway across the room, the dowager paused and looked at Stacie. "By rights, this room should become your domain, my dear. I would be happy to shift to using one of the smaller rooms...?"

"No need." Stacie smiled confidently. "I'm perfectly content that this room remains primarily yours, Mama-in-law." She was surprised by how easily the title tripped off her tongue and immediately saw how much her use of it had pleased Frederick's mother. "Provided, of course, that I may join you here."

The dowager closed a hand on Stacie's arm and gently squeezed.

"You will always be welcome, my dear—never doubt it." She released Stacie and waved them to the chairs; the dowager sank into one of the armchairs by the fireplace, Emily and Ernestine shared the chaise, while Stacie claimed the second armchair.

As soon as she'd settled, the three older ladies fixed eager eyes on her. "Now," the dowager commanded, "tell me—how did you find Brampton Hall?"

Stacie was happy to satisfy their curiosity on the subject, although her unvoiced refusal to touch on anything to do with her and Frederick's relationship caused a certain level of disappointment.

From the corner of her eye, she kept watch on the clock. When the hands stood at two-thirty, she concluded her description of Mr. Camber, who the dowager knew of but had never met, and stated, "Ladies, I must call on my sisters-in-law and let them know I'm back in town." She rose. "Especially with Felicia so near her time, I wouldn't want them to suppose I was still in the country and too far away to summon if there's a need."

"Oh, indeed. You must let them know," Ernestine agreed.

The prospect of an imminent baby obliterated any disappointment the three ladies might have felt. The dowager looked quite pleased. "We'll look forward to hearing whatever news there may be over dinner tonight."

Stacie left them, hurried to her room, summoned Kitty, and gave orders for the town carriage Frederick had said she might use to be brought around, then when Kitty returned, changed into one of her more fashionable walking dresses.

For the visit she was about to make, she wanted to look her best.

By the simple expedient of asking her modiste while being fitted for her wedding gown, she'd learned that Lady Halbertson lived at Number 9, Farm Street. After allowing Fortingale to instruct the coachman to take her to Raventhorne House, she waited until the carriage was on South Audley Street and nearing the corner of Mount Street before rapping on the roof and giving the coachman her revised destination. She fully intended to call on her sisters-in-law, but first, she had a suspicion to either confirm or refute.

She'd spent the hours traveling to town mulling over the possible motives for the incidents at Brampton Hall and had accepted that there was a distant chance that she herself had been the intended target on both occasions. While she considered such a scenario extremely unlikely, it was one she could check, given that the only person who might have reason to attack her was Lady Halbertson.

Stacie had to own to a worm of jealousy where Frances Halbertson was concerned. Her ladyship had known Frederick before Stacie had, and now that she more fully comprehended the sensual delights her husband could bestow, she had to wonder if Lady Halbertson's gentle and unthreatening demeanor cloaked a more devious nature. If, for instance, her ladyship harbored an ambition to do away with Stacie and inveigle Frederick into marriage once the position of his marchioness was, again, vacant.

Stacie didn't want to believe that of Lady Halbertson, but having grown up observing her mother and her cronies, she knew how much duplicitousness could lurk behind a charming façade.

She trod up Lady Halbertson's steps at a few minutes before three o'clock—a time when the lady should, with any luck, be at home. The parlormaid who answered the door confirmed that was so and, on being given Stacie's title, without any show of consciousness, invited Stacie inside and showed her into the small drawing room, then went to fetch her mistress.

Stacie was left to conclude that either the parlormaid was a new addition to the household, or the staff had never known the identity of the gentleman who had, in the not so distant past, called on their mistress.

Lady Halbertson didn't keep her waiting; she swept into the room mere minutes later, a pleasant and intrigued smile on her face. "Lady Albury." Her ladyship curtsied, then gracefully rose. "To what do I owe the pleasure of this visit?"

Nothing in Lady Halbertson's face suggested Stacie's visit wasn't the pleasure she'd termed it. Stacie drew in a breath and opted for blatant honesty. "Lady Halbertson, I hope I may be frank with you."

Her ladyship's gaze grew a touch wary, but her features remained relaxed. "I take it you've heard that I was Frederick's mistress—as far as I'm aware, his last mistress prior to him marrying you." She waved Stacie to the chaise and moved to claim an armchair. "And indeed," she went on, as Stacie sank onto the chaise, and her ladyship sat as well, "I would prefer frankness between us. I have nothing but the greatest respect for you, and as I owe Frederick a genuine and ongoing debt of gratitude, I sincerely want nothing but the best for him. So whatever questions you may have, ask, and I will answer as best as I can."

Stacie studied Frances Halbertson's face; she would take an oath that every word her ladyship had uttered had been the absolute truth—that reality shone in her fine eyes, in the helpful eagerness that infused her. Stacie replayed her ladyship's words, then tilted her head and inquired, "A genuine and ongoing debt?"

Lady Halbertson nodded. "Over his continuing advice and his efforts on Connor's behalf."

"Connor?"

"My son." Lady Halbertson's face transformed; no Madonna had ever looked prouder. "He's just nine years old and has a burning ambition to become a great violinist. Frederick's advice—to both Connor and myself —has been"—her ladyship raised her hands in an expansive gesture —"invaluable. He counseled Connor that he should finish school before exclusively devoting himself to his music and explained why in terms a nine-year-old could understand." Her ladyship caught Stacie's eyes. "If you've ever had to manage a nine-year-old boy, you'll know how impera- tive that is."

Stacie nodded. "I remember my younger brother at that age. You couldn't get him to do anything unless you could explain its purpose. 'Why' was his favorite word."

"Exactly. And Frederick has gone further and spoken to his friends at the Royal Academy, and when Connor leaves Eton, if he still wishes to pursue what he insists is his calling, then the Academy has agreed to assess him and, if he makes the grade, take him in on a scholarship." Her ladyship's eyes shone as she said, "I cannot tell you how much Freder- ick's support and help have meant to Connor and me."

Studying her ladyship's face, Stacie suspected she understood.

Under her gaze, Lady Halbertson sobered. "I should make it plain that Frederick didn't have to do what he did—I never asked it of him. His actions, first to last, were made out of the goodness of his heart. He called one afternoon—purely to check if I would be at some ball that evening— and heard Connor practicing. Nothing would do but for Frederick to climb to the schoolroom and put Connor through his musical paces." Her ladyship seemed to reflect, then confessed, "I must say, I found Freder- ick's commanding attitude rather terrifying, but Connor lapped it up. He was in alt after Frederick left."

Stacie couldn't help smiling. "One does not get between Frederick and music. I've already learned that lesson."

Lady Halbertson tipped her head, her gaze on Stacie. "Would it be appropriate to offer you refreshments?"

Stacie read the question in her ladyship's eyes—*Could they be friends?*—and smiled. "I don't see why not."

Frances Halbertson beamed, rose, and crossed to the bellpull. After giving instructions to the parlormaid, she returned to her armchair. "Now, I hope I've set your mind at rest as to the cause of any lingering interest in this household on Frederick's part. We agreed to speak frankly, so in that vein, allow me to assure you that any more personal connection between Frederick and myself is very definitely in the past."

When Stacie tilted her head, asking an unaskable question with her eyes, her ladyship readily volunteered, "I've decided I'm not cut out for the role of nobleman's mistress. Indeed, I don't think I ever was—my husband left me sufficiently well provided for, and of course, Connor will eventually come into his own—but something in Frederick called to me and..." She shrugged. "He was persistent, yet in matters such as that, once the pursuit is ended and the prize won, for the gentleman, the excitement tends to wear off." For the first time, her ladyship openly studied Stacie. "That said, I would suggest that, with you, he will remain constant. Given the way he looks at you, I would say that you and he have a chance at a match made in heaven."

Unsure what to say in reply, Stacie inclined her head and was glad when the maid reappeared with the tea tray and the delicate moment was at an end.

Over the teacups, Lady Halbertson inquired as to Stacie's plans for future musical events. Perhaps unsurprisingly, her ladyship displayed a genuine interest, and as she inhabited a position of knowing music well enough to appreciate it yet wasn't any sort of aficionado, she proved an excellent sounding board for Stacie's ideas of how to develop her evenings.

They were soon on first-name terms, and when she heard the distant squeak of a violin, Stacie caught the hopeful glint in Frances's eyes and asked whether Connor might be persuaded to play for her.

Connor was duly summoned, and the question put to him; like many a confident nine-year-old possessed of a loving and encouraging mama, he was very ready to demonstrate his skills.

When he finished and bowed, Stacie clapped as loudly as his mama.

After Connor left the room, she answered the question in Frances's eyes. "He definitely has the vital spark. I can see why Frederick supports him."

They continued to chat, mostly about music, but also touching on other ton matters. By the time Stacie rose and touched fingers with Frances—and both agreed that while it might be inappropriate for Frances to call at Albury House, there was no reason Stacie couldn't confound any busybodies and call in Farm Street—Stacie was convinced that Frances wasn't in any way connected to the attacks in Surrey. Aside from entirely lacking in duplicity, let alone malevolence, Frances had revealed via various comments that she thought Brampton Hall lay north of Farnham rather than south of Guildford, and Stacie was quite sure Frances hadn't been lying.

Once back in the Albury carriage, Stacie directed the coachman to drive on to Raventhorne House. Leaning back against the well-padded seat, she smiled. She'd enjoyed a much more pleasant afternoon than she'd anticipated and had made a new friend in the process.

Because of her mother, she'd never had true friends—no close girlhood companions. Other parents hadn't wanted to chance their daughters' reputations by allowing them to associate with the household of a lady, no matter how high-born, who lived her life poised on the brink of major scandal.

Yet Stacie's years under her mother's wing had left her with well-honed skills that allowed her to feel utterly confident that she'd read Frances and her feelings accurately.

"But Mama is long gone, and now, I'm in charge of my life, and the attacks aside, I'm really very pleased with the way that life is evolving."

That realization had come to her in Frances Halbertson's drawing room. Her life now was one she actively wanted, and she would do whatever was necessary to cling to what she now had.

~

The next morning, Frederick and Stacie renewed their habit of riding out early and enjoying a good gallop down Rotten Row.

Reveling in the exhilaration, they reached the Kensington end of the tan and, smiling, side by side, wheeled right, toward the trees.

A shot rang out. Grass erupted between their horses as a ball plowed into the turf.

Both horses reared; his heart in his mouth, Frederick ruthlessly brought his gray's hooves thudding down and, to his immense relief, saw Stacie wrestle her mare back under control, too.

Her eyes, huge, met his.

"Go!" Forcefully, he waved her past him. "Ride!"

She dug in her heels and did. He wheeled behind her, putting his horse and body between her and where he thought the gunman had been, and rode hard after her.

They both stayed low, quickly putting distance between the gunman and themselves.

A group of three riders who had followed them down the tan stared as they thundered past on the grass. Frederick didn't bother warning the trio; they weren't in any danger, but Stacie was.

She slowed as she reached the more populated area toward the beginning of Rotten Row. He caught up with her and glanced back at the now-distant trees and decided it was safe enough to slow to a canter.

When, her face pale, she looked questioningly at him, he nodded grimly ahead. "Home."

There was nothing he could do—or could have done—to identify much less catch the shooter, who would, doubtless, be long gone by now. And regardless of the reason behind the attacks, he was perfectly certain he and Stacie didn't need the ton's attention rabidly refocused on them.

They cantered to the Grosvenor Gate, then walked their horses across Park Lane and into Upper Grosvenor Street. After drawing rein before the steps of Albury House, Frederick dismounted, handed his reins to his waiting groom, and went to lift Stacie down. She'd largely recovered her outward composure, but as he closed his hands about her waist, he felt how tense she was—felt the faint tremors that continued to course through her.

He set her on her feet and firmly clasped his hand about one of hers. He glanced at the grooms holding both horses' reins. "We won't need the horses again today." Then he urged Stacie up the steps and into the safety of the house.

Even with the door closed and all threats held at bay, the clamor of his emotions didn't noticeably ease. Struggling to rein in his rising temper, he followed Stacie into his study. She'd apparently chosen the room without thought, but in this house, it was an excellent place to seek refuge; his mother and Emily rarely came there.

Stacie walked to the wide windows overlooking the side courtyard and halted before them. She crossed her arms, hugged her elbows, and looked out, he assumed unseeingly.

He closed the door and, more slowly, walked across to halt by her side. He'd organized to have men trail her in a protective capacity if she left the house alone, but it hadn't occurred to him to have guards following while she was with him and they were riding. "I'm sorry—that must have been frightening."

She glanced at him—frowned at him. "It was hardly your fault."

He didn't reply. Something inside him insisted that it was his fault, that it was his duty to keep her safe regardless of how random or unpredictable the attack.

She made a disbelieving sound. "You may be a nobleman and used to getting your own way in everything, but you can't control"—she gestured toward the park—"men hiding in bushes with pistols!"

He studied her and realized there was a flush in her cheeks and her eyes glittered. "You're angry."

"Of course, I'm angry! I was enjoying a ride with my husband, and they ruined it! I'm furious! How dare they shoot at us?"

That was precisely how he felt; she'd managed to put his rage into words while he was still grappling with the fury itself. He stood ramrod straight beside her, his hands tightly clasped behind his back, and battled the urge to pace like a madman—he who never paced. He didn't feel like himself—like the self he knew—yet this was him as he now was, now that he'd fallen in love with her and she'd come under attack yet again.

Each time, the effect grew worse—stronger, more powerful, harder to contain and restrain.

He wanted to pace and rage about the room, but the target he wanted to vent his temper on wasn't there.

She gave vent to an angry, frustrated sound, released her elbows, swung around, and paced down the room. She flung up her hands. "There has to be something we can do." She turned, kicked the heavy skirts of her riding habit around, and came storming back toward him. "Someone is doing this." She met his eyes as she halted. "Who?"

When he didn't immediately answer, she swung violently around and paced away again, then turned—viciously kicking her skirts again—and with her lips and chin set and fire in her eyes, came striding back to him.

Having her pace—watching her temper play out—was oddly soothing, almost as if, through watching her, his temper found release, too.

Release enough for the ability to think to return.

He frowned and finally offered, "I can't think why anyone would be doing this—attacking you like this."

"Not me—you." She halted beside him and jabbed a finger into his upper arm. "It's much more likely that it's you who's the target, and I just happened to be there. And before you argue"—she jabbed his arm again—"I'm not the one who owns things other people want."

He wrapped a hand about hers before she could jab him again.

"And"—she determinedly wagged the index finger of her other hand in his face—"before you say I hold the position of your marchioness, which, admittedly, other ladies want, I really can't see any lady hiring a thug to do away with me in order to step into my shoes. The only lady who might even be said to have cause is Frances, and she wouldn't—she's not like that."

"Frances Halbertson?" He nearly goggled. "Good God, no."

"Exactly. So I think we should accept that all these attacks are directed at you, and I was merely an innocent bystander." She'd released most of her frenetic, fright-induced energy; she drew in a breath and, her gaze steadying on his, asked, "So who might be behind attacks on you?"

He stared into her eyes and mentally reviewed the few who, at a very long stretch, might fall into that category. Eventually, he slowly shook his head. "I'm finding it difficult to imagine anyone I know as being the villain behind these attacks. However..."

When he frowned and didn't continue, she prompted, "Yes?"

Jaw setting, he refocused on her face. "There's someone—someone I can't imagine is behind this—but who I believe I need to eliminate as a possibility."

While she remained at risk—and no matter what she said or who the intended target truly was, she'd consistently been threatened by the attacks—then he couldn't sit on his hands and leave any potential avenue unexplored.

She searched his eyes, then nodded. "We need to follow every possible lead, even if it's only to eliminate someone as a suspect."

He didn't point out that, currently, they had no real suspects at all.

When, in clear demand, she arched her brows at him, he replied, "It's Brougham. I can't believe he would ever stoop to this—I've always thought him a sound man. Priggish and stiff, maybe, but at base, a staunchly honorable gentleman. Against that, he must be spitting chips over that recent auction and losing the book to me—and he was at the meeting yesterday, so he knows I'm back in town."

Her eyes widened, and he saw realization dawn.

"Other than this household," she said, "we didn't tell anyone we were coming back. We didn't announce it, and other than your meeting and my visits yesterday, which were private and to people who wouldn't bruit the news abroad, until this morning, we haven't been seen in public."

He nodded. "Whoever sent someone with a pistol to hide in the woodland near the end of Rotten Row knew we were back in town."

"And that, when in town, riding early in the morning is a long-standing habit of yours."

"Indeed. Which is why"—he turned toward the door—"I'm going to Hampstead to have a word with Brougham."

She looped her arm with his and turned to walk with him. "After breakfast."

He slowed as he realized they hadn't yet broken their fast. "Ah—yes."

"And of course, I'll accompany you."

He weighed the pros and cons of that as they walked to the breakfast parlor. By the time they'd helped themselves from the sideboard, and he'd seated her and sunk into his chair, he'd decided that, all in all, taking her with him was a sound idea.

Given Lady Brougham would likely be at home, Stacie's presence might be helpful, but more importantly, having her with him—within arm's reach—would allow him to focus on the matter at hand without being distracted by his otherwise apparently inescapable concern over whether she was safe. Whether she was well and happy and, most important of all, still his.

No one had ever told him that love could be so discombobulating.

Stacie sat beside Frederick on the box seat of his curricle during the unexpectedly pleasant drive to Hampstead. Just beyond the village, they came to a neat redbrick house set back from the road behind a high stone wall. The gates flanking the gravel drive stood propped wide; Frederick turned his curricle through, and they rolled around the curved drive to the steps that led up to a narrow, pillared porch.

Stacie drew in a long breath. Her principal purpose in accompanying Frederick was, first, to bear witness as to what transpired and whatever might be revealed and, secondly, to ensure his safety, whatever that might entail. She was starting to feel distinctly protective of him in what she mentally termed a lioness-like way; she'd originally used the term to describe Mary's fierce protectiveness of Ryder, but apparently, the reaction wasn't peculiar to her sister-in-law.

Frederick drew his horses to a halt before Brougham's front steps. He hadn't previously visited Brougham at home. The house was substantial, in excellent repair, and painstakingly neat, the flower beds regimented even to the colors of the plants growing in them and the drive edged with bricks to prevent the thick, manicured lawn from creating a raggedy edge.

Every element his gaze lit upon spoke of quiet prosperity; Brougham had inherited a tidy estate from his father, more from a doting aunt, and had, as common parlance put it, married well to boot. While with his house, Brougham's outward show of wealth was restrained, when it came to his purchases of rare books, he was significantly less reserved.

Frederick stepped down to the gravel as a groom came running from around the house. Frederick hadn't brought Timson, knowing that during the drive, he and Stacie were likely to mention sensitive subjects and would want privacy.

Brougham's groom slowed, his eyes widening as they took in the magnificence of Frederick's matched bays, then the lad hurried forward to take the reins.

Frederick handed them over. "I'm not sure how long we'll be— perhaps you'd better take them to the stable."

"Aye, m'lord."

Frederick rounded the carriage and handed Stacie down. She'd changed her peacock-blue riding habit for a walking dress in a rich shade of garnet, combined with a bonnet with satin ribbons of the same hue.

Together, arm in arm, they climbed the steps, and Frederick pulled the bell chain.

Seconds later, a little maid opened the door. Her eyes widened, and she instinctively bobbed. "Yes, sir?"

Frederick handed her one of his calling cards. "Lord Albury and Lady Albury to see Lord Brougham."

The maid stared at the embossed card with its coat of arms, blinked up at them, then stood back and waved them inside. "If you'll wait in the drawing room, my lord, my lady, I'll see if the master is receiving."

The maid showed them into a scrupulously neat drawing room. Stacie drew her arm from his and crossed to sit on the chaise. Frederick followed, but rather than sit, remained standing beside her.

Brougham didn't keep them waiting. He walked in, Frederick's card in his hand, with a faintly intrigued expression on his face and a question in his eyes. "Albury?" Then he saw Stacie and, if it were possible, pokered up even more. He bowed. "Lady Albury—a pleasure."

Stacie rose and held out her hand. "Likewise, my lord." As Brougham advanced and very properly shook her hand, she continued, "When my husband said he intended to visit you, I couldn't not come." As if on cue, Lady Brougham followed her husband into the room, and Stacie switched her smile to her ladyship. "I do hope you'll forgive us for calling like this, out of the blue."

Lady Brougham's pleasure appeared genuine as she declared, "On the contrary, we're delighted to receive you." Her ladyship and Frederick exchanged greetings, and she touched fingers with Stacie, then waved at the chaise and armchairs. "Please, sit."

Stacie sank back onto the chaise, and Lady Brougham joined her. Frederick moved to take one of the armchairs facing the ladies as Brougham moved to claim its mate.

Deciding to take the bull by the horns, Frederick fixed his gaze on Brougham. "I'm here about the volume on ancient Egyptian music I recently acquired."

Brougham pulled a face. "Indeed. I had hoped to acquire it for Kings' library—quite obviously the subject matter intersects with my area of expertise—but I admit"—he tipped his head to Frederick—"that I can see how the book also has relevance to your area of study."

Frederick hadn't expected such an amenable reception or such an immediate opening, but he decided to seize it and risk his hand; Brougham had never been good at pulling off even the most minor deception. "Your interest in and knowledge of the volume is, in part, why we are here. Since the day I took possession of the tome, her ladyship and I have been the subject of a spate of attacks. First, we had a burglar who broke into Brampton Hall in the dead of night, and whom her ladyship inadvertently disturbed—he left those bruises you can see about her neck." Stacie drew aside the gauzy scarf she'd looped about her throat; the marks were fading, but still stood out against her pale skin.

The horror on Brougham's face and his wife's as well told Frederick all he needed to know regarding any association with the attacks. "Subsequently," he went on, "when driving the gig on a track on the estate, we came upon rocks strewn across the way—the gig was wrecked, but luckily, we escaped unscathed."

Both Broughams turned to stare at him, astonished and transparently aghast.

"Then this morning, on our early-morning ride in the park, some blighter shot at us."

"Good Lord!" After an instant more of staring at him, Brougham shifted forward and earnestly asked, "Have you notified the authorities? What did they say?"

Frederick grimaced. "I haven't brought any of this to their attention as yet. We have nothing to offer by way of evidence as to who it might be—or even a certain motive for the attacks."

Lady Brougham's eyes widened. She raised a hand to her throat. "You don't think...?"

Frederick met her gaze and forced his features to ease into what he hoped was a reassuring expression. "I don't believe your husband or you are in any way involved."

Brougham made a choked sound—as if he'd been about to hotly protest being named a suspect, then realized he hadn't been.

Frederick returned his attention to Brougham. "I did, however, want to ask if, while in researching the book, you learned of anyone else who had an interest in it—anyone unscrupulous enough to not greatly care by what means they laid their hands upon it."

He and Brougham were both well aware that there were quite a few gentlemen of questionable morals who inhabited the shady edges of the ancient book trade. Consequently, Brougham did not dismiss the question outright but frowned in thought. Eventually, however, he shook his head and met Frederick's gaze. "No. As far as I know, none of that sort were after this particular tome."

"You were at the auction—who else was bidding?"

Brougham humphed. "Other than me and your man, there were a handful of flashy, young, would-be scholars—you know the sort, those who fancy themselves as erudite gentlemen, at least for this year—but I didn't sense they were that put out, especially not when they heard the final price."

Frederick nodded. "Dilettantes."

"Precisely. Other than them, there was no one else."

"No one hanging back on the sidelines, waiting to see who the book went to?"

Clearly thinking back, Brougham slowly shook his head. "I didn't notice anyone, but ask your man—as he didn't start bidding until it was just me left, he had more time to observe the onlookers."

Frederick nodded. "I will." Then he grimaced. "But it doesn't sound as if the book is high in anyone else's mind."

Brougham shrugged. "The subject matter is rather esoteric."

Frederick nodded. "True."

Silence fell, then with determined brightness, Lady Brougham said, "Now you are here, I hope you will take tea with us. We can go into the garden and be comfortable, and I would like to introduce our children to you."

Frederick glanced at Stacie.

Stacie caught his look and saw the hesitancy behind it, but she was fully in agreement with Lady Brougham's transparent wish to foster a closer relationship. The two men were ridiculously stiff and stilted in each other's company, yet she'd detected not the slightest true antipathy between them, and given their shared interests and Brougham's genuine concern over the attacks, the pair would benefit from a closer association, yet apparently it required Lady Brougham and herself to push them together. She smiled, every bit as brightly as her ladyship. "That would be lovely. Thank you."

She rose with Lady Brougham, and together, they walked out of the drawing room. Neither looked back, leaving their husbands to trail after them as they would.

Yet by the time she and her ladyship had progressed through a parlor and out onto a pleasant rear terrace, taken seats at the wrought-iron table there, and finally, looked to see how their menfolk were faring, the pair had their heads together and were deep in some scholarly discussion of musical theory.

They joined the ladies at the table and consumed their share of the tea and cucumber sandwiches placed before them, but their minds barely deflected from the matter under discussion.

And once they'd finished with their first topic, Brougham volunteered, "You were right about Jolyneaux's treatise—once I read it through carefully, I saw the holes in his argument. Quite reprehensible for the journal's board to encourage him to spout such nonsense."

"Indeed." Frederick nodded, then looked at Brougham. "Have you thought of putting your name forward for the editorial board?"

Brougham met Frederick's eyes and, after a moment, said, "I will if you will."

Frederick's brows rose, then he nodded. "Done. We need to get them back on track, at least as far as our specialties go."

And they were off again, diving into what, for all intents and purposes, was the arcane.

Stacie understood perhaps one word in a dozen. She looked at Lady Brougham, who rolled her eyes and tipped her head toward the lawn. "Come and meet our children."

Three young boys had been playing farther down the lawn.

With her ladyship, Stacie walked slowly down the gentle slope.

Lady Brougham cast a glance back at their husbands, then smiled and faced forward. "I cannot tell you, Lady Eustacia, how pleased I am to see them talking. Simply talking and sharing their views. I've been trying to engineer such a meeting for years, but while Albury was unwed, the opportunity to even meet him was rare and usually not in company conducive to persuading him to call here."

Fascinated, Stacie regarded her ladyship. "Please—just Stacie."

Lady Brougham smiled back. "I'm Henrietta, and I do hope we can be friends."

"I hope so, too," Stacie averred. "And in light of that, might I prevail on you to explain just what the situation was between our husbands that, apparently, inhibited them from interacting with each other before today?"

Henrietta made a disapproving sound. "That's just it—there never was any situation as such between them, no difficulty or anything like that. Well, other than their characters, I suppose." She met Stacie's eyes. "Has Albury mentioned that he and Brougham attended Eton together—in the same year?"

"He alluded to it in passing."

"Well, because of that, they shared the same classes throughout their time there, and as far as I've gathered, both were fixated on music and history even then. Brougham's primary instrument is the oboe, and Albury's was always the piano, so not even in that were they in direct competition. Yet instead of their shared interest drawing them together and becoming a source of friendship, it became the source of a muted sort of rivalry. Nothing in any way violent or extreme, of course—just trumping each other over acquiring this book or that, as in this most recent instance. Their areas of interest intersect, but as I understand it, don't overlap by that much that either feels threatened by the success of the other—and of course, they went to and remain affiliated with different universities, so even in that, they don't personally compete." She paused, then went on, "It always seemed to me that they were both, inside, stiff and standoffish with the other—with each of them waiting for the other to make the first move, which ensured that neither did."

"Ah!" Stacie saw the light. "Each wanted the other as a friend, but was uncertain the other felt the same way, so neither wanted to make the first move and risk being rejected."

Henrietta regarded her as if she'd finally found a like-minded ally. "That's exactly it—you've put your finger on it."

They glanced back at the table on the terrace, where their husbands were deep in discussion. Stacie studied the sight. "I have rarely seen Albury so animated. He needs this as much as you suggest Brougham does."

"They should always have been friends." Henrietta looked on the pair with fond pleasure, then met Stacie's gaze. "Although I think it might well fall to us to keep them talking, at least in the short term."

Stacie grinned. "Nothing could be easier. We'll simply have to organize some quiet dinners for just the four of us. Perhaps we can add their museum curator friend, Wiggs?"

Smiling, Henrietta tipped her head in agreement, and they continued to where the children were playing.

The rest of their stay went in meeting and being greeted appropriately by the Broughams' three boys. Stacie was pleased to find that Frederick and Hubert had progressed to first-name terms as well. As soon as the children rushed off, the talk turned once more to musical matters. Both men seemed a trifle stunned by how very much they had in common; it was transparent that both had dispensed with the shields they had, apparently, kept high for well-nigh twenty years.

Men! Stacie had to smile.

By the time Frederick asked for the carriage to be sent for, and he and she rose to depart, and Henrietta and Hubert walked them to the door, it seemed clear, at least to both ladies, that the basis for an ongoing friendship had been laid.

"Perhaps you might come for luncheon next time," Henrietta suggested.

"That would be lovely," Stacie responded. "And we must, at some point, have you come down to stay at Brampton Hall." She caught Hubert's eye. "I'm sure Hubert will be keen to see Frederick's collection."

Although interest flared in Hubert's eyes and Frederick didn't look at all opposed, neither man said yea or nay; instead, they exchanged a somewhat startled look, as if only then realizing that their wives had formed an alliance, possibly even more definitely than they had.

As they shook hands and took their leave, Stacie couldn't help but reflect on the irony that, courtesy of the attacks and whoever was behind them, she had made two female friends in as many days.

The curricle, drawn by Frederick's bays, had been brought around to the gravel before the porch. Frederick and she descended the steps, and he handed her up, then climbed up himself, and with last waves to the Broughams, who were standing on their porch, they rolled off down the drive and turned onto the road back to London.

"Well," Frederick observed, as he tooled the bays along the macadam, "while in the matter of learning who is behind these attacks, that was a waste of time, I'm...happy that Hubert and I had a chance to talk." He glanced sidelong at Stacie. "We never really have, you know."

"So Henrietta told me. Clearly, you both needed a shove, and odd though it seems, this business of the attacks provided it."

"Indeed." After a moment, he sighed. "While we were talking of music, it was easy to forget the reason we were there, yet we're now left with the question of, if not Brougham, then whom?"

From the corner of his eye, he saw Stacie, distinctly sober now, nod.

"More," she said, "I think we need to question whether getting their hands on the book is, in fact, the motive driving whoever is behind the attacks. You questioned that from the first, and I think you're right. It's not about the book—we need to think what other motives someone might possibly have."

Crack!

Stacie shrieked and gripped the railing as the curricle lurched, then an even mightier crack rent the air, and the right wheel spun away, and the seat dipped precariously.

Not again!

Frederick tried to stand, catch Stacie, and fling them from the curricle, but this time, he'd been driving and was on the dipping side. He had a split second to decide—stay clinging to the seat and risk getting trapped under the wreck or leap into the middle of the road?

His earlier imagined vision of Stacie's lifeless body in the wreck of the gig swamped his mind, and he chose the latter. Wrapping his arms around her, he flung himself bodily back—away from the disintegrating curricle and onto the macadam.

He clutched Stacie to him, trying his damnedest to land with her atop him, and caught a fleeting glimpse of a coach and four thundering up the road toward them.

Then he landed on his back on the road. His shoulders thumped down; his head followed.

Sharp pain exploded through his skull, and blackness engulfed him.

CHAPTER 17

*T*hey landed heavily, and Stacie lost her breath. For a second, she lay slumped on Frederick's chest, then she managed to lift her head and haul in some air. She looked up—and saw horses bearing down on them, but before she could even open her mouth to scream, the coachman, shock written all over his face, was hauling on the reins and swerving the beasts to a stamping halt on the verge.

Yells and calls reached her, but she couldn't make sense of them. She looked down at Frederick, "Are you all right?" on her tongue, only to find his eyes were closed. She registered how deathly still he was just as his hands slowly slid from about her and fell, lifeless, to his sides.

"Oh no!" She scrambled off him. Kneeling by his side, she patted his cheek. "Frederick?"

Not so much as a muscle twitched.

She stared at his chest. It rose and fell steadily. "Thank God."

She slid her fingers into his hair, reaching around his head, gently probing. She was dimly aware that the coachman and groom from the halted carriage had leapt down and run to calm Frederick's beautiful bays; panicked, the horses continued to kick at and drag the broken curricle they couldn't get away from.

People came running, some from a nearby farm, others from the carriages now halting on the road behind them.

Stacie's fingers touched a good-sized lump on the back of Frederick's head. Gingerly, she traced its outline; it was large and no doubt painful.

She cast around, but didn't have anything to cushion his head, so she shifted around on her knees, but his shoulders were too heavy for her to lift.

She glanced up to find a wall of men closing around them.

"Is he dead?" one asked.

"No. But he's hit his head, and I can't lift him to get it off the road."

"Here. Let us help."

Several men crowded around, and all she could see were boots, trouser legs, and reaching hands. Then a hand darted in from the side, and silver glinted close by Frederick's throat. Instinctively, she batted the thing—*a knife?*—away, and it vanished; when, shocked, she looked again, there was nothing—not even a hand—there.

She couldn't even be sure it hadn't been some trick of the light.

In the end, two kindly older men in the sober clothes of merchants took charge, urging the other would-be helpers back—sensibly calling on all to give the man air—then they helped her raise Frederick's shoulders enough for her to ease her knees under so that, when the men let Frederick gently down, she could cradle his head in her lap.

She bent over him and, again, patted his cheeks—more firmly, this time. "Frederick?" She hated the way her voice hitched. "Please, darling," she pleaded, "open your eyes."

His brow lightly furrowed, a frown growing, then his lashes fluttered and rose. As she hung over him, upside down, he met her eyes, and she could have wept on seeing lucidity in his golden gaze.

His frown deepened. He raised his hands and clutched his head. She leaned back, and slowly, he sat up; she helped support him.

"Hell!" Frederick briefly closed his eyes, felt Stacie's hand on his back, told himself she was reasonably all right, and ruthlessly stifled the terrified fury that had erupted the instant his wits had returned—pure panic that something had happened to her while he'd been unconscious.

His head felt like it was splitting in two. He eased his lids up again, squinting, then, when the world remained steady, he drew in his legs and tried to stand. Hands—Stacie's and an older gentleman's—helped him to his feet. "Thank you," he told them both.

He draped an arm over Stacie's shoulders and used her to keep his balance as, finally, he looked around.

His horses were apparently unharmed and in the care of someone's groom.

Two coachmen were standing beside the remains of his curricle. On seeing him up and alert, they dipped their heads respectfully, and the older one said, "With your permission, sir, we'll need to drag this clear of the road."

"One moment." Keeping his hold on Stacie, taking her with him—as much to soothe his inner self as to ensure he remained upright—he walked the few steps to where the curricle had fetched up. "Was it the axle?"

Both coachmen nodded.

"Aye, sir," the younger man said. "Split right through. Never seen anything like it in all my born days—not on a rig of this quality."

Frederick looked at where the man pointed and simply nodded. The coachman had never seen anything like it because he hadn't previously seen what happened when an axle was sawn almost through and the carriage subsequently driven.

The older coachman nodded sagely. "Aye." Across the wreck, he met Frederick's gaze. "Axles rarely break like that."

Lips thinning, Frederick tipped his head, indicating he understood the warning, then said, "You may haul it off and leave it. I'll send men to get rid of it."

"Thank ye, sir." The older man called for ropes and volunteers to pull the wreckage clear.

Frederick tightened his hold on Stacie's shoulders. "You didn't leave anything in the carriage, did you?"

She glanced down and seemed surprised to find her reticule still swinging from her wrist; she raised a hand and righted her bonnet, which had slipped askew. "No," she replied. "It appears I have everything."

"Good." Frederick turned to thank the others who had helped, but they'd already retreated back to their carriages. He turned and looked down the road. "There's a decent inn at the base of this hill. We can hire a carriage to take us home from there, and the walk down will help clear my head."

She glanced up at him, concern etched in her eyes and face. "Your head still hurts, doesn't it?"

"Like the devil, but at least the pounding isn't so bad I can't think." He steered her toward the groom who held his horses.

"Lovely pair, m'lord," the groom said, offering up the ribbons he'd fashioned into serviceable leading reins. "Doesn't appear they took any harm."

"Thank you for seeing to them." Frederick accepted the reins and passed the groom a shilling. "They're my favorites."

The groom grinned. "They'd be my favorites, too, if I had 'em." He bowed and returned to where his master's carriage was waiting for the blockage to be cleared.

Frederick and Stacie started down the hill with the bays trailing behind, jibbing every now and then, still unsettled by what had occurred.

A horseman cantered up from behind. "Are you making for the inn?"

Squinting up at him, Frederick nodded.

"If you like, I'll send the ostlers up to help with the horses."

"Thank you," Stacie said. "That would be a great help."

Frederick managed a nod of assent; with the way his head was thudding, it was the best he could do.

With a salute, the horseman rode on.

Two minutes later, two eager young ostlers came running up the hill. Their eyes rounded; in happier circumstances, their expressions of awe would have been comical. They took charge of the bays with all due reverence, which seemed to calm the flighty beasts.

Relieved of the horses' reins, Frederick didn't have to concentrate on anything beyond taking the next step, and they progressed without incident to the inn, where they were received with exclamations and assurances of the very best of care for the horses and for themselves.

By then, the pain in Frederick's head had reduced to a dull ache; the walk had, indeed, helped.

Stacie was relieved when, on entering the inn, Frederick released his hold on her shoulders and, standing straight and tall, with his usual commanding air, issued crisp orders that saw the two ostlers riding his bays back to Albury House, a crew of stable hands dispatched to remove and dispose of the wrecked curricle, and a groom and coachman off readying a carriage to transport him and her back to Albury House.

He looked at her, then ordered tea to be served in a private parlor while they waited for the carriage to be prepared.

Having realized by then that they had real nobility gracing their small inn, the innkeeper's wife broke out her special tea service and served them hot tea and quite scrumptious scones with homemade jam.

Stacie thanked the woman, and she bobbed and withdrew. Stacie poured and was relieved to see Frederick not just sip the tea but devour three scones with obvious relish.

She knew she was staring, but couldn't stop. Relief was like a drug, seeping through her veins as the realization sank in that he was recovering as well as might be expected. The effect of that relief, its depth and intensity, threw the power of her earlier emotions—the shock, the panic, the expectation of devastating grief—into sharp focus.

As she sat staring at her husband—who was looking more disheveled than she'd ever seen him, yet, to her eyes, was the most glorious sight she'd ever beheld—she couldn't avoid recognizing the obvious truth.

Sometime over the past weeks, she'd fallen in love.

~

They reached Albury House after the bays, the arrival of which—sans curricle—had, understandably, caused considerable consternation.

Stacie realized they should have sent a message with the ostlers. "Our apologies, Fortingale—we had other things on our minds."

As Fortingale had, by then, taken stock of his master's state—and Stacie's dusty skirts as well—he regally forgave her. "Quite understandable, my lady."

One hand at his temple, Frederick asked, "Is my mother in, Fortingale?"

"No, my lord. She and Mrs. Weston are attending a luncheon at Lady Harborough's. I could send word, if you wish?"

"Good God, no." Frederick met Stacie's eyes. "It's late for luncheon, and I'm famished." He glanced down at his clothes. "I'm in no fit state to sit down at anyone else's table, but I'd rather eat before going up to change."

She interpreted that as meaning he was still feeling shaky and needed the bolstering food would provide. She looked at Fortingale. "I'm sure Mrs. Macaffrey and Cook can put together a cold collation for us."

"Indeed, my lady." Fortingale bowed. "If you and his lordship will go through to the dining room, I will bring in their offerings within minutes."

Fortingale—and Mrs. Macaffrey and Cook—were as good as his word, and once the food was set before Stacie, she discovered she was ravenous, too. Between them, she and Frederick made decent inroads into the dishes provided, then both sat back with somewhat weary sighs.

She studied Frederick's face; although some of the pain-induced tension had eased, to her, his features still appeared tight. "How's your head?"

He glanced at her, considered, then replied, "Better." He set down his water glass and stretched his back and arms. "I daresay I'll feel better yet after I change."

She readily rose and walked with him slowly up the main stairs and to the large bedroom they now shared. Frederick continued on into his dressing room; Stacie trailed after him and leaned a shoulder against the door frame. He seemed recovered enough—steady enough—yet her concerns remained.

While Frederick shrugged out of his dusty coat and tossed it on a rack for Elliot to resurrect, she seized the moment to revisit the revelation that had struck her in the inn parlor; she wasn't sure she was yet ready to deal with it—to assess what her falling in love with Frederick might mean, whether it would necessitate any change in how she dealt with him or in how they conducted their marriage—but for now, she was rattled enough to discover that the feeling was still there and all too real.

It hadn't been any ephemeral emotion evoked by the danger he'd been in. No—it was solid and visceral and powerful...

She hauled her mind away and refocused on Frederick. He'd peeled off his waistcoat and dropped it on his discarded coat. He reached for his cravat and started tugging the simple knot loose, then he frowned and, holding out one section of the linen band, peered down at it. "What's this?" The tips of his fingers speared through a slit in the material. "How on earth did that happen? It couldn't have been there this morning—Elliot would never have missed it."

Stacie's mind flashed back to the moments in the road—to the glint she'd seen and batted away. "Oh, God." She slumped against the door frame.

Then Frederick was there, standing before her. "What is it?" His eyes searched hers. "You've gone deathly pale."

Her eyes locking with his, she moistened suddenly dry lips. "In the road, when you were still unconscious, lots of men gathered around, and at the edge of my vision, I saw a hand and a flash of something silvery dart toward your throat, and without really looking, I batted it away. By the time I turned my head and looked properly, there was nothing there, and I wasn't sure it hadn't been the light reflecting off a shoe buckle or something similar..." She shoved away from the door frame, raised her hands to the remaining folds of the cravat, and pushed them aside.

His fingers followed hers as they found unmarked skin.

"Not a scratch," he said, his eyes darkening. "Thanks to you."

She stared into his eyes; she had no idea what he might see in hers. "The axle shouldn't have broken, should it?"

"No. It was almost sawn through."

"But…" She felt confounded. "How? Where?"

His lips tightened. "I think it must have been while the curricle was in Brougham's stable. My carriage house is secure—the stablemen sleep there, and there's always someone around."

"You think Brougham…?"

She was relieved when he shook his head decisively.

"No. But while Brougham and I were on the terrace, I saw his groom, coachman, and stable boys hanging on a paddock fence admiring my bays. They were there for quite a while—long enough for someone who had been following us to slip into the stable and saw through the axle."

He paused, then went on, "Whoever it is, they're opportunistic, seizing on any chance that offers." After a moment, he added, "Thus far, we've been lucky. If the axle had held for longer and broken when we were in town, on cobbled streets rather than macadam, and with many more carriages, horses, and people about…"

"I just remembered." She felt suddenly giddy and tightened her fists in his shirt to anchor her. "The first men who reached us asked if you were dead, and I said no. It was after that that everyone gathered around and the knife appeared."

He nodded. "He—whoever the blackguard is—was following close enough to be there when the carriage disintegrated, to see if I was killed outright and, if not, to finish the job." He caught her eyes. "Thanks to you, he didn't succeed."

She released her hold on his shirt, raised her hands, and framed his jaw. "You! It's *you* they're after." Uncaring of what he might read in her face, she clung to him, with her gaze desperately willing him to accept that truth.

Frederick couldn't name the emotion that rose inside him as the meaning of all he could see in her features, in her blue eyes, registered. His hands settled on her waist. "Stop panicking. They're not going to kill me—especially not when I have you by my side."

She wasn't soothed. Her panic seemed to be escalating.

He bent his head and set his lips to hers, demonstrating in the most unequivocal way that he was still there, still hers.

Hers.

That thought—that truth—resonated inside him, and when she

returned his kiss with fervent kisses of her own, he saw no reason not to follow their prompting and show her, prove to her, the full gamut of all that undeniable truth meant.

He set aside all reservation, embraced the passion that so readily flared between them, and shaped it—orchestrated it into a display of all he felt.

Emotion was made real, manifesting in increasingly heated kisses, in the possessive need that infused his touch—and hers. He didn't miss that—mistake that. And the realization sent his own heart—his passion and desire for her—soaring.

Unable, it seemed, to break from the hungry, greedy exchange, by stages, they made their way to the bed, divesting each other of their clothes as they went.

They fell on the silken coverlet in a tangle of limbs and searching hands. Hands intent on using stroking caresses to impress on the other the reverence and devotion that had flowered in their hearts.

Need built, and passion swirled about them.

Desire sharpened to a whip and drove them on.

They came together on a gasp and a cry, fusing their bodies with one aim in both their minds.

To hold, to possess—above all, to love.

There were no reins capable of holding them—they plunged into the heat and the fire and let the conflagration have them, let the flames of a passionate love too searing to deny envelop and consume them.

Fast, hard, they raced to the peak and, with an abandon beyond any either had ever known, flung themselves from its pinnacle.

Into shattering pleasure and scintillating joy.

Into ecstasy so far-reaching and profound it metaphorically stopped their thundering hearts.

Slowly, the starburst of their senses faded, and they fell.

Into an abyss of bliss, fathoms deep.

Untold minutes later, drifting in the calm in the wake of their storm, with her eyes closed, Stacie lay slumped by Frederick's side and, with her head resting against his chest, listened to the steady thud of his heart.

She adored moments like this—held them close in her mind—those times when he was with her, but not aware, and she didn't have to hide…

What she felt for him.

How long had she been in love with him?

Looking back, she couldn't say. Love had crept into her quietly, making no fuss, doing nothing to draw her attention while it found its place and put down roots.

Her love for him was now an intrinsic part of her.

She couldn't rip it out, couldn't even pretend it wasn't there—not when it had grown to possess power enough to rule her.

And it had.

Oh yes, it has.

She'd always recognized that love was a protective emotion—the events of the day, the threats to him, were what had brought it rising so strongly to the surface that she couldn't overlook it, couldn't mistake it or doubt its existence. Couldn't deny that love now very definitely lived in her.

Has he seen it?

She'd learned that he was observant and perceptive—and when it came to her, very much so on both counts. If he'd seen and correctly identified what she now felt for him...she doubted it would bother him. He might even be pleased in a smug male way that his wife's heart as well as her body was his.

Regardless, what did her loving him mean for them?

She'd never imagined falling in love herself. While she'd made him promise not to fall in love with her, she hadn't made any counterstipulation about not falling in love with him. It hadn't occurred to her to do so.

Because it isn't necessary.

That understanding rose through her, and she fell on it with relief. *Of course.* Her loving him meant she would protect him, including from herself, at least as far as she was able. Her loving him was a positive development she hadn't imagined might come to be, but it had, and for that, she could only be grateful.

As had always been the case, the only true threat to him and their marriage lay in him falling in love with her.

Admittedly, he was protective of her, but men of his ilk were innately protective of their ladies and possessive, too; neither protectiveness nor possessiveness necessarily indicated love on his part, and thus far, he'd shown no sign of deviating from his word. She felt confident she could trust him on that; men like him didn't seek to fall in love when they didn't need to.

Feeling soothed, reassured, and secure, she mentally wrapped the knowledge of her love for him around her, curled more definitely against his hard body, and let sleep claim her.

~

Frederick woke in the late afternoon. Somewhat warily, he shifted his head and looked down at Stacie.

She was still asleep, the lingering remnants of desire a delicate tinge on her alabaster cheeks.

He considered the sight, considered the intensity of their most recent lovemaking, and prayed that her lack of prior experience continued to leave her unaware that the emotion that drove him—that invested his every touch and was, to him, so apparent in his worship of her—was anything especially noteworthy.

In truth, he'd had no idea love—the force encompassed by that simple word—would prove so powerful, so impossible to control, so undeniable and compelling.

That she'd been in danger, that she'd been close to some assailant wielding a knife, had chilled him; he'd been battling to hold his reactions inside, but her distress had ripped through all the screens and veils he'd fought to keep in place, and his love had surged free, and he'd reached for her.

He hoped she hadn't seen the truth; he was perfectly certain she hadn't yet reached the point that he could with impunity confess to having slid around her stipulation. Regardless, he was going to have to be more careful in the future.

Love wasn't an emotion to underestimate. There was now very little he would not do to protect her—to hold on to her and keep her safe.

~

In the middle of the following morning, Stacie started down the main stairs and heard distant notes falling upon the air—Frederick was playing the piano in the music room.

She'd just finished her usual morning meeting with Mrs. Macaffrey. When Stacie wasn't in residence, she'd discovered that Mrs. Macaffrey operated at her own discretion; apparently, the dowager had declared some years ago that she no longer considered herself mistress of the house, so Mrs. Macaffrey was free to organize as she wished. However, once Stacie had arrived, the housekeeper had insisted proper protocol be observed, and so they had to meet every morning to review the menus and any pending household business.

On reaching the last step, with her hand on the newel post, Stacie paused to listen. The piece Frederick was playing—practicing, it seemed —had a beautiful lilting melody. As she listened, she realized she'd heard segments of it over the past weeks at the Hall. She wondered what the piece was—it didn't sound like Mendelssohn or Haydn, much less Beethoven. Possibly Bach, although she couldn't place it.

After the excitement of the day before, she and Frederick had enjoyed a quiet dinner with the dowager, Emily, and Ernestine; they'd agreed there was no need to worry the ladies with news of the incident with the curricle, and it was unlikely they would otherwise hear of it.

A series of delicate trills, leaping and dancing, tugged her on.

She stepped onto the hall tiles and turned toward the music room, but before she reached the corridor that led into that wing, the music cut off, then she heard Frederick's footsteps coming toward her.

She halted and waited and was ready with a smile when he emerged from the corridor and saw her.

His answering smile was relaxed and, despite the lurking problem of their unknown villain, held a measure of content. "Ah—you're down."

Before she could ask him what he'd been playing, Frederick continued, "I wondered if you wanted to visit the music school—you mentioned you intended to, and checking up on our protégés sounds an excellent idea, especially if you hope to hold another of your evenings in a few weeks' time."

"Indeed." She widened her eyes at him. "Are you free to accompany me?"

Frederick had decided that, henceforth, nothing would keep him from her side, not until they'd solved the riddle of who was behind the attacks. He wasn't convinced that he was the sole target; she'd always been present as well. "I am. We'll have to take the town carriage, as my curricle is no more."

Fortingale appeared, and Frederick gave orders for the carriage to be brought around. Stacie declared her lemon morning gown perfectly appropriate for the visit; Frederick helped her don her half cape while she quizzed him about ordering a new curricle.

Once in the carriage and on their way, he instigated a discussion of the performers she'd mooted adding to her next event and on whether it might prove useful to focus on the works of one composer per evening and, if so, which one.

She was as easy to distract with music as he was. The options kept them engrossed as the carriage rolled smoothly along Piccadilly, down Haymarket to Pall Mall, and eventually, circled Trafalgar Square.

Jenkins, Frederick's coachman, was an experienced driver; he successfully negotiated the tangle of traffic and pulled up the carriage beside the curb before the steps of St Martin's colonnaded porch.

Frederick opened the door and stepped down. As was usual during the day, the pavements surrounding the raised square with its monumental column were filled with a busy, jostling throng, everyone bustling about their business. Instinctively, he glanced around, then turned and gave Stacie his hand.

She gripped it, and he assisted her to the pavement.

Stacie released Frederick's hand and bent to shake out her skirts, then she straightened and turned to him.

And time seemed to slow.

Frederick was looking at her, smiling, waiting to take her arm and escort her up the steps.

Beyond him, a heavyset man stepped out of the crowd and lunged at Frederick.

Stacie's eyes locked on the knife in the man's hand.

She screamed and flung herself at Frederick, shoving him back against the carriage.

A paving stone tipped, and she stumbled.

Into the path of the oncoming knife.

She felt the cold steel slide into her side, into her flesh.

She gasped. Her knees turned to water, and she started to crumple.

The last thing she knew was Frederick's arms closing around her.

Then chill darkness swallowed her whole.

Frederick swore as Stacie slumped, lifeless, in his arms. Rage erupted; narrow-eyed, he looked up, searching for the attacker, but pandemonium had broken out, and the man had vanished into the melee.

The crowd surged, driven by avid curiosity, yet ready to flee if there was more danger about.

Some helpful woman stepped in. "The lady's fainted—give her room to breathe." She waved her arms and succeeded in forcing the crowd to back away, clearing a small area around where Frederick crouched in the lee of the carriage, cradling Stacie's limp form.

Ignoring everyone and everything else, he looked into Stacie's pale face, noted that her breathing, although shallow, was still steady. He'd seen it happen—seen the knife meant for him slide into her instead. Taken by surprise, the villain had already been pulling back, but the knife had been there, thrust out, and she'd fallen onto it.

The damn coward had wrenched the knife free and fled.

With desperation building, Frederick held on to every ounce of control and searched Stacie's midsection. He found the seeping red stain low on her left side. Supporting her with one arm, he hunted with his other hand, found and hauled out his handkerchief, wadded it, and pressed it to the spot, but the wound itself lay hidden beneath gown, stays, and chemise.

Jenkins appeared beside him. "I saw the blackguard what did it, my lord, but he's away in the crowd, and there's no chance of catching up with him." Jenkins paused, then asked, "Is the mistress all right?"

I don't know. "She's alive." That was the critical fact. "We need to stop the bleeding and tend the wound, but we can't do that here—or in the carriage."

Frederick slid his arms beneath Stacie and lifted her.

Jenkins leapt to open the carriage door.

Frederick paused with his foot on the step and caught Jenkins's eyes. "Use your whip. I don't care how you do it, but get us back to Albury House as fast as humanly possible. Then, once we're inside, fetch Dr. Sanderson. Regardless of where he is or what he's doing, tell him Lady Albury has been stabbed and needs urgent attention."

"Aye, m'lord."

Frederick climbed in, and Jenkins shut the door.

Frederick sat and drew Stacie protectively close.

Jenkins took him at his word; the whip cracked and the carriage lurched into motion, plunging and weaving back around the square.

Frederick looked down at a face more pallid than he'd ever seen it. And prayed.

～

Stacie's senses returned in fits and starts.

She felt as if she was surfacing from a very long sleep, her wits rising through a fog of dreams. She had no idea what time it was—not even what day it was; when she tried to remember, she discovered her recollections of what had happened last, before she'd fallen asleep, were too vague and cloudy to make any sense of them.

It took too much effort to raise her lids, much less shift her limbs. Gradually, she realized there was a tight band wound about her ribs; it prevented her from drawing in a deeper breath.

But she was breathing steadily. Now she thought of it, there was a dull pain radiating from her left side, just above her waist, beneath where the band—*a bandage?*—was so tightly wrapped.

Eventually, it dawned on her that she was lying in a soft bed—it might even be hers. Hers and Frederick's.

Then her hearing sharpened, and she heard voices. Two voices, talking in hushed tones. She made out the comforting rumble of Frederick's voice. The other was lighter, a woman's…Ernestine's.

Stacie concentrated and heard Frederick tell Ernestine to go to bed, that he would stay with her—with his wife.

She heard the door open and softly close, then she sensed Frederick draw near.

She thought he hovered over her, then she felt his lips lightly brush her forehead.

Heard his voice whisper, "Sleep and get well."

She knew he settled in a chair by the bed, knew he was close, but the effort of making out his words had been too much, and the clouds billowed again, and she drifted back into the fog.

The next time she awoke, her wits were her own, and her mind was fully aware and able to focus.

She blinked her eyes open. Judging by the quality of the shadows wreathing the room, it was nighttime. The bed curtains had been left open; she glanced to the side and, through a gap in the curtains drawn across the window, saw the blackness of the night sky.

A lamp had been left burning on the bedside table, its flame turned low.

She shifted her head on the pillow and, in the soft light, saw Frederick, still sitting in the armchair drawn up beside the bed; still holding her hand, he'd fallen asleep with his head and shoulders on the covers by her side.

His grip on her hand remained definite, yet gentle, as if he held the finest porcelain.

Moving slowly, she raised her free hand, reached across, and almost wonderingly, stroked her fingers over his dark hair as the memories, now clear, rolled through her mind.

She remembered the moments before the steps of St Martin's—recalled in vivid detail seeing the knife heading Frederick's way. Relived the panic and desperation the sight had evoked.

More vaguely, she recalled what she'd done, but that didn't matter. He was still there, by her side, and as far as she could see and sense, he was unharmed.

Good.

As she was alive, too, then to her mind, all was well.

She smiled—in relief, in satisfaction—and settled her head back on the pillow.

Her hand shifted in Frederick's hair, and he stirred.

She let her hand fall as he woke and raised his head.

His lids rose, and his eyes met hers—and she saw the leap of joy, the flare of hope.

And so much more.

In that unguarded moment, she saw into his soul.

Saw what lived there.

The sight shook her to the core.

"No," she whispered. Horror gripped her; she couldn't breathe.

All she could do was stare at the mind-numbing truth of what he felt for her, shining undeniably in his eyes.

She was vaguely aware of how haggard he looked, of the contrast between the drawn lines of his face and the welling emotion that was all brightness and light that filled him.

That, steady and sure, radiated from him.

She locked her gaze with his as fear rose up and all but choked her. "You *promised* you wouldn't."

The anguished accusation fell on Frederick's ears—and he realized how much he'd allowed her to see...

It was too late to reassemble the shields shock had ripped away.

Equally impossible to deny the reality of what she'd seen. He wouldn't—didn't think he could—do that.

He couldn't go on that way—denying what was so real and true, so powerful and potent.

They couldn't.

It's time.

Undoubtedly, yet he was drained, wrung dry by the past hours, the past day; he wasn't up to explaining and reassuring her, not yet.

Holding her gaze, refusing to turn aside and hide the truth any longer, he told her, "Sanderson said the baby was unharmed. That as long as you recovered, our child would survive."

Nearly overcome by the tide of emotion the words evoked, he raised her hand and pressed a long, fervent kiss to her knuckles.

Her expression had blanked. She blinked. "Baby?"

He'd wondered if she'd realized. "It's early days yet, but Sanderson's probably the most experienced practitioner around, and he was sure. He said you're somewhere between one and two months along. We're apparently to be blessed in January."

He was somewhat cravenly relieved to see that she was as distracted by the news as he was. Ever since Sanderson had told him, his mind kept returning to and fixing on the fact—on the prospect of holding his own child in the new year. Of sharing those precious moments with her.

Gently, he eased his fingers from hers and rose. "I'll get you some water." He crossed to the side table where a pitcher and glasses stood waiting.

Stacie's eyes tracked Frederick, but she wasn't truly seeing him. Instead, her mind was filled with the vision of her cradling a babe—hers and Frederick's.

If anyone had asked if she wanted children, she would have said yes, but now the prospect was staring her in the face...she wanted it with a desperate ardor that stole her breath.

She hadn't known it—she—would be like this.

Then Frederick was back with a glass of water. Her arms were still weak; he helped her to sit up, helped her guide the glass to her lips so she could drink.

When she pushed the glass away, he turned and placed it on the nightstand, within easy reach.

He wasn't, she realized, meeting her eyes, not even when he glanced back at her and said, "There's color in your cheeks—I think it's safe to say you've turned the corner." His lips quirked a fraction in self-deprecation. "Sanderson felt confident you would."

He hesitated, his fingertips trailing over the back of her hand—as if he'd intended to reach for it, but wasn't sure he should. Then he drew in a deep breath and said, "As you're awake, I'll send for Ernestine."

She would have turned her hand and caught his and argued, but he raised both hands, rubbed his eyes, then drew his hands down over the achingly weary planes of his face.

"I need to get some sleep." Finally, his eyes met hers. "When you're fully recovered, we can...discuss whatever you wish."

Her mind was still reeling as she watched him walk to the bellpull and tug it. She wanted to insist he stay and sleep beside her—where else?— then she realized she wasn't, as she'd supposed, in the bed they now shared but in the one in the marchioness's apartments.

They'd been redecorated, too, using the same garnet-red fabrics as in the main bedchamber. The only real difference was that the furniture in this room was lighter, more feminine in style.

Someone had come to the door, and Frederick had spoken with them. Now, he closed the door, glanced at her, then walked toward the connecting door leading to his bedroom.

The way he moved told her just how dragged down he was; small wonder he wanted to get some rest before discussing the issue that now lay between them.

With his hand on the doorknob, he paused and looked back at her, as if, despite all, he didn't want to leave her.

She summoned a smile, weak though it undoubtedly was, and managed to raise a hand and wave him on. "Go. You need to recover, too."

That he did testified to the reality she dreaded. He held her gaze for an instant more, then dipped his head to her, opened the door, and left.

She watched the door close behind him, then the smile fell from her face. She needed time, too—to assimilate all that had changed between them and decide what she ought to do.

CHAPTER 18

*S*tacie awoke the next morning alone, feeling much improved physically, but with a problem more fraught than any she'd ever faced looming before her.

Her worst fears had come true. Frederick had fallen in love with her. What on earth was she to do?

For long minutes, she lay staring at the canopy overhead, debating unanswerable questions such as: How deeply in love was he? Might he fall out of love if she pushed? What could she do if...?

Regardless of her inability to form any answers, the issue wasn't about to go away; she had to get up and confront it.

She rang for Kitty, who was delighted to see her awake, alert, and—so Kitty claimed—blooming. Stacie allowed the maid to fuss over her and tend to the wound in her side, which, thanks to her stays, had proved less serious than everyone had feared, before helping her dress.

She insisted on donning a new gown, one in a stunning shade of teal; she felt certain she was going to need every ounce of confidence-boosting support she could muster for the upcoming discussion with her loving spouse.

Eventually, she deemed herself as ready as she would ever be. Leaving Kitty tidying the room, Stacie headed for the stairs; she carefully held on to the bannister as she descended, in case she suffered a sudden spell of the fainting sort to which she'd heard ladies in a delicate condition were sometimes prone.

Regardless of what lay between her and its father, she wanted their child with every bone in her body.

She reached the front hall, paused to draw breath, and heard lovely music spilling from the music room. Frederick was playing that lilting, dancing air she'd heard him practicing before, but it seemed he'd finally strung all the segments together; the melody was vibrant yet delicate—a truly glorious piece.

She let her feet follow the sound. Not wanting to interrupt and have him prematurely stop, she paused in the corridor just outside the music room and listened.

And found herself swept into a magical delight of exquisitely playful chords, accented by trills executed as only a player of Frederick's quality could produce.

Finally, the piece drew to a well-rounded conclusion. As the last chords rang out, she drew in a deeper breath and walked into the music room.

"Bravo!" Smiling—with the echoes of the piece still ringing in her ears, she was unable not to—when Frederick looked up from the keyboard, she met his eyes. "That was utterly captivating." She walked to where she could lean against the piano's side. "What is it? I've been meaning to ask."

Any hope she'd entertained that he didn't love her—that she'd imagined it—was slain by the warmth in his gaze.

Although his eyes searched hers, his fingers returned to the keys, idly stringing together bits and pieces of the melody. "I haven't named it yet," he told her. "I wrote it for you."

Understanding rocked her. He hadn't composed for years, not since the piece he'd written for his first love more than a decade ago. All the ton knew that. All the ton hoped he would start composing again—and now he had.

For her.

As if to underscore that, he said, "I'm thinking of calling it 'Anthem to My Muse.'" The devil arched a brow at her, inviting her comment.

What lady in her right mind wouldn't want her musician husband to compose such a wonderful piece in her honor?

Yet such a piece, played for others, would be tantamount to a public avowal of his love for her.

She narrowed her eyes on his face. "You are diabolical."

Unrepentant and assured, he held her gaze. "I'm a man in love with my wife."

And there it was.

Unable to look away, captured not only by his personality but also by all he now meant to her—and all that he was making it abundantly clear she meant to him—she ignored the vise tightening about her lungs, ignored the fear that hovered, waiting to swamp her, and instead, drew in a determined breath and said, "You promised. You gave me your word you wouldn't fall in love with me."

He nodded in ready agreement. His fingers embarked on a succession of trills, and a wistful, almost-artful smile flirted about his lips. "Think back," he said. "I promised I wouldn't fall in love with you *after we were wed*. And I didn't. I couldn't, because I was already very much in love with you by then."

She blinked. "What?"

"Falling in love is one of those peculiar activities you can't really repeat," he explained, "not unless you somehow manage to reverse the state first—and I haven't a clue how to do that, and I daresay, neither do you."

She frowned. "You're saying you were in love with me before we agreed to marry?"

His smile turned self-deprecating, a sight she realized she'd seen often in recent weeks. "Why else do you think I suggested we make our sham engagement a reality?"

She stared at him. "I thought it was because of all the perfectly sensible and logical reasons you gave me."

He inclined his head. "For those as well, but the most compelling reason was that I was in love with you."

Her legs felt weak. She folded her arms and leaned on the piano.

His smile deepened, and he went on, answering her unvoiced questions, "I think I loved you from the first instant I laid eyes on you—when you walked into my mother's drawing room—although I admit it took me a little while to realize what it was I felt, and by then, I was too deeply enthralled to retreat. Put simply, I didn't want to."

His eyes had remained steady on hers throughout his revelations, allowing her to confirm that all he was saying was the truth.

Stacie gnawed her lower lip. One thing she knew about love was that, once it bit, it never, ever, let go. If he truly was in love with her—as she was with him...

He glanced at his fingers on the keys, then looked up and, again, met her eyes; this time, his gaze held a challenge. "What would have happened if I'd confessed at the time that I loved you?"

"I wouldn't have married you." The truth fell from her lips without thought.

His smile took on an edge. "I rest my case."

Her head was spinning; not only was she feeling giddy but also as if the world as she'd known it had shifted beneath her feet. Exasperation wasn't far from her surface. "Men like you," she insisted, "aren't supposed to readily embrace love." She uncrossed her arms and flung up her hands. "You're supposed to need to be dragged, kicking and screaming, to it. Instead, you appear to have taken falling in love in your stride."

"Don't be fooled." His tone sharpened. "I had my moments of resistance, but your brothers seem to thrive on the curse—I couldn't see any reason why they should be unique."

She felt her lips involuntarily twitch and slapped her fingers across them. She stared at him. She didn't want to think of what lay ahead—of the glorious future filled with happiness that would *not* now be theirs, of the forever they would now not have, due to the darkness that lived inside her—but she had to be realistic. For his sake, for the sake of the child she carried, she had to face her reality and act, before it was too late. Now she knew he truly loved her, her inner malevolence would inevitably rise and blight everything—just the thought was enough to shred her heart.

Holding his gaze as those thoughts—that certainty—filled her mind, she quietly stated, "You don't understand."

At the sight of all Frederick saw in her eyes—the rising anguish, the expectation of pain, the hovering shadows of despair, defeat, and devastation—he stopped playing and, fisting his hands, fought not to leap up and seize her and hold her. Instead, he evenly replied, "Don't understand that you fear that you will use me loving you to manipulate and emotionally attack me, causing me infinite pain and grief?"

When she blinked, clearly astonished, he simply arched his brows.

After a long moment of staring, her lips firmed, and she nodded. "Yes. That's exactly what my mother did—she drove my father to his grave by breaking his heart again and again, just because she could. She couldn't resist exercising the power his love for her gave her over him."

He'd thought long and hard on the best way to challenge and overturn a long-held belief and had concluded that unrelenting logic was his only real option. "Your mother was an arch manipulator, and she used those skills to harm your father, correct?"

She frowned, then nodded.

"And you believe you've inherited her manipulative traits."

"There's no belief involved. I've been manipulating others since I could talk—and arguably, even before that. It's second nature. My only saving grace is that, to date, I've striven never to harm others by doing so." Her face set, resolution and determination writ large in every line. "I made a vow on my father's grave, one I've held to unwaveringly ever since. I will never become—I *refuse* to become—my mother."

He allowed a gentle smile to curve his lips. "Please know I'm relieved to hear that."

Temper lit her eyes, and she lost her rigid composure and hotly—a trifle desperately—declared, "It's no laughing matter! And you shouldn't be relieved! There's nothing to say that, earlier in her life, Mama wasn't as I have been, and that her...*unquenchable* desire to hurt Papa only surfaced after she realized he loved her—when she learned she could hurt him in that way. I'm *exactly* like Mama in so many ways. How do I know —how do *you* know—that one day, I won't find the temptation to manipulate you and hurt you purely because I can too much to resist?"

At last! "I know because I know *you*. Because I see you as you truly are, not as you fear you might become." He held her gaze levelly. "There's so much in your view of yourself that's wrong, I'm not sure where to start my rebuttal. But perhaps we should cut to the heart of your worry—I've loved you from the first, yet how successful have you been in manipulating me?"

Stacie scoffed; he was a typical, misguided, arrogant male. "If you recall, I manipulated you into performing for the ton again, entirely against your wishes."

His smile returned, his expression confidence personified. "Think again, sweetheart. It's a well-known fact that you can't manipulate someone who knows all about manipulation themselves."

"Then why did you agree to do it?"

"I believe I mentioned I was in love with you—I was also deeply attracted to you. I decided complying with your wishes was the easiest way to get what I wanted—to spend more time with you. That music was your price only made the decision easier." He paused, then spelled it out for her. "I only ever did what I wanted to do. You never successfully manipulated me—I merely allowed you to think you did."

She frowned at him. "Why would I believe that?"

His smile turned wry. "Aside from knowing in your heart that it's true? If you seek further proof, all you need do is ask anyone who knows me well—George, Percy, my mother, my sisters, even Emily. All will tell you that I am not, and never have been, susceptible to manipulation, that it's utterly impossible to make me do anything I don't wish to." He held her gaze. "Never. Not ever."

She continued to frown at him as she tried to work her way through his assertions, tried to see where he was leading her...

At that very moment, he was endeavoring to manipulate her.

Before she could properly grapple with that insight, he leaned on the piano and, still holding her gaze, stated, "In a nutshell, I'm not your father. I'm more akin to Ryder, and you know how successful your mother was with him."

Not at all. She knew that was true.

But Frederick wasn't finished. "Even more importantly, my one and only love, you are not your mother."

She opened her mouth to protest the obvious, but he raised a staying hand.

"No—hear me out." The gaze he leveled on her held a degree of understanding she'd never encountered in anyone else. "I understand your fear has been there since you were a child, steadily growing through all you saw of your mother's machinations and the effect those had on your father. I know that fear has been constantly fed by all those who incessantly tell you how like your mother you are."

He paused, then more gently said, "You are like her on the outside, but inside...?" He shook his head. "No. Your fear has blinded you to that critical truth. Your mother never loved anyone in her entire life. Not her husband, not her children—not even her closest, oldest friends. And yes, I've checked with her oldest erstwhile friend and with Ryder. Lavinia loved only one person in the entire world—herself. That was why she was as she was—no one else ever mattered to her.

"But that's not how you are. Not at all. You love others—you care about others." He paused, his eyes searching hers as if gauging the impact of his words, then stated, "The strongest and most inviolable bulwark against you ever harming me is the simple fact you love me."

She would have sworn her heart gave a little leap, and a tiny kernel of hope kindled.

As if sensing it, he tilted his head and, his eyes on hers, asked, "You do love me, don't you?"

She'd wanted to hold that secret close, her cross to bear once they parted, as she'd assumed they soon would, yet...there was a shadow of vulnerability in his eyes that tugged at her and made it impossible not to respond, "Yes." She frowned anew. "But—"

"But nothing. I've learned a lot about love over recent weeks, and one thing I now know is that the poets had it right: Love conquers all—everything else." He held her gaze, and she could feel his confidence—the confidence he was trying to instill in her.

"It truly does," he averred. "Always."

He rose, and she watched him round the piano and come to her. She straightened and faced him, and he took her hands, one in each of his.

His gaze trapped hers, and softly, he said, "Place your trust in love—yours for me and mine for you. Love, that combined love, will hold us safe, even from ourselves. Because of that love, I won't ever attempt to manipulate you other than for your own good, and you, my love, won't ever harm me—in your heart, you know you never will."

He was utterly, unswervingly certain; she read that in his eyes. Lost in the promise carried in his gaze, she drew in a breath and told herself she might be able to...

She exhaled. "I...still don't know." She clutched his fingers. "I can't see—can't be sure—that our lives and our marriage will continue as they have to date, that the path ahead will remain one of sunshine and roses."

His expression was the epitome of understanding and support. "Sunshine and roses every day will probably grow boring." Without releasing her from his gaze, he raised one of her hands to his lips and kissed. "Better, I think, that we take our future one day at a time. We'll wake up in each other's arms, live side by side through our day, and come together again at night. Life is like a symphony—it has its various movements, all with different cadence and rhythm, yet in reality, it's played one note, one chord, one beat at a time."

Something inside her shifted, and she felt the hovering darkness thin, then wisp away, and her heart—her hopes—started to rise. "And what of love?" she felt compelled to ask. "What part does love play in life's symphony?"

Frederick smiled; he knew he'd won—this round, at least. There might be more battles in the future, but this had been the first and most difficult. "Love is the emotion each player brings to the performance—

the feelings with which you imbue each note, the touch you infuse into each chord. In life, love provides the most powerful joy that buoys and fills and lifts our hearts."

He let his smile deepen and, once again, raised her hand and brushed his lips to her fingers. "We've already started our symphony, you and I— all we have to do to see it through to a glorious end is to devote ourselves to it and keep playing."

Stacie stood on the cusp of her personal paradise, with the dark cloud of her fear receding—dissipated by him, by his confidence in her, by his love for her and hers for him—and with her most treasured dream blossoming before her. "I want you." She clutched his fingers and heard the words fall from her lips. "I want us—our marriage, our children, our home, our shared life." She gripped tighter. "I'll try." A lingering tendril of doubt intruded. "But if we strike a sour note—"

"We won't." His certainty was absolute. "Trust me, my love. Sour notes are not in our repertoire."

She couldn't hold back any longer, not against the plea in his eyes, not against the emotion he'd evoked that now charged the air between them. She stepped forward into his embrace and, as his arms closed around her, murmured, "I'll place my trust in love and in you. You might outclass me as a manipulator, yet from the first, I trusted you, and I always will."

Although triumph shone in his smile, there was a serious light in his eyes as he said, "I swear to you, here and now, that I will never let you— let us—down."

Frederick started to lower his head.

A flicker of movement outside the window had him glancing that way.

He dived to the floor, taking Stacie, already in his arms, with him.

BANG!

The glass in the window shattered, and a bullet plowed into the parquet floor at the far end of the room.

Frederick didn't waste breath swearing. He shoved Stacie under the piano. "Stay there!" He scrambled up, raced across the room, hauled open the French door, and charged after the man racing up the side lawn, making for the stone wall fronting the street.

The man flung himself at the wall. He reached the top and dropped to the street as Frederick laid hands on the thick ivy.

He hadn't forgotten how to climb. He scaled the wall, swung over the top, and dropped to the pavement.

Just in time to see an older carriage careening up the street, one door still hanging open. The carriage slowed for the turn into Park Lane, and a hand reached out, caught the door, and slammed it shut.

Then the carriage turned the corner and was gone.

He glanced up and down the street, but there were no lurking hackneys to commandeer.

Stacie rushed out of the house and down the steps. She fetched up beside him, one hand gripping his arm as she scanned the street. "Are you all right?"

The breathlessness in the question had him jettisoning any inclination to upbraid her for not staying safely in the house. If he wanted her love—and he did—he had to put up with the consequences. "Yes." He focused on her. "What about you? Did the fall jar your wound?"

She shook her head. "Kitty bound it up tight this morning. The bandage didn't shift at all." She looked toward Park Lane. "Did you see anything useful?"

"Enough to be sure of the sort of man our villain is sending against us."

When she looked at him questioningly, he took her hand and turned back to the house. "The man was a rough sort—the type of man one hires from the taverns down by the docks." That whoever was behind the attacks refused to face him openly—to do the deed himself—only fed Frederick's fury.

Also his frustration. "Using such men leaves us little chance of identifying who our true villain is. That said"—he felt his jaw clench—"I've had enough."

Hand in hand, side by side, they climbed the steps to where Fortingale stood by the door, alert and watchful.

As they reached the porch, Frederick vowed, "One way or another, we're going to get to the bottom of this—whatever it is that's going on."

~

After calming the staff and Ernestine—thankfully, his mother and Emily had yet to come downstairs—Frederick and Stacie repaired to the study. Perhaps unsurprisingly, Ernestine refused to let them out of her sight; while Frederick sat mired in thought behind the desk and Stacie fell to pacing—also deep in thought—across the windows of the alcove, Ernestine sat poker-straight on one of the chairs before the desk and watched them both.

Frowning, Frederick picked up a pencil and let it slide through his fingers, twirled it, and let it slide down to tap his blotter—a habit from his schooldays that helped him think. Eventually, he said, "It occurs to me that, while hiring a thug from some dockside tavern makes it more diffi-cult to trace the man and so learn who hired him, it still tells us something about our villain—namely that he knows dockside taverns well enough to find the right man to hire to kill someone."

Stacie paused in her pacing, then drifted closer and perched on a corner of the desk. "So our villain is someone who knows dockside taverns well."

Frederick nodded. "That seems a reasonable bet. And given how many unsuccessful attempts have thus far been made, I think we can also conclude that our villain, whoever he is, isn't able to pay for a quality assassin—someone who actually knows what he's doing."

He glanced at Stacie and, when she frowned at him in puzzlement, explained, "If he came to Brampton Hall to kill either you or me, then he made a poor fist of it. Breaking into the house in the dead of night—if you hadn't walked in on him in the kitchen, how would he have proceeded? Even if he knew which room we were in, it's a huge house to go tramping around in."

She nodded. "Especially in the dark, walking through areas with which he would have been totally unfamiliar."

"And if he had found his way to the room we were sharing, what then?" Frederick shook his head. "I suppose he might have had a pistol on him, but even so, attacking both of us at once in a large house full of servants would have been a huge risk." He paused, then went on, "Next, he tried the rocks on the track—that had to have been the same man."

Stacie nodded. "Or men."

Frederick narrowed his eyes. "I think just one—if there had been two, there would have been two in the kitchen, and more and more, I'm inclined to think our villain is cash-strapped—that he walked into a dock-side tavern and found a thug willing to do the deed for what our villain was able to pay."

"Hmm." Stacie folded her arms and frowned. "The rocks on the track—overturning a gig is hardly a certain way of killing someone."

"True. But if he'd been hiding in the woods, waiting to finish us off...

He would likely have assumed only one of us would drive out in the gig." Frederick tipped his head. "That might have worked."

"Except it didn't, and we came back to town," Stacie said, "and he shot at us in the park."

"*What?*"

With Stacie, Frederick glanced at Ernestine, who he realized had been hearing of the earlier attempts for the first time.

Looking shocked and pale, she stared at them. "Some blackguard has been trying to kill you both all this time—ever since you married?"

Frederick, hearing what might be the critical point clearly stated, nodded. "Indeed."

Ernestine shifted her gaze to Stacie, then waved a hand before her face and rose. "If you will excuse me, my dears, I believe I need...my smelling salts."

Stacie smiled understandingly. "Yes, of course."

As the door closed behind Ernestine, Frederick returned to their review of events. "Actually, that attempt in the park tells us quite a bit about the hired thug's capabilities. He was about twenty yards away from us, standing still and steady. We were right in front of him, and even though we were moving, we weren't moving fast, and there was nothing more than a light breeze. Anyone familiar with a pistol should have hit one of us, and if not one of us, then at least one of our horses. That he managed to miss us entirely suggests he's not used to handling a gun."

Stacie's brows rose. "Perhaps that's why, for his next two attempts, he opted for a knife."

"Very likely. A thug of that type would be comfortable with knives."

Stacie drew in a breath that wasn't entirely steady. "He nearly managed to kill you on the way back from the Broughams."

Frederick reached across, caught one of her hands, and gently squeezed. "If it hadn't been for you—then, and again, outside St Martin's —he might have succeeded."

Stacie met his eyes. She held his gaze for several seconds, then, as if drawing strength from the contact, filled her lungs and said, "So he came with a gun today."

Frederick nodded. "He came with a gun, and he came to the music room."

She frowned. "That could have been a good guess—you are well known to be a pianist. He might have thought the music room would be the best place to look for you."

"But how did he know where the music room was? In fact, how would a thug of that type know about music rooms at all? Yet he came over the wall in the right spot to approach the music room directly—in fleeing, he would have gone the same way." Frederick leaned back in the chair, grimly accepting what that meant.

Stacie put it into words. "Our villain knows this house or at least where the music room is."

"Which narrows the field to all the guests Mama has entertained here over the decades."

Stacie wrinkled her nose. "And I suppose all the other times, he might simply have been following us."

Frederick tipped his head in agreement. Still holding her hand, his thumb gently rubbing circles over the soft skin, he let his mind skate back over all they'd said. "Our villain is someone familiar with this house, but has insufficient funds to be able to hire a competent assassin. And while I feel Ernestine's point—that the attacks commenced after our wedding—is both correct and somehow relevant, I can't see how it fits."

When Stacie looked at him, he met her gaze.

After a moment of studying him, she said, "I can't help but see a parallel between what's been happening to us and what my mother caused to happen to Mary and Ryder." He frowned, and she went on, "That was all about the succession—so the pertinent question in this case might also be: Who is your heir?"

His face cleared. "Carlisle, who you've met. And with Carlisle, what you see is the genuine man." He shook his head. "I can't see him being in any way involved in this—he's definitely not the bloodthirsty, or even the desperately acquisitive, type."

Stacie's eyes narrowed. "Hmm. But it was Rand who was Ryder's heir, not Mama, and Rand was entirely clueless as to Mama's plotting." She refocused on Frederick's eyes. "What about Aurelia? She wasn't thrilled over me joining the family—I thought she was thawing at our wedding, but when I spoke to her before we left the wedding breakfast, she was still distinctly chilly."

Frederick frowned. "She was?"

Stacie nodded decisively, but after a second's further thought, she grimaced. "Then again, I've heard that Aurelia is frequently chilly to everyone, so I'm not sure that counts."

Frederick forced himself to consider the prospect that the motive behind the attacks was the succession. Eventually, he said, "No matter how I try, no matter what pressure he might be under, I can't see Carlisle doing anything so mercenary and inherently messy and risky as plotting my demise. He would be much more likely to approach me for help. And as for Aurelia"—he shook his head and met Stacie's eyes—"while I accept that she has as much to gain as Carlisle by my death, I can't see her being behind these sorts of attacks, either. Hiring a low-class thug—even through an intermediary—is definitely not Aurelia's style."

Stacie humphed. "I doubt she'd even countenance an intermediary who would associate with thugs."

Frederick grinned and tipped his head. "That's true."

A peremptory rap fell on the study door, then it opened and a determined-looking Mary walked in with Ryder, grim-faced, at her heels. They were closely followed by Frederick's mother and Emily, both looking concerned and, if Frederick was any judge, faintly miffed at not having been summoned sooner.

Ernestine brought up the rear. She shut the door, waited until the others disposed themselves in the various armchairs, then crossed to retake the chair she'd earlier vacated. With a defiant tilt to her chin, she looked at Frederick and Stacie and announced, "This is a time for family to rally around."

Given the expressions on the faces now turned their way, Frederick accepted that there was no point in arguing. In fact, it probably was time to seek wider counsel. He inclined his head in acquiescence and let his gaze touch each face. "Thank you for coming."

Mary, who'd looked poised to annihilate any argument he attempted to make, narrowed her eyes on him. "Perhaps you might open our discussions by telling us all of the attacks that, apparently, you and Stacie have been subjected to."

Frederick exchanged a glance with Stacie and, at her encouraging nod, proceeded to outline all the incidents and included their thoughts on what each suggested about their assailant and who had hired him.

While listening to their observations regarding the thug, and what that might mean, Ryder nodded several times.

Frederick concluded with their recent thoughts on the succession being a possible motive. "But that avenue doesn't seem to get us any further."

Mary and Ryder exchanged a long glance, then Ryder looked at Frederick and said, "Instead of asking who benefits directly by your death—namely Carlisle, who I think we all agree"—he glanced at the dowager,

Emily, and Ernestine—"doesn't have the right character for a villain—perhaps we should be asking who benefits by Carlisle succeeding to the title, other than Carlisle himself?"

Frederick glanced at Stacie, but it was his mother who said, "Aurelia?"

When everyone looked at her, the dowager huffed. "I suppose she's definitely one who will benefit, but although she is not my favorite person—indeed, she's not a particularly likeable person at all—I can't see the change in position, even being elevated to the title of marchioness, as being a sufficient lure to push her into the act of hiring someone to murder another. She's extraordinarily straitlaced, and even a whiff of scandal is, in her terms, something to be avoided at all costs."

The dowager tightened her shawl about her shoulders and looked at Stacie. "I suspect that's why Aurelia has been a trifle stiff with you, my dear. Given your mama's reputation, Aurelia would have feared that your association with our family would bring scandal in its wake—and neither the circumstances surrounding your engagement or your wedding would have allayed those fears in the least."

A short silence ensued.

Mary broke it. "I agree with Ryder. Given we're satisfied these attacks have nothing to do with music and books, the qui bono angle seems the most likely. So if not Carlisle or Aurelia, then who?"

Stacie looked from one face to the other as the silence stretched—and stretched.

Then Emily, looking faintly conscious, suggested, "What about Mr. Barkshaw?"

"Mr. Hadley Barkshaw?" Mary clarified. When Emily nodded, Mary looked at the dowager. "How is Hadley Barkshaw connected to the marquessate?"

"Indirectly." The dowager turned to stare at Emily. "He's Aurelia's brother."

Emily explained, "Aurelia was a Barkshaw before she married Carlisle. Hadley is Aurelia's younger brother. She has an older brother as well, but I believe he spends most of his time in the country with the elder Barkshaws—their parents."

"Who," the dowager added, "are known to be exceedingly strict in their ways. Hence, Aurelia's overreaction to any possible hint of scandal."

Puzzled, Stacie asked, "Why did you suggest Hadley, Emily?"

From the look on Mary's face, she'd taken the words from her sister-in-law's mouth.

Emily colored. "It was just a notion—an impression I've gathered based on what I've seen at various family functions. People—well, those like Hadley, who is very self-centered—often forget I'm there and are wont to speak rather indiscreetly, and I rather suspect that Aurelia has been…" Her gaze grew distant as if she was recalling a conversation, then she refocused and said, "I believe the term Hadley used was 'bailing him out' with funds."

"Well!" the dowager said. A second later, she added, "Not that I find I'm all that surprised—not on either of their parts."

Ryder had been watching Mary's face. When a short silence fell, he prompted, "Mary?"

After Emily's revelation, Mary had been staring at the rug. She blinked and looked at Ryder, and he asked, "Can you add anything regarding Hadley Barkshaw?"

Mary primmed her lips, then eased them and said, "There's nothing I know of as verified fact. However, I do recall that Hadley, who generally presents as being charming and personable, was said to have been sniffing around Miss Dunsworthy's skirts until her father and brother got wind of it and—according to the rumors—saw him off. Given that the Barkshaws and Dunsworthys are of similar social standing, but that Miss Dunsworthy is something of an heiress, one is left to draw the obvious conclusion." She looked around at all their faces and explained, "That the Dunsworthys discovered enough about Hadley to convince them that he was after Miss Dunsworthy's money—more, enough to decide he was an undesirable parti."

Stacie glanced at Frederick and found him exchanging a long look with Ryder, one laden with several layers of meaning.

"I believe," Ryder said, speaking to Frederick, "that you and I should consult with Rand and, through him, with whoever else we need to speak to in order to get a definitive answer regarding Hadley Barkshaw's finances."

Looking increasingly focused, Frederick nodded. "My thoughts exactly." He and Ryder rose. Frederick glanced at Stacie, then at the other ladies. "We'll return as soon as we can, but until then, I believe I speak for both Ryder and myself in asking you all to remain here—in this house."

Safe and surrounded by the Albury House staff, who—Stacie had not the slightest doubt—Frederick would set to guard them.

She wanted to go with him, but it was likely their quest would take them into the gentlemen's clubs and similar places where she couldn't go; they would find what they needed to uncover faster without her.

Before Stacie could, Mary answered, "Of course." She glanced at the others, finally bringing her gaze to rest—wryly understandingly—on Stacie. "We'll wait here—just hurry up and find out if Hadley might be the one behind all this. If he isn't, we'll need to think again."

Stacie met Frederick's eyes. "Perhaps that's something we can do while you and Ryder are out—see if there's anyone else we can think of who might possibly be behind these attacks."

Frederick nodded. "Good idea. We'll leave you to it." He caught her hand, raised it swiftly to his lips, his eyes trapping hers as he briefly kissed her knuckles, then he released her and followed Ryder to the door.

Stacie watched them go—the two men in all the world she held most dear—then she stifled a sigh, rose and rounded the desk, and joined the other ladies.

They put their heads together and wracked their collective brains, but after fifteen minutes, none of them had advanced any other name for the role of possible villain.

Relaxing in the armchairs, the other ladies started to chat about this and that—the usual inconsequential matters that absorbed the ton. Stacie did her best to pay attention and contribute; she was well aware that all four ladies had remained to do their part in keeping her occupied and therefore safe—for no other reason than that they loved and cared for her as she loved and cared for them.

This, she told the tiny child growing inside her, *is the stuff of which families are made.*

CHAPTER 19

Frederick and Ryder returned to Albury House while the ladies were still at the luncheon table.

Frederick walked into his dining room to see Stacie seated in her usual place; she'd been avidly chatting with Mary and Emily and appeared reasonably calm—at least she wasn't pacing.

On his and Ryder's arrival, all five ladies ceased talking and fixed them with expectant looks.

As he and Ryder took their places at the table, Mary, imperious as always, demanded, "Well?"

"In a moment," Frederick returned. He glanced at the two footmen who had been serving, then looked at Fortingale, who promptly directed the footmen to set down the water and wine jugs they were carrying and leave the room.

As the pair passed out of the door, Fortingale caught Frederick's eye and faintly arched his brows—asking if he should depart as well.

Frederick shook his head. Better Fortingale remained and heard the story; if they were to pursue the idea he and Ryder had tossed around in the carriage on the way home, they would need the butler's—indeed, the entire household's—assistance.

Fortingale shut the door and, while Ryder and Frederick served themselves from the platters the ladies readily passed them, circled the table and filled Frederick's and Ryder's water and wine glasses. When Fortingale stepped back to take up his usual position beside the sideboard, Frederick, his fork in his hand, looked around at the ladies' impatient faces and stated, "It seems entirely possible that Hadley Barkshaw is, in fact, behind the attacks on myself and Stacie."

"Well!" The dowager sat back, a host of emotions crossing her face. "That is going to set the cat among the pigeons with the Barkshaws."

Mary leaned forward. "What did you learn?"

Down the length of the table, Stacie met Frederick's eyes. "Start from the beginning—what did Rand say?"

Ryder replied, giving Frederick the chance to eat a few mouthfuls. He'd been seriously impressed that, once Rand had understood what they needed to know, it had taken Stacie's brother a matter of an hour before he handed them the name and address of a Mr. Mordaunt, a major money-lender in the East End, who, according to Rand's sources, was the person they needed to speak with regarding Hadley Barkshaw.

"So," Ryder concluded, "Frederick and I paid Mr. Mordaunt a visit."

Ryder looked at Frederick, and he nodded and took up their tale, allowing Ryder to address his plate.

"Luckily," Frederick said, "Mordaunt was at home and, once we sent in our cards, entirely willing to speak with us. Indeed, he was quite eager to meet me—to actually set eyes on me. It transpired that Mordaunt was laboring under a series of consecutive misapprehensions, on the basis of which he'd loaned Hadley Barkshaw far, *far* more than he otherwise would have."

Eyes on his plate, Ryder snorted. "You really have to hand it to Bark-shaw—Mordaunt is no one's fool, but Hadley hadn't just convinced him with his tale but had strung him along through setback after setback."

"How?" Stacie stared at Frederick. "How on earth did Hadley lure an experienced moneylender—which is what I assume Mordaunt is—in?"

"And then continue to pull the wool over his eyes?" Mary added.

Frederick picked up his wineglass and took a sip while rapidly consid-ering how frank he should be. Lowering the glass, he decided that, given what he knew of the ladies present, none of them were likely to have the vapors. "Initially," he said, "Hadley borrowed on the grounds that, although by then I was in my late twenties, I remained unmarried, lived the life of a scholar, and eschewed the ton, and had shown no interest whatsoever in marriage—or, in fact, in females—at all." Frederick met Stacie's eyes and saw them widen in comprehension.

"And Mordaunt believed that?" she asked, as Mary, Frederick's mother, and Emily all made inelegant sounds of disbelief.

Frederick inclined his head. "In that, Hadley neatly used the discretion I have always practiced, combined it with Mordaunt's apparently somewhat jaundiced view of men who devote themselves to musical pursuits, and came up with a story that worked to Hadley's advantage. Suffice it to say he convinced Mordaunt that there was every likelihood that I would never marry, and that at some point in the future, Carlisle or Carlisle's son, Jonathon, would inherit the title and the estate—and most importantly, the estate's coffers."

"I still can't see..." Frowning, Mary looked at the dowager and Emily. "Would Carlisle have repaid Hadley's loans? Perhaps to placate his wife and his in-laws?"

The dowager considered, but eventually shook her head. "Carlisle is as generous as the next man, but he has sons and two daughters to establish... I really can't see Carlisle, who, while not as priggish at Aurelia, frowns on even the most innocent forms of gaming, being, as the term goes, an easy touch—not for Hadley."

"That wasn't Hadley's pitch to Mordaunt." Having taken the opportunity to clear his plate, Frederick lifted his wineglass, sat back, and sipped.

It was Stacie who guessed, "Aurelia. Hadley told Mordaunt he could bleed what money he needed from the estate through Aurelia. That way, it wouldn't have mattered whether it was Carlisle or Jonathon who inherited. Regardless, Hadley could claim Aurelia would have access to the funds he needed."

Frederick and Ryder nodded.

Ryder touched his napkin to his lips, then lowered it and said, "According to Mordaunt, Hadley claimed Aurelia will give him any money he wishes once she has access to the marquessate's funds—quite how she would do that, Hadley didn't specify, but he had told Mordaunt of Aurelia's fear of scandal and how she would do anything to ensure the Barkshaw family name remained untarnished."

"That was something Mordaunt could and did check," Frederick said. "He had information on the elder Barkshaws and the older brother and his family that confirmed what Hadley had told him—namely, that the Barkshaws value their scandal-free name above all other considerations."

He paused, then went on, "Obviously, when Mordaunt saw the announcement of Stacie's and my engagement—and then the wedding occurred so soon afterward and quietly to boot—he leapt to the obvious conclusion."

The ladies' faces conveyed their dawning comprehension of how, to an outsider, the unexpected betrothal followed by a wedding twenty days later might appear. "Oh," Ernestine said.

Stacie's eyes met Frederick's. "What did Mordaunt do?"

Ryder answered, "Unsurprisingly, Mordaunt wanted to ask Hadley just what your engagement, and then your marriage, meant in terms of his investment, but it took him another few weeks to hunt Hadley down."

"By which time," Frederick took up the tale, "Hadley had decided that —as you and I were conveniently in the country, out of sight of everyone, including Mordaunt—that I was suffering from an incurable illness, and our engagement and marriage was actually a noble kindness arranged by our families designed to give you"—he nodded down the table to Stacie —"an established spinster, the protection of my title and a dower settlement on my death, which was expected at any minute."

Ryder shook his head in disbelief. "I have to admit to being in awe— Hadley shouldn't have been able to worm his way out of such a situation, but he found a story that Mordaunt didn't know enough not to believe. Hadley played on Mordaunt's expectations of ton behavior and got away with it."

Frederick drily added, "Hadley also spun a tale that Mordaunt wanted to believe—he didn't want to think that he'd been played like a fish on a line from the start."

"But," Mary said, "Mordaunt now knows the truth."

"Indeed." Ryder cut a glance at Frederick.

Frederick noted Ryder's look and transferred his gaze to Stacie. "In order to ensure that Hadley didn't, somehow, manage to dream up yet another twist, I felt it wise to tell Mordaunt of our expectations of an addition to our family in January."

"What?" The dowager sat up and, along with the other ladies, looked at Stacie.

She blushed delightfully and tipped her head their way. "We only found out yesterday, when Dr. Sanderson examined me."

As delighted as his wife and proud with it, Frederick smiled as congratulations rained down on both him and Stacie.

Eventually, however, the ladies refocused, and Mary asked, "So what do we do next?" She looked around the table. "I assume we're all in agreement that it's Hadley who has been arranging the attacks on you both?" At the last, she looked from Frederick to Stacie.

It was Ernestine who suggested, "This Mr. Mordaunt doesn't sound as if he would be the most forgiving of men. Is it possible for us to…well, leave it to him to suitably chastise Hadley?"

"No." Both Frederick and Ryder had spoken simultaneously. Ryder looked to Frederick, who explained, "Mordaunt is not a man to cross—Rand and his sources were abundantly clear on that point. And yes, Mordaunt will be exceedingly keen to wreak vengeance on Hadley—not least to ensure the story of how Hadley has effectively swindled him never gets out. However, quite aside from the moral question of consigning even Hadley to the untender mercies of someone of Mordaunt's reputation, I can't be comfortable giving Hadley any chance whatsoever of doing something desperate in a last-ditch effort to placate Mordaunt."

Her features set, Stacie nodded. "For instance, by attempting to kill you himself."

His eyes flicked to meet hers. "Or you."

Their gazes held for an instant, long enough for each to sense the other's resolution.

"Consequently," Frederick said, "as we have no evidence beyond the circumstantial, I believe we need to confront Hadley and force a confession from him."

"Not by—in any way, shape, or form—using yourself as bait." Stacie's words rang with iron-clad determination.

Her tone brought a smile to Frederick's lips. He inclined his head. "No, indeed. I am not of a mind to place either of us at risk."

He glanced at Ryder.

To the ladies, Ryder said, "As we speak, Mordaunt will be arranging to go after Hadley, but first, Mordaunt's men will have to find Hadley, and Hadley's proved adept at avoiding them. However, that does mean that whatever we do, we need to move quickly—before Hadley realizes something's changed and that Mordaunt is after him and, this time, decides to take matters into his own hands and makes a bid to remove Frederick or Stacie." He glanced at Frederick, then at Stacie, and grimly added, "For Hadley's purpose, either of you would do."

Tapping his fingertips on the tablecloth, Frederick said, "While we might, eventually, be able to assemble formal proof of Hadley's involvement in the attacks, to do so, we would need to trace the thug—or possibly thugs—who have been trying to kill us over the past week, and we don't have time for that."

"Nor," stated the dowager, "would we wish to visit a scandal of such magnitude as a criminal trial on this family."

Frederick inclined his head in acknowledgment. "So that leaves us facing the question of inveigling Hadley to say enough before witnesses to implicate himself."

Mary's eyes had narrowed on her husband. Now, she glanced at Frederick, then at Stacie. "With our combined talents, that shouldn't be impossible."

Ryder nodded. "On the way back here, Frederick and I had an idea."

Stacie held up a staying hand and pushed back her chair. "If we're to give this endeavor our best, I suggest we repair to the drawing room."

Readily, indeed eagerly, they all rose and returned to the drawing room.

As Frederick, the last of the group, was about to cross the threshold, Fortingale ventured, "Once you have your plan devised, my lord, rest assured that I and the entire household will stand ready to do whatever is necessary to implement it."

Frederick smiled. "Thank you, Fortingale. Her ladyship and I will inform you of our requirements as soon as we can."

Fortingale bowed, and still smiling, Frederick followed the others into the drawing room. The door shut behind him, and they all found seats. Then, between them, he and Ryder outlined the bare bones of the plan they hoped would lure Hadley Barkshaw into revealing his guilt.

An hour later, Stacie led the others into the room on the first floor she'd elected to use as her private parlor. She crossed to the escritoire, set between two long windows, sat on the chair before it, let down the lid, and reached for a pen and her recently delivered new stationery, embossed with her title and the Albury coat of arms.

The others took up positions around the room—Frederick and Ryder lounging against the mantel, while the other ladies settled on the chaise and the delicate chairs.

"Very well." Stacie dipped her nib into the inkwell. "Tell me how to phrase this."

Emily—who was a dab hand at wording invitations, having assisted the dowager in that capacity for a decade and more—dutifully recited,

"My dearest Carlisle and Aurelia. It is my greatest hope that you will both find yourselves free…"

Emily continued, and Stacie wrote out the two invitations they'd decided to send, one to Carlisle and Aurelia and the other to Hadley, inviting all three to a "family dinner" at Albury House that evening. After apologizing for the short notice, they'd decided to include what Ryder had termed a well-baited hook by declaring that Frederick and Stacie were expecting to return to Brampton Hall again, but wanted to discuss a matter that impacted on the estate prior to leaving London.

Stacie finished the notes and blotted them, and Emily told her the addresses to which to direct them.

Finally, the notes were ready, and Frederick rang and handed them to Fortingale, instructing him to dispatch both notes immediately in the hands of two footmen. "Tell the men that the notes must be delivered as soon as possible—the man you send with the note to Mr. Barkshaw might have to hunt him down—and both men are to wait for a reply and return with it as soon as they're able. If necessary, they may say the message relates to urgent family business and tell them to take hackneys as much as possible—time is of the essence."

"Yes, my lord." Fortingale departed with zeal in his step.

Stacie stretched her arms, then looked at the others. "Tea?"

They could do nothing more until they were assured that Hadley as well as Carlisle and Aurelia would attend their hastily convened dinner party; there was a general consensus that tea would be an excellent way to pass the time.

"In that case"—Stacie rose and motioned the others to their feet —"we'll be much more comfortable in the drawing room."

They returned downstairs and settled to wait.

To everyone's relief, they didn't have to wait for long. Both footmen returned within the hour.

The first, who reported back while the company in the drawing room was still fortifying themselves with tea and scones, relayed Carlisle's and Aurelia's politely worded acceptance. The second, who had set out to find Hadley, eventually arrived as the clock ticked toward the hour.

"I was lucky, my lord," Thomas reported. "Mr. Barkshaw's landlady tried to tell me he was away in the country, but when I showed her the seal on the letter and explained, like you said, that it was a matter of urgent family business, she ummed and aahed and eventually said he was staying with her sister two streets over, but that I wasn't to tell him she'd told. So I headed over to her sister's, but I spotted Mr. Barkshaw walking up the street, so I hailed him and gave him the note—as if I'd just been leaving his old address and happened to see him." Thomas grinned. "He never thought to ask, and once he read the note, he seemed quite eager and said he would attend as requested."

"Excellent." Frederick and Stacie both commended Thomas, then Frederick dismissed him.

Now they knew that their plan could go ahead, the others were already discussing the various steps.

Frederick met Stacie's eyes and, under cover of the others' chatter, said, "I'm determined to see an end to this business tonight." Protecting her and, now, their unborn child had evolved into a compulsion that far exceeded even his previous obsession with the rarest of musical manuscripts.

She smiled and linked her arm in his. "Well, then." She turned him to face the others and, in a tone as resolute as his own, said, "We'd better get to it."

They returned to the group, and Frederick took charge, and together, they turned their minds to defining how their denouement would run.

～

The single, most intractable potential hiccup in their plan was that none of them felt able to definitively absolve Aurelia of complicity in her younger brother's scheme.

If, as Emily maintained, Aurelia had been actively supporting her brother, very likely without Carlisle's knowledge given Carlisle's attitude to gaming, then her involvement, certainly the degree of it, revolved about who sat higher in her loyalties—her husband or her brother, her husband's family or her own, one known to be overly sensitive regarding any hint of scandal.

As Ernestine had said, "Even if she doesn't approve of Hadley's scheme, that doesn't mean she hasn't known about it all along and is simply turning a blind eye." The normally mild companion had set her chin and stated, "In my book, that makes her equally culpable."

No one had argued.

However, when Carlisle and Aurelia were shown into the Albury House drawing room at the not-quite-fashionable hour of seven o'clock, the others all greeted them with easy smiles and outward good humor.

Hadley arrived on their heels, decked out in clothes that were the height of current fashion; both Frederick and Ryder recognized his coat as hailing from the latest premier gentleman's outfitters and whispered as much in their respective wife's ear.

If Hadley saw anything odd in being invited to be part of such a select company, he gave no sign—and Stacie artfully thanked him for helping to balance the numbers about her table, intimating as she did that, given the subject they hoped to discuss after dinner, she'd been limited to inviting only family, and her only unwed brother, Godfrey, had been out of town.

While in the drawing room prior to dinner, the dowager, Mary, and Ernestine were delegated to do their best to calm Aurelia and, if such a thing were possible, to make her feel welcome enough to relax her usual poker-rigid demeanor. Meanwhile, Stacie and Emily joined Frederick and Ryder in chatting with Carlisle and Hadley about inconsequential subjects.

When Hadley could contain his curiosity no longer and inquired, in an airy way, as to the family business that had brought them there, earning a disapproving frown from Carlisle, Frederick smiled and, at his most enigmatic, stated, "I rather think the change I wish to discuss after dinner will please everyone here."

It would have been atrocious manners to insist on hearing further details then and there. Stymied, yet intrigued, Hadley resisted the urge and continued to play the charming and innocuous rakehell, a role he'd obviously spent some time rehearsing; Stacie considered he'd improved since the first time she'd met him.

Just before Fortingale was due to appear and announce that dinner was served, Stacie slipped from Frederick's side and glided across to join the ladies. It seemed they'd expended a significant effort and had achieved a notable result; Stacie saw Aurelia attempt a small smile in response to one of Mary's more outrageous tales about her children.

In discussing Aurelia and her possible involvement, all the ladies had agreed that her stiff behavior might well be the outcome of nervousness and tension occasioned by her overactive fear of scandal—but whether that nervousness and tension was due to concern over how she herself and Carlisle presented themselves to the ton or concern arising from her knowledge of Hadley's scheme, there was really no way to tell.

After Stacie had chatted with the group for several minutes, Mary rose and drew her aside. Lowering her voice, Mary murmured, "I do believe Aurelia's starting to thaw. I wouldn't say she's relaxed, but she's more relaxed than I've ever seen her. I think it's the smaller number of people—I've only previously met her at balls and the like, and she's always struck me as someone who's smiling with her back teeth clenched tight."

Stacie thought back to the earlier occasions on which she'd met Aurelia. "Previously, the smallest gathering I've seen her at was the dinner Frederick's mother hosted before our wedding, and there were many more people here that night—lots more of Frederick's more distant family and connections."

Mary nodded. "I wouldn't say she's absolved of guilt yet, but I would have to admit the possibility exists that her stiff attitude to you and, indeed, all of us might have nothing whatsoever to do with her harboring a dislike sufficient to make her a party to Hadley's scheme."

Stacie nodded, then observed, "If she doesn't know anything of Hadley's scheme..." She met Mary's eyes.

Compassion swam in Mary's gaze, and she dipped her head. "Indeed. If so, we'll need to stand ready to support her, because if she doesn't know of it, given her obsession with avoiding scandal, she's in for a truly horrible shock."

Fortingale appeared in the doorway and announced that dinner was served.

Claiming Ryder's arm, Stacie led the company into the formal dining room, while Frederick escorted Mary, Carlisle gave the dowager his arm, and Hadley gallantly escorted Aurelia, leaving Ernestine and Emily to bring up the rear.

The seating had been carefully arranged, and Emily had set out beautifully lettered cards. Necessarily, Ryder and Mary took the places on Stacie's and Frederick's right, respectively, but rather than Carlisle being on Stacie's left, as he should have been, they'd placed Hadley there, with Carlisle on Frederick's left.

As they all took their seats, Stacie said to Hadley, "I'm sure you won't mind being in Carlisle's place—Frederick wished to sound him out over this latest idea of his."

Hadley's eyes lit. "I see. And what is Frederick's latest idea?"

Stacie smiled fondly up the table at her husband, who had already engaged Carlisle in what, from that distance, appeared to be a serious conversation. "I wouldn't want to steal his thunder, but..."

When she didn't immediately go on, Hadley prompted, "Yes?"

Stacie flung him a conspiratorial look. "Suffice it to say that it's very possible there'll be a change in Carlisle's status soon."

Hadley blinked. "Indeed?"

Fortingale interrupted with the first course, and Stacie turned to Ryder. Hadley had to wait for some considerable time before he managed to extract himself from Ernestine's and Emily's steady stream of comments and, again, snag Stacie's attention.

This time, with an attempt to make the inquiry jovial, he asked, "And how do you feel about your husband's latest notion?"

"Well," Stacie said, "quite obviously, Frederick's interest in music is longstanding, and combined with my interest in supporting worthy local musicians, his idea seems a natural evolution."

Ryder duly chimed in with a tale of a noble acquaintance who had established an arrangement with his heir—a cousin—to take over his estate in order to enable the titled gentleman to go exploring in Egypt. "He managed it so that his heir effectively inherited the estate, yet he kept the title, which was important as that allowed him to trade on it in getting foreign rulers' permission to dig in their lands."

Stacie watched Hadley's eyes grow rounder and rounder as Ryder continued to embroider his entirely fictitious tale.

When, after the end of the final course, Stacie rose to lead the ladies back to the drawing room, she was smiling; before she turned away, she met Frederick's eyes and gave an infinitesimal nod. Between them, via a series of separate but apparently connected comments, she and Ryder had succeeded in planting the notion in Hadley's mind that Frederick was on the cusp of announcing his "retirement" from managing the marquessate's estates, effectively passing Carlisle's potential inheritance on to Carlisle early, freeing Frederick, still retaining the title, to devote himself to the pursuit of his music via an extended sojourn on the Continent, visiting the major composers of the day.

Ernestine had, with absolutely exquisite timing, inserted the last tiny spark designed to ignite Hadley's hopes and send them skyrocketing; in a whispered exchange, she'd confided to Hadley that she believed that, due to a childhood accident, Stacie had always feared she would be unable to conceive—a fact that had inhibited her from accepting any offer prior to Frederick's, who, having Carlisle as his heir, hadn't cared. Ernestine had done a superb job of appearing overcome at the thought of Frederick being so swept away by love, and she'd gabbled just a little in suggesting that a part of Frederick's reason for wanting to travel on the Continent was to spare Stacie the inevitable questions and expectations and the resulting gossip.

Ernestine had been utterly believable; both Stacie and Ryder, pretending to discuss relatives while straining their ears to eavesdrop, had been awed by her performance.

On quitting the dining room, Stacie dropped back and looped her arm through Ernestine's as her erstwhile companion walked sedately beside Emily toward the drawing room. "You were magnificent!" Stacie murmured.

Ernestine blushed. "I have never lied so much in my entire life, but I do believe he accepted every word."

Stacie beamed across Ernestine at Emily, who had been seated opposite Ernestine at the table. "Did you hear it?"

Likewise beaming, Emily nodded. "A more accomplished performance, I have never witnessed."

They walked into the drawing room and settled themselves on the chaise and the chairs in the arrangement they'd decided on. Stacie made for her usual armchair, one of the pair closest to the fireplace. Emily took its mate, while Ernestine left the armchair next to Emily vacant and took the next one down the room.

The dowager, who, with Mary, had accompanied Aurelia from the dining room, steered her to the long chaise. Mary sat at the end closest to Stacie, Aurelia sank down beside her, and the dowager took her usual position at the other end.

As they settled to chat about recent ton events, Stacie covertly observed Aurelia and had to admit that Mary's suggestion that much of Aurelia's rigidity might have its roots in nervousness appeared increasingly correct. Aurelia was gradually relaxing, albeit by painfully slow degrees.

Adhering to their plan, the men didn't dally over their brandy and port. They returned to the drawing room and disposed themselves about the space. Ryder surreptitiously steered Carlisle to the armchair beside the dowager, yet himself remained closest to the door; he drew up a straight-backed chair, set it a little beyond Carlisle, facing the fireplace, and sat, crossing his long legs and giving the impression he was looking forward to hearing some news.

From where he sat, Ryder would be able to see the faces of everyone else in the room.

Frederick, meanwhile, walked to the fireplace and took up a stance before it, gracefully waving Hadley to the vacant armchair between Emily and Ernestine. Smiling easily, Hadley sat, exchanging an idle comment with Ernestine.

Stacie looked up into her husband's eyes and allowed him to read her satisfaction. Thus far, everything had gone more or less as they'd scripted; now, it was Frederick's turn to take center stage.

He smiled in gentle and open affection, then raised his head and looked around the company.

The chatter faded; the others all looked at him, and an expectant silence fell.

Frederick looked at Carlisle and Aurelia. "Now, to our news—mine and Stacie's. The others already know, but I wanted you to be among the first to hear that we're expecting our first child in January."

Carlisle's face broke into a spontaneously beaming smile. "Congratulations! That's wonderful news!" That he was sincere was beyond question.

Aurelia's perennially tight features softened, and she looked at Stacie and smiled—a gesture that reached her eyes and made her appear much more approachable. "My congratulations as well." She raised her gaze to Frederick's face. "You must both be thrilled."

Stacie's smile was entirely genuine. "We are."

Along with everyone else, she looked at Hadley.

All color had drained from his face, and his gaze had grown distant; he'd been frozen in place, but when everyone stared at him, he blinked to attention and babbled, "Yes, congratulations—definitely, er...good news. I...wasn't quite expecting that, but...well." He flung a glance at Ernestine, who blinked innocently back, then Hadley dredged up a somewhat sickly smile for Stacie and Frederick. "I suppose I should have, of course."

Then he stilled and focused on Frederick. "When are you planning to announce the impending birth?"

Carlisle stiffened and directed a disapproving look at his brother-in-law.

Aurelia stared at her brother, a frown forming in her eyes.

Frederick merely smiled, albeit with an edge. "We're not planning on announcing anything at all until our child is born."

Hadley's relief was obvious to everyone—and everyone was watching. Carlisle looked increasingly puzzled, while Aurelia looked increasingly concerned.

Apparently oblivious to the swirling undercurrents, Frederick blithely went on, "However, as it happens, Ryder and I had occasion to meet with a Mr. Mordaunt in Wapping this afternoon—I believe you know him? I did share our news with him."

"What?" Hadley's face lost what little color he'd regained. He goggled at Frederick, then glanced at Ryder. "W-Why on earth did you tell him?"

Ryder smiled chillingly. "Because he was laboring under several misapprehensions regarding the House of Brampton, and as your principal creditor, Mordaunt deserved to know that your attempts to ensure that Carlisle inherits and unwittingly gives you access to the Brampton estate counting room, so to speak, are destined to come to naught."

Ryder's final words, "Mr. Mordaunt is not at all happy with you," were lost beneath Aurelia's gasped, *"Attempts to..."* Her face a mask of horror, she leapt to her feet. "Hadley! What have you done?"

One glance at her face was enough to assure everyone that the only thing Aurelia had known or even suspected was the potential for her younger brother to behave atrociously.

"You don't understand!" Hadley sprang to his feet. Facing his sister across the Aubusson rug, he insisted, "I had to! I had no choice." Abruptly, Hadley rounded on Frederick. "You bastard! I'll never be free of Mordaunt now—I'll have to flee the country!"

"Indeed." Utterly calm, Frederick reached into his coat pocket, withdrew a folded sheet, and held it out to Hadley.

Hadley stared at the paper. "What's that?"

"It's a ticket for passage on the early-morning ferry from Dover to Calais. I suggest you take it."

When Hadley continued to stare at the ticket, Ryder said, "I second that recommendation. And just so you're aware, men—very able men—will be watching you from the moment you leave this house."

Frederick didn't lower the ticket. "In light of the accidents you engineered, if we ask around, I'm sure we'll find people willing to bear witness against you. I'm sure you know the punishment for attempting to murder members of the nobility. However, if you leave the country immediately, we won't have any reason to dig for evidence with which to convict you."

After much debate, they'd decided that the only way to protect those innocent of any wrongdoing—namely, the other Barkshaws—from the inevitable repercussions of Hadley's crimes was to allow him to flee the country. After considering what sort of life a man like Hadley would face, alone, without resources, in a foreign land, Frederick had agreed. He wasn't happy about letting Hadley go, but he accepted it was the best way.

"Accidents?" Aurelia stared at Hadley as if he'd grown two heads. She glanced briefly at Frederick's hard face, then returned her gaze to Hadley's. "What accidents, Hadley?" Her voice had grown harsh and demanding. "What did you do?"

"I had to, I tell you!" Hadley's face contorted; he clutched at his hair with both hands and tugged. "I had no choice! When Frederick married, Mordaunt sent his men around to ask what that meant for the succession, and although I spun him a tale, I had to make sure nothing came of it—you must see that!"

Carlisle had risen when Aurelia had and had watched the unfolding drama in some confusion. "Succession?" he asked, looking even more confused. "What has the succession to do with you?"

When no one offered an answer, Mary, who, along with Stacie, had been watching Aurelia closely, said, "I believe your wife might be able to shed some light on that."

Aurelia's expression turned anguished, and she swung to face Carlisle. "I helped him out—with money. Just here and there, from my pin money and sometimes from the household funds—but only when he was desperate."

She swung back to Hadley and, fists clenching, her whole body vibrating, demanded, "How *could* you? I risked going against my husband's wishes purely so that there would be no scandal. You knew what it would do to Papa and Mama—you always held that over my head. You *knew* that was why I did it! Nothing I did was ever an invitation to use me, to use Carlisle and his connection to Frederick, to borrow funds from some cent-per-cent!"

Far from displaying any remorse, Hadley sneered. "All very well for you—living the life of a lady while I had to scrimp and scrape."

"Enough!" Frederick stepped forward, his gaze taking in the pain and fear written across Aurelia's face. He swung to face Hadley, slapped the ticket against Hadley's chest, caught his eye, and harshly commanded, "Take it and go—before I change my mind."

The threat in the latter phrase was real; Hadley looked into Frederick's eyes, realized that, and snatched the paper.

Hadley glanced at Ryder and Carlisle, both stony faced, then looked at Aurelia, then he shoved the ticket into his pocket. "All right. I'll go."

Ryder stepped back to allow Hadley to stalk past. As he did, Ryder said, "Just in case you're tempted to try it, if you're wise, you won't set foot in England again. Mordaunt's memory is long, and he's said to have a vindictive streak. Many of us here would feel obliged to inform him if you are sighted on English soil." Ryder turned his head and met Hadley's eyes. "It's the least we can do given we're depriving him of all satisfaction by allowing you to flee, thus escaping his retribution."

Frederick watched with grim satisfaction as the last of Hadley's misplaced confidence drained, and he turned and walked, increasingly quickly, to the door. When Hadley opened it, Frederick glimpsed Fortingale, flanked by two footmen, waiting in the hall, and left it to his staff to see Hadley from the house.

The door shut with a click, releasing the tension that had held everyone in its grip.

Aurelia slumped onto the chaise. Stricken, she looked up at Carlisle. "Can you ever forgive me?" She shifted her gaze to Frederick and Stacie. "Can you?" Then she dissolved into gasping, noisy, utterly genuine tears.

The ladies all gathered around, and the gentlemen backed away—even Carlisle, after he'd patted Aurelia's shoulder in a clumsy, comforting way and attempted to assure her he didn't blame her for her brother's actions.

She only sobbed harder.

Emily and Ernestine were inclined to be soothing, but Mary, Stacie, and the dowager quickly adopted a more bracing attitude, promulgating a view that there was no need to overstate, much less overdramatize, Aurelia's involvement, as it was hardly her fault her brother had turned out to be a bad egg.

Ryder and Carlisle joined Frederick by the fireplace, and Carlisle asked and Frederick described the attacks that Hadley's paid thugs had engineered.

Carlisle was shocked, yet his principal concern was for Aurelia. He glanced at her, seated on the sofa, surrounded by the other ladies. "She's always tried to help him," he said, rather sadly. "She could never accept that he wasn't worth it."

Eventually, the storm of Aurelia's sobs abated. The other ladies tried to reassure her that, as long as Hadley quit the country and stayed away, there was no reason the ton would ever hear of his behavior—no reason scandal would engulf her family. Yet still she hung her head; she seemed to want to shrink into the chaise.

Finally, Frederick stepped closer, crouched in front of Aurelia, bringing them eye to eye. "Aurelia." His tone was commanding enough to make her raise her head.

Her eyes, large and swollen, met his, and her breath hitched.

"Listen to all we're saying." Frederick held her gaze. "In everything you've done, you've acted from the best of motives. You thought you had to act as you did in order to save your family from being tainted by scandal—by the scandal Hadley blatantly courted. Your actions are nothing to be ashamed of—if any of us had been placed in a similar situation, chances are, we would have done the same. We all value family, and each family has its vulnerabilities. Acting to protect your family is something we all understand—none of us hold your actions against you, and we never will." He paused, then added, "What Hadley did is in no way your fault—you are not to blame for his transgressions."

Aurelia blinked.

Frederick continued to hold her gaze; slowly, he arched a brow.

At last, Aurelia fractionally nodded. "Thank you," she whispered.

Frederick tipped his head and rose. He hadn't said anything more than the others already had, but because he was the head of the house and arguably the most wronged by Hadley's actions, she could accept absolution from him.

Aurelia looked at Carlisle, who stepped to her side and patted her shoulder. "There, there, m'dear. No need to fear the worst. Like Frederick said, we're all family here, and no one's going to speak about Hadley again."

There was a firmness in Carlisle's tone that didn't surprise Frederick, but of which he saw Stacie, Mary, and Ernestine take note.

Carlisle urged Aurelia to her feet, and they took their leave; Frederick, with Stacie beside him, saw them to the door and waited with them as their carriage was brought around.

When Fortingale had shut the door and Frederick, with Stacie, turned to head back to the drawing room, Stacie leaned close and murmured, "I suspect we could all do with a little uplifting—do you think you might play your new air for us?"

He met her eyes, then smiled and raised her hand to his lips. He kissed her fingers, then said, "As my lady commands."

They parted, she to summon the others to the music room while he went ahead and opened the piano.

As she led the company into the room, the strains of Frederick's "Anthem to My Muse" swelled, then swooped and snared them in its light and airy embrace.

They stood and listened—Ryder and Mary, Frederick's mother, Emily, and Ernestine—and in the center of the group stood the lady who held Frederick's heart.

He played for her, and the music rolled through the house, an anthem in truth, a paean to love.

As the final chord sounded, only Ryder's and Frederick's eyes remained dry.

His audience burst into spontaneous applause and shouts of *Bravo!*

His mother held her hands to her heart and looked thrilled to her soul.

But his eyes were all for his love and all he saw shining in her gaze.

She was and would be his hearth, his home, the lynchpin of his family —his future, his muse, his, forevermore.

～

They persuaded Frederick to play for a while more—light airs that lifted the clouds of the day and blew them away.

Eventually, satisfied with the outcome of their endeavors, Ryder and Mary took their leave, and Emily and Ernestine went upstairs.

Leaving Frederick closing the piano, Stacie walked with the dowager to the music room door.

After casting a swift glance behind them, the dowager grasped Stacie's wrist, leaned close, and murmured, "Thank you! You cannot know what a difference you've made to him—how completely you've lured him back into the world."

Stacie twisted her wrist, caught the dowager's fingers, and lightly squeezed. "If so, it's only fair, given the difference he's made to me."

The dowager's old eyes met hers directly, then Philippa nodded. "You balance each other." She returned the pressure of Stacie's fingers, then released her. "And that's a wonderful thing."

With a smile and a graceful nod, the dowager went ahead.

Stacie heard Frederick's footsteps approaching, glanced back, and met his eyes. He arched a brow at her, but she only shook her head and, when he drew level, linked her arm with his. Together, they went upstairs and walked down the corridor to the room they shared.

He opened the door and followed her in, then closed the door and halted. He drew her to face him and searched her eyes, her face. "I didn't get a chance to ask you before—in all honesty, do you like the piece?"

She read in his eyes that he was serious, that he truly wasn't sure. She smiled and let her love shine in her eyes. "Like is too small a word for how I feel—I adore it."

Relief flitted across his face, softening the hard lines. "Good."

He drew her to him, and she went.

She draped her arms about his shoulders and said, "Now that we've slain all our lurking dragons and seen off all threats, it seems we're free to embrace our marriage and all that comes with it."

She wondered if he would rise to her challenge, if he would continue to match her in directness.

His gaze rock-steady, he didn't disappoint. "Our love, our child—and our children to come."

"Our family." She had never thought to have one of her own—to have all he'd laid at her feet. "I believe, my lord, that we have all we need—secured, safe, and so very much wanted."

His smile wrapped around her heart. "As I said, life is a symphony. You and I have laid down our melody and crafted our first movement—it's time to start work on the next."

She returned his smile with all the love in her soul, stretched up on her toes, and just before her lips met his, whispered, "Yes," and kissed him.

EPILOGUE

APRIL 16, 1845. ALBURY HOUSE, UPPER GROSVENOR STREET, LONDON

The Marchioness of Albury's musical evenings were now widely regarded by the haut ton as must-be-seen-at events. Consequently, her fourth such evening got under way with the reception rooms of Albury House packed to capacity.

As had occurred at the previous evenings, the instant the musical segment of the entertainment commenced, the focus of the entire gathering centered on the music room. Not a single grande dame remained chatting in the drawing room; having learned from past experience, those wily old ladies now claimed seats in the front rows in the music room, the better to assess the quality of the performers for future reference.

The young performers invited to showcase their talents that evening were the same three who had opened the marchioness's near-legendary first event the year before, when she'd still been Lady Eustacia Cavanaugh. As she, now Lady Albury, said in her introduction, all three young men had made strides as, under the patronage of the marquess and herself, their careers had progressed onto a wider stage.

The pianist, Brandon Miller, and the duo of cellist and violinist who followed—Phillip Carpenter and George Goodes—were now familiar to many of those attending, having been hired by ladies to perform at various events through the preceding year. Nevertheless, it was clear to even the most superficial observer that all three had evolved both in skills and in confidence under the Alburys' wing.

Those three were followed by the latest three performers to be admitted to the list of Albury protégés. The cream of the haut ton pricked up their collective ears when her ladyship invited Lord Brougham to introduce the horn and wind ensemble. Subsequently, they listened closely, noting the rich timbre of the performance that Brougham had explained was the hallmark of exceptional performance with such instruments.

When the trio took their final bow, the haut ton was pleased to approve, and ladies could be seen making notes of names and instruments for later consideration.

Finally came the moment that even the most jaded of the audience had waited for. Lord Frederick Brampton, Marquess of Albury—very much one of their own—appeared to rapturous applause. Those in the front rows saw the faintly cynical look he exchanged with his wife, then he bowed, circled the grand piano, and sat before the keyboard.

Then he placed his fingers on the keys and played his latest composition, which he had titled simply "Ode to My Son."

The piece was indescribably moving; not a single matronly eye remained unclouded by tears, and not a few of the gentlemen were similarly afflicted.

When the evocative work finally drew to a close and the marquess took his bow to thunderous applause, then, as was his habit, retreated from the room, all were in agreement that this, his third publicly released composition, was a worthy addition to his catalog, joining the earlier "Anthem to My Muse" and his "Christmas Sonata," which had been delivered to critical acclaim at, respectively, the second and third of Lady Albury's evenings the previous year.

Stacie remained in the music room only long enough to see the guests all moving into the supper room, then she slipped away and joined Frederick where he loitered, waiting for her in the shadows at the top of the stairs.

He smiled when he saw her step into the gallery. "I thought you would come up."

She returned his smile with one even more fond. "I knew you would."

He reached for her hand, and their fingers intertwined as they turned down a corridor, then took another flight of stairs upward.

"Incidentally," she informed him, knowing he needed to hear it, "they loved your Ode." She cast him a laughing glance. "You haven't lost your touch."

He arched his brows, but she could tell he was relieved. "Good to know."

They reached the top of the stairs and fetched up before the door to the nursery.

Frederick watched Stacie grip the doorknob and quietly crack open the door.

The inspiration for his latest opus lay sleeping peacefully in a cot near the window.

The nursemaid on duty smiled and bobbed a curtsy, then withdrew, leaving them with their son.

Lord Edmund Frederick Carlisle Brampton was just three months old and remained blissfully unaware of the doting gazes trained upon him.

Frederick lounged against the window frame and, in the soft moonlight that spilled through the glass, watched Stacie as her gaze traced the small round face, the tiny nose, the delicately pursed lips.

Whether Edmund would have her hair or Frederick's was still moot, but Frederick felt sure his son would inherit her periwinkle-blue eyes.

Yet as he relaxed and the tension of performance sloughed away, it wasn't his son who commanded his attention. He drank in Stacie's Madonna-like expression, the glow of pure love that infused her face, an expression unlike any other in the universe—and inside him, music stirred.

Eventually, she drew back with a sigh, then she looked up and saw his smile. "What?" she whispered.

Smile deepening, he shook his head as he reached out, slid an arm around her waist, and settling her beside him, drew her toward the open door. "I cannot understand how you ever doubted the power of your love —for me and for our children." Through the shadows, he captured her gaze, caught her hand, raised it to his lips, and kissed her fingers. "You are radiant—literally radiant—with it, and as ever, I am in awe."

She smiled, then halted and, stretching up on her toes, kissed him. "I do love you," she whispered against his lips.

Unable to resist, he drew her back for a longer, more thorough kiss, but eventually, albeit reluctantly, they both drew back.

He met her eyes and lightly grimaced. "We have guests."

"And protégés to do our best for."

"Indeed." He guided her through the doorway and nodded to the maid, who slipped back into the room as he and Stacie walked down the corridor.

He and she had carved out a unique position within the haut ton, but along with that much-desired state came responsibilities—responsibilities they both took seriously. Championing the alumni of the music school attached to St Martin-in-the-Fields had become a shared purpose, a joint endeavor.

Another sort of family, in a way.

The thought made him smile as they returned downstairs, and dutifully, with a commitment he'd never expected to possess, he steeled himself to accept with due grace the accolades of their guests.

An hour later, Stacie was circulating among their guests when she came upon her younger brother, Godfrey, taking his leave of Mary.

"I've hardly had a chance to say hello," Stacie protested as she linked her arm in his.

Godfrey grinned and patted her hand. "I'm your younger brother. Hello is optional."

She chuckled. "Do you really have to leave?"

He nodded. "I've a commission in Cornwall—quite an intriguing one. I want to get an early start."

"Very well." Stacie exchanged a look with Mary, who then waved them both away as she returned to Ryder, who was deep in conversation with another peer. Stacie held on to Godfrey's arm. "I'll see you to the door."

"Hmm." Godfrey eyed her warily. "Why do I get the impression that look you just exchanged with dearest Mary bodes me no good at all?"

She shook her head and steered them determinedly through the still-substantial crowd. "You're imagining things. But I've been meaning to point out to you—you who are the last of us to wed—that despite our past, love does, in truth, conquer all." She met his eyes. "I'm a shining— indeed, my husband informs me I'm a radiantly glowing—example of that."

"You are radiantly glowing, but I rather suspect it's Frederick himself who's the cause of that."

Stacie pinched his arm.

"Ow!" He mock-scowled and pretended to rub the hurt. "I knew I should have left you with Mary."

They reached the front hall, and she drew him to one side and halted.

"Stop trying to change the subject. I accept that I was the one most affected by Mama and her machinations, but you were there often as well. As much as I had to, you, too, need to leave behind your years with her and all the twisted lessons she tried to teach us. Quite literally, we need to forget her and all her works and go forward and live our own lives and not allow her to taint those. I know that's not always easy, but if we want happiness in our lives, that's what we have to do."

Stacie looked into Godfrey's eyes and saw the gentle, easy smile curving his lips reflected there.

Godfrey squeezed her hand and held her gaze. "Would you believe me if I told you I'd thrown off Mama's influence years ago?"

When she looked doubtful, he sighed, then more briskly said, "Don't worry about me."

That brought on a very sisterly frown. "Don't be nonsensical. I'm your sister—I'll always worry about you. We're family, and that's what families do."

He had to give her that. "Possibly, but with you and Mary and Felicia and Sylvia all watching out for me, I doubt that even Fate would dare decline to send love my way—eventually."

She knew him well—better than his sisters-in-law, even better than his brothers. She cocked a questioning brow at him. "Eventually?"

"Indeed." It was time to get away, before she could start an inquisition. He moved toward the door, and Fortingale—bless the man—opened it. Godfrey swooped down, pecked Stacie on the cheek, then tapped the tip of her nose, which always made her wrinkle it and was guaranteed to distract her. "Eventually," he said, as he slipped his arm from under her hand, "because at this very moment, I have no time for falling in love. I, dear sister, have another and even more demanding mistress to serve."

Namely, Art, in his drive to become the very best in his chosen field of gentleman-assessors of masterpieces.

Stacie frowned, but before she could say anything more, he turned and walked out of the door and went quickly down the steps.

Without looking back, he waved over his shoulder, then strode off determinedly into the night.

∼

Dear Reader,

Stacie's story was always destined to be one of challenges—that was obvious after the dramatic events at the end of *The Taming of Ryder Cavanaugh*, the book in which she first appeared. It was clear that Stacie's relationship with her mother and the shadow of her mother's actions would inevitably influence who Stacie became, the sort of woman she grew to be, especially in the arena of love and romance.

And because of the hurdles Stacie faced, her hero had to be the right sort of man—one who faced a challenge of his own—and who, through meeting that challenge at Stacie's behest, would in turn challenge Stacie to face her own demons.

I hope you enjoyed following Stacie's path into love, marriage, and happiness with Frederick.

As I'm sure you've realized from the last scene in this book, the final volume in the Cavanaughs, *The Obsessions of Lord Godfrey Cavanaugh*, the tale of how Godfrey finds romance, is on my drawing board and is scheduled for release in July 2020.

Meanwhile, to round out 2019, the third volume of Lady Osbaldestone's Christmas Chronicles, *Lady Osbaldestone's Plum Puddings*, will be released on October 17 for you to enjoy in the lead-up to Christmas.

As ever, I wish you continued happy reading!

Stephanie.

For alerts as new books are released, plus information on upcoming books, exclusive sweepstakes and sneak peeks into upcoming novels, sign up for Stephanie's Private Email Newsletter http://www.stephanielaurens.com/newsletter-signup/

Or if you don't have time to chat and want a quick email alert, sign up and follow me at BookBub https://www.bookbub.com/authors/stephanie-laurens

The ultimate source for detailed information on all Stephanie's published books, including covers, descriptions, and excerpts, is Stephanie's Website www.stephanielaurens.com

You can also follow Stephanie via her Amazon Author Page at http://tinyurl.com/zc3e9mp

Goodreads members can follow Stephanie via her author page https://www.goodreads.com/author/show/9241.Stephanie_Laurens

You can email Stephanie at stephanie@stephanielaurens.com

Or find her on Facebook
https://www.facebook.com/AuthorStephanieLaurens/

COMING NEXT:

**The third instalment in LADY OSBALDESTONE'S CHRISTMAS CHRONICLES
LADY OSBALDESTONE'S PLUM PUDDINGS
To be released on October 17, 2019.**

#1 New York Times *bestselling author Stephanie Laurens brings you the delights of a long-ago country-village Christmas, featuring a grandmother, her grandchildren, an artifact hunter, the lady who catches his eye, and three ancient coins that draw them all together in a Christmas treasure hunt.*

Therese, Lady Osbaldestone, and her household again welcome her younger daughter's children, Jamie, George, and Lottie, plus their cousins Melissa and Mandy, all of whom have insisted on spending the three weeks prior to Christmas at Therese's house, Hartington Manor, in the village of Little Moseley.

The children are looking forward to the village's traditional events, and this year, Therese has arranged a new distraction—the plum puddings she and her staff are making for the entire village. But while cleaning the coins donated as the puddings' good-luck tokens, the children discover that three aren't coins of the realm. When consulted, Reverend Colebatch summons a friend, an archeological scholar from Oxford, who confirms the coins are Roman, raising the possibility of a Roman treasure buried somewhere near. Unfortunately, Professor Webster is facing a deadline and cannot assist in the search, but along with his niece Honor, he will stay in the village, writing, remaining available for consultation should the children and their helpers uncover more treasure.

It soon becomes clear that discovering the source of the coins—or even which villager donated them—isn't a straightforward matter. Then the children come across a personable gentleman who knows a great deal about Roman antiquities. He introduces himself as Callum Harris, and they agree to allow him to help, and he gets their search back on track.

But while the manor five, assisted by the gentlemen from Fulsom Hall, scour the village for who had the coins and search the countryside for signs of excavation and Harris combs through the village's country-house libraries, amassing evidence of a Roman compound somewhere near, the site from which the coins actually came remains a frustrating mystery.

Then Therese recognizes Harris, who is more than he's pretending to be. She also notes the romance burgeoning between Harris and Honor Webster, and given the girl doesn't know Harris's full name, let alone his fraught relationship with her uncle, Therese steps in. But while she can engineer a successful resolution to one romance-of-the-season, as well a reconciliation long overdue, another romance that strikes much closer to home is beyond her ability to manipulate.

Meanwhile, the search for the source of the coins goes on, but time is running out. Will Therese's grandchildren and their Fulsom Hall helpers locate the Roman merchant's villa Harris is sure lies near before they all must leave the village for Christmas with their families?

Third in series. A novel of 70,000 words. A Christmas tale of antiquities, reconciliation, romance, and requited love.

RECENTLY RELEASED:

A CONQUEST IMPOSSIBLE TO RESIST
Cynster Next Generation Novel #7

#1 New York Times *bestselling author Stephanie Laurens returns to the Cynsters' next generation to bring you a thrilling tale of love, intrigue, and fabulous horses.*

A notorious rakehell with a stable of rare Thoroughbreds and a lady on a quest to locate such horses must negotiate personal minefields to forge a greatly desired alliance—one someone is prepared to murder to prevent.

Prudence Cynster has turned her back on husband hunting in favor of horse hunting. As the head of the breeding program underpinning the success of the Cynster racing stables, she's on a quest to acquire the necessary horses to refresh the stable's breeding stock.

On his estranged father's death, Deaglan Fitzgerald, now Earl of Glengarah, left London and the hedonistic life of a wealthy, wellborn rake and returned to Glengarah Castle determined to rectify the harm caused by his father's neglect. Driven by guilt that he hadn't been there to protect his people during the Great Famine, Deaglan holds firm against the lure of his father's extensive collection of horses and, leaving the stable to the care of his brother, Felix, devotes himself to returning the estate to prosperity.

Deaglan had fallen out with his father and been exiled from Glengarah over his drive to have the horses pay their way. Knowing Deaglan's wishes and that restoration of the estate is almost complete, Felix writes to the premier Thoroughbred breeding program in the British Isles to test their interest in the Glengarah horses.

On receiving a letter describing exactly the type of horses she's seeking, Pru overrides her family's reluctance and sets out for Ireland's west coast to visit the now-reclusive wicked Earl of Glengarah. Yet her only interest is in his horses, which she cannot wait to see.

When Felix tells Deaglan that a P. H. Cynster is about to arrive to assess the horses with a view to a breeding arrangement, Deaglan can only be grateful. But then P. H. Cynster turns out to be a lady, one utterly unlike any other he's ever met.

Yet they are who they are, and both understand their world. They battle their instincts and attempt to keep their interactions businesslike, but the sparks are incandescent and inevitably ignite a sexual blaze that consumes them both—and opens their eyes.

But before they can find their way to their now-desired goal, first one accident, then another distracts them. Someone, it seems, doesn't want them to strike a deal. Who? Why?

They need to find out before whoever it is resorts to the ultimate sanction.

A historical romance with neo-Gothic overtones, set in the west of Ireland. A Cynster Next Generation novel—a full-length historical romance of 125,000 words.

And if you haven't already indulged:
PREVIOUS VOLUMES IN THE CAVANAUGHS
The first volume in THE CAVANAUGHS
THE DESIGNS OF LORD RANDOLPH CAVANAUGH

#1 New York Times *bestselling author Stephanie Laurens returns with a new series that captures the simmering desires and intrigues of early Victorians as only she can. Ryder Cavanaugh's step-siblings are determined to make their own marks in London society. Seeking fortune and passion, THE CAVANAUGHS will delight readers with their bold exploits.*

An independent nobleman

Lord Randolph Cavanaugh is loyal and devoted—but only to family. To the rest of the world he's aloof and untouchable, a respected and driven entrepreneur. But Rand yearns for more in life, and when he travels to Buckinghamshire to review a recent investment, he discovers a passionate woman who will challenge his rigid self-control...

A determined lady

Felicia Throgmorton intends to keep her family afloat. For decades, her father was consumed by his inventions and now, months after his death, with their finances in ruins, her brother insists on continuing their father's tinkering. Felicia is desperate to hold together what's left of the estate. Then she discovers she must help persuade their latest investor that her father's follies are a risk worth taking...

Together—the perfect team

Rand arrives at Throgmorton Hall to discover the invention on which he's staked his reputation has exploded, the inventor is not who he expected, and a fiercely intelligent woman now holds the key to his future success. But unflinching courage in the face of dismaying hurdles is a trait they share, and Rand and Felicia are forced to act together against ruthless foes to protect everything they hold dear.

The second volume in THE CAVANAUGHS
THE PURSUITS OF LORD KIT CAVANAUGH

Bold and clever, THE CAVANAUGHS are unlike any other family in early

Victorian England. #1 New York Times bestselling author Stephanie Laurens continues to explore the enthralling world of these dynamic siblings in the eagerly anticipated second volume in her captivating series.

A gentleman of means

One of the most eligible bachelors in London, Lord Christopher "Kit" Cavanaugh has discovered his true path and it doesn't include the expected society marriage. Kit is all business and has chosen the bustling port of Bristol to launch his passion--Cavanaugh Yachts.

A woman of character

Miss Sylvia Buckleberry's passion is her school for impoverished children. When a new business venture forces the school out of its building, she must act quickly. But confronting Kit Cavanaugh is a daunting task made even more difficult by their first and only previous meeting, when, believing she'd never see him again, she'd treated him dismissively. Still, Sylvia is determined to be persuasive.

An unstoppable duo

But it quickly becomes clear there are others who want the school--and Cavanaugh Yachts--closed. Working side by side, Kit and Sylvia fight to secure her school and to expose the blackguard trying to sabotage his business. Yet an even more dastardly villain lurks, one who threatens the future both discover they now hold dear.

ALSO AVAILABLE:

**The first volume in Lady Osbaldestone's Christmas Chronicles
LADY OSBALDESTONE'S CHRISTMAS GOOSE**

#1 New York Times bestselling author Stephanie Laurens brings you a lighthearted tale of Christmas long ago with a grandmother and three of her grandchildren, one lost soul, a lady driven to distraction, a recalcitrant donkey, and a flock of determined geese.

Three years after being widowed, Therese, Lady Osbaldestone finally settles into her dower property of Hartington Manor in the village of Little Moseley in Hampshire. She is in two minds as to whether life in the small village will generate sufficient interest to keep her amused over the months when she is not in London or visiting friends around the country. But she will see.

It's December, 1810, and Therese is looking forward to her usual Christmas with her family at Winslow Abbey, her youngest daughter, Celia's home. But then a carriage rolls up and disgorges Celia's three oldest children. Their father has contracted mumps, and their mother has sent the three—Jamie, George, and Lottie—to spend this Christmas with their grandmama in Little Moseley.

Therese has never had to manage small children, not even her own. She assumes the children will keep themselves amused, but quickly learns that what amuses three inquisitive, curious, and confident youngsters isn't compatible with village peace. Just when it seems she will have to set her mind to inventing something, she and the children learn that with only twelve days to go before Christmas, the village flock of geese has vanished.

Every household in the village is now missing the centerpiece of their Christmas feast. But how could an entire flock go missing without the slightest trace? The children are as mystified and as curious as Therese—and she seizes on the mystery as the perfect distraction for the three children as well as herself.

But while searching for the geese, she and her three helpers stumble on two locals who, it is clear, are in dire need of assistance in sorting out their lives. Never one to shy from a little matchmaking, Therese undertakes to guide Miss Eugenia Fitzgibbon into the arms of the determinedly reclusive Lord Longfellow. To her considerable surprise, she discovers that her grandchildren have inherited skills and talents from both her late husband as well as herself. And with all the customary village events held in the lead up to Christmas, she and her three helpers have opportunities galore in which to subtly nudge and steer.

Yet while their matchmaking appears to be succeeding, neither they nor anyone else have found so much as a feather from the village's geese. Larceny is ruled out; a flock of that size could not have been taken from the area without someone noticing. So where could the birds be? And with the days passing and Christmas inexorably approaching, will they find the blasted birds in time?

First in series. A novel of 60,000 words. A Christmas tale of romance and geese.

The second volume in Lady Osbaldestone's Christmas Chronicles
LADY OSBALDESTONE AND THE MISSING CHRISTMAS CAROLS

#1 New York Times *bestselling author Stephanie Laurens brings you a heartwarming tale of a long-ago country-village Christmas, a grandmother, three eager grandchildren, one moody teenage granddaughter, an earnest young lady, a gentleman in hiding, and an elusive book of Christmas carols.*

Therese, Lady Osbaldestone, and her household are quietly delighted when her younger daughter's three children, Jamie, George, and Lottie, insist on returning to Therese's house, Hartington Manor in the village Little Moseley, to spend the three weeks leading up to Christmas participating in the village's traditional events.

Then out of the blue, one of Therese's older granddaughters, Melissa, arrives on the doorstep. Her mother, Therese's older daughter, begs Therese to take Melissa in until the family gathering at Christmas—otherwise, Melissa has nowhere else to go.

Despite having no experience dealing with moody, reticent teenagers like Melissa, Therese welcomes Melissa warmly. The younger children are happy to include their cousin in their plans—and despite her initial aloofness, Melissa discovers she's not too old to enjoy the simple delights of a village Christmas.

The previous year, Therese learned the trick to keeping her unexpected guests out of mischief. She casts around and discovers that the new organist, who plays superbly, has a strange failing. He requires the written music in front of him before he can play a piece, and the church's book of Christmas carols has gone missing.

Therese immediately volunteers the services of her grandchildren, who are only too happy to fling themselves into the search to find the missing book of carols. Its disappearance threatens one of the village's most-valued Christmas traditions—the Carol Service—yet as the book has always been freely loaned within the village, no one imagines that it won't be found with a little application.

But as Therese's intrepid four follow the trail of the book from house to house, the mystery of where the book has vanished to only deepens. Then the organist hears the children singing and invites them to form a special guest choir. The children love singing, and provided they find the book in time, they'll be able to put on an extra-special service for the village.

While the urgency and their desire to finding the missing book escalates, the children—being Therese's grandchildren—get distracted by the potential for romance that buds, burgeons, and blooms before them.

Yet as Christmas nears, the questions remain: Will the four unravel the twisted trail of the missing book in time to save the village's Carol Service? And will they succeed in nudging the organist and the harpist they've found to play alongside him into seizing the happy-ever-after that hovers before the pair's noses?

Second in series. A novel of 62,000 words. A Christmas tale full of music and romance.

ABOUT THE AUTHOR

#1 *New York Times* bestselling author Stephanie Laurens began writing romances as an escape from the dry world of professional science. Her hobby quickly became a career when her first novel was accepted for publication, and with entirely becoming alacrity, she gave up writing about facts in favor of writing fiction.

All Laurens's works to date are historical romances, ranging from medieval times to the mid-1800s, and her settings range from Scotland to India. The majority of her works are set in the period of the British Regency. Laurens has published more than 70 works of historical romance, including 40 *New York Times* bestsellers. Laurens has sold more than 20 million print, audio, and e-books globally. All her works are continuously available in print and e-book formats in English worldwide, and have been translated into many other languages. An international bestseller, among other accolades, Laurens has received the Romance Writers of America® prestigious RITA® Award for Best Romance Novella 2008 for *The Fall of Rogue Gerrard*.

Laurens's continuing novels featuring the Cynster family are widely regarded as classics of the historical romance genre. Other series include the *Bastion Club Novels*, the *Black Cobra Quartet*, and the *Casebook of Barnaby Adair Novels*. All her previous works remain available in print and all e-book formats.

For information on all published novels and on upcoming releases and updates on novels yet to come, visit Stephanie's website: www.stephanielaurens.com

To sign up for Stephanie's Email Newsletter (a private list) for heads-up alerts as new books are released, exclusive sneak peeks into upcoming books, and exclusive sweepstakes contests, follow the prompts at Stephanie's Email Newsletter Sign-up Page

To follow Stephanie on BookBub, head here https://www.bookbub.com/authors/stephanie-laurens

Stephanie lives with her husband and a goofy black labradoodle in the hills outside Melbourne, Australia. When she isn't writing, she's reading, and if she isn't reading, she'll be tending her garden.

www.stephanielaurens.com
stephanie@stephanielaurens.com